A BLADE THROUGH TIME

A BLADE THROUGH TIME

DESOLADA ✦ 1

LOUIS KALMAN

Podium

To kindred souls and constructive critics

All rights reserved. No part of this publication may be reproduced, stored in a retrieval system, or transmitted in any form or by any means electronic, mechanical, photocopying, recording, or otherwise without prior written permission from Podium Publishing.

This is a work of fiction. Names, characters, places, and incidents are either products of the author's imagination or used fictitiously. Any resemblance to actual events, locales, or persons, living, dead, or undead, is entirely coincidental.

Copyright © 2022 by Louis Kalman

Cover design by Podium Publishing

ISBN: 978-1-0394-1522-5

Published in 2022 by Podium Publishing, ULC
www.podiumaudio.com

Podium

A BLADE THROUGH TIME

1

BURN

Things are transformed one into another according to necessity, and render justice to one another according to the order of time.

—Anaximander

They killed me in the summer of my sixteenth year.

A man and woman in the white robes of the Magistrate strolled down the boulevard leading to my family manor. A retinue of soldiers marched behind them, dressed for war despite the heat. I lounged beneath a lemon tree, oblivious, while my rhetoric teacher rambled about the meaning of language. I offered an occasional grunt to prove I had not fallen asleep.

"Young master," he said. I had never heard Everett sound uncertain before. I opened my eyes.

Two Magisters came through the open gate, their faces hidden behind ivory masks. What were the Archon's justices doing here? They existed in a different world to children like myself, a parallel realm that sometimes drifted past but never truly mixed with my own.

As the ruler of Velassa, Nony brought stability to the area. In a Great City of a hundred thousand people, only the deranged and the desperate broke the law. It wasn't because Velassa was some religious utopia. It was because of monsters like those two in the ivory masks, specters of divine justice.

I was so fixated on the pair I barely noticed as the soldiers circled around the manor. Everett understood the danger before I did. He ran for it.

He made it less than a dozen yards before the female Magister raised her hand. His clothing burst into flames, a white-hot intensity that melted flesh and turned his hair into a torch. His screams pierced through the silence that had settled over the area. I will never forget that acrid stench, the mix of burnt pork and the copper tang of his blood as it boiled.

The Magisters continued along the path toward the manor. A surreal feeling washed over me, as if my body no longer belonged to me. I felt as if I were drifting through some morbid daydream. Everett's screams died away, and that empty silence once again settled over everything. His blackened corpse made no sound as it collapsed onto the grass. The gentle breeze stole swirls of ash from his body.

I flinched as a soldier hoisted me up by the collar. I hadn't even noticed his approach. Bleary eyes looked down at me, bloodshot from a night of drinking. His hands were cracked and calloused, knuckles white with faded scars. Sudden terror turned me into a rag doll in his grip.

"Don't struggle." His voice was little more than a whisper. "Was that man your teacher? Yes? The Increate is the greatest teacher of all. Watch what he has to tell you about sinners."

The manor doors opened, and a few of the servants stepped out. A maid attempted to flee, and she too became a smear of flame. The others slammed the door shut as if wood could protect them from what was coming.

The soldier watched me, lips curved in a small smile, curious as to how I would react. It drifted away when he saw the lack of expression on my face. "Heartless bastard, aren't you?"

I had known Everett for over a decade; one of my earliest memories was of him scolding me. What kind of ending was this for him? What kind of ending for that maid, whose only mistake had been working for us instead of for one of the hundreds of other affluent families in Velassa?

The sight of their bodies, pitiful and twisted, formed a cold pit deep in my chest. So this was death. Casual destruction beneath the afternoon sun. The priests say that death is the next step, a bridge that leads our souls to paradise.

In that moment even I had to shake my head at their naivete. There was no beauty there, nothing divine. The laughable thing was that

Archon Nony had ordered the Magistrate to come to my family manor. He was the flames of heaven made flesh, a blessed child of the Increate. Paradise was his home. Those he condemned went elsewhere.

Shouts rang out from the manor. Even from a distance I could recognize my father's baritone voice cutting through the panic. The door opened, and he stepped out, a giant confined in an expensive suit. He held a saber at his side. Despite his size and cold gray eyes, I had never pictured him as a fighter. The only time I had ever heard him raise his voice was when he roared with laughter. But in that moment, blade in his hand and eyes on the maid's corpse, I saw a different side of him.

"What is the meaning of this?" The savage expression on his face died when he caught sight of me in the soldier's grip. "Leones! He has nothing to do with this."

By now the Magisters were almost at the portico, close enough that I wondered if my father would be able to cut them down. He was like a warrior from legend, facing these demons in their white robes. They stepped forward, and his sword wavered. Another step forward, and he lowered the blade, a lost expression on his face.

The woman trailed her fingers along a colonnade as she ascended the stairs. Her touch left charred streaks along the marble.

"What a lovely home." Her voice drifted out from behind her mask, soft and melodic. "This is the pride and joy of a family. Of a husband, a wife, their precocious son. Fifteen servants. Four rotating tutors. Productive citizens, living an idyllic life in an idyllic city. And what have we asked of you people? Have we taxed you unfairly?"

"Do not pretend," my father said. "Do not pretend that what you do is right. Wanton slaughter of those who disagree with you. What heinous crime have I committed, that you kill these people for simply being around me?"

The woman nodded, then gestured back toward me; the soldier dragged me forward by the arm. When I tried to struggle, he seized me more securely, holding me in a vise-like grip.

She strolled forward until she was almost face-to-face with my father.

"What heinous crimes have you committed?" The woman glanced my way. I could almost sense her smug smile behind her mask. "The most heinous of all. You questioned Archon Nony. Your little secret meetings with your other collaborators. Writings denouncing his divine lineage."

"It's a historical discussion. There have been other Archons who could control fire. There are many powerful creatures in the world with similar powers. I simply compiled research on the topic of the Archons and whether others could become as powerful as they."

The woman raised her hand to her mouth and laughed. "Such ridiculous heresy. You don't even try to deny it. Even if we were to pretend it wasn't heresy, what qualifications do you have to make that assumption? You're a cloth merchant. The things the Archon can do makes us look like children burning ants with a lens. Without the Archons we would be slaves to the Goetia. Demon food."

My father shook his head. He looked beaten, lost, the idea of him being a fighter no more than an illusion. "I can stop looking into it. It was just something I found interesting. Is this . . . is this all really necessary? Killing innocents over research?"

The woman turned my way. I pulled my head away as she reached out, but the soldier held me in place. Her fingers traced along my jaw and cheekbones, suffused with a pleasant warmth that made me think of Everett's smoldering corpse. "You must think me heartless. I have a daughter. She's a bit younger than you. Oh, the things I would do to protect her . . ."

My mind was blank. From what I had gathered my father had been collecting research on the Archons and similar figures. Even among the Archons, Nony was known to be eccentric, not even allowing paintings or any other depiction of himself. A smarter or braver person could have said something to her. Could have done something to convince her to leave. All I could do was look back at her and her surprisingly gentle eyes.

"Perhaps your father really does just have an academic interest in the Archons. They really are such mysterious beings, after all, somewhere between human and a law of nature." She straightened up and brushed her robes. "But do not question them. Ever. They're the reason you live such comfortable lives, in this pretty little manor near the sea. All these lemon trees and chirping birds. A thousand years ago mankind was bred like livestock. There were no happy families. We didn't even have a language."

Farther into the manor there was a scream. Probably one of the maids attempting to escape out of a side door.

That's when Father struck.

The saber chopped deep into the woman's shoulder with a meaty *thunk*. Before he could swing again, the male Magister pointed, and the world flashed orange. When my vision cleared, I saw Father had fallen to one knee; his forearm was incinerated, ending in little more than a charcoal stick. The saber had half-melted into a bar of liquid steel.

The woman leaned against a column, rivulets of blood dripping from beneath her sleeve as her arm hung uselessly at her side. She touched the gaping wound in her shoulder. Flesh sizzled as she cauterized the wound. She took a deep breath to gather her composure, then nodded at her companion.

My father looked at me, his face pale and eyes unfocused. His mouth twisted into a mirthless grin. He breathed "sorry" at me. A moment later, flames washed over him, so intense the soldier had to drag me back a couple of paces.

He did not scream. Such heat scours away everything, even the sensation of pain. The fire consumed him with a merciful swiftness, reducing him to a blackened skeleton. He collapsed not far from the body of the maid who had attempted to escape.

"He should have suffered more," said the woman.

"You should have talked less." The male Magister glanced at the soldier who was holding me. "Put the boy inside. Make sure the perimeter is secure. We've spent enough time here."

With a grunt, the soldier pried open the front door and shoved me toward the manor. The knowledge of what was coming broke through the haze. I grabbed the man's arm, trying to pull him closer or maybe pull myself out. His other fist buried itself in my gut, knocking the wind from my lungs. I kneeled, dry heaving, hardly noticing him plant his boot against my forehead until he shoved me backward into the foyer.

The door slammed shut.

Waiting for my breathing to return to normal, I looked around. Disconcerting how normal everything looked inside the entranceway. I had walked through the foyer a thousand times, past all the plants and tapestries, and it looked the same as ever.

For a moment I found it easy to pretend that nothing had happened. Everett had ended his lesson early. I would walk to the kitchens, where the cook would prepare me a midday snack. Everything was fine.

"Leones!" One of the maids noticed me and hurried over. "What's happening? What happened to your father? Never mind that, come. We'll figure this out, don't you worry."

Recovered enough, I shoved myself to my feet and tried the door. It refused to budge even after I put all my weight behind it; the maid even added her own frantic strength, to no avail. The door began to feel warm to the touch.

"We have to get out of here." My voice sounded strange. High and panicked. "They're going to burn us alive."

The maid stared, her face scrunched in confusion, but after a moment, the gravity of the situation dawned on her. "We'll try another exit."

I stumbled after her, the world a blur. Before long, smoke began to drift through the air.

The manor was made of stone, but nearly everything within it was flammable. Tapestries adorned the walls, the furniture was wood, and my mother's green thumb had given rise to a host of plants and ivy. Perhaps we could have contained a normal fire, but the divine magic of the Magistrate could consume even the stone foundation.

The maid sniffled and wiped her nose. "I have a daughter. I can't . . ."

"You'll see her soon." It sounded feeble, pathetic, but she made eye contact and nodded.

We hurried along. Not far to the side exit leading toward the gardens. Maybe we could even slip past the soldiers. They would be stretched thin along the perimeter of the estate.

We almost made it before smoke roiled past us in a dense fog. The maid inhaled it first and doubled over, coughs wracking her body until tears streamed down her face. Burying my face in my sleeve, I fell to the floor and crawled beneath that dark miasma.

The maid followed suit, still attempting to cough the poison out of her lungs. The heat was insidious, almost pleasant at first, then evolving into an unpleasant warmth that sapped my strength. I thought of Everett, the maid, and my father—burned to nothing in moments. It almost seemed like a merciful death compared to the smoke and building heat.

Flames spread into the room. They raced along the vines of ivy growing along the walls. A tapestry went up, ablaze. The conflagration ate through the room, insatiable, turning my home into a land of oranges and yellows and black smoke.

I whimpered as my skin reddened from the heat. The maid had given up, head buried in her arms, letting out the occasional rumbling cough. Wisps of smoke drifted from her head as her hair curled and burnt. A weak voice muttered something too soft to make out—her daughter's name?

My biggest regret was that I would not see my mother one last time. No, my biggest regret was that I was a weak child. All of our destinies had been snipped away because we had provoked monsters infinitely more powerful than we were. I lay there with my eyes closed, wishing I was one of those monsters. Wishing I could save my family.

My body tingled with a numbness that let me ignore my inflamed skin. I opened my eyes, determined for some reason to face my death with dignity. Not that anyone would remember the stubborn heroism of a teenager buried beneath a spreading inferno. It was impossible to see past the waves of roiling smoke. The heat sapped the moisture from my eyes as I stared at death.

Smoke swirled above. The pattern seemed impossible; I felt as if my vision was fragmented, as if I were watching everything through a dark prism. I could sense something beyond the smoke. It was a promise of power. If only I could reach up, I could grab some tear in reality and reshape it with my will. Perhaps what I sensed was the realm of death, purgatory breaking through to welcome me in.

Slowly, I raised my hand. It took everything I had to move my fingers a few inches. There was a stubbornness deep within me I had never noticed before, an explosion of will that refused to die. I tapped that power to lift my shuddering hand into the smoke.

Heat exploded outward. The flames licking the room flashed into an inferno that consumed everything, a brilliant sky of orange piercing through the miasma.

2

NUMBERS

In numerology, eleven is a sacred number. It represents heaven reflected on itself. One and one. We can find an underlying pattern throughout society that treats this as holy. There are eleven Archons who rule over eleven Great Cities."

I opened my eyes to see Everett sitting on the grass next to me. He was rolling a cigarillo on his lap and winked when he saw he had my attention. His clever fingers manipulated the tobacco leaf in the way I'd watched a hundred times before. There were wrinkles at the corners of his eyes, and gray hair had begun to show at his temples. Still, he gave off the energy of a man in his prime, happily rambling about esoteric knowledge to an audience he knew couldn't care less.

But this time I did care, focusing on every word he said. In fact, they were the same words he had uttered earlier in the day, an hour before the Magisters arrived.

His smile grew larger. "Well look at you, young master. Forgive me if my lesson woke you up from your nap. Honestly, I just enjoy hearing myself speak, and your good parents actually pay me to do it. Don't tell me, do you actually like numerology? It's one of my favorites."

"What?" I stood and looked around. Everything seemed the same as usual. I looked at the back of my shaking hands, expecting them to be cracked and burnt from the flames, but the skin was smooth and tanned.

Birds sang sweet melodies to one another. The breeze contained a hint of salt from the nearby Twilight Sea.

"Numerology." Everett mixed bits of clove into his cigarillo. "It's one of the hard sciences. It's intrinsically linked with logic, philosophy, all the underpinnings of the world. Tarotology and the like are all nonsense, and don't let anyone tell you different."

I stared at him. Had everything before simply been a dream? The things I had touched, the smells, the pain—all had seemed so real at the time. Death was one of the sure ways of waking up from a dream. That must have been what happened. It had been a vivid nightmare, perhaps triggered because Everett had mentioned the Archon while I was drifting off to sleep.

Everett rolled the cigarillo tight and licked it to seal the paper. Rising to his feet, he tucked the cigarillo behind his ear and coughed. "Let me go and light this, supposing you don't mind."

Whistling, he strolled down the avenue toward the manor. Everything about this seemed so familiar.

Most likely it was a coincidence. Everett often smoked during our lectures and went off on tangents about numerology and alchemy. We must have gone through the same motions a dozen times before. But there was a nagging feeling in the back of my mind that I couldn't explain. I sat against the lemon tree until Everett returned.

"Do you think it's possible to tell the future?" I asked as he crouched next to me. "Through dreams or numerology or . . . whatever."

Everett blew a smoke ring off to the side and scrunched his face in thought. "Despite all my talk of numerology and the like, most philosophers agree it's impossible. No prophecy has ever come true unless it was so vague it could apply to a dozen situations. Our ancestors used to practice oracular magic, sure. But our ancestors believed a lot of nonsense without any scientific basis. Smarter men than me could talk to you about causality and the arrow of time. You're a bright kid, but even if I knew how to explain it, I'm not sure you'd understand."

Everett was eccentric, but I trusted him. He had studied under the renowned philosopher Severius and graduated from the Academia Levana. I believed him if he said there was no proven incident of a person accurately predicting the future. He was far too overeducated to be my tutor, and we both knew it. His casual attitude made me think he saw his position as a sort of retirement.

To me he was a mysterious figure. Levana was on the other side of the Civilized Lands, meaning that over the course of his life my tutor had journeyed farther than I could imagine before finally ending up here. Even though the Archons protected mankind from the outside world they were not all-powerful. While I doubted some of the more fantastical stories I'd heard, beyond Velassa's walls there were vast swaths of land best avoided. Chaos from the outside world had found a home in those lost and quiet places.

If he told me no one could predict the future, I trusted him. Yet my heart still raced in my chest. I was old enough that people expected me to leave my childish fantasies behind. I was the son of cloth merchants, expected to learn the ins and outs of the family business.

I told myself this, but my panic continued to grow. I felt as though my dream had merged with reality. Everything around me proceeded as I had remembered. Everett's rant about the number eleven sounded familiar. The words, the cadence . . . despite my nonchalant exterior I did listen to some of what he said. I was certain he had uttered the same speech earlier, right before taking a break to smoke an identical cigarillo.

The entire situation made me feel helpless, as when I had been afraid of the dark as a child. There was the sense that something dangerous and unknowable watched from the shadows, an eerie pressure on the soul.

Sensing my unease, Everett placed a hand on my shoulder. "Is something wrong? You're behaving differently today. I can't recall the last time you actually asked me a question."

I spoke before thinking. "Do you know anything about my father looking into the Archons? Does he ever talk about Archon Nony to you?"

Everett's hand slipped from my shoulder. He exhaled a stream of smoke. The sight of it sent my heart racing.

"Your father is a brilliant man. I've met a lot of smart people so I don't use that term lightly. But there is absolutely no reason a merchant would do something so unbelievably stupid. He didn't tell you he was doing this, did he?"

"Maybe . . . maybe you should go." I tried to smile, but it came out as more of a grimace. "I think my dad made a mistake."

Everett looked down the avenue, eyes wide. There was nothing but rows of trees. "If you're joking, I'm not impressed. Maybe I haven't been the best tutor, but I hope you respect me enough not to lie about that sort of thing. Come, let's go to your father and get to the bottom of this."

"I really think you should go now." Some of the panic crept into my voice.

Everett ran a hand through his hair, a complex expression on his face. I had no idea what he was thinking as he watched me fidget. I thought of the way he had fled when he saw the Magisters, how he hadn't even attempted to help me.

In a way I resented the way he had abandoned me in that moment of panic, regardless of whether it had been dream or prophecy. We had known each other for years. As foolish as it was, I considered him one of my few friends, a familiar face that had laughed with me and sparked my imagination with stories of the outside world.

"Go," I said.

Everett gave me a tight-lipped nod and wandered off. Instead of walking down the avenue he headed toward the back of the manor, avoiding the obvious routes. The sight of his retreating figure eased some of my panic. He was my friend, and I had saved him.

I headed back in the direction of the manor. I walked at first, but all the nervous energy building up in my body demanded I speed up. I was running by the time I reached the portico and leaped up the stairs two at a time. I wrenched the front door open, much to the shock of one of the maids cleaning the foyer.

"What's the fuss?"

It was Velia, a pretty young woman I had developed a bit of a crush on. For a moment I was embarrassed for her to see me in such a state.

"Where's my father? I need to see him."

She offered me an uncertain smile. "He's in his study."

I thanked her before rushing in that direction. As I hurried along, I remembered the way the flames had devoured everything. All the beauty of my home was little more than kindling. After an eternity I arrived outside my father's study.

What if I was wrong? I had sent Everett away and come here based on some nightmare. I knocked before I gave in to my second thoughts.

"Come in," my father called out.

I had only seen the inside of his study a handful of times. It never failed to impress me. Countless books lined the walls; once I had asked him if he had read them all, and with a smile, he claimed to have memorized at least half of them. The rest of the study was an exercise in organized chaos. A vibrant quilt imported from the Turquoise Isles dangled from a bust of some ancient philosopher. The saber he had wielded in my dream was propped against a recliner. Various other baubles cluttered the room, from ancient metal spheres to lewd statuettes.

Father sat behind a mahogany desk like a dragon in the center of its hoard. He looked up from one of the several tomes arrayed before him and steepled his fingers under his chin. "What's the matter, Leones? Shouldn't you be with Everett?"

He poured himself a measure of brandy from a crystal decanter. Sipping it, he waited for me to gather my thoughts.

I was unsure where to start. I clasped my hands behind my back to stop them from trembling. "I sent him away. I didn't want the Magisters to get him."

The glass paused at his lips. "The Magisters? The Magistrate are here?"

"No, not yet," I said. "I had a dream they came here with soldiers. They said you were looking into the Archon. They burned everything. You aren't, are you?"

Father finished the brandy and rose to his feet. He was a tall man, standing head and shoulders above most. He had always been gentle toward me, but many people found him imposing. The intensity in his gray eyes made me realize why.

Even his voice was deeper, a husky growl I had never heard from him. "A dream? This happened in a dream? Tell me the truth. How did you learn about this? Did your mother say something?"

I felt overwhelmed by all of my fear and uncertainty, by the abandonment and disbelief from the people I looked up to. Most damning of all, my father had essentially admitted that he had been looking into the Archon. All of my life I had seen him as someone holy, someone beyond reproach. I believed in him the way I believed the sun would rise in the morning. In the end it turned out he was just a man.

His voice was little more than a whisper. "How could they know? This doesn't make any sense. Tell me what you saw, Leones."

It took a moment to find my voice. Slowly, haltingly, I described my dream. How the Magisters came with a retinue of soldiers and brought ruin to everything we knew. He poured himself more brandy as I told him how our home had burned around me. In a small voice, I explained how the world had warped and I had woken up to Everett's voice.

All the blood drained from my father's face. "You used magic? Has this ever happened before?"

Out of all the responses I had braced myself for I had never imagined he would say such a thing. Seeing my confusion, Father choked out a laugh. He walked across the room and touched the spine of an ancient leather-bound book. Eyes closed, he muttered to himself under his breath.

I had seen him do this before as a parlor trick. Years ago, he had challenged me to pick a page from a book in his library. After I told him, he laid his hand on the book and after a moment was able to recite the entire passage from memory.

He opened his eyes and glanced my way. "It doesn't make sense. There's no true divinatory magic. It's impossible to tell the future. I need you to focus, son. Remember exactly how you felt in that moment. Try to recreate that exact sensation. If you are able to repeat what you did, explain everything again, but start with the phrase 'phoenix burn.'"

Despite everything he was still my father. I couldn't disappoint him. Even at my worst he never offered more than harsh words and disappointed glares. Especially when I was younger, I had been prone to mischief; every time I went too far, he would sit me down and explain what I had done wrong. Sometimes when my mother wasn't around he would even put on a secretive smile and tell me how I could have done it better. He had given me everything. If he wanted me to try, I would try.

I remembered the way the flames had closed in around me. At first my mind shied away from the memory of my skin blistering and beginning to slough away. I gritted my teeth and focused. I felt an echo of that agony, of the primal terror I felt as black smoke roiled around me. How in the end the world had fractured around me.

And just like that a wisp of that bizarre power drifted past my consciousness. I noticed it, and it noticed me. I abandoned the memory of death and reached out. That force was like lightning on a summer day. It was an orchid in the desert and a shadow in the valley of heaven. It was the anger hiding deep within the prayers of a saint. It was all of that and more.

A bright explosion of pain forced me back to reality. It felt as if someone was twisting a knife in the front of my skull. Tiny stars drifted through my vision; the world around me was blurred, unfocused. I sat on the floor and buried my face in my hands, waiting for the pain to subside.

I heard my father's voice. "What's wrong, Leones? Why aren't you with Everett?"

3

MUSIC

I repeated everything to him again, but this time I started with the phrase he had given me: phoenix burn. After that, he sat rigidly in his chair, hands clenched on the desk in front of me. Occasionally he looked as if he wanted to speak, but the code and my descriptions were enough to keep him silent. It was a testament to his intelligence that he could take my insane ramblings and form them into a logical sequence of events. Between my migraine and the overlapping memories, I had lost touch with reality.

"So you're manipulating time." He placed his coin purse on the desk. With trembling fingers, he removed a gold sovereign and set it spinning. "What you're telling me is so convoluted that I believe you. I can't imagine you would make this up or someone would set you up to this. You . . . saw the Magistrate come, you activated your magic, and then you went back approximately an hour into the past. You came here, used your magic when I asked you to, and went back another ten minutes or so."

The migraine had faded slightly. I was unsure how to respond. Separate memories competed in my head. Parts of my mind insisted that the past had occurred in completely different ways. Even worse, another part of my brain insisted that it was remembering the future. All I could do was focus on what was happening each moment. Only the present was real.

The gold sovereign wobbled before coming to a stop. Father nodded as if he had come to a decision and removed his golden rings. "This is what's going to happen. I'm going to give you some things to take with you."

"To take with me?"

"Yes." He sighed. "I can't give you anything that makes it obvious you are part of this family. Nobody can know who you are."

A lump formed in my throat. Exiled from everything I knew. No longer could I wear the surname Ansteri with pride. A childish thought, one I tried my best to push away.

"Your mother is in the city," Father continued. "If the Increate is kind they won't find her. I'm going to tell everyone in the manor what is coming. Hopefully they will not hunt down the servants and make them suffer for my sins. You have maybe half an hour to run. If this power is real, it may be what you need to survive. You must be very careful as well. If someone helps you and is caught, they will burn."

"Why are you talking like you aren't coming with me?" The migraine continued to fade. The world started to make more sense. Like specters, my feelings of loss and abandonment drifted back. Who would I have to rely on?

"I can't. Maybe if I had a couple of days' notice." Father placed the sovereign and his rings into the coin purse and rose to his feet. He walked over to the saber and grabbed it before continuing over to me. "So what you have to do is become powerful. If you are somehow going back in time, I want you to become strong enough to give me those couple of days. I've put a lot of blood and tears into building up our family legacy. You're still just a boy, but I'm asking you to help me."

He handed me the coin purse and kept the sword for himself. "Take this. You know Volario Faske? You've met him before. Little fellow. He has the tailor's shop in the Market District. Go there and tell him to get you out of the city. Go to Odena. It's close, and Archon Vasely rules fairly. I've given you a very unconventional education, and I know you're a smart boy. You'll do fine."

"What am I supposed to do?" The wool pouch was heavy with coin. A man like my father mostly dealt with gold. Though it was nothing to him, it was enough to live a simple life for a few decades. But that was not my path in life.

He selected a couple of books from his library, including the leather-bound tome he had touched before. "You need to learn more. Don't join the Academia. Find the philosophers and impress them without letting them know the truth. They know me. Don't reveal your heritage, though some of them will figure it out easily enough. Don't flaunt this money. Get a travel bag."

He barked out each sentence in a commanding tone. As he looked down at me his eyes softened. "I can't tell you how sorry I am that I have failed you and your mother like this. Now please, go. "

"I don't want you to die." By now I had begun to feel like myself again. I knew we were saying our goodbyes. This would be one of the last memories of my old life. A childhood severed away, and over what?

"Get far away and don't look back. The Magistrate are thorough. Once they get close enough it's impossible to slip through their grasp." Father held the scabbard in front of his face and unsheathed a few inches of the saber's blade. Even after decades he had kept the blade polished and well-honed. "Strength on your journey; journey strong."

I hugged him for as long as he allowed me to.

I wandered through the city, down familiar streets filled with unfamiliar faces.

No matter how far I walked, my thoughts kept returning home. I remembered looking back at my father, seeing the sadness in his face as he held his saber. After a while I thought I could smell smoke in the air, but it may have been my mind playing tricks.

I considered my future in a futile attempt to ignore the present. Others had provided for my every need as I grew up. Servants washed my clothes and prepared my food. Tutors instructed me how to think. Now Father had stitched together a plan for my survival, trying to provide for me even in the shadow of death. He had held my hand for so long that I was determined to pull him back to his feet.

My mother was somewhere in the city. I wanted to look for her, but how could I? I had no idea where she was. Velassa was a Great City, and the Magistrate would be looking for her. Most of all, this way I would never know her true fate. There would always be the chance that she was still alive.

I promised that one day, when I became strong enough, I would look for her.

I had used magic. What that fully entailed remained a mystery to me. Most powers were linked to the material plane, though some were more ethereal than others. Archon Nony wielded the spark of purgatory. Vasely held dominion over sound. The Huntress walked from shadow to shadow. The idea of being able to return to the past seemed far more mystical in comparison. What does a child know of time?

After a few miles I entered Market Street. Vendors presented their wares, a hectic mix of jewelry and weapons and clothing and anything else they felt would attract customers. The smell of grilled meat offered a welcome distraction.

I weaved my way through the crowd, keeping my eyes open for a particular sign. Eventually I spotted a wooden board swinging in the breeze, engraved with a pair of crossed needles above the word FASKE. Unlike most of the proprietors of Market Street, he had no need to advertise his services beyond simply displaying his name.

A bell tinkled overhead as I entered the shop.

A man sitting on a stool glanced up with a frown. He was hardly taller than a child, but there was no mistaking his age. Sunlight gleamed off his bald pate, and a heavy white mustachio drooped past his chin. He wore simple cotton clothing in defiance of the luxurious outfits arranged around the store. Beside him was a wooden mannequin in a half-finished dress, covered with a gaudy collection of lace and sequins.

"Please schedule an appointment in advance, boy. I'm very busy." Volario Faske studied his fingernails as if to emphasize his point. His guard, a brute of a man sitting on a chair that threatened to collapse under his weight, didn't even bother to glance up from his book. The cover depicted a fair maiden fainting into a knight's arms.

"I don't care how busy you are." The words slipped out before I could stop myself. "This is important."

Volario snapped his fingers without bothering to look back at me.

The guard sighed and closed his book. The chair creaked as his massive bulk slowly rose. "Have some respect for your elders, boy. You are in the presence of my brother Volario Faske, whose legend eclipses the Civilized Lands. It is said that even the Archons seek out his talents."

Volario started worrying at a dress sleeve, unraveling an errant thread. "Yes, some have certainly said such a thing."

When I had come here with my father a few years ago he had warned me about the eccentric clothier. The more ancient he became the more liberties he took in dealing with people. Half of his fame came from the notoriety of offending a host of folk. Father found him amusing; their conversation had mostly consisted of insults and thinly-veiled threats that somehow concluded with an invitation for him to eat dinner with us.

I bit my tongue and forced myself to speak calmly. "I need your help getting out of the city."

This caught the little old man's attention. He raised his hand, and the guard stopped shuffling toward me. "I remember you. An upstart squirt who could barely let go of his mom's hand long enough to pick up a fork. How is Jansen, that smug prick?"

The look on my face must have told him all he needed to know.

"Ah, so it's like that." Volario hopped to his feet with the vigor of a man half his age. "I knew that fairy-footed bastard would slip up one day. I don't want to know what he did or what's happening. There's a lot of trouble out there waiting to be found. People like me and him were born with more balls than brains, so we go hunting for it."

"How did you meet?" The question sounded absurd in my ears. More important things to do than idle chatter. But I needed to get on the dwarf's good side.

Volario sauntered over to me and gave me a thorough look from head to toe. "Oh, we weren't much older than you. You can imagine how dashing I was back then. Jansen and I were acolyte philosophers. It was a lot of getting in touch with nature and stuffy discussions, but we had some good times."

"I never knew he was a philosopher." It seemed like a strange thing to never mention. Nothing to be ashamed about.

"Technically not. The entire process takes damn near a decade. Your father never had much patience. Went to the Frontier to test his mettle." He jerked a thumb at the massive guard. "That's where he and Dondarrio became fast friends. Never had much in common before that."

"You were an acolyte as well?" I asked the guard.

He shut his book again and closed his eyes as if the conversation pained him. His deep voice rumbled through the store. "No. Not much for fancy words. I've always been a soldier. So was your father. Much more than some silver-tongued philosopher."

The mention of soldiers sparked a thrill of panic in my gut. "Do many people know you're friends? Father . . . upset the Archon. They sent Magisters to our home. And soldiers. He told me they might come for anyone who helps me."

I expected Volario to throw me out. Instead, his eyes became even more lively. He snapped at his brother; with a heavy sigh the guard lumbered to his feet and headed toward a back room.

Volario slapped his thigh. "Jansen really fucked it up this time. We haven't talked much recently, but in the end, he knows the best man to patch this up. Let's find you some clothes."

The dwarf sped around his shop, gathering simple yet well-crafted clothing that wouldn't draw attention. Two outfits and an elegant fur jacket.

"My clientele tends to run toward women," he said, holding up a pair of trousers against my waist. "But these should do nicely. Ignore the frills. Supposed to be another mild winter, but preparation always wins out."

The giant returned with a cloth-covered object balanced between his arms. When he deposited it on the floor, groaning as he bent over, it landed with a heavy clatter. Volario skipped over and pulled back the cloth, revealing a sword shaped like a giant cleaver and a pair of wicked stilettos. He flourished the knives with glee, the tip of his tongue clamped between his teeth.

"It's been a while," he said.

The giant—Dondarrio Faske—grasped his weapon and held it aloft. Joints popped, but he held it as if it weighed nothing. Slightly more intimidating than his lesser half.

I considered asking if they had any spare iron lying around, but I had never held a real weapon in my life. Better to know my place for now. And I had something more effective—a power lingering at the back of my mind. The ability to return to the past. An unreliable ability, and I had no idea what its limitations were, but I suspected being able to flee would serve me well.

"How long ago did the Magisters arrive at your home?" asked Volario.

I had walked several miles to get here, at a pace just short of frantic, trying not to draw too much attention. Forty minutes, perhaps? That meant that I had departed before the Magisters arrived, though I had no intention of explaining the finer details.

"Twenty minutes ago, maybe?"

Thankfully they asked no more questions. Volario patted me on the hip and told me to follow him as he surged toward the door. Before he could escape, Dondarrio rested a hand on his back, large enough to eclipse the dwarf's shoulders.

"Stay," he said. "I will get the boy to Odena."

"Oh? You don't think I can fight anymore?"

Dondarrio grunted. "Never could. Times are even worse now."

I thought the dwarf would press the issue, but he relented with a good-natured shrug. He twirled my way, clasped his hands together, and bowed. "Strength on your journey. Journey strong."

Unsure what to do, I returned the bow before falling in behind Dondarrio. He moved at a serene pace, but his long legs ate up the distance. I stayed off to the side, head tilted away from the crowd, wondering if my attempts to look inconspicuous would only draw more attention. The lumbering giant with a giant cleaver propped against his shoulder certainly didn't help.

My eyes kept drifting toward the Panopticon, a looming edifice of steel and glass and hard lines that dwarfed every other building in the city. Archon Nony's residence. Rumor had it that Magisters stood vigil day and night, peering into the soul of the citizens below. Searching for kindling to feed the divine flame.

"Dondarrio, is it?" I asked to distract myself. "Thank you."

"Just Faske," he said.

We passed by a few guardsmen who were leaning against a building. Their eyes tracked the giant, completely ignoring me. After we passed, they laughed amongst themselves, whispering.

My heart thundered in my chest. No way they had recognized me. No one besides the Magisters would know I had escaped. My description would be passed around, but it was still too early for every random guardsman to be on alert.

"Where are we going?" I asked.

"Caravans," said Faske. "Many leave this time of day. Some bound to head toward Odena. You act too suspicious. Breathe. In. And out."

His advice was surprisingly useful. I focused on the air flowing through my lungs, allowing myself to be swallowed up in the giant's shadow. After fifteen minutes of pretending my heart wasn't on the verge of failure we arrived at the caravans.

Shouting. Men bustling about, hauling crates and cursing. Sweat and tar and other random, contradictory scents. Spices and herbs and metal.

Faske lumbered through it all, carving a path through the chaos with his bulk.

Then, a different type of shout. A Magister stood in the center of a group of distraught men. They knew better than to contradict a divine official, but from the looks on their faces, they were seething.

The Magister was a middle-aged gentleman with refined features. An orb of white flame whirled around his head like some orbiting crown. He shouted again, his voice slicing through the clamor. "I repeat, all caravans must be thoroughly searched before departure."

Faske stopped, pressing a hand against my chest—as if I had any intention of approaching the Magister. "We find another way."

Before we turned back, I noticed something disturbing. The white orb stopped revolving around the Magister's head. After a moment he looked straight at me.

He pointed.

"Run," said Faske.

A spark ignited at the tip of the Magister's finger. The distressed looks on the faces of the men around him transformed into horror. They scurried away as the immediate area brightened, the midday light turned blinding.

Faske shoved me, and I finally took the hint, scrambling toward safety.

A faint buzz, then screams. A blast of heat washed against my back. Concern for the giant made me look behind.

A perfect line had carved through the flagstones where we were standing, at least two dozen paces long. In its path lay several men, screaming or staring at missing limbs, bloodlessly cauterized. Two halves of a crate fell in opposite directions, revealing bags of smoldering herbs.

The sight etched itself in my memory.

Fortunately, none of the fallen men was Faske.

The giant charged toward the Magister, hollering some wordless battle cry. I wondered for a moment if time had become distorted, but no—he was simply that fast, eating up the distance between him and the Magister in seconds, heedless of the panicked crowd surging against him.

For a moment I thought he was going to chop the bastard in half.

Then another beam of light erupted from the Magister's finger. It lasted only for a second, lancing through the giant before winking out of existence. Faske's momentum brought him forward a few steps before he collapsed, neatly bisected in half.

No...

The power in the back of my mind activated. Back ten minutes.

"We can't take the caravans," was the first thing I said to Faske. "They're being watched."

"You know this now? Not ten seconds ago?"

The giant shook his head but agreed to take another route. We headed toward the Western Gate, where Faske said he knew a smuggler who would be willing to take me to Odena.

The only problem was a matter of money. I thought the passage should not have cost more than a few silvers, but Faske removed two golden sovs.

"To keep him hush," said the giant.

The smuggler turned out to be a completely normal looking fellow. The kind of face that would blend in with any crowd. He sat on a crate in an alleyway, legs swinging, taking great bites from a loaf of hardbread.

Faske, the man of few words, shoved the gold into his hands, jerked a finger at the two of us, and muttered, "Odena. Fast."

We were in the back of his wagon in three minutes. The crates smelled moldy, and I did not relish spending a week back here, but as far as options went, it won out over being burned alive. I would not mind the giant's company either. The man had elevated himself several leagues in my eyes by willing to die for a random kid, charging a Magister. When I closed my eyes, I sometimes imagined his bisected figure collapsing to the flagstones.

The week, at least, was peaceful.

In the morning I would stretch and work through the calisthenic routines I had always neglected in the past. I fancied I could feel myself becoming stronger. It felt like a sort of meditation, allowing me to purge my thoughts for a short while.

When I was finished, I would join the others to break my fast, a simple meal of bread and salted halibut. The smuggler and Faske would talk—mostly the smuggler, making recommendations or idle conversation while the giant grunted. I ate in silence, memorizing what they said and the ways they said it. Their speech had a different cadence, rough and uneducated. Mother would've hated it.

From my past knowledge and the smuggler's chatter I formed a rough idea of Odena, the Great City of music and the arts. It was the throbbing pulse of the Civilized Lands, its streets clogged with bards and firedancers and every other manner of performer. A place where people let their muse drink and revel until the early hours of the morning. It was a triumph of mankind, a tribute to the old days when our ancestors sang stories around a campfire to forget the surrounding dark.

Out of the Great Cities, Odena was the only one that did not fully isolate itself from the outside world. The smuggler claimed that in his youth he had witnessed the Serpent Prince of the Narahven Desert enter the city. Supposedly every hundred years the perennial lord from the South would make a pilgrimage to meet with Archon Vasely.

After my meal I would return to the wagon. Faske would lie there and read his romance novels, rarely bothering to acknowledge my existence. I welcomed the silence. Occasionally I would pull the book Father had given me from my bag and flip through the pages. Most of it was nonsense to me. It was full of inscrutable passages such as:

The kings from the core sea speak the truth when they lie. Their realm of fire and air came before ours of earth and water; they float and watch us drown. We see the Aspect of the Increate as a thousand entrances to a temple, and they see it as a temple with a thousand holes.

Father had written little notes on the margins of the pages. Next to this paragraph he had inked "all is one" in a tight, cramped script that took me half an hour to decipher. I thought of the way Everett would ramble about such esoteric nonsense and realized this was the language of philosophers. Father thought I would benefit from studying under them, though I found it difficult to imagine what my future held.

When I became too frustrated to continue reading the book I experimented with my magic.

Hesitantly I opened my mind to that power. At first it seemed chaotic and mysterious, but eventually I began to identify its edges.

I found that if I thought about a specific memory within the past hour I could go back to that moment. If I reversed time more than two total hours in a day a migraine would begin to set in. After the third I had to curl up in a dark corner until the pain and nausea passed.

There seemed to be no limit as to how many times I could use the power within those three hours. Returning five minutes into the past a dozen times caused no more strain than reversing an entire hour. But no matter what I did, I could not return more than an hour in the past from the initial activation of my power. Any attempt to consecutively use magic to break through that barrier accomplished nothing. The limitations seemed arbitrary, but I learned to begrudgingly accept them.

Over the course of the week, I felt my understanding slowly begin to blossom. I trained my body and mind, attempting one more second, one more repetition. It was the slow and steady progress of a man exploring his limits.

Faske rarely spoke, but over time our proximity forged a bond between us. Sometimes he would watch me go through my daily routine, and after a while he started offering small tips to improve my form as I exercised.

It was a tranquil journey. The worst were the quiet moments where I laid in the back of the wagon, a scratchy blanket pulled up to my chest, fighting to forget the faces of the dead. Everett's charred corpse. Father on his knees, looking up at the female Magister before she ended him. The maid, sobbing as she suffocated.

A deep heaviness would weigh down on my chest. Eventually sleep relieved me from my memories, morphing them into vague nightmares. In the morning I would remember them only as a lingering anxiety.

Once we stopped at a roadside inn at my insistence. My power would make things safe enough, and Velassa could not spare enough guards to patrol every inn. I took the opportunity to bathe and eat something besides salted fish. Mostly I kept my chin down and avoided eye contact with others, but the inn had a small library that drew my attention. I browsed through the books until I found one on introductory philosophy.

It seemed like a flight of fancy. What if the Magisters tracked us down and discovered, on the route to Odena, I had bought a book on philosophy? But I couldn't live the rest of my life being too paranoid to interact with other people.

Father had cautioned that I would have to intrigue the philosophers of Odena in order to become their student. I paid a silver denari for the book and a set of writing utensils.

The book offered a broad overview of topics I had already studied, such as ethics, logic, and language. Feeling foolish, I scrawled notes in the margins like my father. My insights seemed hollow and ridiculous as I attempted to mimic the writer's vague musings. Most promising were mental exercises purporting to expand the mind and cultivate willpower. I integrated these into my daily routine, hoping they would help control my magic.

Despite these distractions I had more spare time than I wanted. I would watch the landscape drift past, feeling lost and uncertain. I was barely a young man, and the future seemed insurmountable. The first step would be to join the ranks of Odena's philosophers, and that was only the beginning. Even worse, I had no concrete goal besides the desire to become powerful.

Eventually Odena appeared on the horizon. Like all Great Cities it was encircled by a perfect stone wall raised from the earth by Archon Aramadat. Splotches of color marred the walls; as we approached, I realized these were decorative murals depicting all manner of fantastic scenes. Winged men hovered over a battlefield. Nagas emerged from water with their tridents held aloft. An unfathomably large golem loomed over a village.

The peaks and spires of a castle poked above the wall. This was Archon Vasely's residence, and despite its elegance it seemed very reserved in comparison to Nony's Panopticon. Nony's fortress was like a pillar stretching to the heavens, a constant reminder of his presence. After living in its shadow my whole life, I had never imagined an Archon would reside within a simple palace.

For the first time since the Magistrate destroyed my home, I felt hopeful. As our wagon approached the gates, I heard music drifting through the air. The smuggler had mentioned it before: a soothing melody, almost like a lullaby. It was a manifestation of Vasely's power, a sort of aura that radiated out for miles around him whenever he meditated. After a few minutes I barely noticed unless I focused on it.

The guards waved us into the city without a second glance. An eclectic crowd bustled through the streets. Strange and colorful figures mingled with the familiar commonfolk. I saw a shirtless man with a lute strapped to his back, his body wreathed in geometric tattoos. A woman in a yellow robe twirled through the streets, her face turned toward the sky, occasionally bumping into folk who all but ignored her presence.

After a few minutes the caravan came to a stop.

"Welcome to Odena, boy." Faske pocketed his book and rose to his feet. "Damned sinful place that it is."

4

NOTHING

I wanted to go to the philosophers immediately, but Faske insisted that I spend at least a day in the city preparing myself. He lamented about the impatience of youth when I told him I had spent the entire journey planning how to impress them. Appearance, he insisted, was one of the most important qualities in a candidate. I found it amusing that he said this while patting his prodigious gut, but when he showed me my reflection in a mirror, I conceded he may have a point.

We stayed at an upscale tavern named The Golden Crown. I sipped lavender tea while I watched musicians perform in the common area, trying to ignore the voice in the back of my head telling me I was wasting valuable time.

I brought the book on introductory philosophy, intending to read through it once more, but as the day wore on, I set it to one side. Remembering the wild look in my reflection's eyes, I surrendered to the soothing effects of the tea and the music. The bards sang of summer love and the innocent joys of life. It wasn't until I finally relaxed that I realized how close to the edge I was.

Faske was right. Constant studying and exercise had pushed my body to its limits. My jaw ached from grinding my teeth, and a heavy dullness had settled into my muscles. Experimenting with my power left me in a fugue as my mind attempted to make sense of my overlapping memories.

Best not to focus overly much on piecing together a coherent reality. Whatever was happening, happened.

I succumbed to the simple pleasures of living. After a while the musicians stopped playing. Faske joined me for lunch and a few words. The philosophy book received some attention, and in my relaxed mindstate I actually understood most of what I read.

After a few hours an older woman took a seat next to me and struck up a conversation about the book. I wondered what her motive was as she reminisced about her academy days studying philosophy. Somehow that segued into an explanation of her life story.

In the end I chalked it up to a much more relaxed atmosphere between strangers in this city. She paid for my tab and even bought me a delicious plate of thinly sliced raw fish unlike anything I'd had before.

She eventually wandered off, thanking me for listening. Likely I had not said more than a dozen words myself, but there was comfort in such a simple, pleasant encounter. New musicians took over as the night wore on, playing rowdier tunes. The alcohol started to flow, and I waved off a server who offered me some wine, wondering how old they thought I was or whether they cared.

After finishing my day with a hot bath, I felt almost like my old self. My eyes closed the second my head hit the pillow, and the next morning I woke up with a smile on my face. For once, no nightmares had troubled me. But soon enough dark thoughts fluttered at the edges of my consciousness.

Careful not to wake Faske, I slipped out of bed and went through the motions of my morning routine. I had to admit the giant's advice was sound. If I had gone to the philosophers immediately, they would have seen a young man toeing the edge of the abyss. Even if I joined their ranks their impression of me would have been forever tainted.

Faske knocked on the door. After entering he gave me an appraising look and nodded. "Better."

I returned his nod. The giant and I had not spoken much over the last week, but I felt as if we communicated as much as was necessary. His reserved demeanor had taught me more than any of the philosophical nonsense I had studied during our journey. Despite his grumbling and solemn stares there was something comforting about his presence—something solid. After living around garrulous folk like Everett and my father I had never before considered the value of silence.

In the afternoon we headed toward the home of the philosophers. When I asked the giant what he knew about them he shrugged.

My heart pounded in my chest as I considered what lay ahead. For the past sixteen years my life had followed a comfortable routine. I had never truly faced the unknown. What if the philosophers saw right through my tricks? How could it be simple to fool those who studied the mind and soul?

I took a deep breath and focused on my surroundings. One of the core teachings of the philosophers was the concept of mindfulness: to live in the moment and ignore the mind's attempts to sabotage itself. The streets of Odena offered plenty of distractions.

I followed behind Faske, allowing his bulk to part the crowd. Commonfolk passed us, their faces blank as they trod the familiar paths of their lives. Dondarrio moved out of the way of a group of women with powdered faces and dark rings of kohl around their eyes. They wore voluminous robes, striped black-and-white, and when they passed, I noticed each of them had a wooden stave strapped onto her back.

Faske paused and watched them disappear into the throng. "The Lunatic Daughters. You would never see them in Velassa. Nony doesn't take kindly to pagans, especially ones that worship the moon."

As we walked through the city, he named more bizarre figures I had never seen before. Rosegolds lounged on the porch of a high-end brothel, men and women who moved with casual sensuality as they puffed husk-pipes and brushed one another's hair. A Narahven bowed to Faske, which was apparently a challenge to unarmed combat. The giant ignored him.

Pagans from uncivilized territories, heretics, the impure and the unclean, all of them found sanctuary in Odena. There were no hostile stares, no grumbling. The lullaby of Vasely's presence wound through the streets like a gentle breeze.

The innkeeper had given us directions to the home of the philosophers. They lived in the Verdant Gardens, a vast botanical landscape in the middle of the city, fed by a natural hot spring.

Guarding the entrance was a marble statue of a physicker, a flower in one hand and a scalpel in the other. The occasional botany student knelt amongst the countless herbs and shrubs, carefully attempting to identify medicinal plants hidden amongst their poisonous cousins. Deeper within the Gardens we came upon an arboretum of strange trees.

One of them, a gnarled monstrosity with a lightning-hollowed trunk, loomed over the others. A smattering of autumnal leaves sprouted from its branches in defiance of the cycle of life.

A small hut had been erected in the shadow of that great tree. A stream of pure water burbled behind the building, winding between the trees to nourish their ancient roots. It seemed like an oasis that the city had been built around, a slice of nature hidden inside of a civilization which had twisted wood and stone to its own ends.

A philosopher sat with his feet in the river, the bottom of his dark brown robes bunched around him. A sword pierced the soil beside him, tilted so that he would be able to grab the handle at a moment's notice.

It should have been a tranquil sight, but when I looked at the man, I felt a sense of unease. Perhaps I was merely nervous about my future, but his perfectly straight back and bare weapon lent him a martial aura that made me hesitate.

"Boy," said Faske. The giant looked down at me, showing a few teeth in what I imagined was an attempt at a smile. "This is a hard world. No shame in breaking every once in a while. If you need anyone, you know where to find me and my brother."

I stared at the philosopher's back. There was something unyielding about his posture. This was not a man who would break. A tempest could sweep through the arboretum, tearing those ancient trees out by their roots, and still, he would sit there, just like that, the river water whipping around him in a frenzy.

I nodded at the giant, keeping my true thoughts unvoiced. I would not break. One day I would reach a point where I didn't need anyone. I wouldn't need a protector to guide me through the streets of some foreign city. On that day no corrupt god, let alone his disciples, would threaten me or mine.

I think Faske sensed my resolve and approved.

Our farewells were silent, a clasping of wrists.

The world around me seemed etched in perfect clarity. This, I thought, was mindfulness. I was aware of the tension in my shoulders, the heaviness of my tongue, the whisper of the wind around me. The giant shuffled into the distance. There were a lot of words I could have said to him.

I walked toward the philosopher. He turned toward me sooner than I expected.

His features were sharp, but the tranquil expression on his face softened the edges. Pale scribbles of scar tissue traced along his exposed skin as if he had rolled through a briar of devilthorn. His thin lips stretched into a smile as I approached. I should have felt at ease, but I found something about him disturbing. Familiar yet unknown.

"You seem so purposeful." He had a sly voice, the kind you would expect from an elder brother about to deceive his sibling.

I clasped my hands in front of me and bowed my head. "Do I have the privilege of speaking with a philosopher?"

The man rose to his feet and brushed the soil from his robes. In one smooth flourish he pulled his sword from the ground and sheathed it at his side. Even I could realize the blade was of superb quality as it slid home. "You do."

"I wish to join as an apprentice." The words came out with surprising confidence. The man blinked a few times then glanced back at the river. Silence stretched between us as he pretended I had never said anything. "Are you accepting new disciples?"

"Oh, I wouldn't think so." His smile didn't reach his eyes. "We already have eight from your generation. Of course, we historically have gone out and invited promising candidates. If we accepted every rich child that was dropped off by his guardian, well, we'd be a veritable guild."

I set my pack down and sat at the edge of the river. I removed my boots and socks before submerging my feet in the water. It felt like the right thing to do.

From what I knew about philosophers, they were the sort who would test others from the beginning. They had carved out their place in the world through their deep understanding of the mind and soul. One did not need to wield some powerful weapon or control the elements; better to be the ideal that they pledged themself to. Even the Archons could be influenced by the words of a philosopher, and through the gods they could change the consciousness of the world.

So I ignored his rejection and relaxed. After a few minutes he sat beside me, dipping his feet in the pristine waters. We enjoyed the slow decline of the sun, hours passing in an endless moment. I thought of nothing, only experiencing the world around me, the unfurling of time as the shadows of the great boughs shifted across the ground, and the sun flared purple and orange as it collided with the horizon.

At one point I felt that strange power flicker in the back of my mind. I acknowledged it without attempting to understand it.

According to the Church, the Archons could accomplish miraculous feats because of the divine insights bestowed upon them. Nony could conjure an inferno because he had a nearly complete mastery of the essence of fire—what formed it, its purpose. Once he achieved a perfect understanding his soul would become a flame itself, and he would become one with each ember that flickered across the world.

As nebulous as fire may be, it pales in comparison with time. Nony was supposedly a god who had spent centuries honing his skills. I barely understood the present, let alone the past or the future; at my age a decade seemed like an eternity. Yet, as we sat there in silence, I felt myself living in the moment. The mental exercises from my book had prepared me to enter that meditative trance.

"Why do you wish to become an apprentice?" The man's voice crashed through the silence of the past eight hours. I had wondered how long it would take him before one of us spoke. I gambled that he had more important things to do than sit beside me, while I had little more than a coin purse and an empty future.

I could barely make out his silhouette beside me in the moonlight. "I respect the mind and the truths that the philosophers seek."

"And why should we teach you these truths?"

We went back and forth for a while. I tried to speak in the vague and mysterious dialect of the philosophers. Often, I rambled a nonsensical answer, and the man would sigh or lapse into silence. I felt my power drifting in the back of my mind, closer than ever, as if waiting for me to reach for it. Whenever I sensed I had made a misstep I would reverse time and offer a better answer.

Though it was a simple application of my power I had to use it more frequently than I would like to admit. The philosopher would have laughed me out of the arboretum if I hadn't had this advantage. After the tenth reversal I felt the familiar throbbing of a migraine at my temples.

As the night wore on, I was able to get a feel of the man's psyche. He seemed to approve of the tenets of Ivarius, an ascetic who believed that self-reflection was an act of purification.

No doubt he thought there was something strange about my behavior. A true philosopher would be able to see through the illusions of some sixteen-year-old boy. But there were no rules to our conversation. He was attempting to determine whether I met the minimum requirements to succeed as an apprentice, nothing else. His questions became more esoteric until I could even begin to formulate an answer to a question like *which iteration of reality are we?*

After that question, I shook my head, and no more questions came. His face was like a mask, barely visible in the soft glow of the moon, but I had the impression I hadn't convinced him quite yet.

"Why did you want to be a philosopher?" I asked.

The man chuckled. When he spoke, he dropped the sly tone and high-class mannerisms from before. "That's an interesting question to ask me in particular. Many of my brothers would say that they felt some divine calling. Some of them sought power for selfish or noble ideals. I'm a bit different. My father was a nightman. They paid him five copper a week to clean out privies and cesspits. He would come home right before sunrise and drink himself into oblivion, absolutely reeking of human filth. He slept on the floor because my mother couldn't stand his smell.

"Like all children I idolized my father. I saw him as a great man, and in the brief periods of time that I saw him awake, we would talk about all manner of things. He had taught himself to read and was very eloquent. He had a little library that he treasured, mostly books thrown out because they were beyond repair. There were a few treasures he found abandoned around the city at night. His favorite was a copy of *Machineries* by the great inventor Veracles. Once he told me he had thought up an improvement to the printing press, something to do with hand moulds. I was nine and had no idea what he was talking about at the time.

"He did nothing with it, of course. He thought nobody would care about a nightman who thought he was a better inventor than Veracles. He slept on the floor and drank himself into oblivion, and five years later he died from a wasting illness. My mother didn't want to be around him in his final days so he died alone—except for his library, I suppose. She always said I had my father's mind so she dropped me off here, specifically where I built this hut. Back then, the philosophers used to take pity on lost children, and they accepted me into their midst.

"So, what does this story tell you about me?"

I said the first thing that came to mind. "Nothing."

The philosopher nodded and clapped a hand on my shoulder. "My name is Brother Augur. Come, get some sleep. You will have a busy day ahead of you tomorrow."

5

VERDANT

"Wake up."

I opened my eyes blearily. The philosopher stood in the entrance of the hut, the gray sky peeking over his shoulder. The birds had yet to even begin their dawn chorus.

Though I had achieved a sense of perfect clarity before falling asleep, once I closed my eyes I could have slept through the winter. Instead, the philosopher had allowed me at most a couple of hours of rest. Given that I had slept on the floor with only a rolled-up blanket as a pillow, I may have been better off without any sleep. A dull headache lurked behind my eyes.

I heaved myself into a sitting position. A couple of weeks of exercise and studying on the journey to Odena had not been enough to shake off a lifetime of pampering. I tried to keep the resentment off my face as I stared up at the philosopher, blinking the sleep out of my eyes.

"Are you certain this is what you want to do?" Though Brother Augur's face remained tranquil, a hint of derision colored his tone. Again, I was struck by his discordant nature. He seemed like both an enlightened hermit and an imperious philosopher, as if two souls inhabited one body.

Two weeks of studying was not enough time for me to truly clash wits with a man like this. I felt a measure of confidence due to my magic. I had thought of the many potential applications of my power, from gambling to assassination. Unlike the ability to manipulate sound or generate massive infernos, my magic was one of opportunity. Its limitations were based on my limitations as a person; even with a dozen chances I would lose a duel against a blademaster every time.

Yet even for a naive boy it had its advantages. Namely, I could ask stupid questions or give terrible responses and learn from them without suffering any consequences.

"Do all philosophers act like you?" I asked.

He smiled. "Not everyone recognizes the staccato. It is, in essence, the study of body language, charisma, the first impression. The way I am using it now confuses you, makes you unsure of what you are dealing with. Confusion opens you to suggestion. A master of the staccato can disguise himself as anything with the proper resources. As for how the others behave, they are generally tough but fair. My generation were all raised by the same sour old hag. Strong personalities leave their mark."

The philosopher wandered about the hut as he talked. The room consisted of little more than a chair that seemed to have organically grown into its shape, a table that was more of a protrusion of smooth wood extending from the wall, and a row of potted herbs in the windowsill. He gathered a few mint leaves and disappeared outside.

I followed, lost in thought. This lesson was a sign that, for the time being, I had been accepted as an apprentice. I thought of interrogating him about the future—when would I meet the others, how were the philosophers organized, what was expected of me?

My headache proved I had overexerted myself last night. For now, it would be best to play the role of observant pupil.

Brother Augur leaned over a small firepit beside the hut and reached his hand into the hungry flames. His expression remained neutral as he grasped a heating stone from the center of the pit and transferred it to a clay bowl filled with water. Steam erupted outwards. He settled into a lotus position beside the bowl, waiting patiently as the water began to boil.

"You are, of course, wondering what comes next," he said. "You chose to join the philosophers, not the Academia or the soldiery. They would have been the superior option. Discipline is the foundation of a great man. You have a spark, granted, but you look like someone new to suffering. No one will whip you for breaking rules or force you to attend seminars. Here you earn your knowledge."

"That's fine."

His eyes chastised me for breaking his monologue. "If Avarus takes a shine to you he may teach you the secrets of the blade. Others may teach you to play music so beautiful it sends listeners into a frenzy. When you're older some may invite you on expeditions beyond the Frontier in search of glory. If you walk away, no one will chase you unless they have taken personal offense. You control your own fate."

I blinked up at the sky, thinking of the world outside of the Great Cities, all the mysteries waiting to be discovered. Though I had been raised to take control of the family business, unlikely to personally venture far outside of Velassa, my imagination had always wandered far.

Here, in the middle of the Civilized Lands, everything I encountered was the domain of man. Yet if I went far enough away from Odena I would find cracks in the shield. Our world was filled with amazing stories, some of which may have been false reports or old legends, but all of them agreed that the world was a realm of bizarre danger and strange beauty.

Far enough outside of the Great Cities were places where demons had formed cults in the wilderness; if I stumbled into the wrong forest I might find myself under the thrall of the Goetia. Farther along, close to the Frontier, there were forgotten villages where ethereal arachnids scuttled between buildings on dream-webs.

The lands beyond gave birth to even more fantastical places such as Daevadastra, the underwater hive of the nagas, formed from coral that glimmered with colors beyond the spectrum of the human eye. There were places that existed even beyond our world—most notably Desolada, the realm of the Goetic demon lords, floating in the hollow core of the moon.

Brother Augur coughed, bringing me back to reality. He poured boiling water into a cup and, retrieving the mint leaves from a pocket, brewed himself a cup of tea. "That faraway look in your eyes tells me you're a dreamer. I mention searching the world for glory, and off you go. A word of caution, though. Dreams do not translate well to reality. They are distorted things, unstable, but the mind pretends they are coherent."

"So you don't agree with searching for glory?"

"Glory." The philosopher blew on his tea, face scrunched in thought. "Seeking things—glory, power, fame—is one of the ways the mind sabotages itself. Not that I wish to dissuade you from living a life full of mistakes. Knowing something and experiencing it are completely different. Your mistakes shape the person you become. They keep you humble."

I considered his words carefully. He tended to ramble, but he was certainly more accessible than the convoluted writings of most philosophers.

"Do the others think like you?" I asked.

He finished his tea and poured water over the firepit. For a long moment he considered my question. Though the silence dragged on, at least he respected my questions enough to offer them proper consideration.

"Each of us are different, of course," he said at last. "The only true commonality between us is our mutual respect and the desire to conquer ourselves. Hedonism is always popular and not always bad. Some want solitude, free from convoluted social plots and disappointment. In the end we're just people, learning together."

He gestured for me to follow him. We walked deeper in the Gardens, toward the center. Past the stone pathway, past legions of forget-me-nots and roses and violets. Deeper we went, until familiar flowers segued into exotic plants from around the world. Iridescent trees began to loom over the path, the dance of colors along their great expanses shifting in hypnotic patterns. Glacial flowers gleamed blue-silver in the twilight; when the wind stirred their petals they would suddenly blossom and release spores that drifted through the area like diamond dust.

A man in honey-colored robes rested in a hammock strung up between a pair of trees. I walked on my toes, careful not to disturb him, but as I snuck past, his eyes opened and focused on me. The intensity of his gaze made me take a step back. After a moment he snorted and fell back asleep.

I hurried to catch up to Brother Augur, who strolled along with the confidence of a respected elder returning home.

A dozen feet later we passed a gargantuan tree, a hollow carved into the side of its vast trunk. It was one large room, veins of sap glistening along wooden walls the color of bone. A circle of candles flickered around an old woman meditating on a pile of furs. I tore my eyes away from her as I followed behind Brother Augur.

"When will we be there?" I regretted the words the second they came out of my mouth. It sounded like the whine of a petulant child.

A flicker of disappointment crossed his face. "We are already here."

He refused to elaborate further. Hands folded behind his back, soft steps carried him farther along the path. Cursing myself, I considered reversing time to escape his chastisement. What had I been expecting, anyway? A palace deep within the Gardens, where pretty women lounged about as bearded sages announced ancient wisdom?

I should have known better than to assume anything. Groups of philosophers mingled throughout the Civilized Lands, but they lacked the structure of the Academies. No matter where you went you could expect the Academies to behave in a similar fashion. Five years of studying until you earned the bronze ring of a generalist. If you wished, you could delve deeper into subjects of interest such as surgery or alchemy—some revered academics were rumored to have so many metallic rings they had to thread them through a necklace.

The philosophers did not dispense trinkets to display how educated they were. They were all individuals pursuing different paths through life. No committee had created a strict set of rules they were obliged to follow. I thought back on my tutor, Everett, who followed the teachings of Severius. Though he agreed with most of his mentor's words, his own experiences had shaped his mentality, personalizing his own branch of philosophy.

The memory of my old tutor brought a smile to my face. By now my migraine had faded, and I was confident I would be able to use my power without much pain. With the confidence of a fool who could reverse time, I asked, "Do you know of Everett? He's a Levenan philosopher who moved to Velassa."

Brother Augur raised an eyebrow. I thought of his earlier explanation of the staccato—he claimed to be the perfect actor, able to fill any role he wished. It would be worse than useless to attempt to infer anything from his body language. He shrugged and continued walking along the pathway.

Feeling ashamed at my silly questions, I reached for my magic. The world fractured around me as I reversed time to the moment we encountered the man in the hammock. This time I ignored his stare, likewise strolling past the old woman meditating in the tree without a glance. If Brother Augur wanted to give off an air of inscrutability, I should too. Feeling a bit ridiculous, I copied his posture, hands folded behind the small of my back.

Not for the first time I reflected on how strange my life had become. Everett had been somewhat of a novelty in my life. Everyone else whom my father knew behaved in a way I had considered "normal"—merchants, the gentry, and other members of privileged society, all following the same general etiquette. Nothing in my life had prepared me for smart-mouthed dwarfs like Volario and eccentric philosophers living in a massive garden.

I knew little of my father's past beyond him becoming a wealthy merchant, only that he had served for some period of time as a soldier on the Frontier. Understandably he did not like to speak about whatever horrors he encountered there. What connection did he have with these people? Despite my curiosity I thought it would be best not to reveal my relationship with a man who had suffered Nony's wrath, even among people he apparently trusted.

We carried along in silence until we came upon three youths lounging around a tree, each clad in the simple gray wool of the acolytes. They were around my age, perhaps a year or two my senior. Only one of them looked up, a girl with a smattering of freckles across her cheeks. Her red hair and clever face reminded me of a fox, especially when her lips twisted into a playful smirk.

"Who's this now?" She looked me up and down. I wondered what she thought when she saw me, with my fine clothes and smooth face. She had a way of immediately making me feel self-conscious, as if I was some imposter brought before her for interrogation.

An awkward silence stretched between us. I had expected Brother Augur to introduce me, but when I turned, he was already a dozen feet away, his casual stroll leading him back along the path. Dismissing the sudden urge to chase him and offer my thanks, I focused on the other acolytes. Better to make a good impression with the girl and her companions.

"My name's Leones," I said, bowing my head. "I came here to study."

The young man at her side shook his head slightly, a mocking smile flickering about his lips. "Great. Well, I'm sure Brother Augur saw something in you. Even if he is one of the more . . . eccentric philosophers."

It was an obvious challenge. He sat close to the girl, their knees touching with a casual familiarity.

Ah, so that was his game. This was the dance mankind had performed since our history had been recorded.

The Goetia had enslaved our ancestors for millennia. The whole time we had fought each other for women or food or for the entertainment of our masters, never daring to raise a hand against our true enemies. For all the philosophy and art and good we had brought into the world since gaining our independence, we were no different than our ancestors, who would slit another man's throat for looking at their wives.

I thought of reversing time and trying again but thought better of it. I would have to at least attempt to put in an effort instead of relying on my power the moment I felt pressured. Either way it was pointless. The youth was looking for a fight, and nothing would change that.

Instead, I ignored them and continued along the path, deeper into the territory of the philosophers. I had no particular plan in mind. Brother Augur said there were five others of my generation I had yet to meet. Chances were that at least one of them would welcome me with more than mockery.

I barely made it a few steps before the young man yelled at my back. "I was speaking to you. Do you have no manners?"

That made me turn. He had stood to his full height. Stubble covered his square jawline and veins stood out along his muscular forearms.

"We're here to become philosophers," I said, "not court ladies."

My words gave him pause. An incredulous look spread across his face. Before he could respond the third member of the group threw back his head and laughed.

Until now he had ignored us, sitting off to the side with his back against the tree, whittling away at a chunk of wood roughly the shape of a person. Unlike the older boy he was slender, his face too sharp and asymmetrical to be considered attractive, but he had the most striking blue eyes.

"Do I amuse you, Felix?" The older boy faced his companion.

Felix slid his paring knife along the wooden figurine one last time before pausing, staring down at the blade in his hand. There was no sound except for the wind and the susurrus of dead leaves skipping along in its wake.

The girl stood and rested her hand on the older boy's shoulder. "Is all this necessary? If it makes you feel better, all of you are very masculine and respectable. I for one am very impressed with this display of virility."

Felix resumed his whittling as if nothing had happened.

"A pleasure to meet you. I'm Mara." She looked up at the youth beside her, wrinkling her nose and laughing. He offered me a pained smile but remained silent. "This fine specimen of a man is Caedius. Come, we'll show you around. And just so you know, there's nothing wrong with wanting to be a court lady."

6

POSTURE

"Wrong." Avarus walked over to me and adjusted my fingers along the grip of the wooden practice sword. Still unsatisfied, he snatched the weapon from my limp grasp and demonstrated the proper way to hold it. The weapon looked natural in his gnarled fingers, an extension of his arm as he held it straight in front of him.

"Mimic my posture," he said, returning the sword. I had captured his exact image in my head and felt confident as I adjusted my feet and stretched the weapon out before me.

The older philosopher grunted and slapped the flat of the blade with his knuckles. The blow looked casual, yet the shock of it numbed my arm; the weapon slipped out of my fingers and clattered to the ground.

Avarus circled me as if scrutinizing a horse for sale. Five other acolytes had gathered in the clearing, each a witness to my failure. Embarrassment formed a hard lump in my throat, and I considered using my power to reverse time. It was not too late to back out completely.

Caedius had invited me to join in Avarus's daily lesson. Despite his gruff demeanor the philosopher always set aside several hours in the evening to spread the gospel of the sword. Before the lesson Caedius had taken me to watch the older man practicing his bladeforms. He must have been in his fifth decade, yet he moved like a man half his age, a blur of fluid motion as he thrust and pivoted and weaved through the air.

The display was convincing, though now with the others' eyes burning into my back I wondered why I had ever thought I was suited to learning the blade.

Avarus had shed his honey-brown robes and wore only a pair of simple woolen trousers. He looked like he had been carved out of driftwood, sun-dark skin marred with the evidence of old wounds. Most prominent was a jagged pucker of scar tissue near his heart where someone must have skewered him with a polearm.

Shaking his head, Avarus turned and moved toward the next acolyte. Examining the fist-sized exit wound under his left shoulder, I wondered for the hundredth time if I had made the right decision in coming here.

The blademaster stopped in front of Caedius next. He unsheathed the weapon at his side—a true steel blade—and demonstrated a sequence of lightning-fast strikes. Caedius echoed the flurry of sword strokes; though I could see no difference, Avarus shook his head and repeated the movement. After two more attempts the blademaster nodded in satisfaction and moved along.

Next was Felix.

I was unsure what to think of the other disciple. I had spent most of the day with Mara's group, attempting to memorize their advice and the locations they pointed out. Caedius would laugh and slap me on the back around the others, even though his gaze would linger on mine a second too long, a brittle hardness behind his smile. On the other hand, Felix had ignored my existence completely, lingering behind the three of us, his eyes downturned.

Avarus demonstrated another sequence of moves, longer and more elegant than before. Felix watched, unblinking, then repeated the movements exactly, his wooden sword tracing elegant patterns in the air. Avarus nodded and launched into a more complex dance, this one lasting twenty seconds.

This time Felix stumbled at the end. He snarled, baring his teeth like some feral animal. The blademaster clapped him on the shoulder and whispered in his ear. I thought back to earlier, when I had first met the other disciples, the promise of violence that hung in the air after Caedius chastised Felix, and decided he was someone to tread lightly around. A temper like that meant nothing good.

Avarus rounded on the other three disciples. The other two boys were roughly equal to Caedius, able to repeat a few seconds of complex strokes and footwork. None came even close to Felix. The willowy youth did not even bother to watch the others. His eyes remained on the ground, jaw muscles clenching and unclenching.

The final acolyte was a broad-shouldered girl, taller than everyone except Caedius, sweat running down her face in rivulets as she stumbled through the motions. I took some small solace in her failure even though I doubted I would last more than a few moves against her.

When he finished tormenting the next two disciples, the blademaster sauntered into the middle of the clearing. "We have a new face among us today, courtesy of Brother Augur."

I forced myself to meet their gaze, keeping my expression neutral. Caedius offered a shrug.

Avarus sheathed his blade. "I have made it my life's work to teach the legato to those who seek it. I have not stepped foot outside of the Gardens in a decade, though I am told the bards still sing of me. You may think pretty words sufficient to protect you, but they only work against pretty people."

Again, I resisted the urge to reverse time and end this lesson in my inadequacy. I could no longer be that lazy child sleeping beneath a lemon tree, content with a simple life. The Magisters had taken that away. I closed my eyes, remembering the way Everett's corpse had smoldered in the grass. I couldn't run from every harsh word and mocking gaze.

The lesson resumed as the other disciples lined up and began to work through the bladeforms. The beginning was simple, an exercise in footwork like some bizarre waltz that I attempted to mimic. Soon they integrated their weapons into the dance, wooden blades swishing in identical arcs.

Here I did use my power, the world warping and twisting around me each time I stumbled through the movements, again and again as I attempted to master the bladeform. I made it through the footwork, ten seconds of precise steps, before that familiar migraine returned, warning me I was overusing my power.

After that I stood off to the side, hands clasped behind my back. The tall girl fell out of step after a half-minute and, cheeks flushing red, stepped away from the others. After a minute Caedius broke away as well, chest working like a bellows as he sucked in air. The other two joined shortly after, leaving only Felix to work through the forms. His wooden sword flickered, the movements becoming more and more complex, blocking attacks from multiple imaginary foes, a constant whirl of motion.

After another thirty seconds Felix brought his feet together, back straight as a blade, the dance ended.

"Excellent," said Avarus. "The first form of the legato. Most of you will be lucky to master this within your lifetime. It is the simplest of the eleven. I have heard that a true master may challenge the Archon of Blades, though none has emerged in the past three centuries. It is the dream of all blademasters to face him on the Diamond Plains. Perhaps young Felix here will one day find himself on that hallowed ground."

Felix bowed, his face blank. There was something unnerving about him, the way he avoided eye contact, how he had lingered behind Mara and Caedius while they showed me around the area. I had not expected him to participate in the lesson, but his bladework turned out to be beautiful. The work of a prodigy. I had misjudged him over a little perceived awkwardness.

The rest of the class was spent with the students sparring amongst one another. Avarus pulled me to the side. If I could not even hold a sword properly there was no use embarrassing myself against the others.

"I have to admit," he said, "your footwork during the beginning of the first legato was good. Perhaps you have some promise. For the past decade I have never turned any prospective students away. You are welcome here, but you must understand that when I criticize you I do so for your benefit. You should tolerate no flaw in yourself. Surrender your pride when you seek perfection. Now, show me your grip once more."

This time when he adjusted my fingers, I felt no embarrassment. With patience he demonstrated proper form, nudging my knee a few degrees, tilting my chin upward. He was right, of course—there was no shame in being corrected.

After one last adjustment he told me to hold the position for five minutes. It felt unnatural, muscles I hadn't been aware of quivering with effort, but I focused on memorizing the precise angles of my body.

My wrist felt as though it was about to collapse under the weight of the extended sword. A deep burn spread through my hamstrings and calves, building to a bright crescendo of agony. A voice in the back of my head roared to surrender, to fall to my knees. Taking a deep breath, I attempted to clear my mind and enter the trance-like state I had experienced with Brother Augur, but the pain was impossible to ignore.

Finally, my legs buckled, and I fell to my knees.

"Forty-six seconds," said Avarus. "Do better tomorrow."

After the lesson, Caedius and I headed toward the cookshop, Felix trailing at our heels. I slowed my pace until the silent boy fell in at my side. Caedius glanced back, a curious look on his face, and stopped until we were walking together.

To my surprise Felix made eye contact for a moment, his stare so intense I had to force myself to meet his gaze. After a moment his gaze returned to the ground. Still, it felt like he was at least acknowledging my acknowledgment. I had planted a seed, and in due time I hoped to see it flourish.

Despite Brother Augur leading me to believe that the camp of the philosophers consisted of little more than the occasional man in a hammock, there were a few stone buildings scattered around the area. The cookshop—or as Caedius insisted on calling it, the *thermopolium*—was a single room. It contained a terra-cotta counter embedded with earthenware vessels, offering an assortment of salted beef, almonds, mushrooms, and sour cherries.

As I heaped food onto my plate, I remembered the meals I used to eat with my parents, especially when my mother donned her apron and became a tyrant in the kitchen. Tuna baked in banana leaves with mint and thyme, boiled eggs drizzled in honey, sugared pastries bursting with cream. There was always so much warmth around the dinner table, my parents holding hands, all of us laughing and teasing one another.

I shook my head and poured myself a healthy portion of mulled wine after watching the others do the same. The three of us sat on a pile of furs in the corner, eating in silence. The memory of my parents weighed heavily on my mind. I considered making small talk, but the others seemed lost in their thoughts as well. I finished my meal quickly, the wine filling my stomach with warmth, and walked outside. The alcohol muddled my mind. Weakened me.

I leaned against the wall, the evening breeze ruffling my hair. Foolish, childish tears slipped down my cheeks. On the road to Odena I had promised myself I would never cry again. It was weakness. Weakness that I could no longer afford. With a choked laugh I thought, well, it didn't take long to break that oath. Not that my word could be considered very sacred; after all, I had promised my father I would attempt to save him when I couldn't even hold a sword properly.

How could he ask me to come back and help him? No matter how hard I tried I could not go back in time more than an hour. Even if I could, how was I supposed to take on the Magisters? Perhaps after a few years of feverish training I could defeat their retinue of soldiers, assuming they were all kind enough to challenge me to single combat. But even if I could go back to that moment in time, I would have to face them in the body of a boy who could barely touch his toes.

It all seemed so ridiculous. Coming here, learning to swing a sword and meditate. Sharing a meal with some companions. None of it would matter if I came face to face with one of the Magisters. No philosophical text could protect me from a snap of their fingers.

I closed my eyes against the tears. Pointless. Stupid.

"I came here when I was nine." A soft voice said from behind. Felix. "I may as well tell you myself since it's common knowledge around here. The Increate blessed me with luck, which is the sort of cosmic irony I'm sure He enjoys deeply. So much luck, in fact, that I was accused of consorting with demons because I turned a copper penny into a small fortune playing dice."

"Where I come from, an accusation like that would see a boy burned to death."

"You're Velassan, then?" Felix grunted. "In Odena we are far too high-minded to execute children. They threw me in the dungeons instead, living in my own filth for a month until Avarus heard about me and came to my rescue.

"Never be ashamed to cry, Leones. There are plenty of things in this world worthy of your tears."

7

CORRUPT

Months passed. The trees shed the last of their autumnal leaves, and the wind grew chill. Winter in Odena was nothing compared to the arctic north, where spit would freeze before hitting the ground. Still, the little stone barracks reserved for us acolytes offered little protection from the cold.

In the beginning I wore a fur cloak from my travel bag, a luxurious thing entirely at odds with the natural simplicity cultivated by the philosophers. Mara mocked me relentlessly for it, and the next day I suffered the cold in my thin uniform.

Avarus, that old whipmaster, taught me new exercises to fill out my frame. Acrobatics on the branches of the iridescent trees, starting with simply pulling myself up from a deadhang, each week going for one or two more. I ran through the Gardens in the early morning to clear my head, exploring off-trail paths to marvel at the slice of nature Archon Vasely had grown in the stone jungle of the city. Those initial months of physical training were lovely, the kind of rapid progress that makes you think that in a few years you'll be punching trees in half.

After two months I was able to follow a half-minute of the first legato—with generous use of my power, of course—which occasioned a thoughtful nod and smile from Avarus. While I had managed fifteen seconds on my first lesson, the legato became increasingly complex the longer it went. Being able to shuffle my feet around in the appropriate rhythm paled in comparison to actually swinging the sword, especially considering the evolution of footwork involved.

I met many of the elder philosophers, a menagerie of twenty-odd folk. Though perhaps "meeting" was too strong of a term. Most preferred solitude whenever they came to the Gardens. My imagination was filled with thoughts of the secrets they would be able to teach me. I introduced myself to a few but quickly learned that Brother Augur's openness was not the norm among them.

Discouraged, I asked the other disciples how I could earn the elders' respect. They laughed and told me to let them know when I figured it out.

Not to say that I learned nothing. Far from it. While no one seemed impressed enough with me for individual lessons, they would hold impromptu classes and debates on a variety of topics. I listened to a thorough analysis of the aqueducts and sewage system of Odena; an impassioned deconstruction of Yanesai's *Analects* that lasted for hours; an epic poem about the Tragedy of Aleras, a man who was perfect and was slaughtered by his neighbors because of it; and a dozen other eclectic tales and entreaties. The worst of them was an explanation about the meaning of metaphysics that concluded the meaning could not be explained.

There was no obvious pattern or structure to our education. The philosophers just rambled about whatever they felt like sharing. Somehow, I began to make sense of the chaos, their stilted language slowly becoming comprehensible. To my surprise I even found myself gaining some insights.

Lakken was my favorite philosopher, an ancient man who spent his days on a cushion in front of a roaring fire and the only one besides Augur who seemed to enjoy speaking with me. Crescents of yellowed sclera peeked out from beneath his perpetually drooping eyelids. Palsy had claimed his hands, contorting them into twitching claws he kept folded on his lap. His granddaughter Elys stayed at his side, always rubbing ointments into his misshapen fingers or singing or cooking.

Despite his poor health he spoke with vigor. He must have commanded quite an audience in his youth. He claimed he had been a great warrior up until a decade ago, though rumor had him to be over a century old. He taught that the secrets to long living were daily walks and red wine with meals, encouraging me to spend more time around the city to absorb its eccentric culture.

I liked him most of all because of the stories he told. While not all of them were new to me, his versions differed from the official histories in subtle ways, revealing flaws in their narratives I had never before considered.

"We believe we are the crown of creation," Lakken told me one day. He let out a parched cough, and Elys brought a flagon of wine to his lips. He drank deeply, his wizened face radiating pleasure. He nodded and his granddaughter returned to tending the fire.

"Ha. The Goetia precede us by a thousand thousand years. First, the Increate shaped their realm from air and fire, the esoteric elements. Long after that, He created our world from water and earth, populating it with countless races, many of them superior to mankind. The Goetia were intrigued by our diametric universe, and some of them decided they preferred it to Desolada. They enslaved our ancestors because we are a feeble race, our minds easily shaped. The perfect servants, emotional enough to be manipulated and logical enough to accept our fate."

"Until the Archons came and freed us," I said.

The old man smiled, displaying his set of wooden teeth. "According to the clergy. They would have us believe mankind has conquered a great empire. The Civilized Lands, we call it. The sun shines brighter here; we are closer to the heavens. In truth the world is far more vast than you could ever imagine. I will make you prove this to yourself. Have you heard of the Corruption of Arostara?"

I shook my head. I had heard the name before: one of the Great Cities, lost centuries ago. An arctic deadzone. Everett had mentioned it before as one of the great mysteries of the modern world. It existed, in a sense, far to the northeast, silhouettes of buildings encased within a colossal glacier. Supposedly Winter, most powerful of the Archons, had frozen the city for all eternity. No one knew why.

With an effort Lakken lifted a trembling hand. Elys clasped it and helped him to his feet, wrapping her other arm around his waist for support.

"Come inside, come inside. My knees hate this cold."

Slowly he hobbled toward his home. It was the largest building in the Gardens, a show of respect to the eldest philosopher. It would have barely passed as a servant's house in the city, but here it was the closest thing to a palace.

The interior was just as sparse as any other philosopher's home. The greatest luxury was the feather bed tucked into the corner. Beside it was a plush cushion where I assumed Elys slept, close by in case he needed anything in the night. Along one wall was a bookcase, carved from the bone-white wood of one of the iridescent trees, containing hundreds of thin tomes in identical leather binding. The main area branched off into a small room, containing a chair and a wooden desk topped with writing utensils.

Lakken led us toward the bookcase and ran his fingers along the collection, peering at the titles written in small golden script. I wasn't familiar with the language; even the letters appeared slightly warped, as if the alphabet was some foreign corruption of my native tongue.

"Here we are." The old man tapped one of the tomes. Elys snatched it from the shelf and flipped to a page in one smooth motion, seemingly at random. For the first time I noticed there was a disconcerting fluidity to the way she moved—an almost unnatural grace. I had never focused on her much because she remained silent, her eyes averted, but she must have been a fully-fledged philosopher in her own right. If Lakken was willing to divulge some of his secrets to a random acolyte of a few months, what must she have learned?

She passed me the book. Unlike the lettering on the spine, the contents were written in Avanchean, the primary language shared in the delta of land between Velassa, Odena, and Mosatte.

The Corruption of Arostara

In the city of Arostara they observed no festivals, no shabbath or religious rites. For three centuries Archon Tenlas ruled, and not once did a priest bless a newborn or sing the final hymn to those near the gates of Death. The clergy were not to step foot within the city at all.

None of these ceremonies had been devised by the Increate, he decreed. Each ritual was dedicated to the Goetia and only served to strengthen the lunar gods.

At winter solstice the rest of mankind would paint runes of health and fortune on their walls. All would gather in the streets to dance for the souls of the departed. The rich would leave carafes of wine at their doorstep; the poor would leave bowls of water; and those with nothing would leave a thimble of blood. They would feast late into the night, on suckling pig, or boiled pheasant, or on warm memories.

In Arostara they went to sleep early.

The city was near the Frontier, ever besieged by the minions of the Goetia and mankind's countless other enemies. To light a candle for the dead would draw their attention. To wish for joy and peace would open your heart to their influence. There was no worship in Arostara, no one to be more revered than Tenlas the Iconoclast.

Then, on the winter solstice of the three hundredth year of his reign, when the moon reached its zenith and cast its foul light all throughout the world, every citizen woke in unison. All of Arostara gathered in the streets and danced, wild and panicked. Their mouths gibbered dark words in forbidden languages. They were puppets, one and all possessed by the pallid splendor of the moon, trapped within their corrupted flesh.

They did not pray for salvation. They did not know how.

Tenlas watched from his castle, high above those lost and frantic souls. He entered his Aspect, and water flooded through the streets, sweeping some off their feet, on occasion swelling to great waves that crushed his citizens to death. Still, they whirled and flailed and sang, unseen tears melding with the snow.

Angered, the Iconoclast descended among them. They ignored his commands, praising the lords of Desolada in the high tongue of Hell. He walked amongst them, demanding answers, and when none came, he agitated the water in their bodies until they bled from their eyes and their ears and their mouths.

From each corpse would sprout a single white rose, and so it was that Tenlas knew who had come to Arostara.

In the middle of the city was a Fountain, and within it a massive statue depicting the Iconoclast, sword held aloft, pointing toward the heavens. Only, now the statue was different. It wore no clothes and had no face; the upraised hand grasped only emptiness. The water of the Fountain had become blood, gathered from the covenant of those who had nothing else to offer.

In front of the Fountain stood an abomination in a child's skin, clad all in white. His eyes were completely devoid of color, staring into the infinite. Venom dripped from his fingers, this too a brilliant white, speckling the snow at his feet and birthing plumes of sulphurous smoke. An intricate seal blazed upon his brow, and along its borders was the name S I T R I.

Leave now, in the name of our Father, *said Tenlas. From his scabbard he withdrew Demiurge, forged from brilliant naga-coral. His people cavorted about the immortals, divine in their suffering.*

The Child whispered to him clever words. Words that cannot be committed to paper lest they tempt even the most pure. For a day and a night, he talked, Tenlas absorbing each and every word without comment. The people of Arostara danced and danced, feet bleeding and black from the cold, until their hearts stopped and they found the sweetest mercy of all.

When the child's mouth finally stopped moving the Iconoclast fell to his knees, head bowed. Sitri touched him on the brow, and there appeared a sigil. Hand in hand they walked into the Fountain and disappeared.

Winter, most blessed of the heavens, came to Arostara too late to help, since Tenlas had been too proud to contact the others. He wept when he saw the bodies, fifty thousand men and women and children, preserved in the blood-black snow. From each of them sprouted a single white rose.

I looked up from the page, unsure what to think of the story. The Church acknowledged the existence of the Goetia, the dark children born when the Increate cast the darkness from His heart. There had been stories about their appearance in this world, summoned with rings of salt and occult runes. The ones I heard were allegories meant for children. People blamed them for distant plagues and outbursts of violence in small communities.

They were the answer the clergyman gave when nonbelievers asked why there was still evil in the world if the Increate had formed us from his love.

"What is wrong with this story?" asked Lakken.

"It's impossible for anyone besides Winter to know what happened there," I said. "He completely sealed the city in ice."

"You know so little yet you use words like 'impossible'. The human understanding of reality is so limited, so narrow." The passion on the old man's face surprised me. "We cannot even begin to conceive of the truth, the same way a grain of sand cannot imagine what it is like to be a human. The first step to developing the soul of a philosopher is to realize you know nothing. Question every thought you have."

I tapped the book with my fingers as if trying to summon the meaning of the story from the page. The entire tale had a sort of eerie mysticism to it. What sort of power did the Goetia wield, to make men into slaves and alter reality at will? I still knew little about magic powers, but at least they seemed to be associated with some sort of element or concept, something recognizably native to the world. Time, sound, flames—all existed in accordance with the will of the Increate. The power of the Goetia was a sort of perversion, warping the natural order to suit their desires.

But that couldn't be the answer Lakken was looking for. His tirade was focused on making me think differently, to search for cracks in the foundation of my worldview. The philosophers loved to point out our inherent biases, to question every presupposition. I mentally divided the story into characters, actions, motivations, then pieced them back together into chimeras.

The problem was Sitri. I knew he was one of the Goetia but could not remember anything about him in particular. He was a Prince of Desolada and historically known for making trouble along the Frontier. The story could very well be true, at least partially. His sixty legions of demons had not marched against mankind since around the time of the Freezing. He was little more than a footnote in history, another foe vanquished by the Archons.

As soon as that thought crossed my mind it seemed obvious. "Sitri is only a Prince. One of the most powerful of them, but all of the Dukes and Kings are a tier above. He was still able to corrupt Archon Tenlas."

"And why does that matter?" Lakken gestured, and Elys took the book from my hands, returning it to the bookshelf.

"If one of the Princes can defeat one of the Archons, then how did mankind ever gain their independence? There are seventy-seven of the Goetia and only eleven Archons. For the past thousand years the Civilized Lands have only been growing. How?"

Lakken chuckled. "How, indeed?"

8

LUCK

Time continued inexorably forward. To the glee of children and the consternation of adults, snow began to fall on the day of the winter solstice. The cold deepened, and frost clung to the world, transforming the lands of the north into a winter landscape for the first time in over a decade.

I was meditating with Brother Augur when a snowflake fell on my hand. I glanced up in time to catch another on my face. After realizing it was snowing, I could no longer focus on my meditation. Lost in his trance, Augur paid no attention when I left his arboretum. With a small smile I tried to imagine how the other disciples would react.

Few philosophers remained within the Gardens. By now most had returned to warm homes with sturdy walls.

Avarus was one of the few who remained. I never missed one of his lessons, though the other disciples had left until the only remaining acolytes were Felix and Irele. Felix and I rarely spoke, only interacting when Avarus would have him spar with Irele and myself at the same time. Our wooden swords would clack together, and more often than not it would end with her disarmed and me on the ground.

Avarus would lecture about precisely what we had done and why it was wrong, and each time I lost I learned a little more.

I was unsure what to think of Felix. His arrogance and temper were off-putting, but nothing about him was malicious. He seemed like the lost and broken type. Too much like myself.

Caedius was spending the winter with an aunt in the city. Proximity had forced us into a shallow friendship, but I was by no means sad to see him go. While he was harmless, he seemed to consider me something of a rival. Likely as a result of how greatly Felix eclipsed both of us, he enjoyed his temporary superiority. Mara encouraged this one-sided competition in a half-joking attempt to brew up a little chaos.

The other five acolytes spared me little attention. Sometimes two brothers named Soren and Parish joined Avarus's lessons, but they kept to themselves and treated it as more of a novelty than anything. Mara was certain at least one of them had a crush on Irele. The other two were Meli, who spent most of her time reading in quiet places and wandering off whenever someone intruded, and Roshe, who hadn't made an appearance in the Gardens since before I arrived.

I walked through the empty Gardens feeling very alone. It hadn't snowed this far north since I was a child. One of my earliest memories was spending an afternoon watching snow drift past a window. The memory was a bittersweet fragment from my childhood. Back then the winter meant heated cocoa with cinnamon sticks. Now it made me think of corpses in the snow, marked with a white rose.

I paused outside of the barracks, collecting my thoughts. My mind had started wandering down some dark paths. I made sure that the others never saw me appear uncertain or troubled. Always polite, always controlled. For the past four months I had interacted with the others, and the only happiness I saw was between Caedius and Mara. Everyone else remained silent, together but distant.

Truthfully, I did like the others. The issue was that I had no idea how to make them like me. It felt as if an invisible barrier separated all of us, and I lacked the courage to reach out and see if it was only an illusion. I took one last glance back at the falling snow and leafless trees before entering the barracks.

Mara was the only one there, lounging on her cot, lost in thought. When I entered, she glanced my way, then looked again after something grabbed her attention. Her smile was charming in its wickedness. "Is that snow in your hair?"

She looked surprised when I returned her smile. Absently I realized I hadn't actually smiled in months. She set her book aside and joined me at the entrance, holding out a hand to catch snowflakes. Her perfume smelled of vanilla and rose in olive oil.

"It's been so long since I've seen the snow," she said, a beatific smile on her face. "My sister and I were little terrors. We pelted each other with snowballs all afternoon until I got her with a chunk of ice. Cut her forehead up real good, blood everywhere."

"Sounds like a cherished memory," I said.

"It's a warning, actually." She grabbed her boots and began pulling them on with characteristic fervor. "You boys play with swords all day and think I'm over here sewing quilts. I've been practicing my aim, waiting for this day to come."

I snagged my fur cloak from my pack and slipped it around my shoulders. She had mocked me for wearing it when it was not quite so cold. Now she glanced at me with purse-lipped envy as we walked out into the snow. She wore only a thin woolen jacket over her gray uniform. Gooseflesh prickled her exposed skin.

"It's the winter solstice," I said. "We should go and celebrate."

I waited for her to laugh. It would be easy enough to correct the embarrassment with my power. I had learned to rely on it, perhaps a bit too much.

Surprisingly, she shrugged and brushed the hair from her eyes. "Sure. I haven't been to town in a while, and there's nothing to do here. Most of the philosophers couldn't care less whether we froze to death or ended up in jail."

"Those are our only options, then?"

Without answering, she set off along the path, decision made; we were heading to the city, and that was that. Was this the secret behind friendship? A shared smile, an invitation? I had grown up around others my age: the scions of Velassan wealth and old blood, even the children of the servants whenever they had reason to come to our manor. With the highborn our conversations were little more than diversions demanded by etiquette. Talking with the servants always made me self-conscious. I slept in a big, warm house while they lived with a dozen other families in insulae complexes like concrete honeycombs.

Mara was different. I couldn't quite call her approachable, but she had a caustic warmth to her; she was perceptive and honest the way children are, blind to any social boundaries or consequences. Her temperament, mixed with her education as a disciple, would have seemed arrogant if she had not been so self-aware. But there was a warmth to her nonetheless, the flame that can warm or burn, depending.

The exotic forestry began to thin as we walked, the landscape becoming tamed into carefully plotted rows of shrubs and flowers, wilted in the sudden frost. The paths were empty, abandoned in favor of solstice festivities or a warm hearth.

"You've been with us for a while now." Mara broke the lingering silence. "What do you think?"

I exhaled a plume of cold air. She would appreciate honesty the most. "It's different. My whole life was simple. Planned out. My education came with curriculums. Others cooked my meals. It was a very small world, but I liked it. There's some joy to be found here, too, I think."

Mara held out a hand to catch snowflakes. "You think we have joy? The Gardens must be the strangest place I've ever been."

"Brother Augur can meditate for days, only pausing to drink water, and the whole time he looks blissful. Sometimes Avarus smiles, and I know he would rather be doing nothing else besides criticizing my form. There are a lot of strange little joys in life."

Mara stopped, hugging her thin jacket closer. There was a mischievous glint in her eye. "Interesting speech. That may be more words than you've said to me the whole time you've been here. Do you know why Caedius didn't like you the first time we met? Why he still stares daggers at you from time to time?"

It occurred to me there was a certain impropriety to us standing there together, in the same Gardens where lovers would promenade about with bottles of wine. I glanced about, as if looking for Caedius, and laughed. "No, not exactly."

"Because you had curriculums and cooks." Her red hair whipped about in the wind like a fan. "You came in one day, unannounced, with nobody knowing who you were or what you wanted. You never deigned to tell us either. Kept to yourself, as if you were better than us."

I had introduced myself, in fact, but now didn't seem like the time to argue. Or had I? Did I turn back time in that conversation? Hard to keep things straight.

"That's a big assumption to make based on me being quiet." I continued walking down the path, hiding my face from her.

She must have heard the annoyance in my tone. "Felix is quiet around most people, too. Have you talked with him much?"

"Not exactly conversations."

"He can be charming in the right place and time, with the right people. Strangest boy I've ever met, and all teenage boys are a little off. I don't mind him, but Caedius is more sensitive. It's one thing to act superior to other people. It's another thing to prove it to them. Felix proves it." She paused for a moment, as if remembering some incident from the past.

I scratched my chin. "He's definitely talented."

She snorted. "He's the philosophers' golden boy. They brought him here when he was so young. Give a child that age to a group of philosophers, and they're going to see him as an experiment. I've only been here for a year, and I can already tell something about me is different. You know about Felix's gift, right?"

I remembered the night Felix saw me crying. Of course, I had reversed time to erase the moment—that was too personal, too weak for anyone else to witness. But I remembered his words, a memory from a phantom reality. *The Increate blessed me with luck . . .*

"I've heard of it," I said, "but how can luck be a gift?"

"I'm going to let you see for yourself."

In the distance drums beat and muffled shouts of delight became audible. We left the Gardens through the eastern gate into a district of gabled manors and lively taverns. The buildings here had windows of fine glass, permitting glimpses of laughing families and servants balancing trays heaped with food.

The sun had barely begun its early descent, and already Odena was feasting and drinking. After living in the Gardens, it seemed impossibly welcoming.

And, of course, it was the winter solstice. In Velassa festivities were subdued, at least in my household. Here a pair of men wrestled in the streets, shirtless despite the cold, while strangers gathered to shout encouragement and insults. From the taverns and the wealthy homes came music, mingling and discordant, on occasion punctuated with laughter.

We passed a troupe of firetwirlers, and beyond them a crone with milky eyes who claimed she could tell me my future. Mara had to drag me after her when I stopped to watch a man tilt his head back and swallow the blade of a sword.

We came to a large tavern named Amelie in Yellow. A pretty young woman in an appropriately colored dress sat by the door, holding a parasol against the snow.

Mara bared her teeth at me in mock sternness. "I hope you can handle your drink."

I almost responded that I was too young for the taverns to serve but thought better of it. In the past few months, my voice had become more husky. Rigorous exercise had sliced away the fat of an easy youth. My shoulders had grown broader, and stubble marked my lip.

"One silver apiece." There was a dullness to the doorwoman's voice and movements that made me take a closer look. Her eyes were glazed over, pupils constricted into pinpoints. Recognition slowly broke through her haze at the sight of our gray uniforms. "Your friend is upstairs."

Mara slapped a pair of denarii into the woman's hand and gave her a tight-lipped nod. I followed her in, bracing myself for a rowdy affair, patrons singing bawdy songs and spilling ale all over one another. The entrance fee of one silver should have alerted me Amelie in Yellow catered to a different type of clientele.

Everyone inside wore masks, from battered iron to jade and gold, each unique in their own way. Figures lounged on beds and cushions along the sides of the room, barely visible behind diaphanous silk curtains hanging from the low walls. A quintet of flutes and violin played a haunting melody, a reminder that the nights had become long and cold. Strangely, a few couples danced, holding each other, slow and solemn. The smell of lavender was cloying but failed to mask the sickly sweet smell of what I suspected was opium.

Women in yellow dresses glided about, their hair done up in intricate arrangements, long legs flashing. The closest one stepped toward us, but Mara waved her off. Up to the back, past the dancers, up a spiral staircase to the next floor.

A guard in a bronze mask stood at the top, stout and serious, hand casually resting on the pommel of his sword. He stepped aside and gestured for us to continue; his hand never left his weapon, and I could feel his eyes boring into our backs.

The second floor of Amelie in Yellow was a gambling den, dim in the guttering light of candles spaced along the walls. Thirty or so people had come to test their luck with games of dice and cards. Amusement for the rich and the addicted. They made their bets in gold or tidy stacks of silver, more money than a commoner would make in a month changing hands over a pair of sixes.

"Not exactly what I was expecting," I said. "Should we be wearing masks?"

Mara held up a pair of fingers and locked eyes with the nearest servant in yellow. "Not completely necessary if you don't mind being seen. What do I care about these people? One of the philosophers owns this place, actually. Sensi's never around in the Gardens, though. She probably has a score of different places like this that she manages. Odena is the city of arts and vices, after all. Poetry from the end of a pipe."

The servant answered Mara's summons, the heels of her calfskin boots clicking along the tiled floor. Like the others she was strikingly beautiful, lips painted black to offset her porcelain half-mask and blonde hair. She spoke in a voice like smoke. "Welcome. Lady Mara, a pleasure to see you again. And an unfamiliar face."

"Leones. And you are?"

She raised an eyebrow. "I would be ruining the game if I told you that. One of us is Amelie, and I could not possibly deceive the two of you. Better to say nothing at all."

"Lovely," said Mara. "Do you know what I drink?"

The servant gave no sign she minded the younger woman's curtness. "Of course. And for yourself, Master Leones?"

I thought of the decanter my father used to keep on his desk. "Your finest brandy."

She waited as if expecting more. Seeing my uncertain smile, she winked conspiratorially and swished away.

"'Your finest brandy.'" Mara's lips twitched. She held a hand to her mouth as if trying to hold back laughter. "Bless your heart."

I followed the servant's lead and ignored her attitude. "What game was she talking about?"

"Forget about it," she said. "Even Felix can't figure it out. There are at least twenty women who work here at any given time. Sensi and all of her disciples are experts in the staccato. If you identify the real Amelie, you win the game."

"What's the prize?"

"You get a chance to meet Sensi and possibly become one of her personal apprentices. You may even get to own a weird place like this. Can you imagine? *Leones in Gray* has a certain ring to it."

"So you have a one-in-twenty chance."

"Right." Mara patted me on the shoulder, as if impressed at my display of mathematical prowess. "Far more than twenty people have tried and failed. Perhaps it's just bad luck. Not everyone makes an attempt, of course. The stipulation is that you only get one guess, and if you're wrong you owe her a favor. Anything she asks of you. You can refuse, but I'm sure that path leads nowhere good."

"Amelie is trained as a philosopher, right?" I picked at my chapped lower lip absently. "You could ask her questions other people wouldn't know."

Mara tapped the side of her nose. "Think about it. All of the women here are highly educated. They're some of the best-paid workers in the city, often hand-selected from the graduating classes of the Academia. And forgetting that, you could be speaking with the real Amelie, and she could just pretend not to know the answer."

All right, my question was a bit stupid. I mulled over potential ways to turn the game in my favor.

The servant returned, balancing a pair of crystal glasses on a tray. "For Lady Mara. A favorite of mine as well, an Avanchean white. Our sommelier assures me this bottle is a fine vintage, personally sampled. And for the master, a Raisso private brandy with just a touch of sugar and water."

I accepted my glass, trying not to frown at the amber drink. The sliver of orange peel garnish did little to ease my uncertainty. I took a small sip, keeping the glass pressed against my lips to mask an involuntary spasm as the brandy burned its way down. After the initial shock it was not unpleasant, a sweet blend of oak and spice and dried fruit.

"Perfect," I managed, after taking a moment to compose myself.

The servant flashed her dazzling smile. "Consider it on the house. Is there any other way I can offer my assistance?"

"Take us to Felix," said Mara.

She dipped her head in an obedient nod and led us through the tables. Taking delicate sips of my drink, I considered the mystery game. It was a battle of wits and perception and, as always, the house had the advantage. Unfortunately for them, I had my own. The most important question was, how could I shape my power to form the perfect key for this lock?

"What happens if I accuse one of you of being Amelie?" I asked the servant.

"In a week you will be summoned. If you guessed correctly, Sensi will greet you. If not, we will ask something of you, immediately or sometime in the future. Perhaps far in the future, for people with great potential."

"What if someone guesses right, and you just pretend they didn't?" I asked.

The servant stopped, head swiveling to face me. All mirth had drained from her voice. "Do not call us liars."

My cheeks flushed. A little smile broke her painted lips. I resisted the urge to reverse time, especially since Mara elbowed me in annoyance.

That answered some of my questions, at least. With my talent it wouldn't be difficult to accuse every woman in yellow of being Amelie; if I was wrong, I could simply try again. Forcing me to wait a week removed that possibility. I also had the feeling that bending the rules of the game would make it pointless. The reward for identifying the real Amelie was the chance to catch Sensi's eye. A useless prize if I won it through obvious trickery.

Still, what if there simply was no Amelie, so anyone destined to play the game would lose? In that case Sensi would just accumulate favors with no risk to herself.

I caught sight of Felix sitting at a table near the back, playing cards with two others. He was one of the only other people without a mask. The stack of coins in front of him dwarfed those of the other players. He caught sight of us and lifted a long wooden pipe to his lips. The opium nugget kindled, and he blew plumes of smoke from his nose.

The sight of him shocked me. I knew him as a somber, eloquent young man who continued practicing the sword by himself after Avarus's lessons. It was difficult to imagine that person playing cards in a high-class opium den.

The brandy filled my head with a pleasant warmth, for a moment quieting the constantly worried voice in the back of my mind. Perhaps it was not so strange that Felix found comfort in these sorts of vices. After all, they were made for lost folk like us.

"My friends," he said. "Can't say I was expecting this. I thought you disapproved of this place, Mara. And you've brought Leones." He nodded at the servant. "Bring them chairs, please."

"An audience, then?" asked the woman to Felix's right. A few years older than myself, with dark hair stacked in curls and a tattoo around her neck of a serpent eating its own tail. She rested her chin in her hand, observing me with a little smile.

The other man at the table wore an owl-face mask. Dark hair framed his face in oiled curls. "New fans for you. Introductions are in order. This is the fabulous painter Lyra Incada. I am the tragically unappreciated poet known as Ontos."

I nodded. "A pleasure."

The servant returned with our chairs. We seated ourselves and thanked her.

Felix set his opium pipe down and glanced my way. "I didn't expect to see you in this sort of place."

I looked around. "I was thinking the same about you."

"I grew up in places like this before I joined the philosophers. Not quite as opulent as this, of course. Some select places allow children to gamble as long as they have the coin. Guaranteed food in my belly and a little extra for my friends. Now they pay me back."

He smiled and revealed his hand. The other players groaned, and he scooped up his winnings.

"Still, it's a surprise," I said. "I've never been in a place like this."

Felix stacked his new winnings in one fluid motion. "One of my favorites. Deal the next hand please, Lyra. So, Leones, what is it that you thought I did in my spare time? Stare off into space, brooding?"

I sipped my brandy and gestured for Lyra to include me in the next round. "I never thought much of it. I see you practicing with the sword by yourself in the morning. We have lessons with Avarus. Outside of that I'm not sure."

"Is he much of a swordsman?" Lyra turned toward me, running a hand through her hair. "The way he talks himself up, you would think he's ready to challenge the Archon of Blades."

Mara waved away the other woman's offer to deal her cards. "The best out of our lot, I would say."

"I prefer a more realistic challenge." Felix glanced at his cards, shook his head, and took up his pipe again. After a short puff he glanced my way. "Have you heard of the house game? Attempting to identify Amelie. Any insights?"

His question caught me by surprise since I was focused on the card game. We were playing Kettle, a game where you can fold your hand with no penalty. The rest of the game relied on luck: whose cards totaled up to the greatest value. I could see why Felix liked it.

"Maybe," I said. "If Amelie is the owner of this place, you could create a situation where she would have to assume authority. A brawl or a fire could work."

Ontos shoved his cards away with a small grimace. "Your idea is to destroy her business to make her reveal herself? Not that we have come up with better. Felix isn't willing to take the risk of choosing at random."

"It's an unwinnable game meant to drive men like you crazy," said Mara. "You sort think you can solve every problem. It's all a ploy to add to the mystique. They're cultivating an atmosphere."

"I like you already," said Lyra.

"Thanks." Mara nodded at her. "How did you all meet?"

Ontos and Lyra glanced at Felix. He spoke for them. "Street urchins, all of us. There used to be others, but we drifted apart for different reasons. Lyra is a renowned artist now. She painted the mural on the wall there, the golden skull. That's why we always sit here."

Lyra frowned at her cards. "I fold. I'm not sure why I keep getting involved in these games. Charity toward Felix, maybe."

The scoundrel smiled. "So, Leones. Fold or challenge?"

After glancing down at my cards, I took a sip of brandy. I did end up winning. It only took ten rounds.

After that night the others treated me more warmly. The three of us agreed to try to meet at least once a week for what Mara called bonding sessions. Caedius occasionally stopped by the Gardens; he still didn't seem impressed but acted more to appease Mara than anything. On the third meeting he joined us, and after a couple drinks I found him to be surprisingly easygoing. Sometimes his laughter seemed forced, but he generally was content to sit back and observe.

I did discover he loved the art of combat. Despite his confidence he realized he was no prodigy blademaster. He instead worshipped martial figures from the past and devoured tales of their exploits. If someone wanted him to speak up, they would only have to mention Champion Jokul or Brys Three-Eyes. He never struck me as charming or interesting, but Mara insisted there was more to him than he showed.

We visited other establishments, though none held the same appeal as Amelie in Yellow. I would lay awake in our little barracks some nights and wonder about the riddle of the real Amelie, worrying at the problem like a loose tooth. All the obvious solutions seemed unnecessarily morbid. This birthed a new moral predicament for me: if I tortured someone and reversed time so that it never happened, would I have committed any lasting sin?

I had no intention of torturing anyone, but sometimes those dark thoughts crept through.

People began to discuss how curious the snow was. It continued the whole time in a light little flurry. There were some breaks where the sun would shine warm, but the snow would always return. A layer of white powder settled over the world and began to accumulate, slow but endless.

I attempted to visit Augur, but he had disappeared. According to the others, that was nothing out of the ordinary. Sometimes he would just leave and one day return, unannounced and uninterested in discussing where he had been.

Avarus continued to teach in the same simple outfit, immune to the cold. One day he led our dwindling group of acolytes to some hills outside of the city. He thought it great fun to have us race down the slopes until we fell, sputtering, then scramble back up to try again.

I began to look forward to his classes. His methods were brutal, but the progress was addicting. A couple more seconds of footwork, a little more speed behind my wooden blade. Sometimes I did worse than the previous day due to exhaustion or simply an off day, but in the end, there was always something to be proud of.

All the while I honed my magic. Gambling proved to be excellent practice in exploring my limits. My control improved, and I began to record my capabilities within a journal. I was careful to write in ways that would be inscrutable to others. My fondness for them continued growing, but I could not let them discover my power.

To my disappointment I was never able to go back farther than one hour from the initial activation of my magic. I tested myself against the most reliable clocks I could find. Always the same result.

I discovered that I was able to reduce the amount of fatigue each use of my powers caused, so that I could repeat events within the same hour more frequently. It took three months of exhausting experiments to be able to reverse an entire hour four times instead of three. Likewise, I could go back a half-hour eight times. It was easier to track my progress with large amounts of smaller increments.

It took around a week to fully replenish my magic. I tried to work out how long it would take to be able to repeat the same hour infinitely, assuming there was a point where I would recharge faster than I expended my magic. Eventually I decided to stop torturing myself with my inadequacy at math, especially since it seemed unlikely my growth would be linear.

Days began to blur together. Routines are easy to fall into. There were small variations, like the night I visited an art show hosted by Lyra in some rich patron's manor. I had to admit she had talent, and the other viewers murmured appreciatively amongst themselves.

Great understanding of lighting and contrast, a stranger mentioned to me. Clearly a student of Tarrare's pupil Iserus, who really emphasized the use of chiaroscuro in her works. I nodded and kept silent, feeling rather uncultured.

Fiery nightmares and fantasies about revenge no longer haunted me as much. Still, there was always that contradictory voice in the back of my mind, the unabashed critic, who pestered me about how a little comfort proved enough to erode my resolve. Sometimes I lay on my cot, fantasizing about breaking into forbidden libraries or impressing some influential patron until I drifted to sleep. In the morning it all seemed rather ridiculous.

One night Felix and I headed toward one of the local taverns. Just us. He hoped to find a group of gamblers willing to let us join, but he had developed enough of a reputation to usually encounter polite refusal. On occasion people mentioned that I seemed rather fortunate myself. I made sure not to win too much, at least compared to Felix. The earnings were beginning to overfill my coin purse, and I was exploring ways to spend my newfound wealth.

"I think Lyra has taken a fancy to you," Felix told me.

"You think so? Because I noticed nothing of the sort."

"This snow is becoming annoying." On his next step he kicked up enough snow to reveal the flagstones. "At least three inches. Terrible for footwork. Anyway, women are a game we will never win. They keep the rules a secret, then act frustrated when we aren't sure how to play. I do know she talks about you more than she should, and that is an opportunity for you. Don't laugh, it's the truth. You always laugh when you feel awkward."

The idea of anyone discussing me behind my back seemed odd. I thought of myself as a shadow, drifting about unnoticed.

"You know me that well already?" I asked. "You're a true master of the staccato."

"I know enough."

We stopped to allow a funeral procession to pass. The deceased was one of the gentry, judging from the fine clothing and garish jewelry of the mourners. A pair of little girls threw rose petals over their shoulders as they marched along. To my surprise Felix watched them with a look of disdain.

We continued on after they passed. Felix's good humor had vanished. Silence stretched between us until I felt compelled to speak. "Bad memory?"

"Do you know," he asked, "the reason you never see dead birds? They sense the end coming and hide away. They don't want to be a bother. How strange is it that we make these grand shows out of our deaths? All the rites and ceremonies. We're too arrogant to hide and let ourselves be forgotten."

The venom in his voice shocked me. I smiled, unsure how to respond.

"Mankind, mankind." He had the bitter voice of someone discussing a former lover. "I find it hard to connect with most people. I have a conversation with them and look into their eyes, and it feels like I'm speaking with a puppet. You look and only see yourself reflected back. I know you must see it, too, how strange and unnatural all of this is. There is something fundamentally wrong with our world."

"Sometimes I think like that." I swallowed, thinking carefully about my next words. "What if there is nothing wrong with those other people? What if you and I are the ones with something fundamentally wrong?"

A muscle in his cheek twitched. We walked in silence until it became unbearable. I reversed time to a minute before we stopped at the funeral procession.

"Why don't we go this way?" I pointed in a direction that would avoid the mourners.

"If you insist." Felix grinned. "You know, I wasn't sure if I was going to mention it, but I think Lyra has taken a fancy to you . . ."

I sat on the edge of Lyra's bed, naked.

We had seen each other around a few times in the past month. Eventually she took the initiative to have me walk her home after a night out. It had been a week since then, and we had spent several nights together. I had lain with another woman once before, a servant's daughter who decided it was best to end our impropriety sooner rather than later, but being with Lyra felt easy. Natural.

I had to admit Felix knew a bit more about women than me. It wasn't some storybook romance, but any teenage boy can appreciate the company of a lovely girl.

"What are you thinking about?" Lyra laid on her stomach behind me, legs bent, feet curled. She was dissecting a pomegranate with her hands, a cloth spread beneath to protect her sheets. She slipped individual arils between her full lips. Their juice stained her fingers purple.

"Nothing," I said.

"You are focusing very intently on nothing." She rolled onto her back and stretched. The moonlight through the window illuminated her body in fascinating ways. Chiaroscuro. "Most men would take more interest in a pretty girl lying next to them. Naked."

How to explain this to her? One benefit of experimenting with my power over time is that I had developed a precise mental clock. I knew that Philosopher Jonos's lecture that day on free will had lasted twenty-seven minutes and eighteen seconds. Despite this talent I still felt disoriented from exploring my power so often. Time would overlap as my consciousness experienced the same moment over again. There must be an objective time, what the rest of the world experiences, and then for me a subjective time, separate but still real . . .

"I was thinking about time. Do you think you and I experience it the same way?

"That is a question for your philosopher friends." She flipped back onto her stomach and continued her work on the pomegranate. "Ask me something I know."

I ran a finger along her tattooed neck. "Why the ouroboros?"

"Oh, you recognize it. Maybe it's a symbol of fertility. Silly girls like me only think about babies and romance."

"Seriously."

She touched her neck and looked away. "I like the idea of the infinite, all right? The idea that our lives repeat in a cycle. That death isn't the end. That's one of the great human fears, isn't it?"

I pushed lank hair back out of my eyes. "Good answer. You had me worried. I doubt anyone would call me romantic."

She shrugged. "Any asshole can be romantic. Not all men are capable of love."

Silence settled between us. I looked around her room—slightly disheveled, random paintbrush marks on the walls, a half-finished canvas of a skeletal face in profile. Morbid.

"Do you think Felix is capable of love?"

She set her fruit down on the cloth and rested her chin on her hands. "Bringing Felix up right now is very awkward. I brought up love and babies first, so I can forgive you. Felix is like a brother to me, and I think he views me as a sister. He has done a lot for me and Ontos. But true love? The act of baring your soul to another person? Being vulnerable? No, I don't think he's capable of that type of love."

"Why not?"

Lyra heaved a sigh. "Why don't you ask him? Felix is different from other people. It has gotten him into trouble his whole life, and it has also worked in his favor. I've only seen him truly angry one time, and it was the most terrifying thing I have ever seen."

"What happened?"

"I really hate talking about Felix like this," she said. "I'm telling you as a warning. Do not bring up his father. We were thirteen and walking down the street when we spotted a man coming out of a bakery. He never noticed us."

"Felix's dad."

"Right. I never realized anything had happened until we turned down an empty alley. Felix absolutely lost his mind. Like an animal. After a while he started punching these stone walls until his hands were mangled. Apparently that old blademaster nearly threw a tantrum himself when he learned his favorite pupil couldn't hold a sword for months."

I pushed a strand of hair away from her face and tucked it behind her ear. "For someone who keeps saying they don't want to talk about Felix, you certainly just gave me his life story."

She tried to push me off the bed playfully. "Get out of here."

"Relax, pomegranate-fingers."

9

MEMORY

After months of snowfall the number of philosophers staying in the Gardens dwindled near to nothing. Most of the elders realized their golden ages were behind them and they had nothing to prove by suffering the weather.

Travelers from across the Civilized Lands claimed snow blanketed half the territory. To the Great Cities it was little more than an inconvenience. For the majority of the population, who lived on farmland and in remote villages, it was a tragedy. Only the Increate knows how many families succumbed, holding one another in their cold, dark homes, waiting for someone to come to lay their souls to rest.

Many folk passed through Odena on their way to Velassa. Rumor had it that Archon Nony kept the city safe and well-heated. The same rumor left out the fact that Nony did not approve of vagrants.

Now that I had acquired some funds, I sent out some queries regarding the fate of Jansen Ansteri. A month later, a report arrived detailing how he had surrendered himself to the Magistrate, along with a piece of paper recording the public executions that week. My eyes lingered on his name for a long time, tears stinging at the corners. No mention of my name, and the rest of the household looked to have been spared. I tore the papers into tiny pieces and let the wind carry them away.

I found myself spending more time at Amelie in Yellow than I should. Mostly with Felix in the beginning, though as of late he had invested himself fully into training with the blade. His sudden coldness, as well as Lyra's increasingly distant demeanor, kept me awake late some nights, wondering what I had done to ruin everything. We skipped one of our weekly card sessions, and no one ever mentioned when we would gather next.

You have more important things to worry about, I told myself. Revenge. Mysteries. Becoming stronger. What does it matter if a couple of new friendships turn to ash? The logic made perfect sense, but the hollowness remained.

One night I sat alone at Amelie in Yellow, drinking a snifter of brandy. The sting of the alcohol no longer bothered me, but I was careful not to drink too much or too often. Never touched the opium. I had no intention of joining those sad, limpid souls lounging on the first floor, drool trickling down their chin.

Some men at a nearby table were discussing the snow. They argued about different theories. One of them was new. Winter had used a colossal amount of power, and all of this cold was the result of the backlash. Not the worst idea, but it raised more questions than it answered.

"I've never seen you here alone." A soft voice, warped behind a dragon mask. One of the Amelies slipped into the seat beside me. Olive-skinned, her dark hair tamed into a long braid.

"The others are busy," I said. "I kept thinking of the mystery of this place today. A silly thing to obsess over. Smarter people than I have thought about it, and no one has ever won. I think I'll solve it, though."

She crossed her legs and folded her hands on her lap. "Sensi is an excellent teacher. Best of luck."

I finished my drink and left a denarius as a tip. By the time I descended the staircase and reached the exit, one of the Amelies had located my cloak and slipped me into it. Only the best service.

It was early in the night. Lyra would be awake. Her recent paintings had sold for a tidy sum, and she was home working on her next series, a commission from a new patron. Two weeks ago, she had told me that she needed to completely isolate to focus on her work. Perfectly normal, she had assured me. I found myself thinking of her more often than I should.

I liked her, but I suspected I liked the idea of her more. Mature, intelligent, charming. Well-known enough to be recognized in public. When some of her admirers learned I was an acolyte of the philosophers, they would challenge me on esoterica. Fortunately, my power to give them their own answer mitigated most of their attempts. Proving myself was the first challenge; next came the long discussions about aesthetics, reinforced with multilingual posturing like *negativo chromoso* and *arteste pestere*.

Despite their arrogance I actually liked most of the bohemians. They viewed themselves as overlooked geniuses but in a playful way, as if the world was playing a joke by ignoring their masterpieces. I heard more lewd metaphors and brothel discussions than I cared to remember, enough to convince me the entire artistic community consists of unapologetic degenerates——but at least the amusing sort.

Anest, a handsome youth with swept-back hair who had earned some recognition as a sculptor, could always reduce me to laughter. He was the only one of Lyra's friends I met multiple times during those weeks. On our second encounter I paid for his drinks and listened to his solemn witticisms all night. At the end Lyra said, if I was so enamored with him, I should invite him to join us at her place. I chuckled and only realized a couple days later what she meant and that she was quite serious.

Still, when I was with them, I always found myself wishing I was reading or practicing my swordwork. None of that appealed to me tonight. I needed rest and some time to reflect on the Amelie mystery.

Lost in thought, I returned to the Gardens. With my winnings from gambling, I could have rented a cozy private room; instead, I invested in a safe haven in one of the less populated areas, well-stocked in case I had to hide for a few days and flee the city. Felix continued to sleep in the barracks, and so would I. Avarus took it a step further and still refused to wear a cloak.

I intended to forge myself into a weapon. A little cold shouldn't make me brittle.

Every night I stopped by Augur's hut to see if he had returned. More out of habit than any real expectation of seeing him.

To my surprise, that night the firepit was roaring, and he meditated beside it, oblivious to the licking flames. Shadows played across his face. Eyes closed, peaceful as a figure in some chapel mural. My desire for solitude immediately evaporated.

I approached, trying my best to mask my presence.

"Hail, Leones," he said before I made it within twenty feet.

I fell back a step in surprise. "How did you know I was here?"

He opened his eyes and grinned. "Who else would you be? I don't have many visitors, especially in this cold. Such a shame. Winter is the perfect time for contemplation."

"You've been gone."

"I have. There is a big, strange world out there. Have you kept up with your meditating?"

Lying to him would be pointless. "Not as much as I should. I'm too easily distracted." He stood, waving his hand in dismissal. "You're the right age for distractions. Come in, I'll make some tea."

I followed him into his hut, attempting to stifle the burning question that had been plaguing me for some time. The battle didn't last long. "Could you teach me the staccato?"

"You're not keeping up with your meditation, but you want me to teach you one of the most complex skills a philosopher can learn?" Augur stroked the leaves of one of his potted plants between thumb and forefinger. "Why the sudden interest?"

"I've been going to Amelie in Yellow recently."

Augur chuckled. "I can't say I approve, but you're free to do as you wish. Sensi has created quite the trap for people like you. Are you trying to win the guessing game? You should realize you're at a great disadvantage here."

"I know," I said, "but I want to learn as much as I can."

The philosopher fell into a coughing fit. Afterward he looked at his hand in distaste as if there was something there. Blood? "The staccato is a difficult thing to learn. An even harder thing to teach. The more you learn, the more it will change you. It's a method of dissecting your experiences, which makes it a personal journey. But I will try my best."

I nodded and swallowed a knot of tension I hadn't realized was there. "Thank you."

"You heard none of my warning, only my agreement," he said. "The power of mankind comes from our delusions. To survive in this harsh world, we developed a sense of self. To thrive in it, we created the lie of civilization. The staccato teaches us that society is only a dream we share. Even deeper, the self is a fabrication."

During my time with the philosophers, I had been drowned in various grand claims about the nature of reality. Feeling I should say something, I grunted in agreement. It must not have been very convincing.

"I remember being young. I never listened to good advice either." He sighed. "You are certain you wish to learn?"

I nodded again.

So he explained the way I had been learning was fundamentally flawed. I had neglected training my memory, the foundation of the staccato. If I wanted to be able to read someone, I would have to remember every facial muscle, how they interacted to form complex expressions. If I expected to travel throughout the Civilized Lands I would encounter a dozen common languages, each with a litter of dialects so diverse that two people could claim to speak the same language without understanding the other.

He claimed there were methods of remembering entire tomes of information and, in light of my father's eidetic recall of his library, I believed him.

"The mind must be honed through meditation and techniques such as the creation of memory palaces," he said. "Our memory is imperfect because our minds are imperfect. It is the skill of the artist that brings his work to life: the better he is, the more real it seems."

Brother Augur had created an imaginary arboretum in his mind that mirrored his surroundings exactly. He stored memories of love in the river, his favorite songs and stories in the firepit.

He encouraged me to use a location that I remembered well. I immediately thought of my family manor: the heat and smells of the kitchens, my room with its gorgeous view of Tailors' Avenue, the chaotic splendor of my father's study. According to Augur, if I formed a connection between information and specific parts of my memory palace, I would be more likely to form an accurate recollection. Each connection would have a special resonance that made it easy to remember.

Whatever doubts I had were extinguished after he demonstrated the usefulness of the technique. He had me attempt to remember a list of thirty words through my usual method of staring at them intently—an abject failure.

After that he told me to form a mental image of each word, a unique and memorable creation. For "fish" he had me visualize a salmon the size of a horse laying on one of the kitchen floors. For "yellow" I imagined one of the Amelies, proud and straight-backed in one of the sitting room recliners. To recall them in order I wandered through the halls of my memory palace, noting each part of this bizarre menagerie as I passed.

I recited all thirty back to him.

"You have a talent for visualization," he said, nodding. It was a bit pathetic how much I enjoyed his praise.

This, he told me, was the most valuable gift he had to offer, concluding the lesson. He offered a few more pointers, such as changing the lighting to see how it affected my mental state. To my surprise, illuminating the rooms well seemed to improve my overall mood. Over time I would discover the unique features of my own memory palace.

I agreed to stay a few hours and dine with him. Silence stretched between us and, even though Brother Augur appeared comfortable, I had to admit I was dissatisfied. What had I been expecting—my first lesson to be spent with us walking through the streets, convincing old ladies to hand over their jewelry?

We shared a meal of fish and berries around his firepit. After we finished, Augur retrieved a sketchpad and began to draw, refusing to reveal his illustration. On occasion he would glance up at the sky, as if mesmerized by something lurking there.

I meditated to pass the time. Clarity of mind eluded me more than usual. Unwelcome thoughts rushed past my half-hearted defenses.

I found myself wandering through the memory of my family manor. There were no comically large salmon or other anomalies. It was as I remembered it: perfect and welcoming. Home.

Part of my consciousness remembered that I was sitting in the lotus position, meditating, but I must have fallen half into the land of sleep, pressing against the thin barrier of a dream. I walked through familiar halls until I came across a servant, a shadow like a brushstroke of black. Though I shouted for its attention the not-person drifted past. I increased my pace, quickly coming to my father's study.

I remembered it perfectly, the familiar chaos. But when I opened the door, I saw only emptiness beyond. It was not darkness. It was an absence. Nothingness. I sensed something, a presence in the void, then in a moment it vanished.

My eyes snapped open. My heart fluttered in my chest, panic-fast. Breath struggled through a throat shrunk to the size of a reed. I leaned forward, balancing myself on one hand, ragged gasps leaking out.

Augur turned back to watch, then his head twisted to the side faster than a falcon's. I followed his gaze and saw nothing in the distance. His gaze snapped up to the evening sky, where the moon watched over us.

There his eyes remained, and when my breathing gradually returned to normal and my heart settled once more, I looked there too.

I saw nothing.

"Tell me what you have been doing recently," said Augur. "Now."

I began to talk about Lyra and my visits to gambling dens, but he waved that away with an incredulous look on his face. I had never seen such a disturbed expression on his face and, in a ridiculous way, I was hurt by it.

"None of that is important," he said. "What do you know of Desolada? Have you been using the names of the Goetia? Some of them are not even safe to think about."

Desolada. The home of the demon lords, associated with the moon and the aether, a place of terrible beauty. Some claimed that the wicked went there after death, to exist in thrall for all eternity. The priests did not preach this publicly, and none of the holy texts made the claim, but it was the sort of thing mothers told their children, and that was a greater authority.

Now it was my turn to look incredulous. "I've done no more than any other."

"What is it that you think others do?" His voice held a sharp anger that I had not suspected lurked inside.

Memories came to me in a jumble. What had I done? He insinuated that I had been dealing with the Goetia—a death sentence even in Odena. In Velassa the rumor of it could see you roasted slow in the public square.

"I read the story of the fall of Arostara. Lakken has it in his library."

Brother Augur's hand beat a frantic rhythm against his hip. "Prince Sitri is supposedly no more. While many claim the Goetia cannot be destroyed, Winter is said to have sealed him for eternity. Since then, Sitri has never answered any summons. Of the demon lords he was one of the weakest as well. He would never have dared to step foot so far within the Civilized Lands. This is far beyond him."

I thought back to the story of the Fall of Arostara and the Iconoclast. "If Prince Sitri was one of the weakest of the Seventy-Seven, then how did the Archons defeat them?"

The tension evaporated from his face, and he once more assumed the visage of a teacher, lofty and aloof. "Not all of them seek dominion over man. They are not of this world, perhaps not even of our cosmos.

We cannot know them, just as we cannot know the will of the wind or the deep thoughts of the ocean. Some of them find us interesting, like a butterfly collector who admires his specimen on the killing board. Others use men as their tools. The men they enslave are called many things—Heralds, Harbingers, Echoes. Their relationship seems beneficial at first, but I know full well how easily a man is deceived. Nothing good comes from associating with the Lords of Desolada."

I nodded, trying not to seem too interested. Augur's agitation already seemed like a distant memory, his face now carved from stone. But his iron will had cracked, and that was no small thing.

I tried to coax more information from him, to no avail. There was always the option of using my power to go back in time before I caught the attention of whatever demon lord lurked about. Both for my own safety and for the possibility of squeezing more information from Brother Augur. Several excuses held me back, but I knew they were just that—excuses.

I wanted to know and be known.

The idea of Echoes had caught my attention and would not release me from its dark grip. They sounded like ambassadors of the Goetia, imbued with special powers and privileges. From Frontier to Frontier the Goetia were cursed as monsters, yet Augur had admitted they were not united against mankind. He compared them to forces of nature. The sea did not hate. It may go into frenzies and destroy everything in its path, but it did so with utter indifference.

I did know one thing: at least one of the Archons was my enemy. Demons had not killed my family.

Since birth I had been told this world was a battlefield between mankind and everything else under the sun. When we expanded the Frontier, we took the land from others. Not just demons, but nagas, giants, mind-arachnids, and a thousand others.

I never questioned our place in the world until that moment. The church claimed that we had a divine right to rule after existing under the yoke of the Goetia for so long, as if revenge was a mandate of heaven. Yet what of the sapient creatures fortunate enough to never encounter us until we marched on their lands with steel and flame?

I could not have blamed Brother Augur if he had killed me where I stood. He must have seen some of my thoughts written clearly on my face. Who knows if he would have been doing the world a favor? If all of my future deeds were weighed on the scales of justice, I could not say which way it would tip. Whose scales, whose justice?

Of Brother Augur himself I knew little. His past must have haunted him enough that he secluded himself from the world. At that point in his life, he must not have been able to bear the sin of killing a boy just because the Goetia interested him.

He said nothing when I offered my farewells and departed.

10

OTHERS

The next day Felix sought me out after Avarus's blade lesson. Over the past few weeks, he had done little more than acknowledge my existence. Curt nods when we crossed paths. Vapid conversations at the barracks—sometimes just a grunt at his end. During the lessons we would stand with Irele listening to the old blademaster, occasionally sparring together or working through forms of the legato side-by-side.

I was so used to him ignoring my presence that I failed to notice his approach until he clapped a hand on my shoulder.

"I need a sparring partner," he said, blue eyes intense.

As resentful as I felt toward him and Lyra, the request tugged a smile from the corner of my lips. No matter how much I chastised myself for wasting time drinking and gambling, those nights had soothed my soul. We are social creatures, after all. Staying out until early morning laughing and winning gold felt more refreshing than a long night's sleep.

"Of course," I said. "Though I'm sure you could afford the best blademaster in the city."

He frowned, eyebrows drawing in. "If you don't want to, just say no."

"I'll spar with you."

Felix tapped the blade of his wooden sword against his boot. "Good. I'm asking you because I saw you a couple of nights ago. Here, around midnight. Swinging your sword around and yelling like a madman.

Don't look so embarrassed, Leones. I respect that passion. You're fighting for something as well. No one becomes the best without the perfect balance of passion and insanity."

"You're right," I said.

He laughed. A rare sound, surprisingly hearty and carefree. "I am. May as well tell you now. I've been chosen to compete in the upcoming Games. Avarus agreed, though it wasn't easy to convince him. A battle between his hatred of spectacles and the pride of hearing them announce his name to half the city."

The news rooted me in place. Competing in the Games meant a public display of your abilities as a warrior. Most of the Great Cities had their own Amphitheater, including Velassa. In my home city, criminals would fight one another to the death in rings of fire or compete against wild beasts driven into a panic. The thought left a sour taste in my mouth. My parents had rightfully forbidden me from attending, even though it was considered a religious ceremony.

The Amphitheater in Odena did not pretend to be holy and was supposedly less sinful. All combatants volunteered to fight, lured by dreams of greed and glory. Lethal strikes were banned even though they used edged weapons; accidents had killed countless fighters in the last couple of centuries, but such inevitabilities were excused under the pretext that they knew what they were signing up for.

Despite the usual soreness from Avarus's lessons, I agreed to spar another hour or two with Felix. Irele departed, casting a questioning glance at us over her shoulder. I respected the tall girl for continuing to attend the daily lessons even when she lived outside the Gardens.

The old blademaster shrugged when we asked if we could continue sparring. He gathered up the rest of his equipment and left without another word.

With a sigh, I faced Felix, wooden sword in hand. When I used my powers, I could keep up with Irele in a friendly match—even scoring a few points, a fact which would make her neck flush scarlet. Likely she believed I possessed a quirk, like Felix's luck. She had around a year's more experience than myself as one of Avarus's pupils, so I could not blame her for becoming upset at my seemingly preternatural ability to sense her incoming strikes.

Felix always made sure to humble me. That day was no different.

He proved that, no matter how many times I could repeat a duel, there were some opponents I could simply not defeat. I could reverse time whenever he scored a point or disarmed me, but if I blocked one attack the next one was always close behind. He combined the movements of the first legato and the beginning of second into something cohesive, organic. Eventually I would grow tired of the farce and let him finish the match.

Worst of all was that quirk of his. Whenever I thought I had an opening, my foot would slip on a random patch of ice, or the wind would blow snow into my eyes. Nothing he seemed to do consciously. Nature just favored him.

After another humiliating defeat we separated to take a break. I planned on asking Felix why he had seemed so distant recently. Had he withdrawn simply because he wanted to focus on his upcoming exhibition at the Games?

Before I could question him, I noticed Avarus had returned with company. Four youths stood off to the side watching us. They wore the gray of acolytes and looked as though they were our elders by a few years. Each held a spear with a wooden blade.

"We have company." Avarus folded his arms. "From our brothers and sisters in Karysto. Their teacher is a dear old friend. I ask him to send his best every year or so. Since everyone else besides Irele ran off after it stopped snowing, I asked if they could visit early. They are more than familiar with Felix at this point. "

Felix offered them a little wave.

"I see there are four of them and two of us," I said. "Are you planning to join us, master?"

Avarus shook his head. "I no longer take much pleasure in smacking children around. Single duels. Their best against Felix. Second best against you."

"I've only been an acolyte for five months."

"Then this should be a humbling experience for someone."

Felix sheathed his wooden sword and strolled over to the group from Karysto. "I thought Lisara was your best."

One of the acolytes was a portly young man with an earnest face. He blushed. "She doesn't like being out in the cold. I would be honored if I could face you this time. After my match with Leones. If you don't mind, of course."

Felix looked at me and blinked rapidly, trying to hold back a smile. "They have manners in Karysto. Not even the servants in Odena are polite."

"I came to the wrong city," I said.

"You're stuck with us now. Shall we show these nice boys some hospitality?"

Avarus cleared his throat. "Remember that this is a friendly competition between peers. It is also a learning opportunity for everyone involved."

In other words, Felix should not embarrass his opponent.

The first duel was between me and the portly acolyte. We assumed our positions, ten feet apart, weapons held at the ready. No trace of friendliness remained on his face. Acceptable posture, tight grip on his spear.

Avarus whistled.

The Karystan charged. Plodding, inelegant, but damn, he was big. My heart pounded, vision sharpening. The first time we fought he tackled me to the ground, and there was no getting back up.

I reversed time.

On the second attempt I bided my time as he charged. At the last second, I danced to the side and swept at the snow with my boot. When he turned to me, a face full of powder blinded him. The spear licked out at me; I deflected his desperate blow, turning aside the shaft and stepping into his reach.

To my surprise he dropped his spear and tried grappling. I struck his chin with the pommel of my sword once, twice, but we had never agreed to any rules for ending the match. The blows did nothing but enrage him. Between his bulk and the look on his face, it felt like wrestling with a bear. He tore the weapon from my hands and pawed at me. No technique, but damn, he was strong.

I tried to pivot and toss him over my shoulder, but his weight barely shifted. With a bellow he pushed out, throwing me off my feet. I rolled to the closest weapon—his spear—and, grabbing it, came to my feet in one smooth motion. The spear whipped around just in time to halt his wild charge; he came to a stop with the wooden blade pressing a furrow into his thick jowls.

The bloodlust in the boy's eyes disappeared. He took a step back and bowed his head in respect. I returned his spear, nodding. Without a word he retreated to his friends, shoulders slumped.

Avarus did not even favor me with a look. He clapped his hands. "Leones is the victor. Now for the real match. Hopefully more of a bout between gentlemen. Felix, Rayen, step to."

Even though the others seemed to have already forgotten my victory, I could not help but grin. I would have been crushed in a true grappling match, but the thought did little to dim my smile. Sure, I used my power, but he had years of training and close to a hundred pounds on me, and I had finished him in less than fifteen seconds.

I stood beside Avarus and the other acolytes from Karysto as the next two combatants assumed their positions.

The portly boy stuck his hand out. "Name's Johan. You're damn fast."

I clasped his wrist. "Leones. You're damn strong."

Avarus whistled for the next match to begin.

They circled each other until Rayen closed the distance with a jab. Felix turned his head just enough to avoid the spear blade. After a few near misses, the Karystan lost his temper and attempted to pin him down with a flurry of strikes.

Felix weaved between the blows like a dancer, beautiful in his fluidity, not even bothering to use his sword. I understood his plan moments before it materialized. He favored this clearing because of all the tricky stones and holes obscured under the snow. Rayen stumbled into the same trap I had fallen into several times before learning my lesson.

The acolyte lost his footing on a concealed rock and fell on his ass. Felix pinned the spear to the ground with his blade and aimed a savage kick at Rayen's head; the blow might have killed him if Felix hadn't stopped it a hair's-breadth from the acolyte's temple.

Avarus clapped. "Felix is the victor. Did I not say this was supposed to be a learning activity? It's a shame Lisara isn't here to humble these two. She will have her opportunity in the next couple of weeks. The Karystan acolytes will be staying for a while to attend my classes."

Felix turned and walked away. I crushed the urge to follow him. What was I, his pet?

"Well," said Avarus, "I guess he will not be joining this impromptu lesson. I think an extra hour today will help us tighten up a few things. Particularly you, Leones. I have several criticisms."

I sighed.

* * *

Felix and I celebrated that night at Amelie's. We were not exactly sure what we were celebrating—perhaps Avarus agreeing to allow his star pupil to compete in such a violent endeavor. Most combatants did not try their luck until later into adulthood. However, since Avarus was last recorded as competing as a fourth-legato blademaster, his word carried enough weight for the officials to agree.

That bought Felix a place in the Games to be held in ten days.

No matter the occasion, the return of Felix's company was welcome. I drank a glass of wine, and he worked on the rest of the bottle. That night we relaxed on a divan pulled up on the first floor. Instead of musicians, a trio of Amelies performed in an aerial silk ballet, lithe forms contorting in a pattern I could not quite follow.

"Bless me," said Felix. "I won't tell Lyra about this."

"I think she's more interested in her paintings nowadays."

"Her paintings are important. Jealousy is ugly."

I still found it strange that Felix and I had become friends in the first place. The youth was not someone whom I would ever have associated with in my past life. He was arrogant and off-putting but had never done anything to harm or offend me. He could be witty, and the more he explained his worldview to me the more sense it made, though I never really empathized with it. There were worse people to spend time with.

Felix gestured to the entrance, wearing a sour expression. Mara stood at the head of the Karystans. Still no sign of their leader, Lisara. The lads watched the aerial silk show with a variety of expressions I couldn't help but find comedic.

Mara spotted us and directed their group toward our divan. Judging from the complaints in her wake she was not careful in avoiding others.

"If I saw Caedius here . . ." said Mara.

"This area is reserved," said Felix. "Private celebration."

Johan, the large one I had sparred with earlier, stepped to the front. He pulled a spectacles case from his pocket and retrieved from it a pair of dainty eyeglasses. When he pressed them against his broad face, he looked absurd. "Avarus asked Mara to show us around. She thought it'd be a good idea for us all to meet up."

Felix did not look impressed. The other boy met his unblinking gaze. My friend shifted and pulled a deck of cards from his pocket, slow and deliberate. He selected a single one and held it out to Johan, clenched between his second and third fingers. "Take this card from my hand, and you can sit down."

Without further prompting Johan made a snatch for the card. Not even close.

"One more try?" asked Felix.

This time, right before Johan made his attempt, I reached out and seized Felix by the wrist. Caught off guard, he turned toward me; the Karystan seized his moment and plundered the immobilized hand.

Felix looked like he had a lot to say. Instead, he gestured beside him. Mara took the seat, and the Karystans gathered around, awkwardly hunched to minimize the amount of space they occupied.

Rayen, the one Felix had defeated earlier, spoke up. "We don't have places like this in Karysto."

To my surprise, my friend responded. "You just don't know the right people. Don't talk too much, you'll ruin the show."

An Amelie with black hair and a cat mask maneuvered her way to our little group and began taking orders. Rayen eyed the pipe loosely clutched in Felix's hand before ordering an ale. The other Karystans followed Johan's lead and chose to remain sober. The other two boys introduced themselves as Kass and Pol. Felix grunted in response.

We watched the remaining fifteen minutes of the show together. Mara grew more interested as the show went on, drinking wine straight out of the bottle with Felix. At the finale when the dancers clambered to the top of their silks then let themselves fall, gyrating and shedding folds of cloth until they came to a sudden stop a few paces above the floor, Mara stood and clapped longer than anyone.

"But you'd be mad if Caedius was here?" I asked, sharing a little grin with Johan. He tilted his head and shrugged, as if saying he couldn't understand women either.

"I can appreciate beauty," she said after another swig of wine. "Caedius goes wild over the Games and his favorite warriors. He still wouldn't want me ogling them with a group of desperate women."

"I'm not desperate," said Rayen, scrunching up his mouse-like face. We ignored him.

Felix adjusted himself on the divan. "So why are you all here again?"

"I told you. Avarus asked me to show them around," said Mara. "Where else should we have gone this late at night?"

"There are about fifty other taverns, ancient temples, the Gardens, brothels, ice sculptures, pit fights, musical performances. Off the top of my head. All this time you've spent recently, hunting me down without your boyfriend latched onto you. I'm starting to wonder if you have a little crush, Mara."

Flushing, she tossed a copper at Felix to pay for her share of the wine. He caught it, rolled it around in his palm, then bit into it as if testing the metal for authenticity. Mara stormed off, waving away one of the Amelies who moved to intercept her path. Johan and Rayen stayed behind while the more taciturn Karystans followed her outside.

"Well," I said. "Did you really have to antagonize her?"

"I didn't invite her. Or them. Is it not rude to just barge in on us when we're relaxing? Should I just let her do whatever she wants because I'm terrified of hurting her feelings?"

Rayen set aside his half-finished mug. "That's how you get a princess like Lisara."

Johan slapped his companion's arm hard enough to make him grunt. "Lisara is the strongest of us so she's the leader. Felix is the strongest overall so we must respect his wishes. We can leave, if we are still disturbing you two."

Felix looked tempted to take them up on that offer. Then he smiled. "A man that respects the hierarchy. You two aren't shabby with the spear. I never gave you that match you asked for, by the way. Maybe we should have a little bout. You two against me."

Rayen did little to conceal his grimace but still nodded. Johan clapped once, face brightening. He gestured for one of the Amelies and ordered a celebratory glass of brandy.

"Go for the Raisso private reserve," I said. "Touch of water and sugar."

We stayed longer than expected, chatting amongst ourselves as the other clientele dispersed. Johan complimented me on my recommendation as if it wasn't the only thing in my repertoire. Rayen in particular loosened up the more we talked, burying a second mug of ale before asking Felix if he could try the opium. My friend wiped his saliva from the pipe and passed it along. The Karystan's eyes widened after he took a small hit. Johan and I declined his offer to pass it along to us.

"So there is a separate legato for the spear as well?" I asked.

Johan nodded, staring at the bottom of his empty glass. "The legato is originally a sword art, but around a hundred years ago Master Jappa made a . . . translation to the spear. Not quite the same, and he only created up to the fourth form. It's the dream of every spearman to continue the song by discovering what comes after."

How interesting. By that point I had finished a brandy myself, turning my thoughts into pretty mush. Rayen took up as much space on the divan as he could; he looked to be in no shape to fight Felix, let alone walk back by himself.

I found myself attempting to teach the others how to create mind palaces. Rayen lacked the focus, but Johan seemed to take my advice well enough, constructing a small room in his head, though he said it was obviously flawed. Perhaps the alcohol interfered. Felix, on the other hand, revealed he was completely incapable of visualization.

"You mean to tell me you can see images in your head?" he asked. "You can close your eyes and see a painting?"

I chuckled. "Of course. You can't? Try imagining a red triangle."

He closed his eyes for an eternity before biting his lip. "No. There's something there, a kind of impression, but that's all. I know what they look like, but I can't create an image of it."

"You have dreams though, right?"

"Yes, but that's completely different."

How bizarre. The philosophers had a concept known as qualia, vaguely the idea that while there is a universally recognized "red," the actual color I and someone else saw may be completely different, but we could never know without merging consciousness. Tutors had praised my memory and learning abilities, and I knew my sense of sight and smell surpassed most, but I wondered just how different my reality was from everyone else's. If someone else experienced my thoughts and perspective, would it be completely unrecognizable?

My musings were interrupted by an emaciated figure buried beneath a dark robe, strolling toward the exit. Long black hair obscured their profile. Not the strangest looking person I had seen that night, but something about their gait seemed off. As if sensing my gaze, she turned toward me—definitely a woman, features sharp and graceful, skin so pale it was near translucent. We made eye contact long enough for me to notice the black depths of her pupilless eyes.

Quicker than my eyes could register, she disappeared from the first floor. The door did not even open. She simply vanished.

"Did anyone else see that?" I asked.

The others denied noticing anything. Felix was trying to concentrate on his visualization, and the Karystans had been facing away.

I reversed time a few minutes, but the lady in the dark robe never returned. Even when I went back an entire hour and excused myself from the group, I could find no trace of her within Amelie in Yellow. Questioning the servants revealed nothing.

Consumed by curiosity, I could not stand to repeat my conversation with the others. I excused myself and wandered around the city, attempting to locate her, but I knew it was a fool's errand. It was late before I returned to the disciples' barracks, now crammed with the Karystans as well as Felix and Mara.

Even when morning came, I could not fall asleep.

That woman was not a human.

11

LYRA

"Nice call." The bookkeeper pawed at his ruddy nose. "What made you choose Slipfoot?"

Offering a fake smile, I accepted the heavy purse of coins. "Liked the look of him."

Emptying the purse onto the encounter revealed eighteen golden sols, a smattering of silver denarii, and a few coppers that I set back on the counter as a tip. Altogether more than a skilled laborer would earn in a year. The odds against my winning horse had been long even if he was part of some bloodline reserved for high-ranking officers. Suspicious, but one chance victory with a modest investment would go unnoticed. I had been tempted to slap a small fortune on the counter, but that much attention would have been unwelcome.

"Good eye," said the bookkeeper, gathering up the coppers. "Come back anytime."

"Of course."

The coins jingled together pleasantly as I returned them to their purse. I took my leave, hand resting on the pommel of my new sword. This piece came from Bakkel, the same smith who had created Felix's sword of choice and that of most serious combatants within the city. Their distinct handles were something of a mark of pride; mine was hatched white-and-gold with a matching scabbard. Any blademaster who saw a teenager walking around with one would likely challenge me to a duel over its ownership, but such bets were illegal with anyone under eighteen. As long as the officials found out, of course.

Three days had passed since I encountered the woman in dark robes. The sword did little to soothe my worries. More powerful weapons did exist, of course. Legendary blades with names and blessings that granted powers to their wielders. Their cost, though ludicrous, would not have been a problem if I utilized the full potential of my power. The issue was that random blacksmiths did not stock them on their shelves. A few may have existed within Odena, jealously guarded by their owners, but most were lent out by the Archons to promising warriors on the Frontier.

If I had simply seen that woman's pale skin and strange eyes I would not have been so paranoid. But for her to disappear like that, I was either losing my mind or had encountered a being that should not exist this deep within human territory.

But even then, my biggest worry was not for myself. Not directly. If that woman was truly a demon, her presence in the city meant nothing good. Wards existed against her kind, not to mention the Archon himself. While Odena had no official counterpart to the Magisters, there would be powerful enforcers within the city with a duty to prevent something like this.

So how was a demon walking around Odena?

Part of me wanted nothing to do with her. The more mischievous parts wanted to find her. That plan went down some dangerous paths. The greatest question was whether to go to the authorities and reveal the sighting. Amelie in Yellow would be closed. Likely nothing would be found. But I was part of the city of Odena now, a citizen of this glorious mess.

I sighed. The choice was obvious in the end.

A street merchant directed me to the closest guard station. I adjusted the sword at my waist before approaching.

The man at the door inclined his chin as I approached. His cuirass and helmet looked battered, but at least he was no helpless teenager.

"I have a report to make," I said, "to your superior."

My Bakkel and fine clothing must not have impressed him.

"You can tell me first."

I took a deep breath. "I spotted what I believe may have been a demon at the establishment Amelie in Yellow last night."

The timing was off, but there was no great explanation for why an innocent civilian would wait so long to report something like this. Fortunately, he did not take me seriously enough to ask.

The guard looked up at the sky as if seeking an answer there. "Amelie in Yellow. Are you telling me you smoked some opium and wish to report a demon sighting?"

"I don't smoke opium," I said. "I gamble. It's legal. If you don't believe me, I'll go around telling every guard until one does. And when it's true, I'll spread the word that you thought I was lying. What's your name?"

"Yarv. In that case, we should report this to Barrow. Let me find a replacement, and I'll take you to him myself."

"My thanks."

The guard didn't move. "Barrow is one of the Four Winds. The Archon's youngest son. There are severe punishments for lying to the man. Meaning if you stop wasting my time I'll let you walk away and forget this ever happened."

Ah, so that was his game. Trying to scare me off with naming one of the highest authorities in the city.

"Well," I said, "it did happen. So I would appreciate you taking me to him."

After a few minutes of Yarv conversing with his companions and all of them sending dirty looks my way, the guard led me down the street in silence.

The Four Winds. The Archon's half-divine children, blessed with mastery over air and, to some lesser degree, sound. Barrow was the only one I knew of; Caedius had mentioned him as a former fixture of the Amphitheater, deadly with the spear even without his magic. Such a man holding authority over the city guard made sense.

Barrow resided in a manor next to the Archon's palace. We passed the training grounds for the soldiery along the way, formations of shabby soldiers plodding away. All Great Cities maintained their own force, some with more attention than others. While I was loath to praise Velassa, at least the legions there looked impressive during their demonstrations. When I was a child I even once blabbered to my parents about how I wanted to be a soldier, entranced by their performance at a parade.

Yarv slowed his pace the closer we came to the manor. The guard at its gates looked far more like the ideal soldier, fully clad in gleaming plate, halberd planted at his side.

Yarv explained the reason for our presence, carefully emphasizing my insistence on coming. The other guard stared at us for a few moments before unlocking the gate and disappearing inside the manor. Yarv took his post, refusing to acknowledge my presence. From the look on his face, he seemed to take pride in his temporary promotion to gateboy.

I waited for over ten minutes. Did they expect me to just leave if I was ignored long enough? Should have brought a book.

Eventually several figures filed out of the manor and approached. Two men flanked by soldiers. The first had delicate features and an emerald-green flower tucked behind one ear matching the exact color of his eyes. Spotless white suit, expensive shoes. At his hip he wore a white-handled sword with a green ribbon sprouting from the pommel.

The other was Barrow, the North Wind. His skin was deeply tanned like most Narahvens, head shaved like a monk's, with a square jaw and high cheekbones hinting at his noble lineage. Simple but finely crafted clothes clung to a muscular frame. His legendary spear was nowhere to be seen, at least.

They stopped a dozen paces away. Barrow whispered with the guard from the gate before addressing me. His voice was deep and husky, each word enunciated precisely.

"I am Barrow, the North Wind, Lord of this manor and Commander of Odena's legions. I am told you have some concerns about a potential infiltration within the city. To whom do I speak?"

Should so many people be present while discussing such a sensitive topic? If he thought it was appropriate, who was I to question him? After dealing with Yarv my respect for authority could not fall much lower, but at least Barrow seemed willing to listen.

"My name is Leones. I'm an acolyte of the philosophers."

The man with the emerald eyes muttered something in Barrow's ear. A bolt of panic shot through my chest. Could they possibly recognize my name? The search for Jansen's lost son was never mentioned within the city, but if the Magistrate had made my escape known to the surrounding Great Cities, Barrow would know of me.

I already regretted coming here. Hell, I should have changed my name when I first came to the city, but it was too late now. Reversing time seemed like the smart choice, but I should at least discover where this conversation led. As long as I was not executed with no warning, I could use my power to escape.

"Greetings, Leones," said the North Wind. "I have much respect for the philosophers. I am told you believe you sighted a demon inside Amelie in Yellow?"

"Well," I said, "she was leaving when I was there. I noticed how pale her skin was. Then I saw her eyes. Black and inhuman. Just looking at her terrified me. I fled, unsure of what she was until I asked one of the philosophers. Lakken. He said that sounded like a demon."

That last part was true enough. Last night I visited Lakken and confirmed my suspicions with him. The old man could verify at least that much of my story.

Barrow rubbed his jaw. "You waited so long to report this?"

"I thought about it all night and day. I meditated. Thought back so many times on what I saw. I didn't want to waste anyone's time if it was just a mistake. But I figured it was best to let the authorities decide."

The North Wind thought for a while before gesturing. "Come."

Yarv stayed behind, happy to return to his original post.

The inside of his manor was simple yet tasteful. A suit of ancient armor decorated the wall; an heirloom, perhaps. Four cushioned chairs had been arranged in the side room for a proper discussion. I settled into one. The man with the emerald eyes unbuckled the scabbard from his waist and rested it across his lap after taking his seat. Barrow sat with his legs crossed, fingers steepled under his chin, face blank. A pair of guards loomed behind them.

"Tell me," said Barrow, "did you imbibe any mind-altering substances before your visit to Amelie in Yellow?"

"No. I'm certain of what I saw."

"We will, of course, investigate the establishment to determine how something like this could occur. Did you inform anyone else?"

"No. Only that man, Yarv, and the guard at the entrance."

The North Wind turned to his companion. "How could something like this happen? Leones, this is Champion Jokul, a sixth-legato blademaster. The greatest swordsman in Avanche. He will personally investigate this matter until we discover the truth. I will also look into it, but so many responsibilities spread me thin. For now, I must take my leave. Tell Jokul everything you remember."

The Champion nodded slowly, unblinking eyes fixated on me. His intensity was unnerving, not to mention the blade across his lap. Barrow departed, and with him went the guards.

"Tell me, then." Jokul's voice was high-pitched, almost feminine.

I spent the next five minutes rambling about everything I knew, which wasn't much. The Champion mostly remained silent as I talked about bringing my suspicions to Lakken, how I had never noticed any demonic activity before this, and attempted to verbalize my initial certainty that the woman was not human.

"That is enough." The Champion stood and held out a hand toward the exit. "You may leave. Remain within the city. Tell no one else what you saw while I investigate. I will not mention your name to Sensi so that there are no repercussions to yourself. That woman very much does not appreciate being questioned."

I brought my power to the forefront of my mind as I turned my back to the Champion to leave. Half-expecting his sword to pierce my heart from behind, I hardly breathed until I made it past the gates, out into the public.

Was I being paranoid? Both of them had been attentive and polite. I could have imagined the tension between us while trying my best to keep my story straight. Men like the Champion had a natural aura of intimidation. I knew of Jokul, of course. The most talented blademaster within a hundred miles, undefeated in the Amphitheater and in personal duels. Caedius's hero. While him acting as Barrow's personal blade seemed somewhat bizarre, even the greatest warriors often had patrons.

I relaxed the farther I walked. The matter of the demon woman was out of my hands. Perhaps I should have sent an anonymous letter instead of revealing myself, but that seemed far more likely to be ignored. If they discovered nothing, at worst I would suffer a verbal reprimand. Perhaps a fine. But if demons were roaming through the city, it was my responsibility to do something about it. Right?

I needed a distraction. My feet carried me in the direction of Lyra's residence, a long-term rental at a fancy inn called The Mellow Heart. Until now I had respected her privacy, but speaking with some of the most powerful men in the city had emboldened me.

"I'm here to see Lyra Incada," I said to the woman at the front counter.

She might not want to see me, of course. But we hadn't spoken in weeks. If my presence offended her for whatever reason, I could always turn back time. Crossing my arms, I waited as the employee went to speak with Lyra.

From where I was standing, I could see the large mural she had painted in the main room. A lovely piece, very unlike her usual morbid art. A knight and a rich lady lounging beside a river, presumably a scene from some romantic tale. I knew she had painted it as part of an agreement with the owner in exchange for six months of rent, no meals included.

The woman returned with bad news. No response to her knocking. As far as she was aware, Lyra had not been seen for at least a week now. No meals in the common area, no word of her departure, though she may have said something to the owner.

"Can you at least check to make sure she's all right?" I asked. "I haven't heard from her either. A girl like her, what if some obsessed stalker broke in?"

"The door is locked," said the woman. From her expression she likely suspected I was an obsessed stalker myself.

When I refused to leave, she glanced at the sword at my hip and, with a sigh, grabbed a ring of keys.

Intimidating some random woman into helping me was not my proudest moment, but after I talked with Lyra it was probably best to reverse time and pretend this never happened. Felix's words from that night at Amelie's came back to me: *Jealousy is ugly.* I knew coming here to bother her was pathetic, but at least I could find some closure.

I tried not to loom over the woman's shoulder as she unlocked the door. Already I could smell something offensive. Spoiled food and something deeper—putrescent—-a thick wrongness. After she opened the door, I had to cover my mouth and nose against the stench.

A cloud of flies assaulted a half-finished meal and the bowl of desiccated oranges on her dining table. While Lyra was never the cleanest person, it looked as if she had ceased caring altogether. Random clothes littered the floor as if she had tossed them aside.

"Heavens above." The employee stumbled out of the room, retching.

Deeper into the suite the smell only worsened. The dining area branched off into her bedroom and the larger, open area she called her studio. Usually, she kept several of her favorite canvases along the walls for inspiration. All of them were missing. Coughing against the miasma of rot, I pushed open the door to her bedroom. An absolute mess. The contents of an overturned bottle of wine stained the bottom of her bed.

I found her in the studio.

Congealed splashes of blood. An empty easel dominated the center of the room. In the corner, a heap of flesh I could hardly consider a person. Decapitated, clothes in tatters.

The smell of her decomposition invaded my nostrils and the back of my throat. My stomach twisted. Hot vomit scalded the back of my throat. I kept going until only splashes of burning bile remained.

Lyra.

12

GAMES

Felix refused to attend Lyra's funeral.

It was a simple but elegant affair, arranged four days after I discovered her body, with a respectable showing of mourners. I stood off to one side, hands clasped behind my back, unsure how I was expected to behave. To my relief no one approached me. The looks and pointing fingers did nothing to improve my mood. The jilted lover, they must have thought. The obsessed lunatic. Who else would do such a thing? Such a talented, beautiful young woman. What kind of monster . . .

The whole time I felt numb, detached. As if I were watching some tragic play for the hundredth time. I left before the ceremony ended. No one stopped me.

I did not wish to disrespect Lyra's spirit, but I was beginning to think Felix had a point. Her immortal soul was not watching us from some perch in the clouds, deeply offended that I had no desire to stand there any longer, listening to a priest who never knew her sing her praises.

There was at least one more selfish reason I chose to leave: I felt naked without a sword by my side. It was my constant companion now, never farther than an arm's reach away. Mara had convinced me not to wear it to the funeral.

She wanted to attend as well, but I insisted it was unnecessary. Those two had only met once and exchanged some pleasantries. Undaunted, Mara held a small ceremony in the acolyte's barracks, lighting incense and praying for Lyra's soul's safe passage. Felix refused to attend that as well.

I found him in his favorite clearing, working through the beginnings of the second legato. Unnoticed, I leaned against a tree, observing his halting attempts and mounting frustration. After losing his balance and stumbling a few steps he reached his limit; with all the fury he could muster, he threw his sword side-hand across the clearing. His shoulders shook as he gasped for breath.

"The ceremony was awful," I said.

He spun on his heels. His face was flushed scarlet "Why kill Lyra? She never hurt another soul in her life. She was innocent, just playing the role life gave her."

Bad enough for the guards to pester me. Bad enough to weather all those glances at the funeral. Felix's words were like a knife in the gut.

I bit down my own anger. "That sounds like an accusation."

"Of course it's not an accusation," he said. "I've never even seen you upset. You're like a statue. None of this is your fault. There's nothing you could have done."

Emotion crept into my voice unbidden. "A statue? I've barely slept since I found her. I don't know how many baths I took to try and scrub that smell away. It's still there."

The anger drained from Felix's face. He walked over to his sword, brushed the snow off, and sheathed it. "She was the brightest little girl. A ball of energy. It's hard to watch the world strip that away. One day at a time, until she was no better than me. I'm sorry you had to find her like that."

"It wasn't a human," I said. "No human kills like that. It tore her apart. All the paintings were gone. What does that?"

"You know what does that."

Yes. I knew. "There was a demon at Amelie in Yellow. You remember when the Karystans joined us the other night and I left all of a sudden? It looked like a woman with black eyes. I chased her down, but she just vanished. Like she was never there."

Felix took a deep, shuddering breath. "You think the same one killed Lyra? Of course it did. How many of them can there be, running around in this city? I'm guessing you went to the authorities?"

"I told the North Wind. Maybe a few hours before I found her corpse. At first, I thought it was revenge, but . . . the body was too old. She must've been there for days."

Felix stomped toward me, face blank. Lost in my own self-pity, I never saw his fist coming until it connected with my nose. Warm blood tickled my upper lip. Blackness crept into the corners of my vision. Instinctually I reached for him, binding him in my grasp, and with a savage glee smashed my forehead into his face.

We spent the next minute brawling in the snow, tripping over each other, pawing at clothes and exposed flesh. At some point Felix remembered some technique and threw me over his shoulder. The snow made the impact annoyingly soft.

I scrambled back to my feet, managed to deflect a wild punch on my forearm. We grappled for a while before finally breaking away, bent over and panting, our bloody noses speckling the snow red.

I managed to speak between gasps. "What was that about?"

"You feel better, don't you?"

"Maybe." I sat down with my back against a tree and closed my eyes. My lungs burned fiercely. "There's something wrong with this city. We should leave."

Felix paused a moment before responding. "I still have so much to do here. The Games are in a few days."

"You can tell there's something wrong, can't you?" I wiped my bloody nose on my sleeve. "With our talents we can go anywhere. Money's no problem. If you want to remain an acolyte, we can transfer to another sect."

"No," he said. "I've been here my whole life. This is my city. Even if demons are roaming around. If they are brazen enough to come here, where can we safely go? Velassa? I could never live there."

I opened my eyes.

Felix stood with his fists clenched at his sides, face serious. "You can go. I won't blame you. But I'm staying. And I'm going to find the bastard who did that to Lyra."

All I could do was nod.

I spent the rest of that day wandering aimlessly through the city. Felix wanted to join me, and I was tempted, but I was still unwilling to reveal my power, and his presence wouldn't accomplish much. A few times I used my magic to interrogate random people—the woman behind the counter of an occult trinket shop, Lakken, some nobleman rumored to specialize in demonology. Nothing.

I sought Champion Jokul, but he was not an easy man to track down; after a couple of hours, I resigned myself to waiting to hear from him.

My failure weighed on me. I excused myself from attending any lessons or sparring with Felix. He trained with the Karystans instead, claiming he was more than happy to practice against the spear. Mara kept pestering me to stop lying around and staring at the same pages of my book. I should have been searching for the demon, but it felt as if a crushing weight held me in place.

When the day of Games arrived, I agreed to attend. Strangely this one was held in the evening, something of a novelty. I spent all day scrounging up the motivation.

Mara barged into the barracks long before the opening ceremony. Like a child she leaped onto my cot, balancing herself on her knees, and bounced in place until I stood up.

Grumbling, I started putting on my boots. "Felix doesn't fight for another two hours."

"Yes, but we have to be there early to encourage him!" said Mara.

I slipped on my fur cloak, and we headed outside. Caedius leaned against the side of the building, arms crossed, his attempt to look imposing ruined by the smile stretching across his face. The man had probably never missed a Game since he was born. He loved to tell the story about his parents buying seats in the very front for his sixth birthday. Always a heartwarming tale.

"I think you're more excited about this than Felix is," Mara said to him.

He swooped over and lifted her up by her armpits, twirling her around until she laughed and swatted at him. Once she was back on the ground Caedius slipped an arm around her shoulders. Watching them only deepened my self-pity, but I would not let my moping ruin their mood.

"This will be different," he said. "They never have the Games at night. They must have something special planned."

Mara wrinkled her nose. "Lucky us."

As we walked into the city proper, he rambled about the history of the Amphitheater.

"The great architect Van Rijn envisioned it three hundred and forty years ago, and it has remained unchanged to this day. The Odenan Amphitheater was one of several historic buildings to suffer massive damage in the Great Fire. A collective effort of all the people in the city restored it to perfection within six months."

Mara patted his shoulder "Very nice. You're awfully quiet, Leones."

"Yeah," I said. She took the hint and dropped the conversation. At least it was better than the awkward condolences everyone offered before.

Once we exited the Gardens, I hailed a coach to take us the rest of the way. Caedius continued to ramble the entire ride, the passion in his voice the only thing saving him from being annoying. I only really paid attention when he brought up the North Wind.

"Barrow is the host tonight. He's one of the most famous combatants to come out of the Odenan Amphitheater in recent times. No one was surprised to see a half-divine child succeed. The surprising thing is that witnesses say he never used any of his powers. Felix is a prodigy with the blade, granted, but they say Barrow was fighting on the Frontier when he was only thirteen years old."

Traffic became congested as we neared the Amphitheater. I told the driver we would continue on foot.

The massive edifice loomed over this part of the city, nearly a district itself. It reminded me of an elaborate seashell, roughly oval in shape, the tiered rows of seating like ridges along its interior. A sailcloth awning shielded the audience from the snow, a feat of engineering that Caedius was all too happy to explain.

Only a quarter of the seats were filled, but the opening ceremony had yet to begin. Etiquette in Odena dictated that one should never arrive at formal events too early. I wished someone had explained that to Mara. Caedius at least had the good manners to purchase me a medicinal drink from a roadside vendor.

"Can't tell you how many times I've drunk this," he told me. "Powdered sweetbark mixed with honey wine. You'll feel amazing in about an hour. Eliminates muscle fatigue and gives you a nice rush of energy. Don't drink too much of it in one day or it destroys your liver. Ever see those old-time fighters with yellow skin? Too much of this."

I put the wooden mug to my lips and muttered into it, "Increate bless me."

After swallowing the concoction in several gulps, I squeezed my eyes against the bitterness. It took several seconds to recover.

"You're not supposed to drink it like someone challenged you to a race at the tavern," said Caedius.

I wiped the residue off my tongue. "This is called sweetbark?"

He shrugged. "I didn't name it."

Caedius returned my mug and returned with one of his own, sipping it as if it were divine nectar. He motioned us to follow him before diving into the crowd at the entrance.

Guardsmen herded the mass of people into approximate lines. Vasely hosted the Games as a public service, ensuring that general seating was free. The wait was not long, though the press of unwashed bodies made me grimace.

An old man reeking of alcohol stumbled into me. I pushed him in the direction of the nearest guard.

Mara shook her head. "Be gentle."

I kept my thoughts to myself.

The beauty of the Amphitheater increased the farther we went. Ornate fountains spaced along the way promised refreshment. The noise of the crowd drowned out Caedius's attempts to explain the origins of the various murals and statuary.

We emerged into the interior of the Amphitheater. On the far side figures scrambled about like colorful ants. Caedius's awe of the building began to make more sense. There were thousands of people here, maybe tens of thousands, more than I had ever seen gathered in one place. I had read about much larger groups before but could never visualize the true scale of those numbers. So many people, each one a distinct soul with their own thoughts and feelings. It stole my breath away.

We found some decent seats in one of the middle tiers and settled in. Caedius nursed his mug of sweetbark between his hands, watching the crowd with the simple contentment of a grandfather at a large family gathering.

Mara sat between us. She drummed the fingers of one hand against her thigh. "Can't we talk to Felix somehow?"

"I told you," said Caedius, "there's no way to see him before the fights. They're kept in their own separate waiting area. They enter the battlefield from the Gates of Death and exit through the Gates of Life. We won't be able to see him until he leaves."

"Do you have to call it a battlefield?"

He shook his head. "You see this, Leones? I've been trying to get her to come to the Games as long as I've known her. She's told me she wouldn't come even if I myself fought, but she's here for Felix. Really makes you wonder."

"Don't talk about me like I'm not here," said Mara. "I wouldn't come and watch you because I don't want to see you get killed."

After the words left her mouth, she realized her mistake and glanced my way. Caedius continued on, oblivious.

"There's a better chance of getting murdered on the way here than dying in the arena."

"Is that supposed to make me feel better?"

I kept my thoughts to myself. The stranger to my right watched us in amusement. After a few moments of pointed eye contact he looked away.

I had to admit I was just as nervous as Mara. There was the sheer presence of the crowd. The thought of my friend dying and, even worse in his own eyes, failing. On top of that I kept remembering the contempt my parents had for the Velassan Games, how my mother would shake her head anytime someone brought them up in conversation.

To my surprise four people in acolyte grays approached our seats. Rayen and Johan followed a young woman, presumably Lisara. A braid of black hair fell to her lower back. Her light blue eyes and the blank expression on her face lent her a frigid appearance.

Johan towered over his companions. He waved. "May we join you?"

"Do you mind?" I asked the stranger next to me. He held his hands out in surrender and left to find another seat.

Mara and Caedius introduced themselves. The Karystans squeezed in between me and my next closest neighbor. Johan had to hunch over and lock his knees together to make room.

"How did you find us in this crowd?" asked Mara.

"Lisara has amazing eyesight," said Johan. "She could probably read the lips of people on the other side of the stadium. Picking out your uniforms is easy. Not like me, I can't see a dozen paces without my spectacles."

Lisara lifted a hand in acknowledgement, not even bothering to glance in our direction.

Mara nudged me and rolled her eyes. I began to wonder if bringing these two groups together was a good call. Hard to deny Johan's company when he behaved in such a friendly way.

The opening ceremony rescued me. Lines of priests in gold robes emerged from each of the four entrances onto the sands of the arena. A high priest led each procession, holding aloft a scepter with a flaming head; albino lions stalked next to them, searching the crowd with hostile pink eyes. The priest's low chanting became discernible as the chatter of the crowd died away. The words were in Old Avanchean, an entirely different language spoken only by the clergy.

At the end of each line came one of the Four Winds: three men and a woman in green cloaks, faces hidden beneath their hoods.

The separate groups of priests joined together in the middle of the arena, forming a circle around the Four who joined their voices to the chanting. Wind swirled through the arena, gathering the sand into complex spirals that weaved amongst the priests without touching them.

The priests stopped chanting all at once, and the swirls of sand disintegrated.

One of the Four threw back his hood. Barrow. "We have gathered on this sacred night to honor the strength of our city."

Complete silence greeted his words.

"It is rare that we fight in the light of the moon. It is tradition not to attract the attention of our ancient enemies. This is a tradition of fear, something that has echoed in the hearts of mankind for millennia. They are the memories of our ancestors passed on to us. The unwritten story of our struggle for freedom against the Goetia. But it is time to supplant tradition and to make our ancestors proud. Tonight, we show them we are strong."

The crowd cheered, though there was an undercurrent of uncertainty.

"Tonight," he continued, "we host a special Game in Odena. You have the option to leave at any time, but there is no cause for alarm. The Four Winds are here to protect you, and there are others hidden among you. Tonight, the warriors of Odena will face demons."

13

DEMON

The crowd went frantic. Caedius stood, clasping Mara's hand as she looked around in confusion. I sat there, frozen, repeating Barrow's last words in my head.

"Peace, my friends, peace," he said. "No demon has invaded our city in centuries. They have been brought from the Frontier for this special purpose. Every warrior has been personally evaluated to make sure they are not in danger. The demons are oracles, unused to combat. Those who refuse to slay these abominations will face one another as usual. Let it be said that no one is forced to participate."

Lisara spoke for the first time, her sharp voice cutting through the uproar. "They can't do this. It's sacrilege to bring demons into the city."

Johan scratched his cheek. "They're divine, aren't they? Can they be sacrilegious toward themselves? Surely they must have the Archon's approval."

"I want to go," said Mara. "Now."

She ignored Caedius's pleas and, assuring him that she did not expect him to come, joined the flood of citizens leaving the Amphitheater. He watched her retreating form with a small frown.

Remaining in formation, the priests returned to the gates, leaving the Four Winds behind. Barrow kept silent, hands clasped behind his back, until the last of them dispersed.

Stuck to my seat, I squeezed my knees with terrified strength. I was afraid for Felix, not myself. All I could do was hope he was not foolish enough to agree to this.

Johan and Lisara stayed as well. I expected the young man to have fled at the first opportunity, but instead he leaned forward, hand to his mouth, the very image of excitement. Lisara's face was carefully blank. Caedius remained standing as if uncertain whether or not to follow Mara; eventually he sat back down.

Lost in thought, I barely paid attention to the rest of the ceremony. Had they captured Lyra's killer for a public execution? But Barrow had claimed the demons were oracles, brought here for that specific purpose. What would possess someone to do that? The Archon wanted to spit in the face of the Goetia and terrify his own populace? I had never heard of any of the Great Cities doing something like this—maybe something similar was done centuries ago, lost in history for good reason.

The Four Winds chanted and danced for several minutes, their shadows grotesque in the torchlight. When the ritual ended the three hooded figures left through their respective gates, leaving Barrow behind.

"We begin," he said, "with the conventional fights. There will be four bouts of single combat, followed by an interlude before the main event."

He bowed to the crowd four times, turning smartly on his heels to face each direction. Silence followed him as he disappeared into the northern gate.

An announcer declared the combatants of the first match. I forgot their names the moment after he said them. Two scarred brutes emerged onto the sands, facing each other with weapons at the ready. They saluted each other by holding their weapons to their foreheads.

The announcer blew his horn, and they charged. None of the careful circling of duelists or the finesse of the legato, just a roared challenge and a clash. The wielder of the short sword used a buckler, slapping the spear away and attempting to slip within the reach of his opponent's weapon. The spear wielder respected his opponent's defense after their first exchange and moved backward with tight, careful steps to stymie his advance.

As they fought, I realized how childish my own fight with Johan had been. The wisps of pride from my victory faded away. Either of these men would have made short work of me. Their styles lacked refinement, but they were confident and disciplined.

People throughout the crowd held up their fingers and pointed at one another, shouting names and numbers. Caedius explained these were bets being formed throughout the stadium. The participants signaled odds and verdicts for others to challenge. How tempting.

The match lasted for several minutes until the swordsman won out on stamina. The spearman missed a beat and was punished with a deep gash to his left forearm. After that it was a matter of cleanup. The swordsman chipped away at his opponent until he wore down his defenses and sent his weapon flying.

Disarmed, the spearman knelt in defeat. The victor tapped him on the shoulder with the flat of his blade, granting him mercy. An old tradition; the unwritten rules of most City Games expected the fighters not to act like bloodthirsty animals.

The next four matches followed the same pattern. Felix competed in none of them, though I held out hope that he had refused to participate altogether. A silly wish. He would never back down from something like this. The idea would have amused him or, depending on his mood, caused deep offense.

After the last bout Barrow emerged from the north gate.

"The prima morte will now commence. Those who doubt our wisdom, this is your last chance to depart." He turned on his heels slowly, his intense gaze washing over the arena. When he faced my way, I clenched my hands in my lap. Barrow nodded. "Then, brave souls, I announce to you the first hero of the night: Onash!"

Onash was the second greatest fighter in Odena, though he was no real competition for Jokul. He was a brute of a man with a sword nearly as notched as himself. Between the plates of his half-armor peeked an impressive assortment of scars. The cheers of the crowd, though subdued, energized him to lift his greatsword to the opponent's gate and roar.

Over a minute passed before the oracle made its appearance. Golden robes adorned with full moons and withered trees trailed behind it in the sand. White skin stretched tight over an angular skull. Though the distance made it impossible to be certain, it appeared to have no facial features at all, like one of Volario Faske's mannequins fitted in the costume of a play wizard.

The oracle appeared to glide over the sand as it approached Onash in the middle. Taking its spot in the center of the arena, it slipped its hands out of its sleeves and bowed over them. Its fingernails were golden talons.

"Greetings, Tec Cithun." No visible mouth moved. Its voice was a low buzz, like an insect speaking. It spoke softly, but its words penetrated deep.

Onash roared.

Creases appeared along the oracle's skin; all at once dozens of eyes opened along its exposed body, frantic and disconcertingly human. The demon began to glide backward, but it was far too slow. Onash charged. His first swing was not a killing blow, merely taking off the hand of its upraised arm in a spray of blue ichor. The second opened the oracle up from shoulder to hip.

The demon attempted to push itself back together, and for a moment I expected it to succeed. It fell to its knees, arms at its side, and the great wound gaped wider and wider until the oracle's upper body collapsed into the sand. Its lower body remained upright. Organs the color of an old bruise glistened within its torso.

Onash took careful aim before removing its head in one chop. Heedless of the ichor staining his skin, the warrior lifted the demon's head from the ground, turning so all could witness his kill. The applause was hesitant.

Barrow emerged from the north gate. "For the first time in centuries, a demon has been killed in Avanchean territory. We have all been raised with myths and legends about the Goetia's immortal servants. Here you see the truth for yourselves. They fear us. They bleed. They can be killed."

He waved a hand, and the oracle's body floated away through the north gate. A flip of his wrist sent sand swirling until a fresh layer obscured the demon's blood.

"Well," said Johan, leaning back, chin propped up on his fist, "as tactless as it may be to say this out loud, I believe most people understand the difference between an oracle and a warrior. This is no different than the demons throwing a pregnant woman into combat with their elite."

"I think there is quite a difference," said Caedius.

"Do you?" Lisara stood, still not bothering to glance at any of us. "I'm growing weary of this spectacle."

"Let me walk you back," said Johan.

"No, I am quite capable of walking by myself. Stay here with your new friends."

The big acolyte looked crestfallen as she walked away. He removed his spectacles, folded them, unfolded them, and slid them back onto his nose. "Lisara is sensitive. She doesn't like large crowds."

When no one responded, the big man lapsed into silence. I tried to eavesdrop on the conversations around us, but most people were smart enough to keep their voices hushed. After Onash departed through the Gate of Life, half of the remaining crowd dispersed, their bloodlust sated or the novelty of the situation usurped by common sense.

I, of course, was not wise enough to leave. If anything occurred I had up to an hour's warning to get my friends as far as possible. I couldn't stay much longer, but I wanted to at least see if Felix was here.

"Next," said Barrow, "The third-legato warrior Larosso will pit himself against our ancestral foes."

Spear clenched at his side, Larosso jogged into the middle of the sand, waving at the crowd with his free hand as if unsure of what to do. The few cheers and claps rang out awkwardly over the near-total silence of the crowd. What kind of people chose to remain here, watching this spectacle? It felt like a fatal curiosity.

The second oracle was identical to the first, and when it glided to the middle of the arena it also greeted its opponent as Tec Cithun. Perhaps they were all one great, interconnected mind, expressing itself through a multitude of oracles.

Larosso also had no interest in the oracle's words. The demon resigned itself to its fate, bowing over its hands as the spearman lunged forward. Even when the blade and haft of the spear skewered it through the heart, the oracle did not so much as flinch. No eyes appeared along its exposed skin.

Perhaps each of them were different individuals after all. What kind of role did they play in the society of the Goetia? Were they monks or priests, being slaughtered for entertainment?

Barrow announced Felix next.

My friend looked very small and alone in that arena. He held his head straight, shoulders back, like a soldier ready for inspection. I knew he would have no trouble. His opponent would not even fight back. Still, I couldn't help but imagine how I would feel down there, a thousand faces watching, the hilt of my sword slick with sweat. My stomach felt queasy even as I told myself Felix wouldn't care, that he lived for combat. But this was an execution. This wasn't what he trained so hard for.

His oracle glided out to meet him. Unlike its predecessors this one tilted its head to the side as it faced him. A single eye opened in the center of its forehead. They faced each other for at least ten seconds, and though I could hear nothing, I was certain the demon was communicating with him.

Then Felix nodded sharply and drove his sword through the demon's chest. The oracle looked down at the blossoming blue stain on its robes as if surprised. Felix's next blow chopped halfway through its neck. The third finished the deed.

The demon's head rolled in the sand. Its unblinking eye stared up at the heavens.

My friend disappeared into the Gate of Life without glancing once at the crowd. Time to leave. If I used my power now, I could still depart around the time that the first matches between the warriors had begun. Before I could make my decision, Barrow made his final appearance on the sand.

"For those that have remained, a final display between a true demon warrior and the greatest swordsman in Avanche: Champion Jokul."

What little remained of the initial crowd made enough noise to put the previous cheers to shame. Caedius shook my shoulder and whistled until he was red in the face. I smiled indulgently. Maniacs, all of them.

Jokul had remained undefeated for over a hundred bouts. Rumors told of superior swordsmen, reclusive monks with no name, and quasi-divine beings who chose to remain in the shadows. But no one mattered more to blood sport enthusiasts and the countless children who fought one another with wooden swords.

That night he wore only a pair of woolen trousers, his sharp cheek bones and the hard lines of his body limned in shadow. He held his green-ribboned sword at his side. After emerging from the Gate of Death he waited in the center of the arena, ignoring the crowd completely, focused on the opposite gate.

The woman in the dark robes nearly flew out, a single leap eating half the distance between her and the Champion. She tossed her robes away, revealing a parody of the human body—near skeletal, too many joints crammed together, smooth skin so translucent one could see the cords of muscle shifting beneath. Chitinous plating gleamed blackly along her arms and up the sides of her neck; the talons at her fingertips ended in wicked points.

My fingernails bit into my palms as I clenched my hands. This was the demon from Amelie in Yellow—the one that killed Lyra. And here, in front of everyone, Jokul would execute it. If not, I would finish it myself, consequences be damned. This whole thing was foolish, but there was no chance this would have been allowed if the Champion had a chance of losing.

Her next leap carried her into Jokul's waiting sword. Steel sparked against chitinous plating as she deflected with one of her arms. The force of their awkward impact thrust them in opposite directions, the Champion backpedaling to avoid falling backward. He recovered an instant before she did, his stumbling transforming into fluid footwork as he went on the offensive.

I recognized part of what he was doing from manuals about the legato. Diagrams did no justice compared to watching the forms performed by a master. The Champion attacked in a series of strikes that flowed into one another, and though the demon turned them aside, his movements appeared so natural it seemed as if the demon's responses were all part of some choreographed dance.

They sped up as the clash continued, sand spraying about. The legato came from a musical term meaning a smooth, continuous sequence. Within them was every movement a fighter could make, and a true master could find the way each movement was connected, even if one note was from the first legato and another from the ninth. Jokul seemed to allow the momentum of their battle to increase his speed, even spinning once—something any blademaster would scold a student for.

He drew first blood, a shallow laceration along the demon's neck and clavicle. Despite all her agility and the unnatural movement granted by her many-jointed body, that moment sealed her fate. The whirlwind of the Champion only grew stronger, his blade chipping away at the plating on her arms, tempo building until, in her desperation, the demon left her lower half completely exposed.

He ducked low and swept her legs out from underneath her. In the air there is only so much a body can do, bound as it was by the laws of gravity. Jokul spun once more and, using all of the force he had been accumulating since their first touch, chopped precisely through her neck before she hit the ground.

After the demon collapsed her head rolled away, making it a few feet before coming to a stop facing upward. Ichor sprayed onto the sand from the demon's neck. The body twitched a few times before coming to a standstill, the arterial gush of blue declining to a trickle.

Dead. The bastard who killed Lyra was dead. But still, the disconcerting expression on her face wiped away any pleasure I felt at the fact. She was smiling at the moon.

14

DISTURBANCE

Felix did not return to the barracks that night. I tossed and turned on my cot, unable to sleep, waiting for the door to creak open. Around midnight I had enough and dressed myself. The walk into the city proper passed in a blur. How many times had I trodden this same path? Hundreds?

My feet carried me to Amelie in Yellow.

The doorwoman smiled. "Nice to see you again, Leones. Your friend's in there."

I thanked her and stepped inside. That strange sense of familiarity intensified as I ascended the staircase. All this time spent in Odena and what had I accomplished? Days spent studying and training, nights of drinking and gambling. My swordwork was going well, and I was amassing a small fortune. Still, it felt as if I was treading water, exhausting myself to get nowhere.

Felix slouched at a table in the back, his only company an empty bottle of wine. He did not have the dreamer's look that betrayed his opium habit, but his eyes were listless and unfocused. I sat beside him. The scraping of the chair legs caught his attention for a moment before he glanced away.

"Felix," I said.

He ignored me.

"Felix," I said, louder.

He tilted the wine bottle in front of him as if testing to make sure it was empty. "I'm not deaf."

"You are drunk."

He gestured with two fingers to summon a servant. "That I am."

A woman in a fox mask hurried over. "Gentlemen."

"Another of the Moravy," said Felix.

Depending on how long he had lingered around the Amphitheater, Felix could not have been here for more than a couple of hours.

"Far be it from me to dissuade a generous tipper," said Fox-Amelie, "but are you sure that's a good idea?"

"Did your parents think it was a good idea for their daughter to become a half-dressed den girl?"

Her smile was like a wolf baring its teeth. "Another bottle of the Moravy for the young sir."

I sighed after she departed. "Do you feel like a big man now?"

He pointed the empty bottle at me. "Don't fuck with me, Leones."

I slapped it aside. "I was there tonight. At the Amphitheater. What's wrong? You can tell me."

"Oh, are we best friends now?" asked Felix. "I have shirts I've known longer than you. But what's the point of keeping it a secret? Why not just shout it into the night? It's not like it's a bad thing. You want to know what the oracle told me? It said 'you will never betray your brothers,' and it laughed."

"And that made you down a bottle of cheap red?"

"There will be repercussions for what I did tonight," he said.

"Then why did you go through with it?"

He held up his clenched fists. "I could never not do it. I might be an asshole, but if you give me a challenge, I'll see it through. Do you have any idea how angry I am? How much I have to prove?"

"No."

"No," he said. "You don't. Because you don't know what it's like to be fucking crazy."

Unsure how to respond, I folded my hands on the table and stared at them. "The woman that Champion Jokul fought at the end. She was the one who killed Lyra."

A complex array of emotions shifted across his face, from anger to curiosity before settling on a sort of vindictive pleasure. "Good."

A woman came to our table with a fresh candle and an identical bottle to the first. She filled half of Felix's glass with the red. After wafting its aroma, he nodded his approval. The woman bowed and set the bottle down. It amused me in a theatrical way, this elaborate ritual over a wine they sold in the cheapest taverns anywhere.

The woman was older than the other Amelies by several decades. She wore a black dress and an assortment of thin golden jewelry that lent her a subdued but dignified appearance. A thick needle secured her dark hair into an austere bun. The lines of her face recalled a lifetime of laughter, though her expression was anything but pleased.

Felix looked her up and down. "The lady of the house, is it?"

"I'm curious," she said, "what makes you think you can insult one of my girls?"

"Bad night."

"Are you a child with so little control over yourself that you lash out at others for your own shortcomings? Is this what my so-called fellow philosophers are teaching you boys?" The woman—Sensi—glanced at me. "And you. You think your friend's behavior is acceptable?"

"His manners could certainly be improved," I said.

Felix snorted. "I've been coming here for a while now. There are as many scumbags here as anywhere else. I've never seen you personally come out to chastise someone for being rude."

"Granted," she said, settling into a chair at an adjacent table, "I usually don't hear such concerning rumors. Supposedly some demons were slaughtered in the Amphitheater tonight. Even worse, one of the executors is a young philosopher, here in my establishment before the blood on his hands finished drying."

"I'll be leaving, then, if my presence is so upsetting." Felix pushed himself to his feet.

"No one here is upset," she said. "Well, one of my best girls is yelling about you in the back, but she has a temper worse than yours. I stopped by to offer you some advice."

"What have I done to deserve such kindness?"

Her glare softened. "Why do you think kindness is something you have to earn?"

Felix opened his mouth, thought for a second, then closed it. She gestured for him to return to his seat, and to my surprise he did.

"I shouldn't have agreed to it," he said. "I'm not that stupid."

Sensi smiled. "It is a difficult thing to control yourself. To acknowledge that you could do better, if only you were stronger, more in control. Sometimes you feel the weight of the whole universe crushing down on you, even though you know you really are insignificant in the grand scheme of things."

"I know all of that," he said.

I shifted in my seat uncomfortably, feeling much like an awkward intruder in this conversation. The moment seemed very intimate between the two of them. Her soft, rhythmic voice; his desperately unhappy eyes.

"It is even more difficult to do something about it," said Sensi, a wistful look on her face. "To cultivate yourself, to blossom, not in one glorious moment but in a succession of little triumphs. You are, after all, a man, not a noble ideal, mindless and uncompromising. You want that little surge when you roll a lucky pair. There's the touch of a woman, the way they look in your eyes that isolates a big, dark eternity to just the two of you. Let the past be the past, you tell yourself. If mankind excels at one thing, it's realizing its vices. Bury yourself. Hide under comfort like a child scared beneath its blanket.

"We can't forget the past. The memories fade, but there are always the scars. It's like we start whole and wholesome, and time chips away at us. You erode, you wither. It hollows you out. You must do what you can to build yourself up. Everything else will wear you down."

Felix ran his fingers through his hair. "Where is that from?"

"Pardon?" said Sensi.

"You didn't make it up off the top of your head."

The woman stood and tucked the chair back under the table. "It's from the letters of Van Rijn to his eldest son, Yuren. Yuren had forsaken all of his duties to pursue a life of drinking and gambling. The letter that is taken from was found on his body. He died on the streets from illness after his father disowned him. It's a lesson on folly and, of course, the unique problems of being the procuress of a gambling den."

Felix's expression grew even more annoyed by the end of her speech. I remembered what Lyra had said once: to never bring his father up around him. Sensi, mistress of Amelie in Yellow and master of the staccato, had chosen the wrong parable.

"Thank you for the lesson," he said, bowing his head mockingly over clasped hands—uncomfortably similar to the oracles' gesture.

"I have much to teach you," said Sensi. "Though I'm not sure how wise it would be to speak openly around others. Including—Leones, was it? Would you mind waiting down on the first floor while we have a conversation? I suspect you'll encounter a familiar face or two down there."

I had long obsessed over the guessing game and how to catch her attention. Now that she was in front of me, all my planning and imagined conversations seemed rather silly. In the end I simply nodded and took my leave.

Hands in my pockets, I strolled down the staircase to the first floor, where a solo fiddler played a solemn tune. The usual assortment of half-sedated addicts occupied the area. The Amelie with the dragon mask stalked through the crowd, stopping on occasion to check on someone's breathing or palpate a pulse. After encountering a particularly unresponsive man, she dug her knuckles into his sternum until he moaned and pushed feebly at her arm. Satisfied, she continued making her rounds.

I doubted she was the familiar face Sensi meant. I settled into a divan, one of the few people paying attention to the performer as he sawed away at his instrument, eyes closed, lost in his music. Dragon-Amelie set a snifter of brandy on the table in front of me. Excellent service as always, but in this instance, I felt no desire to muddy my thoughts, so I left the drink untouched.

What could Sensi and Felix be talking about? Five minutes passed, and I felt my eyelids beginning to droop. Given the company here no one would mind if I took a short nap. Before I settled into sleep's embrace, the person I was waiting for made his entrance. A new emerald-green flower sprouted from behind his ear. The blade that ended Lyra's killer dangled at his side, a legendary weapon far beyond mortal craftsmen like Bakkel, now consecrated in a demon's blood. With a jolt I sat upward, waving away a haze of opium smoke beginning to permeate the area.

Champion Jokul sauntered toward the staircase before noticing me. Between the distance and my sleep-blurred vision it was hard to tell, but it looked like his eyes narrowed and a frown pulled at the corner of his lips. He changed direction, coming to a stop in front of me. Uncomfortable with his looming, I gestured at the seat beside me.

"I'll stand," he said. "Acolyte Leones. Fortunate to meet you here."

"You didn't come for me?"

He ignored the question. "I suspect your friend told you the news, assuming you didn't already see for yourself. I found the killer and put an end to it for all to see. Miss Incada is avenged. May her soul find peace."

"Did you discover anything?" I asked. "Why the demon killed her? What it's doing here?"

"Such information is far too sensitive for me to reveal. Rest assured that the matter has been taken care of. Odena is safe, in no small part due to your intervention. This city owes you its thanks."

Telling me would be a sufficient reward, I thought to myself. The more I discovered, the more questions I had. Loath as I was to antagonize the Champion, there should be no consequences if I used my magic.

"My friend was slaughtered," I said. "Demons are roaming through the city, killing citizens under the direct protection of the Archon. I'm supposed to take your word for it that we're safe? I haven't told anyone besides Felix about what I saw. Now I'm starting to wonder if I should reveal everything to the public."

Face blank, the Champion brushed the cushion off before taking a seat next to me. He clasped his hands on his laps, eyes focused on the violinist. This close, his presence felt overwhelming. "I am not the type of person you threaten."

"Why," I said, "did Barrow lie and say the demons came from the Frontier? Maybe the oracles were, but that woman was already in the city. How did you find her?"

"I am not the type of person you ask silly questions, either."

I reversed time just enough to restart the interrogation. This time I led with the question about Barrow lying, only to meet the same response. I tried a few different tactics, from pleading to arrogance, and none of them had any impact on the iron wall that was the Champion. Frustrated, I blurted out one final accusation, just to see how he would respond.

"Why are you working with demons?"

The Champion froze. His head swiveled my way, green eyes burning. Something in his expression made me reach for my power again. Just in time. One hand slipped over my mouth while the other darted to his side. Time slowed to a crawl as I realized his intent.

I threw myself away from him, just enough that the knife missed my heart. The blade grinded against my ribcage, a white-hot lance of pain. The Champion twisted the blade. All the scrapes and bruises I had experienced were nothing compared to that invasive wrongness in my chest.

My power thrust me back in time as far as I could go.

I fell to my knees, hand pressed against my frantically beating heart. Though my wounds had been erased from existence, I could still feel the phantom presence of that blade twisting inside of me. A distant part of me noted that I was near the exit of the Gardens, surrounded by the plots of medicinal herbs turned barren from the long winter.

How foolish I was. I had never expected that Champion Jokul would attempt to kill me in public. Even a respected authority like him could not expect to walk away from a teenager's corpse. I would have gone unnoticed for a while, another unconscious body in the crowd, but Dragon-Amelie would have noticed me within a few minutes. Not to mention Sensi's confirmed presence. They would know. Would she really tolerate Jokul murdering an acolyte not a hundred paces away from her?

I had to go back and warn Felix. Something was absolutely wrong with this city. For a moment I entertained the thought of going to Barrow. Bad idea. If the Champion actually was working with the demons, chances were the North Wind was involved as well. I had survived Jokul's attack, but I had no intention of testing my luck a second time. Sensi was even more of an unknown factor.

The Bakkel at my side felt like a toy. Useless. I needed to get to my safe house and leave the city with Felix as soon as possible. How could I expect—

I shook my head. What was I doing, kneeling on the path like this? It was late, near midnight. Had I been sleepwalking, disturbed by the events from the Amphitheater earlier?

After watching the Odenan warriors execute the oracles and Jokul's breathtaking fight against Lyra's killer I had been exhausted, falling asleep the moment I laid down on my cot. Likely the rush of energy from the sweetbark concoction Caedius bought me had worn off around the same time—the comedown from those sorts of elixirs is always nasty.

I had never sleepwalked before. Disturbing.

I attempted to use my power to save myself a bit of time walking back to the barracks. My magic failed, only bringing me back a few seconds to when I was kneeling on the ground.

Also disturbing, but my power over time had some interesting limitations. My experiments had shown that, if I tried to reverse time immediately after waking up, I would only return to the point where I became conscious. Presumably my body reverted back to its prior sleeping state, making such an effort useless. Sleepwalking must have been the same. Predictably, that experiment always caused the same amount of fatigue as reverting time an hour back while conscious. Now I could have sworn that I felt that exhaustion before using my power, not after. And why was my heart pounding in my chest?

It was a nice night, just chilly enough to be refreshing. Lost in thought, I retraced my path back to the barracks.

15

F O R G O T T E N

I woke up the next day several hours later than usual. Opening my eyes to reality was a welcome relief after a night of chaotic dreams. The details slipped from my mind after waking, but they left behind a sense of unease. Best to forget them. No surprise that my imagination had run away after witnessing the spectacle at the Amphitheater and the sleepwalking afterward.

I sat on the side of my cot, blinking sleep out of my eyes. Mara was awake before me, for once. She stood at an unused cot off in one of the corners, arms crossed. The blanket and pillow looked ruffled. Strange, for an unused bed. Several pairs of expensive leather shoes and a locked storage chest stood at the foot of the cot. The boots were a top-quality style favored by duelists.

"Did someone move in?" I asked.

She jerked, startled by my voice. An embarrassed smile spread across her face. "This wasn't here last night, was it?"

I scratched my neck. "I don't think so. Maybe Irele or Avarus know something?"

Mara shook her head. "How would someone move here in the middle of the night without us noticing?"

"One of the acolytes decided to come back? Soren or Parish, maybe?"

"Only one of them?" She raised an eyebrow.

"Brotherly spat. Maybe not, though. I don't recognize the belongings."

"We'll find out soon enough, I suppose."

I dressed myself and looked into the full-length mirror near the front door. The figure blinking back at me looked like it could use a good meal and a hot bath. The sword suited me, especially since my frame had grown to the point my clothing squeezed uncomfortably at the arms and shoulders. Ignoring a comment from Mara about preening in the mirror, I strolled outside to begin my morning routine.

Hopefully the new acolyte would turn out to be friendly. The barracks could use another masculine touch. Caedius visited sometimes and was pleasant enough, but we had never become more than casual acquaintances. After Mara and I spent the night of the solstice at Heaven's Gate, we gathered there once a week for a few drinks and some conversation. Her remaining in the barracks with me had caused no end of arguments between the two, but at least the big lad kept me out of them.

Outside of that I rarely associated with anyone my own age. The Karystans were the exception to the rule, but they would return home soon. Despite my initial hope they would remain in the barracks, they were staying in an inn bordering the Gardens, citing Lisara's intolerance for the cold.

After arriving at my favorite clearing, I began my warmup stretches.

I could reach out to one of Lyra's friends. Given the looks and whispers about me at her funeral I doubted it was worth my time. Just thinking about her hurt. Everything about our relationship had been strange and confusing, ever since the first time I met her at that art gallery of hers.

Something about that thought made me pause. We hadn't met at her art gallery, had we? Why would I have attended an exhibition for a local painter I had not heard of, held in the manor of some random member of the gentry? The more I thought about it, the more absurd it seemed. I could still vividly recall the details of my fourth birthday, but I couldn't remember my first time meeting Lyra?

Unconsciously I finished my warmup and unsheathed my sword. The beginning of the first legato came easily enough, but the discord in my mind held me back from progressing much further. My thoughts felt scattered, dampened, as if I were in a dream. But the cool breeze and the pleasant burn in my muscles felt real. I pricked my fingertip on the tip of my sword. Real pain. Real blood.

Many things could explain my bizarre mental state, none of which I liked. The conflicting memories from reversing time. The stress of Lyra's death and my deep loneliness. Perhaps the Goetia had even cast a spell over the city. Mara was the only person I had spoken to since my sleepwalking, and she had also seemed confused. If Prince Sitri could make an entire Great City dance until their hearts gave out, what were higher ranking demons capable of?

Focus. Empty your mind of thoughts. Remember only the steps of the first legato. I flowed through them, following the notes etched onto my soul, step by step leaving my mark in the snow. When the time came my sword added its accompaniment to the song, flickering through the air, no heavier than a current of wind. For a minute I moved perfectly, but no longer. After all my training, with all my advantages, I still could barely make it through two-thirds of the first form. Progress would become no easier as I advanced.

Cursing, I ran my hand through my hair. Not good enough. Not fast enough. With unwavering focus and judicious use of my magic I could maybe reach the fourth legato in the next five years. Fast enough to be considered a rare talent, but at that age there were hundreds of better swordsmen who had held a blade since they took their first steps. None of them could kill an Archon.

To progress, I needed to calm my mind. I sheathed my sword and settled down into the lotus position Augur had taught me. Breathe in, breathe out; feel the wintry air circulating through your body. Invigorating. Nourishing. Nothing exists but the clearing and the young man in that clearing. Ignore the uncertainties. Ignore even that you are ignoring them.

For thirty minutes I struggled to fall into a trance, repeating useless mantras in my head. Then, finally, I stopped trying to force myself to relax and just . . . relaxed.

Emptiness. I felt as if I drifted in a void.

I stood in front of my memory palace, the ghost of my family manor. I had not exactly planned on coming here, but I was not entirely surprised.

The front door opened at the touch of my fingertips. Into the familiar entranceway. Beyond that, past the welcoming hall, into the skylit atrium, where the shallow pool of rainwater in the middle glowed with the moon's luminescence. I resisted the temptation to dip my hands into it.

I continued along, toward the back of the house, avoiding my father's office. A presence lurked there. That presence had alarmed Brother Augur enough that I had not seen him since. Now seemed like the worst time to investigate that mystery.

Finally, I came to my old bedroom and found the inside exactly as I remembered it. The bed, the lounging chair, the small library I was building as a pathetic rival to my father's.

An irresistible curiosity pulled me toward my books. Were the entire contents replicated perfectly within, proof that the unconscious mind stores everything? I selected one from the shelf. The title read *Staccato*.

Frowning, I flipped to the first page. An introduction to the staccato, explained in simple terms that encompassed my general knowledge of the art. The author continued on to detail memory palaces, though referred to another book known as *Mental* for a better primer. Descriptions of the facial muscles, how they interacted to form some basic expressions, followed by a shoddy analysis of body language. After around twenty pages of that came several hundred blank ones.

Of course, I recognized the handwriting. It was my own.

I selected each book from the shelf and read their titles. *Legato. Magic. Demons. Divine. Velassa. Odena.* Around thirty in total, most of them pitifully destitute. I would have to review each in time. Whenever I was not meditating in the middle of a clearing during a snowfall.

My curiosity demanded time to read one more book. I selected the *Legato* and settled into my lounging chair.

This book consisted primarily of images of myself performing the first form. They were perfect—a product of my visualization, not my ability to draw. Footnotes accompanied the images, reminders to breathe at certain points or other details impossible to illustrate.

Everything looked right until the sixty-fifth second. The moment I had failed earlier. After that the illustrations became increasingly vague.

I examined the sequence leading up to my failure for several minutes before discovering the problem. My damned footwork. The movement I was supposed to make would be impossible from that position. Everything collapsed from that point.

I leaned back and considered the motions involved. What would feel natural?

With a nod, I came to my feet. Slowly I went through the motions, experimenting to determine what felt like the right note. On the third try it felt perfect, and in this imaginary mental landscape I moved just as gracefully as I wished, unhampering by my physical form.

I made it seventy-six seconds into the first legato. More progress than I could hope for in a week. With solitude and the right location, how far could I advance?

The illustrations in the book had changed to reflect my progress, right up until my new stumbling point.

The absurdity of the whole situation occurred to me: mentally training myself physically.

My eyes opened back in the real world. The trickle of snow melting into a rivulet down my back wiped the smile from my face.

A half hour of meditation had provided plenty of time for my body to recover. I leaped to my feet and drew my sword. The first form of the legato felt natural, even if my body could not do it justice. Seventy-six seconds, though not without a few missteps.

A familiar migraine pounded between my temples. No need to force anything. Later tonight I would experiment more with the memory palace.

I returned to the barracks, wondering about what I had discovered. How was Brother Augur's technique not more well known? Such a useful skill, acquirable within an afternoon, would be a boon throughout the Civilized Lands. If everyone had the same ability to read and improve their own memories, mankind would experience an unparalleled enlightenment. And yet it hadn't.

Next time I saw Brother Augur, I would have to get some answers.

Heated voices from within the barracks. Pushing open the door revealed Mara and Irele facing each other in the middle of the room, cheeks flushed. When she saw me, Mara hurried over and dragged me to the mystery cot.

Her voice was frantic, elated. "Irele says these things have been here for the past few months, but she doesn't know who they belong to. Tell her what we talked about earlier. You said the same as me. This wasn't here before. We were arguing about it until you came in."

Irele glared as if daring me to choose a side.

"I have to agree with Mara," I said. "I'm absolutely certain I've never seen those things before."

"Of course you agree with her," said Irele. "I'll be back later."

Mara waved at her back as the tall girl flung the front door open and trudged out into the snow.

The red-headed acolyte strolled over to the chest and tapped it with her foot. "Let's go to Heaven's Gate tonight. We'll invite the new guy if he shows up. You look like you need a strong drink either way. If I recall correctly, you have pretty eyes hidden somewhere in that withered skull."

"Sure," I said.

I grunted my way through the rest of the conversation as Mara complained about the other girl. Hard to focus on our conversation when a million possibilities were coursing through my head. Damn, I wished I had someone to confide in.

Best to take it easy over the next few days. Experiment with the memory palace. Nothing that would draw too much attention. My father's office was a short walk away from my bedroom, and something was in there, waiting. After the events at the Amphitheater last night, I had some inkling of what lurked inside.

Scholars tracked the passage of the world's shadow across the moon during lunar eclipses to determine the distance between us. Two hundred thousand miles proved insufficient to deter the Goetia. Some claimed the moon used to be an unfathomable distance away before the demon lords locked it into orbit around our world. Either way, the Goetia descended amongst us, claiming to be our gods. Millennia of servitude followed before the Archons emerged, driving the demon lords back to Desolada.

At least, so the priests claimed.

16

JUDGMENT

When we arrived at Heaven's Gate I realized I had never been there before.

Mara acted as if we came here often and, on the surface, my memories seemed to agree. But the details were indistinct, and as Mara, Caedius, and I walked there I recognized none of the surrounding area.

An elderly gentleman greeted us at the door. He seemed confused when I tried to pay him with a silver denarii, insisting there was no charge to enter.

"Consider it a tip," I said.

The doorman seized my hand in his gnarled grip and pumped it with vigor. After a few seconds I managed to pry myself away, following the others inside.

"Feeling generous?" asked Caedius. "That could have paid for our entire night."

I shrugged. "Fine, I'll pay for our drinks."

Satisfied, Caedius led us to an empty table. The place attracted a decent crowd, folk in tasteful clothing, mostly gathered in groups who talked amongst themselves. The blazing hearth suffused the main room with a homey warmth. No guards anywhere. The only thing familiar about the place was the men a few tables down bickering over a card game.

"Did you really need to bring your sword?" asked Mara.

"I always bring it. It's fashionable." Truth be told, between all the friendly faces and lack of visible weapons, the steel at my hip did feel a touch ridiculous. Bringing my sword had felt so natural I had not even considered whether I should.

A young woman with blonde hair and flushed cheeks interrupted our conversation.

"Mara, Caedius, a pleasure to see you both again. You've brought a friend? My name is Eres, I will be your server tonight."

Mara frowned. "You know Leones."

Eres smiled uncertainly. "Sorry, I must not have the best memory. Excuse me, Master Leones. What can I get for you?"

We ordered our drinks. After the attendant departed, Mara crossed her arms. "She was our server two weeks ago. How does she not remember?"

"Truth be told," I said. "I don't remember this place either."

The other two stared.

Hiding the truth from them would accomplish nothing. Something had tampered with our memories. The most obvious culprit was the mysterious acolyte. No trace of him existed outside of the barracks. I had even asked Avarus, assuming he would know of a duelist joining the philosophers, and he was unaware of any such person.

"Has anything seemed wrong to you recently, Caedius?" I asked. "Especially in the last day?"

The big man rubbed the stubble along his jaw. His eyes flicked over toward Mara. "Not in particular."

"Any false memories?"

"No? Not that I can tell."

Mara shook her head. "You think we have false memories? There could be a hundred other reasons for this."

"Demonic magic is not the same as ours," I said. "The Archons have powers over elements and the like. Demons have some method of altering reality itself."

We lapsed into the silence as the attendant returned with our drinks. She gave me a long, uncertain look before retreating from our table. Mara kept glancing over my shoulder like some sort of nervous tic.

"I'm still not even sure what's wrong," said Caedius.

"I was arguing with Irele earlier," said Mara. "There are some new belongings in the barracks that I don't recognize. She says they've been there for weeks now. Leones agrees. Never seen 'em. Now Leones says that he doesn't recognize this place, when I'm certain we've been coming here for a while. It doesn't make sense."

By the time she finished speaking, most of the tavern had lapsed into silence. Mara looked over my shoulder, eyes widening. Resting my hand on the hilt of my sword, I turned to the front door.

At the entrance was a person I had not seen in almost a year: a middle-aged man in the white robes of the Magistrate. A pair of soldiers flanked him on either side. The one on the left had a haggard face shrouded with stubble. Scarred knuckles and dead eyes. Their faces came to mind more easily than my mother's; I often remembered them during my training sessions, in those moments when my mind screamed to rest for just a few minutes. The other guard, a pock-faced bastard with a shaved head, did not look familiar, but I'd make him touch Hell too.

"In the name of Archon Nony," said the Magister, "we are here to apprehend the fugitive known as Leones Ansteri."

His voice set my heart racing in my chest. This isn't fear, I told myself. This is excitement. Opportunity. After all those daydreams of hunting the Magisters down, in the end they came to me.

My vision darkened at the corners. I leaped out of my chair so fast I sent it clattering behind me. A rapid dash carried me forward—suicidal in an open field, but my bet was that the Magister would not be willing to throw flame magic about in a crowded tavern. And if he did, my power was flaring in the back of my mind. Fire wouldn't kill me immediately. It would just be excruciating.

The Magister fell behind his two guards, who drew their blades and, side-by-side, met me in the middle. People began to shout as my sword clashed with one of the guards'; I was probably one of them. The jarring impact of our blades distracted me as the dead-eyed guard circled around to my side, coming from another direction.

Deep breaths. Don't let the bloodlust take over. Remember the legato. Fluid movements. I intercepted each blow, a frantic dance that drove me backward, sword sweeping in wide arcs. Between the two of them there was no opening to switch to the offensive.

Be mindful of surroundings, I told myself, like you learned when sparring with . . . who?

I stumbled. One of the tavern patrons had mustered up the nerve to come from behind and shove me into a nearby table. A woman screamed as I rolled across her meal of pheasant and wine. Somehow getting twisted in the tablecloth, I brought the table down as I tumbled across the other side. That barrier saved my life as a conflagration of fire magic blossomed into existence, swallowing the woman and billowing over my head. Her screaming turned into a high-pitched squeal.

I flexed my magic, reversing time thirty minutes.

Back to the moment before we departed from the barracks that evening. Caedius, Mara, and I were still within eyesight of the barracks. As tempted as it was to return a full hour, my experiments in the memory palace earlier had exhausted much of my mental energy. Surviving the night would require careful rationing of my power.

I took a few moments to steady my voice against the bloodlust surging through my body.

"I'm actually starting to get a nasty headache," I said, mostly keeping it together. "I think I'm just going to sleep early tonight."

Mara pouted. "Come on. We have a surprise for you there!"

That made me pause. My heart still raged in my chest. Dry mouthed, hands shaking, I unsheathed my sword and pointed it at Caedius.

He held out his hands, bewildered. "Calm down. You don't know what you're doing."

"A surprise waiting for me?" I asked. "Like a Magister? Tell me what's happening or I'll kill both of you."

I doubted I could have followed through with the threat, but they valued their lives too much to take that chance. Tears glistened at the corner of Mara's eyes. They only enraged me further.

"You're a criminal," she said. "You're endangering all of our lives by being here. Some men approached Caedius when he was staying at his aunt's manor and started asking about you. About when you came here. What you call yourself. What you've told us. How could you do this?"

"I did it to survive," I backed away, keeping my sword pointed at Caedius. There was a dangerous look on his face, like he was considering a bad idea.

"So did we," he said, bending slightly at the knees

I reversed time again before the situation turned ugly.

* * *

Mara pouted. "Come on. We have a surprise for you there!"

"No," I said. "I think I'm turning in early for the night."

"We'll stay then," said Caedius.

"Don't be bothered on my account. Go."

To my relief they exchanged glances and set off along the path. I waited in the barracks for a minute until they were out of sight. Lakken's home was a brief run away; my energized body ate up the distance in no time. A candle guttered in the window of his reading room. At least one of them was still awake.

His caretaker, Elys, answered the door, scolding me for my frantic knocking. She invited me inside, leading me to where the old man lay in bed, his eyes half-open.

"What brings you barging in here so late at night?" asked Lakken.

"You heard about what happened last night at the Amphitheater?" I asked. "Ever since then everything has seemed wrong. I woke up outside of the barracks in the middle of the night as if I had been sleepwalking. Then . . ."

The old man listened patiently while I explained. When I finished, he gestured for Elys to help him to the side of the bed. For a moment my panic subsided as I worried for the old man's health. Ever since the snow started, he had become increasingly frail. A few months ago, he would not have needed Elys to help swing his legs off his bed and hoist him into a sitting position with the support of both hands.

"Most accurate accounts of demon magic are scoured from the records," he said after catching his breath. "Foolish, to hide your enemy's tricks for them, but the Archons fear revealing the whole truth. Instead, they teach us not to make deals with demons and other ways to avoid falling victim. If you think this through and consider the lesson behind the story of Arostara, eventually you would discover the truth for yourself."

I said nothing, wishing he would get to the point.

Lakken took a deep, steadying breath. "The Goetia are masters of karma. It's an innate magical gift among their kind. Karma is a delicate thing, difficult to explain succinctly. It encompasses a variety of esoteric connections. Oaths, promises, destiny, and the like. In a sense it makes them far more honorable than mankind, as they are incapable of uttering lies. They will dance around the truth instead. They are far greater masters of the staccato than any mortal."

"I don't understand the connection to Arostara."

"Consider what you know about Odena. Something like this would never happen within most of the other Great Cities. All sorts of pagans congregate here. The traditional morals and adherence to religion that protect us against the Lords of Desolada are not observed as strictly. That freedom allows them to corrupt the hearts of men."

I froze in place. If this city was like Arostara, I needed to get as far from here as possible. After Lakken told me as much as possible.

If Mara and Caedius headed straight toward the guards, they would still have to find the Magisters and inform them that I had canceled my plans with the other acolytes. Another ten minutes' worth of magic would test my limits. That left five minutes to figure out as much as possible.

Elys kneeled beside her grandfather and whispered in his ear. The old man looked like he wanted to argue until she rested a hand on his shoulder and shook her head.

"You being here is too dangerous," she said. "For your safety and ours, please leave."

"You should both get out of the city," I said.

Lakken grunted. "We are prepared for whatever may come"

For a moment I considered pressing the issue. I cast one last glance around his home. To the library of forbidden knowledge, mostly about the Goetia. Lakken's information was invaluable, but the very nature of it was suspicious.

I chose not to reverse time on that particular conversation. There was some chance they would heed my warning.

I set off into the city at a sprint. The few times I almost slipped along ice, I reversed time a second and corrected my movements.

My safehouse was less than a mile away. Slowed by the ice-slick ground, I wasted seven minutes getting there. A few more seconds fumbling at my key to open the door.

The safehouse was a single room. Several packs along the closest wall contained an assortment of necessary supplies. At minimum they held a week of dry rations, a pouch containing five golden solareum, a large canteen, and several pairs of clothing, including gloves and a woolen cap.

At the back of the room was the real prize: a weapon trove of several swords inferior to the Bakkel at my side, a spear, a selection of knives, and, most importantly, a crossbow. I selected the last weapon and its quiver.

Cranking the windlass ate up another seventy seconds, but testing the weapon now would save me some potential trouble later. I fired a bolt into a nearby wall; it punched through with the satisfying thump. The weapon was supposed to make short work of even plate armor.

Another seventy seconds to reload. In a fight I would realistically only be able to fire once, but with my magic that one bolt would be enough.

Ignoring the urge to flee the city, I returned to the Gardens. If anyone thought much of a teenager with a heavy satchel over one shoulder, a crossbow, and a sword at his side, they kept their comments to themselves.

When I came to Brother Augur's arboretum I sighed, wishing the man was around. His home was as good an ambush spot as any. I settled behind a thicket of trees near the path, at an angle where the shadows hid my presence, but I could still make out the flagstone trail stretching into the misty gloom.

After thirty minutes I almost stood up and left. Taking deep, slow breaths, I did my best to settle into a trance. A short while later my patience was rewarded when a trio of figures came into view. The Magister and his guards, unmistakable in the light of the dead-eyed man's torch. Pressing myself closer against the tree, I aimed the crossbow along the path.

Not an easy shot even if I had any actual experience with a crossbow. There was only a short window for me to make the shot as well. I reached for my power.

The first bolt missed entirely. Cursing, I reversed time.

The second attempt clipped the closest guard in the thigh.

The third punched through the dead-eyed man's neck. I waited a few seconds to reverse that one, savoring their panic and the evil bastard pawing at his mangled throat.

The fourth time I cleared my mind and waited until they almost disappeared from sight. That angle offered the best view of the Magister's back.

I pulled the trigger.

The bolt blew through his chest. If not his heart, a lung. The Magister fell to his knees while the guards shouted and grabbed at him. Was he dead? Such an injury should have elicited some sort of reaction; the lack of a raging inferno consuming the Gardens was a good sign. I would have to be ready to reverse time just in case.

The dead-eyed man pointed my way. Slipping around the other side of the wide trunk, I tossed the crossbow aside and unsheathed my sword. Their footsteps crunched in the snow as they approached.

I came at them from an unexpected angle. The dead-eyed man managed to parry my swing, but the force of it sent him stumbling into his companion. Both fell in a tangle of limbs. But these were the personal guards of a Magister, a grade above most others. With coordinated precision they returned to their feet before I could take advantage.

The pock-faced guard recovered first. Snarling, he leveled a devastating swing at my throat. I deflected it at the last moment, trying to get my breathing under control. The next attacks were almost predictable, something even a novice could see through. Now that I knew I could match blades with him, I resisted the mad urge to smile.

He was off-balance for only a moment. It was enough. Using a move from the beginning of the second legato, I propelled myself into a quick leap, no more than a twitch of my calves, blade whipping out sideways. I was so prepared to reverse time and attempt the move again that I nearly lost my grip on my sword when it connected. The blade sank deep into the guard's shoulder. He stumbled away, shouting. Yet again the guards got in each other's way.

Deep breath. Don't let him get away.

With only the briefest resistance as steel met bone, my next slash sheared the lower half of his jaw from his face. He collapsed, screams mangled through the ruin of his face.

One against one, his Magister and the other guard dead or close enough, the remaining bastard stood no chance. In normal circumstances he was stronger than me, taller, more experienced, but he was terrified. He knew I was their target, but to him it would seem as if a demon hunted them in the night. He had grossly overestimated me, and that was all I needed.

For a minute I defended against his savage assault. If Avarus had not taught me the proper way to hold a sword, the first blow would have knocked it from my hands. His panic gave him strength, but it also disrupted his breathing, and as I turned aside each strike, the terror began to wear away at him. There was almost a look of surrender on his face when he relented, so exhausted he could barely hold his sword up.

I skewered him through the heart with a single thrust. The bastard bled all over my boots.

The Magister was crawling away, leaving behind a trail of crimson. He wheezed, blood bubbling at his lips in a pink froth. Mustering all his strength, he pointed at me. A pathetic flame guttered on his fingertip, vanished as his arm fell back to the ground.

Interesting. Could he not use his magic because of the injury? Because he couldn't focus?

I planted my foot on his head and rested my sword against the base of his skull. Both hands clasped on the pommel, I thrust downward. He stopped moving.

Pain screaming between my ears, having just survived a fight for my life, I fell onto my ass. And that's when I remembered.

My friend Felix.

The establishment named Amelie in Yellow.

Jokul stabbing me. Barely surviving.

Using my sword as a cane, I heaved myself to my feet. The smart thing to do would be to leave the city. Make it out of there as fast as I could. Few people strolled the Gardens at night since the snow began. No one would discover these bodies for a while. Probably Mara and Caedius when they returned to see what they had wrought.

The pock-faced man was still alive for now and could probably find some help. Best to finish him off. I did not recognize him as one of the soldiers who burned down my family manor. Did this man deserve to die just because he happened to guard this particular Magister?

I had already made my decision. If I spared him, it would be nothing but trouble for me. Hand trembling, I rested the tip of my sword against his neck. He spasmed at the touch of the sword, eyes opening, trying to speak through his ruined mouth.

I finished him.

With shaky knees I stumbled over to gather my pack before continuing along the path back to the city. Toward Amelie in Yellow and hopefully some answers.

17

RECURSION (I)

My breathing recovered by the time I reached Amelie in Yellow, though the migraine splitting my head continued to worsen. Three separate people asked if I was all right and needed help, likely because of the blood splashed across my clothing. I did not think much of it was mine.

I needed to find Felix and figure out what was going on. Until I was able to recuperate, I could not afford to stress myself. I would spend fifteen minutes inside at most. After that I would have to head somewhere far away. Preferably on the other side of the Civilized Lands.

It had been less than a day since the events at the Amphitheater. The Goetia were the most logical explanation behind my memory being altered. Such workings could fall under the domain of karmic magic, though I still had little idea what exactly the demon lords were capable of.

On the other hand, the spell had been broken after I killed the Magister and his guards, so perhaps they were the culprits. In the worst-case scenario, Magisters with fire and karma magic were hunting me. An unlikely union.

Answers waited inside.

No woman in yellow waited at the door. My chest tightened. Readying my time magic, I unsheathed my sword and pushed open the door.

After walking inside, I immediately noticed something was wrong with Amelie in Yellow. All of the lights had died out. Only pallid moonlight from the high windows illuminated the first floor. The diaphanous silks that usually curtained off the beds puddled on the floor as if someone had torn them down. A few figures lounged about. One moaned, low and pitiful.

I stood at the bottom of the stairs leading to the upper floor. Sounds and light drifted down, warped as if I were looking up from the bottom of a lake. Disconcerted, I turned to leave. Before I reached the door, I collided with an invisible barrier that yielded slightly before thrusting me backward.

After a moment of panic, I reached for my power. For the first time since it manifested, I was unable to sense anything. Even when the backlash of abusing my power became excruciating, I could always squeeze out another second or two. Now there was simply nothing.

I pressed the tip of my scabbard against the barrier. It recoiled a few inches before repelling the leather with equal force. Something about it made me think of a living membrane, more complex than a simple area-restricting spell.

I approached the closest person. Lifeless eyes stared out from a slack face. Gray and cold.

The second was dead as well.

The final man watched me with crazed eyes, mouthing silent nonsense. When I shook his shoulder, he withdrew with a low whimper, feeble arms pushing away at me.

"What's happening here?"

His eyes widened, mouth gibbering in a silent frenzy. Completely mad.

Nowhere to go but up. A terrifying thought, but I had no choice.

I ascended the stairs, hand on the rail to steady myself. No guards in sight. When I reached the second floor I felt as if I had stepped into a play, nervous actors all too aware of their role. Men drank and played cards and dice, their faces gleaming oily in the dim tallow-light. I saw only one Amelie, maskless and staring at the floor, the kohl around her eyes streaked down her cheeks like painted tears. Her hands trembled in her lap.

There seemed to be a pressure to the air, an eddy of unease focused on the center of the room. My mind shied away from the source, the same instinct we develop when we learn not to look too closely at the sun. Again and again, my gaze wandered from that focus, but too stubborn to be deceived, I willed myself to look at the lone figure perched behind the table. Nobody stood within a dozen feet of the thing.

Gray pupils stared out from pools of yellowed sclera. Its many-fingered hands were clasped on the pitted wood, the nails like shards of chipped obsidian. I could not tell if it was a man or woman or beyond such things. There was a sickly beauty to it despite its state of decay; ulcers along the cheeks exposed perfect teeth, a jagged expanse of scar marred its swan-like neck.

Its robes were fine-cut, dyed purple like those of the merchant lords of the Twilight Isles. A sword pierced its chest where its heart would be, a strange weapon with a blade made of porcelain or ivory. Blue ichor stained the fabric around it.

The demon stood, an unfolding of limbs, half-again the height of a man. It extended a hand toward me. Its voice was airy, mocking. "Welcome, my friend."

My heartbeat pounded at my temple. I reached for my magic again. Nothing. I felt like I had lost my sense of balance, head swimming. The demon tilted its head, the lines around its eyes crinkling in amusement.

I looked around. Everyone pretended that nothing amiss was happening in front of them. They were poor actors.

"Are you one of the Goetia?" I asked.

The demon giggled, the carefree sound of a little girl at play. "If my master's master descended upon this city you would know. The wings of Duke Astaroth would flatten the world from horizon to horizon. His breath would turn all these works of stone and wood to chaos. I am but a humble emissary, a Captain of one of His forty legions."

A Captain. Not as bad but certainly bad enough. I clasped my hands behind my back to keep them from trembling. It didn't help.

"To capture Astaroth's attention is a great honor." The demon rested a hand on the handle of the sword impaled through its chest. "Of all the silly men that walk upon this earth, philosophers delight him the most. How far off you all are. Your humanity eclipses the truth. This is a universe of formulae, perfectly tuned. Even the void obeys the fundamental laws. In his realm he keeps a great Tome, larger than this city, detailing the path of every world and the path of everything upon them. Through his wisdom, you too may know the truth one day."

I took the demon speaking instead of slaying me where I stood to be a good sign. The occupants of Amelie in Yellow looked haggard and sullen, but at least they were alive. There must be an actual plan at work here instead of mindless revenge. Still, whatever these people had experienced to shatter their spirits in one night was concerning.

"What is happening?" I asked.

The demon placed the fingers of one hand against its lips. "The Great Lord has decided to plant this tesseract within your so-called Civilized Lands. Such an honor is rarely bestowed upon mere mortals. I am the overseer of this new domain until I see fit to end our time together."

"A tesseract?" I had never heard the word before.

"I could explain," it said, "but oh, how marvelous it is when each of you discovers the truth for yourself! Please, feel obliged to introduce yourself to your fellow prisoners. I, of course, already know much about you, young Leones. One of Astaroth's closest viziers personally updated me when you met the qualifications to enter."

The sinking feeling in my gut deepened.

"What qualifications?"

The demon's long, gray tongue snaked out and licked the lower half of its face. "A sufficient amount of corruption. As your soul has grown more tainted, you have started to become aware of our presence. And now you have done a great favor for us by ridding the world of one of the Magisters. To murder three fellow humans with no remorse shows promise. How truly delicious. But please, go introduce yourself to the others."

I stood there speechless. The Captain returned to its seat. Upon its table lay a number of parchments, along with a red ink I had no doubt was blood. The demon took up its quill and began to write. Eventually it broke through that the Captain, my jailor, had dismissed me.

Once again, I tried using my power without success. Trapped.

Perhaps I could at least find some familiar faces. I prowled through the area, recognizing a few people I had seen here before but never spoken with. Everyone here must have met the qualifications to enter in their own way. They did look like a disreputable bunch, most of them armed, faces suspicious.

Off in a corner, I spotted Felix.

I hurried over, calling his name. Blearily he looked up at me, an opium pipe clutched between his hands. A humorless smile twisted his face.

"Another hallucination, is it?" he said. "Why do you keep torturing me, Leones?"

Taken aback, I paused for a moment before grabbing his shoulder. My friend looked shocked at the physical contact. He tossed his pipe aside and snatched my hand in both of his, squeezing as if unable to believe I was actually there.

"How long has it been now?" he asked.

"A day."

He dropped my hand. "It must be true, then. Some new people like yourself have appeared over the past few weeks, claiming it has only been a few hours. I've been tracking how long I've been here, though it is difficult to tell days apart. It's always nighttime out the windows. I've been here forty days now, I think. Forty days, Leones."

Time distortion? That only raised more questions.

"If it's been that long," I said, "how does everyone look so relatively clean? Not that this looks like a formal ball, but the smell alone should be horrendous."

"That's how I've been keeping track of time. Approximately every twenty-four hours the entire place returns to how it used to be. Our clothes are repaired, the furniture returns. Can't tell you how many chairs I've broken. The only good part is endless opium and alcohol."

"Not the worst prison for you, then," I said.

Felix did not even bother acknowledging my awful joke. "I feel like I'm losing my mind. If that's really you, Leones, I can't tell you how happy I am to see you. Even if it means you are stuck here as well."

He walked over the bar and climbed over the counter. Despite their daily regeneration, several of the bottles of alcohol had already been drained. My friend selected a bottle of brandy, squinted at the label, and poured us both a drink. I kept my eyes on the Captain the whole time, but the demon seemed content with its writing.

I accepted the brandy, certain I was in a nightmare and equally certain that I was not. The glass was cool and smooth in my hand. The liquor smelled like smoke and burned my sinuses. Real. Absolutely real.

"When did this happen?" I asked.

"A little before midnight." He took several large swallows at once, eyes squeezed shut. "The night was already starting to wind down, but suddenly most of the crowd up and left. Most of them didn't even say anything. Just grabbed their coats and walked out the door. A few minutes later, one of the prisoners attempted to leave and found himself repulsed by the barrier. That's when we knew something was wrong. Everyone was panicking, trying to escape, until the Captain showed up and demanded we calm down."

"We have to fight our way out," I said. "We can beat this thing. They do it all the time on the Frontier."

He shook his head. "We've tried. We've tried everything. I doubt Champion Jokul could even put a scratch on it. I mean, the bastard is wearing a sword in its heart like a piece of jewelry. Even if we defeat the Captain, that doesn't mean the tesseract will end. Perhaps the next demon won't be so accommodating."

"Then what—?"

"Take a seat and try to enjoy yourself at least. As terrible as it is to say, I'm glad to see you here. The others don't exactly provide the greatest entertainment. No one wants to practice with swords unless it's a serious fight. And all this demon does is praise its master and draw runes all day."

I drained the brandy as quickly as possible.

"I have to admit," he said, pouring us both another drink, "this has been a great opportunity to practice my bladeforms. Not much else to do."

"Aren't you going to ask the obvious?" I gestured at my clothing.

He laughed. "I figured you would explain all the blood at some point."

So I told him about my encounter with the Magister and his guards. I was unsure how Felix would react to the story, but he merely nodded along, sipping his drink and fiddling with his pipe.

When I was finished, he removed a box of matches from his pocket. From it he selected a sulphur match and struck it against his thumbnail. He lifted the opium pipe to his mouth and relit the nugget, then flicked his wrist to extinguish the flame. It was smooth, practiced, as if he had done it thousands of times.

"That is . . . unexpected, to say the least. I imagine there's some bad blood between you. You can tell me some day, if you feel comfortable with it. I'd like to share my own story with you, if you don't mind. A confession of sorts."

"Sure," I said.

He closed his eyes in pleasure and exhaled a cloud of pungent smoke. "Thank you. Like I said, don't feel compelled to tell me about your past. If we remain here for a while, I think you will."

It was a story I did not want to hear, but he had to tell it.

Felix was from the slums of Odena, born to an opiate addict mother and a religious father who found pleasure to be an abomination. Complete opposites, but they stuck with each other for no apparent reason. Felix barely survived his birth, little larger than a hand. His mother died from hemorrhage.

His father raised him the best he could, which meant the fist and the belt. Felix was a clever boy, curious about the world, always asking questions his father could never answer. Religious texts did not explain why water became ice at a certain temperature or why the sky was blue, thus such knowledge was unnecessary, even blasphemous. One day when he was around seven, his father lashed out in annoyance. When Felix fell, he twisted and struck the ground, caving in part of his skull. Here he tapped a spot hidden behind his bangs.

Modern anatomy claims that the soul resides in the front of the brain. To protect it the Increate shaped the human skull so that the brow is the thickest section of bone. For Felix it proved insufficient, and so he received the absurd diagnosis of fragmentation of the soul.

The kind and curious boy became erratic and self-destructive. One day he learned where his father stashed his meager savings and, hoping to double his father's money and earn his respect, lost it all gambling. The beating left him in an infirmary for months, recovering slowly and developing a laudanum addiction along the way. His father never visited, and when some of the nurses pressured him into coming, he disowned Felix and refused to pay the physikers.

To settle his debt Felix was forced to work as an assistant for two years, bandaging the gangrenous legs of vagrants and stealing laudanum when the opportunity presented itself. The Church owned the infirmary and staffed it with matrons who found Felix's behavior less than holy. He had never imagined he would miss his father until then. Their lectures and disappointment bothered him in a way the fist never could.

During this time, he met Lyra and some other street urchins whom he spent most of his free time with. He ran away often. The matrons hunted him down until he was a month from completing his indenture. They no longer cared enough to waste their time.

While wandering the streets he came across a duel between two swordsmen. A large crowd had gathered, and he managed to weave his way to the front. The duel lasted for less than five seconds. Asalen de

Odena parried his opponent's blow and killed him with a counterthrust to the neck. The man drowned in his own blood. Asalen reminded Felix of his father: tall, graying at the temples, and quick to violence.

The duel occurred because the man's eyes had lingered a bit too long on Asalen's wife as they strolled through the streets. She loved the duels as much as he did. Both were quite convinced of their greatness. When Felix begged them to accept him as a squire, Asalen agreed with the solemnity of a lord accepting a new vassal. They must have sensed Felix was broken too.

Thus, at nine years of age, Felix became a swordsman. Too good a swordsman too quickly, to Asalen's annoyance. His father and the matrons of the infirmary had taught him how to take a beating too well; he would always stand back up.

As long as Felix appealed to his pride Asalen would spare him the flat of his blade. One day Felix slashed his master's forearm, and he was beaten within an inch of his life. The wife had been only too happy to join in. This beating he did not stand up from.

It took Felix another two months to recover. Asalen and his wife returned to Odena, forgetting the boy they had left bleeding in the streets. He did not forget them.

Here Felix paused, tears in his eyes. The grin on his face made me think he was closer to madness than I suspected. He found them and killed them in the night. He was only nine years old, but they weren't expecting the knife. He made it fast—he was no monster, no matter what his father and the matrons claimed.

From there on he lived on the streets, until one day his luck ran out and he ended up in the dungeons. Too lucky with the dice. Avarus had eventually rescued him, and ever since, he had lived among the philosophers.

"Not that my life has been an endless stream of beatings and misery," said Felix, his words slurred. "But that's human, to focus on all the wrongs that we suffered. Maybe I deserved it, too. I stole, and my father beat me. I brought others misery, and they brought misery to me. That's justice, isn't it? It didn't feel just to me. It's like water in a cup. Maybe that doesn't make sense. I'm like water without a cup, and people become upset because I can't hold the shape they want me to. All that water wants is a cup."

"I see."

"That made no sense. It made sense in my head." He drummed his fingers along the counter, eyes downcast. His movements became more languid, more relaxed, as if he had unloaded some great weight off his shoulders.

"I see," I said again to fill the silence.

His chin drifted down to his chest. His eyes closed.

I came to my feet and counted his slow, ragged breaths for a minute. Nine. I copied what I had seen Amelies do before, grinding my knuckles into his sternum. He moaned and slapped my hand away before returning to his slumber. At least he seemed peaceful at rest.

I considered his story for a long time. It explained quite a bit. He had revealed himself as a murderer, but given the circumstances, I found I didn't care. The worst of my nightmares came from when the Magisters destroyed my home. I could still picture their faces, their flames, and though he was not present in reality, sometimes I saw the bandaged figure of Archon Nony, looming over everything. No, what Felix had done made perfect sense to me.

18

RECURSION (II)

Unsure what to do while Felix rested at the table next to me, I waited.

A scarred man at a nearby table shaved with his knife. It was an unsettling sight—I could almost sense the thoughts whirling inside his head as he held the blade to his neck. After a long moment the blade continued, leaving a spot of blood along his throat. We made eye contact for a second. His grin was horrifying.

I decided that was enough interaction with my fellow prisoners.

Fortunately, none of them paid me much heed. I appreciated their silence. There was much to think about. So much had happened recently that I needed some time to center myself. I wanted to meditate, but clearing my mind seemed quite unlikely under these circumstances.

Instead, I reached for my power again, straining for a glimpse. For anything.

During my physical training the connection between my mind and muscles had improved. Before, I had never bothered to consider how every part interacted outside of some rudimentary interest in studying anatomy. Now I could sense specific muscle groups I had been unaware of before, a side effect of gaining a greater mastery over myself.

Similarly, what had started as a vague feeling of magic in the back of my mind had improved as I became more familiar with it. The shape of my power became clearer, more defined. So I did not search for my magic, not exactly. I looked for anything inside of me that may be related to it.

And there was something. Just a sensation, hard to pin down, in my general vicinity. I closed my eyes and turned my head like a hound locking onto a scent. When I opened them I was facing the Captain. Unsurprising. The demon would have powers of its own, perhaps even beyond its innate mastery of karma. Very useful to be able to sense other magical beings. Even if that meant they could also sense me.

I closed my eyes and continued to explore. Controlling my breathing helped, and though it had seemed impossible before, I found myself naturally drifting into the trance state of meditation. My awareness brushed around the area, forming an image of the surroundings in my mind. It stopped whenever it encountered the boundary of the tesseract, a tightly-woven net of silver threads that repulsed anything it touched.

At first, I wondered if I was experiencing some sort of astral projection, my spirit slipping from my body to view the immaterial plane. Supposedly some individuals could navigate through this mental realm, though it was rare among humans. More likely this was some sort of new sense, like a blind man gaining the ability to see. Maybe it was both, a concept greater than a single, narrow definition.

Then a hand clapped down on my shoulder.

My eyes snapped open. Vertigo washed over me at the sudden disorientation as I readjusted to my normal vision. Annoyed, I looked over to see Sensi looming over me. She held an amber-and-ivory cigarette holder, a curlicue of smoke drifting past her expressionless face.

"We need to talk," she said.

"Yes, we do."

"Follow me, then." She turned away and glanced back over her shoulder. "Bring Felix, if you can."

I knuckled his sternum again until he woke up. Once more he tried to shove my arm aside, but this time I refused to relent. His attempts gathered strength until he was forced to regard me with a baleful look.

"We're moving," I said. "I'm not leaving you passed out here."

He muttered something that sounded vaguely like, "Do it all the time . . ."

I slipped his shoulder over mine, supporting him as we followed Sensi. I had no idea where she planned to move us, as that portion of the room seemed just as good as any other. As we approached the far wall, she raised one hand.

Perhaps it was a trick of my eyes, but all the shadows around us appeared to shift slightly.

A black door materialized on the wall.

Inside was a lush suite, tasteful and expensive, just as large as either of Amelie in Yellow's floors. A roaring fireplace filled the area with drowsy warmth. Most of the area was open, including a small, stocked kitchen and the central meeting room, but there were a few closed doors I assumed were bedrooms.

Wherever this was, it was not physically attached to Amelie in Yellow—at least, not in a way that was visible from the exterior. And all this meant one thing: she was able to use magic.

I helped Felix onto a divan in the meeting room before taking my own seat. "Let's talk, then."

"We were never formally introduced," she said. "My name is Sensi. I'm the owner of this establishment and many others. An elder philosopher of the Odena sect. And as you have now seen, an Echo of the Huntress."

"An Echo?" I had heard the term before. Augur had used it to describe mortals who made a pact with the Goetia in return for some of their power, but the Huntress was the Archon of Shadows, not a demon.

"The Archons are the only humans able to cast magic of their own volition," she said. "Everyone else is borrowing from them. They in turn are borrowing their power from the Increate, who blesses them with a partial understanding of the anima."

"The anima?"

She gave me a look that revealed her opinion of my education. "The anima is the universal force of law and order, forming the foundation of all existence. The Archons impart an echo of their knowledge unto others through a reflection of their consciousness. This in turn grants us some small fraction of their powers."

That didn't sound exactly right. My power was not borrowed from anyone else, and I was certainly no Archon. Either way, it was not my place to correct her.

I resisted the urge to scratch my cheek. To keep my hands busy I examined my fingernails, realizing a moment later that this seemed even more suspicious. "I think I understand to some extent. Many philosophers have theorized on the source of the Archon's divinity. Still, I am not sure I follow when you say that your power is a reflection of the Huntress's consciousness onto yours."

Sensi folded her arms. "The process of becoming an Echo is not like joining the soldiery and receiving a spear. The Huntress merged her consciousness with mine in order to introduce me to the realm of shadows. It is a spiritual intimacy unlike anything I have ever experienced. Sex, romantic love, the bond between mother and child—nothing compares."

"So magic is simply a profound understanding of the universe and how to shape it. It's something that can be taught."

"Yes, to some extent," she said. "The anima is linked to consciousness. You will never see a horse burn a city with its mind, though they possess some degree of intelligence. Consciousness has no link to reasoning or learning or anything of the sort. For instance, the nagas operate as a hive mind where only the queen could be considered sapient. Yet despite their lack of consciousness, they are capable of functioning when their queen perishes. Their society will stagnate, but their daily routines are unchanged. They are known to be highly adaptable in individual combat and are even capable of mobilizing as self-sufficient groups. Demons are another excellent example. The Goetia are certainly conscious, but their minions are not."

"What about the Captain?" I asked. "It spoke to me. We had a conversation."

"Even speech is not indicative of consciousness. The lion roars, the horse neighs, but they do not sit at the high table. Language no doubt affects the shape of our thoughts and may even be the foundation of consciousness. Still, it is not the same thing as true understanding. The Captain is simply following its orders with a high degree of intelligence. It is possible that its link to Astaroth grants it some rudimentary consciousness through a reflected anima, but it has no individual self beyond that."

I rubbed my jaw. "So are there people that have multiple magical abilities? Can you be an Echo of multiple different beings?"

"There are a few," she said, "but they become unstable. Some people with strong willpower can handle two, but as you go beyond that, the mental strain is untenable. Having a *single* consciousness, let alone multiple ones, reflected onto your own causes problems. I have memories of another life, another time. On occasion I look at myself in the mirror and feel that I am looking at a complete stranger. It is not an easy way to live. It must also take its toll on the Archons themselves or they would create armies of us. Their magic is intrinsically linked with their being; to give some away, they must lose part of themselves."

I thought of the power that lived in the back of my mind. Part of the anima. Sensi was the first person to reveal any insight on the topic, and I intended to find out as much as possible. She must have suspected I possessed some magic of my own. As a master of the staccato, she would have watched for a tell-tale flush of my cheeks, a widening of my eyes, perhaps my shoulders leaning forward a touch too far.

To be an Archon meant incomprehensible power. I could reverse time for an hour: a useful trick but several orders of magnitude below conjuring infernos from the air and freezing entire cities. Yet I could not shake the feeling that my situation was altogether different from Sensi's. Occasionally I felt a sense of derealization, as if the universe around me was wrong and existence itself utterly bizarre, but I had never experienced anyone else's memories. Not that I could tell. They were mine, just jumbled occasionally from living the same moment multiple times.

"I want to try something with you," said Sensi. She held a deck of cards that seemed to have appeared from nowhere. I wondered if that was part of her power or if she just wanted to throw me off with some clever sleight of hand.

"Gambling? Maybe you should have talked to Felix instead."

"That boy has gone mad. I suspect he was on the edge before being trapped here. He used to come here all the time, one of the only people who didn't wear a mask. When I look at him, I feel like his face is a better mask than any costume we wear."

I blinked in surprise. He had not seemed too bad to me, but maybe that meant I was on the edge myself. It is hard to recognize you are heading down a dangerous path with someone walking just a step ahead of you.

Another thing to think about later. I changed the subject. "What are the cards for?"

She stared at me for an uncomfortably long time before spreading the cards on the table before us. At quick count I guessed there were around fifteen. They seemed sturdy and gleamed in the candlelight as if made of thin wafers of metal. Runes of gold paint covered their gray surfaces, the lines so small and delicate I wondered if any human hand could have formed them.

"Tarot cards," she said. "Descended from one of the ancient methods of divination. Sortilege, also known as casting the lots. Priests claimed they could read the future by throwing the knucklebones of saints. They tended only to be as accurate as random guesswork. But sometimes, in some unique situations, they were accurate in ways you would never expect."

I looked at the cards with suspicion. "And you think this is an accurate way of reading the future?"

"I certainly enjoy doing it, at least. Do you have any better ideas on how we can spend the foreseeable eternity?"

Not the response I was expecting, but she had a point. I offered her a small shrug.

She kept her eyes on me as if to make a point as her fingers roamed over the card backs. "Each of these cards symbolizes a different destiny. One of them shows Paradise, another shows War, and so on. Each may show hundreds of different pictures depending on who they are flipped for. If someone flipped War for me, it would show something completely different than War for you."

She must have noticed my skeptical look. One by one she flipped the tarot cards over, revealing their blank surfaces before returning them face-down.

"Choose," she said.

I tapped one at random. It felt more like wood, unnaturally smooth beneath my fingertip. She flipped the card to reveal an intricate painting.

It was pure white except for two figures etched in such perfect detail that I became certain that no human artist had created this deck. A golden dragon with three heads lay on its side, a splash of red around its neck. The other figure was much smaller, a silhouette in the shape of a man, shaded in a more yellow-tinged white reminiscent of bone. At the bottom was a sigil I vaguely recognized as one of the marks of the Goetia.

Sensi looked down in surprise, her lips parted. She considered it for a long while before I spoke up.

"And that means?"

She pushed the card until it was in front of me. "This card symbolizes the Goetia. Not surprising since we are in the presence of one of their Captains. In theory this card could reveal scenes linked to each of the Seventy-Seven, but we will never see some of them. Many of the Goetia never involve themselves in human affairs, so no one will ever see their depiction. This is a symbol of the Lord of the Void."

"Does that refer to one in particular?"

"Yes," she said, "which is what concerns me. Since the Captain is one of Astaroth's minions, I would expect to see the Lord of the Tome. He usually is seen in a library or standing against a background of writing. If I had flipped Morningstar, I would have burned this deck. His appearance means the end has come. Your card is more neutral, but I would hesitate to call this a good omen."

"So which one of the Goetia is he?"

Sensi looked around the room as if searching for an invisible presence. It reminded me of the last time I saw Augur, right before he asked me if I was conspiring with demons. "Paimon."

19

RECURSION (III)

"Paimon is one of the oldest and most clever of the Goetia," said Sensi. "He has three recorded appearances in the cards. This scene depicts him standing victorious over the last of the angels that protected this world. The white background symbolizes the moon. Though Paimon killed the last angel he is not considered an enemy of mankind. Some say he views himself as a sort of overseer of this world but, again, that is simply an attempt to make sense of him in our terms. By slaying the angel, he ensured that no more divine immortals would stand against the Goetia."

"So what does this have to do with me?" I asked. "You said that these cards change what they show based on the person they are being read for? I'm having trouble interpreting anything good out of this."

"I never promised you anything good."

"Why Paimon? Astaroth is responsible for all of this, right?"

Sensi tapped the card with one finger. "I also never promised that the reading would be completely accurate. Divination is widely considered a false science, but that is not always the case. Especially in a place like this, under the influence of karmic magic. If you have no real reason to suspect Paimon is involved, the simplest explanation is that it is a complete mistake. That would be best, since two demon lords being focused on this location does not bode well."

I bit the knuckle of my thumb. "Paimon is called the Lord of the Void? Brother Augur taught me a mental technique called the memory palace. When I made mine, there was a room inside that contained some sort of presence. When I opened the door there was nothing, just an emptiness and the sensation of being watched. I think you could call that a void."

"That was Paimon, then, watching you," Sensi crossed and uncrossed her legs. "He was observing you in the Mental Realm. As you have discovered, it is not a safe place for the likes of us. Our minds are weak and unguarded. There are beings like the Goetia that have mastered the landscapes of consciousness. To them it is only natural to dominate a lesser mind."

I had some idea what the Mental Realm was at this point. I was tempted to ask what she knew, but she started speaking again before I could. Philosophers do like to hear themselves talk.

"You said Brother Augur taught you a mental technique? I have never known him to take an apprentice or teach anyone in general. As a show of respect, he is allowed to stay within the Gardens despite not being involved at all. What is this memory palace? And why did he accept you?"

Her sudden interest in Augur caught me off guard—she thought that was more important than my revelation about Paimon? Should I reveal his methods to another philosopher? Sensi had been nothing but helpful so far. Augur had never told me to keep the technique a secret, and I had already tried to teach my friends without a second thought. Though calling Mara and Caedius my friends seemed like a cruel joke now.

I told Sensi the truth: that I did not know why Augur had expressed interest in me. I came with no recommendation and not a particularly grand first impression. The ease with which he accepted me struck me as generous from the little I knew about the process of becoming an acolyte. While there were no standardized tests involved in the selection of acolytes, full philosophers were considered among society's elite.

The only answer seemed to be that he could sense my power, though I did not tell her about that. If he knew, perhaps she did as well.

She seemed uninterested in that response, but her attention became apparent when I explained the principles behind the memory palace.

To my surprise she also did not appear as capable of visualization as myself. I spent the next fifteen minutes fumbling through an explanation of how to associate concepts with images to make memorization easy. I kept silent about the strange library in my room that recorded my knowledge. If similar things existed in her memory palace, she would discover them.

When I finished, Sensi thanked me. "Speaking to you was an excellent decision. I will have to explore this in my own time. I do not think this technique is dangerous as long as you keep your mind confined to the specific memory palace. Paimon could not intrude on you without an invitation. I wonder, do you happen to have any insight into the tesseract?"

"I've been thinking about what to call the time loop that restores everything to its original shape. Recursion, maybe? So the tesseract is related to time somehow." I thought of the network of silver threads composing the barrier. "It could even be made out of time itself, twisted in some way. I've heard about some occult branch of mathematics known as dimensionalism. Maybe it's related to that. I tried to read about it, but none of it made sense to me. Just pages of formulae."

"Your education is rather skewed," she said. "You have not learned many of the basic tenets of magic, but you have seen books on dimensionalism? That's a forbidden subject, since understanding it requires knowledge only the Goetia can bestow. Where would you learn such a thing?"

I read it in Lakken's library, but again I wondered how many secrets I should reveal. The philosophers clearly did not freely exchange knowledge among their peers. "I would rather not say."

She stared for several seconds before nodding. "There is one last thing it appears you are not aware of, though I am not certain how you could have reached this point without knowing. The philosopher sect of Odena is completely compromised. The entire city is riddled with so much demonic activity it is a miracle Vasely has not decimated the populace. Even he may be involved."

I heard what she said without registering it at first. "You said you're an Echo of one of the Archons. You still chose the Goetia's side?"

"I am an old woman." She ran a hand along her hairbun, which was a uniform black. "My limits were reached some time ago. I am wealthy beyond any real material needs. At this point, my life is an endless plateau. Giving up everything and starting a new life elsewhere is a waste of my energy. But the corruption is already so deep, why not cast my lots with the demons? The Goetia may grant wishes and powers to take me farther than I could otherwise go. I admit it, I am selfish. Are you not?"

"I have not made any deal with any of the Goetia, if that's what you're asking," I said.

"Then that means they are the ones pursuing you," she said. "Even if you are trapped here, that means you have some power to bargain. Do not give into temptation unless it is completely necessary. But in the end, if you can break everyone out of here, I would be entirely in your debt."

That seemed like another unwelcome burden. "Is Paimon able to do that?"

"His exact ranking in the demon hierarchy is unknown. Different sources say different things. But they all agree he is a frightening individual if he was able to slay the last angel. The void is a bizarre power, and a lot of what we know about it seems very contradictory." Sensi collected her cigarette holder from the table. "Now, if you don't mind, I would like to meditate on what you told me. I would invite you and your friend to stay, but maintaining this area becomes more difficult the more people that are here. I could afford to keep you, but I can't justify Felix."

"I'll stay with him, then," I said. "Can we at least remain here until he wakes up?"

"Of course," she said.

It took several hours for Felix to return to a lucid enough state that I felt comfortable going back outside. Sensi meditated in the lotus position, eyes closed. I did the same, mulling over what she had told me, unable to slip into a true meditative trance.

Her refusal to house us struck a nerve, but she promised that Amelie in Yellow was not any more dangerous than her suite. That seemed like a brazen lie, but I had no real claim to her home in the first place. Felix knew when he wasn't wanted and was happy to leave.

She did redeem herself in some small way by feeding us. The suite was not stocked with a grand feast, but the hearty meal of soft bread, cheese, cured meat, and olives was more than sufficient. The water was stale, but given the circumstances, even thinking about it seemed petulant.

When we indicated we were ready to leave, Sensi materialized the black door again. This time, I reached out with my fledgling awareness and could sense some faint fluctuations of power as she worked her magic.

Before we left, Sensi pulled me aside to say one last thing. She spoke too softly for Felix to overhear. "I may be mistaken, but I suspect even your father was involved in this. I assumed that is why Archon Nony killed him. This started before you were born, and somehow you came to be involved. Everything is connected."

"You knew I'm Jansen's son?" I asked, shouldering my pack.

Felix glanced over, curious about our soft conversation, but remained silent.

"I knew since the first moment I saw you," said Sensi. "You have his jaw and his eyes. If I needed any more confirmation, I saw the look on your face when you saw my fireplace. Velassan children are all scared of fire to some degree. They grow up with stories about how Archon Nony can peer through any flame to watch them. And, of course, I was deeply sorry to hear of your father's passing."

"Will you tell me about him?" I asked.

"He could be frightening sometimes. It was all in those eyes. But overall, he was a great man. One of those people who left a mark on everyone he touched. We were sad to see him go, especially when he joined the war on the Frontier. Whatever he saw there must have changed him, but even afterward he was still a very special person."

"Thank you," I said.

Then Felix and I headed back through the door.

Amelie in Yellow looked the same as before. People had switched positions, but they still wore the same dour expressions. The demon remained in the center of the room, though it had ceased its writing. It sat there with its eyes closed. Sleeping? Meditating?

Felix had remained silent most of the time in the suite, but now that we were out, he had some choice words about Sensi. I nodded along, not really paying attention.

"So what did the old hag tell you?" he asked.

Now would be the best time to reveal some of my powers to Felix. My time magic could be kept a secret for now, since it was useless within the tesseract. If everyone told the truth before it came to this point, perhaps this could have been avoided, but being the only honest person among liars would be a dangerous naivete.

"You know that memory palace technique I tried to teach you?" I asked. "Ever since I've been meddling with it, I've gained . . . I suppose you could call it magical senses. I can feel a barrier around us now. The borders of the tesseract. She explained a bit of how it works, the origin of magic and so on."

Felix nodded. "The anima."

I blinked in surprise. "You already know it, then."

"Of course." He slapped me on the arm. "You think I wouldn't look into how I'm so damned lucky? Should have just asked me in the first place. I knew there was more to you than you were letting on. Where do you think these powers are coming from?"

Hesitant at first, I explained Sensi's tarot reading and Paimon's apparent interest. Felix nodded along as if all of this was perfectly normal. Once the words were out, I felt better, though a voice in the back of my head cautioned that I was revealing too much. Revealing my time magic to anyone would remain a last resort.

"So did you figure out anything to help us get out of here?" asked Felix.

I placed a hand against the wall. "The more I focus on the barrier, the better I understand it. Maybe 'understand' is too strong a word for something so complex. But destroying something is always far simpler than creating it. Maybe we can find a way to disrupt it."

Closing my eyes, I reached out with my awareness. The cocoon of silver threads materialized in my mind's eye. That could not be exactly how the barrier looked; it was, after all, a mental image conjured by my mind to symbolize the energy I sensed. It was still a useful representation.

Again, I detected something coming from the Captain, but this time it seemed a little more detailed. A cage of silver threads surrounded the demon.

I looked closer, deeper. Hundreds of threads no wider than a hair connected the Captain with the boundary of the tesseract, congregating into a cage that was more a tangled knot of time energy.

Could the demon be a time magician as well? If Astaroth was capable of producing the tesseract, then he could make Echoes of Time. And in that case . . . was I one of them? Had my memories been altered so that I had forgotten making an oath with Astaroth? The thought of someone playing with my mind enraged me.

My anger sharpened my senses, allowing me to see a level deeper. The time knot did not originate from the demon. It came from the ivory sword piercing its chest. The Captain had its own gray swirl of energy that made Sensi's tremor of magic seem pitiful in comparison, but the sword's output utterly eclipsed it.

The weapon must be some sort of divine artifact. One of Astaroth's personal treasures? That meant it was the keystone of this barrier. The only problem was how useless that knowledge was. I would never get the sword out of the Captain's chest, and even if I did, could I even destroy such a powerful object?

I opened my eyes, ending the visualization.

"The tesseract is powered by that sword," I said.

He laughed bitterly. "Great. That's a hell of an ability. Too bad I can't visualize a thing."

I placed a hand on his shoulder and looked at him until he made sustained eye contact. "Well, I'm here, and I can do it. You can also do things I can't. You don't have to be able to do everything by yourself, Felix. Together we can figure this out and escape."

His face became very serious. "Yes, we can."

I had meant the words to be placating. But after saying them, I suspected they might actually be true.

The demon sat in the center of the room, its eyes still closed. That sword . . . something about it felt so familiar.

20
INTRUSION

I spent the next week plotting our escape.
While my thoughts wandered, I resumed my physical training: sparring with my friend, practicing bladeforms, improving my calisthenics. Felix seemed pleased with my progress with the legato since the last time we trained together. Not that I was able to lay a touch on him. Eight years of experience and honing himself surpassed being able to mimic particular postures.

Since the outcome was inevitable, there was no pride involved in our matches. This made the training invaluable. Felix used our matches to experiment with the way one pose segued into another, or how a certain arrangement was discordant against the flow. Being able to recognize this pleased me. Mimicking his steps felt awkward, but simply exercising helped keep me steady.

Curious and slightly predatory eyes watched us as we sparred. Everyone here had committed grave sins, though that did not make them unreasonable or needlessly violent. Surviving their pasts made them wary. From Felix's accounts, those who fancied themselves petty tyrants were culled early. Out of those remaining, no one was foolish enough to draw attention to themselves. Except for the two teenagers sparring with table legs, or at half-speed with steel blades, their exaggerated dancing almost ludicrous given the somber atmosphere.

I assumed most of the attention was for Felix, though a few passing strangers offered me nods of respect. I returned the gesture and memorized their faces. After a few days of watching us, some of the prisoners started exercising as well. Groups held their own mock battles. In a sense, we were demonstrating how strong we were, which seemed like a dangerous invitation. But at least it stirred something in those other lost souls.

The Captain paid no attention, absorbed in its writing. Every so often it threw its head back and giggled, disturbingly childlike. Otherwise, it kept to itself as much as any of the prisoners.

I focused on more than the legato. My awareness sharpened as I spent more time developing it. The mental fatigue was negligible as long as I merely observed. I began using it during my sparring matches with Felix, eyes open, focusing on integrating it with my other senses instead of having to blind myself to experience it. The threads of time energy everywhere sharpened the more I honed my ability. The other acolyte had his own little core of green energy centered around his forehead. Some of the prisoners had their own visual markers of power; I studied each of them as subtly as possible. All of this was little more than a distraction during our sparring sessions, but in a fight against someone like a Magister it would be an incalculable advantage.

All the information I had learned formed a tempest in my mind. I needed to focus on how to escape, but connections sprouted up between seemingly unrelated things, and as I explored them, I went down paths of thought that may have been profound or insane. I tried to involve Felix in my musings, but his entire life perspective seemed so different from mine that we could never understand each other on that sort of deeply personal level.

As such, my plans to escape did not amount to much. Discovering more about the tesseract remained at the forefront. The better I learned to sense it, the more obvious it became that nothing I could do would affect it in any measurable way. Felix joined me in throwing chairs with all our might against the barrier, though he confessed it no longer brought him much satisfaction. Particularly when they returned to their prior location the next day, identical down to the smallest surface marking.

I insisted the sword was the key. Every time, Felix asked me how I expected to get it, let alone use it. Great questions.

Every night ended the same way. Some drinks, becoming maudlin, making up ridiculous stories about other prisoners, and sleeping on the wooden floor, waiting for the same thing to occur the next day. It was no surprise this routine was driving people to insanity.

On the seventh day I stood in front of the mural that Lyra had painted on the second floor, arms crossed. I spent almost all of my time up here—the sick, mad, and dying on the beds downstairs made poor company—but I had been avoiding this particular area until now.

Felix was the one who convinced me to come here, saying it was ridiculous to avoid her painting as if that accomplished something. He had known her much longer than I had, after all, and he still enjoyed the bittersweet sight of her art.

The painting was of a golden skull with black runes along the border. The runes reminded me almost of the Goetia's sigils, though they had no obvious relationship. The sigils were circular and contained geometric shapes, while the runes were angular, individual scratchings that could have been inspired by any number of alphabets from around the world. But given the circumstances it seemed almost obvious.

Sensi had told me, after all. The entire city of Odena was corrupt.

"How long were you both involved with the Goetia?" I asked my friend.

He ran a hand through his hair, taking his time before responding. "She only started helping them within the past year. They would have never approached her if it wasn't for me. I warned her so many times. I don't know why she would agree, or what exactly she was doing for them."

I swallowed, my mouth dry after his confession. "And when did you join them?"

"I've heard demons ever since I was a kid. After my father damaged my soul or whatever nonsense the infirmary claimed. One spoke to me in my own voice, but in a way I would have never talked. So formal and educated, knowing things I couldn't. Which is the sort of thing an insane person would say, I know. I thought I was crazy, and so did my father. It made sense."

"Astaroth?"

"No. As far as I'm aware you would have to go to Desolada to speak with them. I personally have no way of reaching the moon. But something came to me and chose me. It told me to learn the sword, so when I saw Asalen, I followed its commands. When Avarus freed me, it told me to trust him, so I listened. Then that being came to the Gardens three years ago, not long after my fourteenth birthday."

"What was it?"

Felix stared at his hands. "It wasn't something you could really see. Almost like a shadow but less material. I could only see how it manipulated the world around it. Like a mirage. Maybe that's a better word for it. That night it revealed itself to many of us. I would prefer not to talk about what the demon said to me. But I didn't refuse it, and here we are."

"Do you know what this tesseract is?" I asked.

"No, not really. Only that it is some sort of test. It's not a tournament to see who is strongest. Not in a conventional sense, at least. After everything I have seen, my best guess is that they're trying to see who survives until the end. They don't care about the method."

I smothered a rising fury of emotions. This whole time, he had kept this a secret. But what right did I have to be angry at him? He had revealed much more about himself than I had volunteered in the past week.

He called me out on it perfectly. "You are awful at hiding how you feel. You could at least look ashamed about it. Take some of that anger out on me with your sword, if it makes you feel any better."

Something about the way he said it drained all my anger and disappointment. I exhaled deeply and drew my sword, an unspoken challenge between us. The way we had started probably a hundred other duels in the last week.

Felix drew his sword in response.

We whirled against each other at half-speed. An impractical way of fighting, but it allowed me to focus on the way my body moved. Though a hint of anger remained, the legato provided a welcome distraction. For a few minutes we sparred and all was well.

Then he nicked my forearm after a particularly abysmal parry. I paid no attention to the welling blood until the Captain began to giggle—a horrible, high-pitched sound that gathered strength the longer it went on. Face buried in its hand, shoulders wracking with laughter, the demon stood from the central table. Its mirth came to a crescendo as it approached us until, coming within arm's reach, it suddenly stopped. Its face turned serious, unblinking.

"You have spilled blood on sacred ground," it said. "It is my honor to serve as arbiter during this sacrifice."

Felix bowed, a gesture I would have never expected. "Our deepest apologies for the misunderstanding. We were merely practicing."

The demon giggled into its hand. "How absurd. Repeating a duel against a foe you should have ended a hundred bouts ago. Such a method fosters nothing but arrogance. Allow me to humble you."

A blur of motion, the Captain seized Felix by the throat with one hand and held him up like a child playing with a doll. It cocked its head to the side as my friend stared in defiance, refusing to make a sound as the pressure on his windpipe intensified. The demon was so tall that Felix's boots drifted near my shoulder.

"Do not waste my time with your pretend games," it said.

It flung him halfway across the second floor.

My friend knew how to take a tumble. He tucked himself into a ball and protected his head with his arms, angling his body to land in a roll against the ground. All this despite the chaos of flying through the air.

Unfortunately, the demon's casual toss sent him into a table. Wood cracked. Chairs flew everywhere.

The demon muttered to itself, staring at the hand it had used to throw Felix. Not sparing either of us a glance, the Captain returned to its table in the center of the room. I released a breath I hadn't realized I was holding and hurried after my friend.

He had managed to haul himself into a sitting position. Blood leaked from a wicked abrasion along his right arm. Thick splinters pierced his shirt in several places. From the dazed look on his face he must have hit his head, though maintaining consciousness was always a good sign. With the ease the Captain had thrown him around, if it had wanted to kill Felix it could have put him through the far wall.

The intent was clear enough. A reminder we were prisoners, completely at the mercy of its whims.

I could not stay here any longer. Not just for myself but for my friend as well. Whatever death found him here would not be merciful. Though perhaps death would be preferable to his mind slowly fracturing. It seemed a cruel fate, for a boy scared of being crazy to find his nightmares realized.

The demon returned to writing.

I knew what I had to do.

I sliced a clean tablecloth into strips with my sword and wound it around the abrasion. A large chunk of Felix's right forearm was a mass of raw flesh, not deep enough to expose fatty tissue but with enough surface area to ooze a concerning amount of blood. He could not keep quiet, a low groan escaping between clenched teeth.

My urging helped coax him to his feet. I supported him under one shoulder. He was so used to that position that his body stumbled through the motions semi-consciously. The walk to Sensi's wall was not far. Though no hint of it remained, in my mind's eye I could see the perfect outline of the black door in front of me. Feeling a bit ridiculous, I knocked.

The door materialized immediately.

Resigned to my fate, I walked inside.

"I hope you don't think the knocking worked," she said. "I have been watching this the whole time."

I had no interest in swapping banter. "Just as safe out there, is it?"

Felix bled next to me. His knees wobbled.

Sensi looked like she wanted to make a smart comment before reconsidering. She helped Felix onto the divan he had slept on before, looking far more motherly now that he wasn't in an opium daze.

"To answer your question, yes, actually," she said. "The Captain can come here as easily as any other place in Amelie in Yellow. My petty magic only stops other humans from intruding. Even then, there are people out there who could come in here if they truly wanted to press the issue."

"Well, you know why I'm here."

Sensi smiled. "I have waited all week for you to come to your senses. I should not complain, considering how long most of us have spent here already. Thank you."

I laughed. "You know, I used to be obsessed with the idea of the guessing game. Which Amelie is real. It seems like such a ridiculous thing to think about now. Is there a way to win?"

"Of course not," she said. "Anyone who can win the challenge has no need to do so. They already have my attention."

I shook my head. "Just teach me how to summon Paimon."

21

DESOLADA

Within Sensi's suite, I prepared to drink a tea made from mesfera leaves.

Mesfera was a potent hallucinogen, used in various spiritual tribes as a way of communion with the universe at large. As far as I knew, it was banned within the Civilized Lands, though plenty of forbidden treasures existed if one had the money and power.

"Opium is not enough to fully penetrate the barrier between the Physical and Mental Realms," she said. "Your mind may already know how to access the realm of thought, and perhaps you can even contact Paimon within your memory palace, but it would not be a true communion. All sentient creatures have a natural protection against mental manipulation from others. The hallucinogen will help overcome those barriers."

That did nothing to help my nerves. My hands shook as I grasped the cup. "Are you sure that's something I should be doing?"

"We have no good options," she said. "The Increate never intended for mortals to enter Desolada. This will facilitate your passage. If Paimon is truly watching you, he will guide you the rest of the way."

"And if he isn't?"

Her face remained blank. "Remember what you're experiencing does not really exist in a way that can harm your physical form. Mesfera lasts around six hours. Wait it out and keep your wits about you."

That sounded suspiciously like telling me to resist losing my mind.

Felix stirred from his divan, turning to look in our direction. He had mostly recovered over the past few hours, though I sympathized with his pounding migraine. At least Sensi had dosed him with laudanum before putting his dislocated shoulder back into place. On top of that he suffered from several cracked ribs. He would recover in time. The Captain had never meant to truly cripple one of his prisoners.

"You don't have to do this, Leones," he said.

The only other path led toward certain insanity and death. There was never any other choice to be made.

The mesfera tea was bitter enough to set my eyes watering. I finished it to the dregs. Sensi poured more water over it and forced me to finish it again. Cursed woman.

After a few minutes Felix rested his head back on a cushion. From his steady breathing he had gone back to sleep.

For the first half hour nothing happened. Sensi continued to drill me on behavior toward Paimon. Respect. Bravery. Though I was now the one approaching him, I still had the power to bargain in my own favor if I did not like the terms of his contract.

Finally, the world began to twist. For the first thirty seconds it was only a distortion before objects began shifting in place. Furniture walked about the room on wooden legs. The array of candles lighting the suite threw off streamers of brilliance; if I turned my head side to side, they left afterimages along my vision.

Sensi directed me to lay supine on an unoccupied divan, my hands crossed against my chest. I closed my eyes.

From the little I knew of hallucinogens I expected to venture through some brilliant universe of vague shapes and vivid colors. I was prepared to lose myself, or at least my sense of self. When I constructed my memory palace, it was more defined—more real—than ever. The sensation of the divan underneath my physical body faded until it barely existed. The mental realm consumed me.

I could feel the wooden floorboards under my feet as I stood in the foyer. The scent of cinnamon bread wafted through the halls. My lip quivered.

Remember why you're here, I told myself.

Through the corridors I strolled, head held high. I dragged the tips of my fingers along one of the walls; when I rubbed them together, I could feel the residue of dust left behind on my skin. How certain was Sensi that I could not truly be harmed here?

I paused in front of the door leading to my father's manor. Beyond that lay something I could never come back from. A death sentence anywhere within the Civilized Lands and not much different in human territories beyond the Frontier.

I opened the door, revealing the void beyond. I stepped through.

Blink.

A vast gray plain stretched out to infinity. Chunks of obsidian floated through the air; the ones near me were the size of fists. Beyond my immediate vicinity my perspective was warped. Depth in particular seemed wrong, as if I was a third-dimensional being captured within a two-dimensional painting. The sky was an endless sheet of white; the false-moon, a perfect black orb, looked more like a hole cut into the fabric of reality.

A figure materialized beside me. I did not turn to look at it. I felt its presence the way a child senses creatures in the dark. A bloodviolet star flickered to life in the sky and, like slowed lightning, spread in a geometric frenzy of lines.

"Another broken mortal finds his way."

It spoke into my mind, with my own voice. At first, I dismissed it as a strange thought, but there was a certain tenor beneath the words—something both impossibly deep and unfathomably empty. He spoke to me the way the Increate spoke to his oracles, burrowing into my consciousness.

Now that I was here, I had no idea what to say. Frozen, I stared at the spread of light across the sky.

"I know you," said Paimon in my head, "and I see you. Gaze upon me and bow not. I cannot abide men whose nature is to kneel."

By degrees I tilted my head until I saw him in the corner of my eye. He loomed beside me, shaped like a man but twice my height. I kept turning until I viewed him head-on.

He appeared to be carved from solid moonlight except for the vast crown of antlers sprouting from his head. His eyes were a pair of bloodviolet sparks. Looking at him I had the sense of great and unknowable depth, as if I were peering down through the surface of an ocean.

"Lord Paimon," I said. My tongue felt heavy in my mouth.

He touched his hands together and bowed his head over them. He had the long, graceful fingers of a master sculptor or musician. "The mortal pays his respects. I welcome you to Desolada. You have not come completely of your own volition. I sense your fear, your uncertainty. This aspect of Desolada does not please you. Be at ease."

The world around us flickered, changed. We were now in my father's study, the colors faded like an old, sunworn painting.

Paimon sat behind my father's desk, but the demon had enough sense not to steal his appearance. Instead, he looked more like the older brother that I had never had. This man must have been nearing thirty. Mother's light blue eyes and long eyelashes added a touch of softness to his face. He wore a military uniform centuries out of style, high-collared and stiff with starch.

"I extracted this vision from one of your dreams," he said in a voice quite similar to my own. At least he was no longer projecting thoughts into my head. "You must not mind this one—you have had it several times. All of your dreams are harsh and lonely, though you are fond of this one. It was only natural you fashioned your memory palace in this likeness."

So much information there, much of it concerning. *Extracted* from one of my dreams, as if my thoughts were some ore to be mined. Did he know everything I thought, everything I felt?

"You understand the situation I am in?" I asked, choosing for now to ignore the implications of Paimon's words.

"In much greater detail than yourself. Astaroth has trapped many of you within a tesseract. It is a four-dimensional construct, encompassing time as well as your physical reality. There is a level of complexity to this that makes it impossible to translate into your understanding. In most circumstances, mortals like yourself would be helpless against a construct by one as powerful as Astaroth. Fortunately, this power is similar to your own, and Astaroth possesses only a tangential understanding of time."

Eyes closed, I took my time absorbing the demon lord's words. "Which means I can escape."

"Even with a thousand years of meditation you would never unravel the tesseract alone." Paimon clasped his hands on the desk and leaned forward. "I have long watched your world. I know the songs of its winds, the eddies of its oceans. The fates of its people are no greater mystery. Nothing happens in this universe that has not happened before. Astaroth knows this. I know this."

"I am not sure I understand," I said.

"Let me speak plainly, then. Astaroth has constructed this tesseract for a particular reason. He is searching for new Echoes to carry out his will. He lures all of his prospects into this tesseract and, when they have all converged, reveals parts of his design. It is a bloody and brutal war that he makes mortals wage amongst themselves. Only one of you will emerge from this tesseract, broken and empty, enslaved to his will. You understand this much?"

I took a deep breath. "So I would have to defeat Felix. Sensi. Everyone else there, until there is only one of us left?"

"Every person there is meant to be there," said Paimon. "Most remain unaware of the particulars, though some came of their own accord. Sensi welcomed Astaroth and his Captain into her establishment. She knew I would tell you this, but she only now realizes the consequences of her actions. I lend her no assistance, but you—you lost little rose—I would welcome you into my garden."

"I would be your Echo," I said. "Not Astaroth's."

Paimon clapped his hands together. A simple gesture, but its vibrations coursed through my soul. "Astaroth does not realize your potential. You must be cultivated. Clipped, where necessary. Your thorns, I hope, will cut deep."

"There are many stories about deals with the demon lords," I said, looking back at him. "None of them end well."

Paimon spread his arms. "They do not tell those stories to little children. In the heart of the Civilized Lands, you live in a safety that few could ever imagine. Savra is a beautiful and terrible world, full of dreams and blood. It has birthed many desperate souls, and many of them seek out the Goetia. That tragedy befalls them is the natural course of the desperate. I accept no responsibility for their fate."

"Is that the secret of the powerful? You decide whether or not to accept responsibility?"

The colors around us seemed to brighten when Paimon laughed. "You act as if I am obliged to shackle myself with your human ethics. The tribunes of your world decree that I must be charged with foul misdeeds. I whisper lies, but against what truth? Others serve me and are rewarded so. For these sins you may imprison me, but I warn you: not even the Increate has devised a dungeon so worthy, lest the cosmos itself is my prison."

We locked eyes for what felt like a long time, though it felt different to staring at another person. There is a certain electricity to maintaining eye contact, whether it's with a lover across the table or an opponent facing you in the dueling circle. Here there was nothing. The figure behind the desk was little more than a puppet, and I imagined Paimon far above this scene, manipulating the strings.

He blinked and the spell ended. "You have a profound issue with authority. You seem to think there is a fault in your teachers, but instead they are sensing this fault in you. As your master I would correct this flaw. Much of what you have been taught is mistaken or altogether wrong; because of this, you are hesitant to trust others. Even that woman Sensi speaks drivel. Revealing myself upon her false tarot cards brought me much pleasure. I will reveal the truth to you, as evil as it may be. If you have no desire to accept my offer, leave, for now. We shall meet again in due time."

I spoke through gritted teeth. "And what is your offer, exactly?"

He smiled. "You and your friend Felix are rarities amongst mortals. Few humans develop power over abstract concepts like time and luck. Likewise, I am somewhat of a rarity amongst the Goetia." He ran his fingers along the desk. The wood disappeared beneath his touch, erased from existence. "I am nullification. The Lord of the Void. This power is the antithesis of the Increate, who embodies infinity. It is nothingness. Zero."

"You offer me nothing," I said.

Paimon stood, stretched his hand toward me. "And you would be wise to accept it. For now, I can only offer you a rudimentary understanding of nullification. Enough to counteract the abilities of others around you and, if you prove worthy, unravel the tesseract. Savra is a world of many dangers. It would not do for my Echo to have no aegis."

"And what do I have to offer you in return?"

"Your loyalty," said the demon lord. "Other than that, we shall discuss the terms of our contract as we go along. If, in the end, you are dissatisfied with the power I will bestow upon you, we may discuss some alterations. Once you begin to understand the extent of my gift, you will have no reason to complain."

I felt as if I stood on the edge, looking down into the abyss. My decision here would shape the rest of my life. This was what the Goetia did: they backed people into corners and turned them into traitors. Yet demons were not the ones who had slaughtered the people closest to me.

There was a very real possibility that Paimon and Astaroth had orchestrated everything. They were brothers of a sort and, though collaboration among the Goetia was rare, it was not unheard of. But even without the threat of the tesseract I still would have considered the offer.

Ever since I first heard of Echoes, I had thought of seeking out the Goetia. The thought slipped into my mind while I lay in bed at night, staring at the ceiling, worrying at the thought like a sore in my mouth.

"I accept."

Paimon nodded slowly. "Take my hand, then, and I will show you the path."

And without a further thought I did.

The void is clarity. It is simplicity itself. All matter is an intrusion on the natural state of the universe. Even energy leaves its mark. The void is what the blind man sees, what the deaf man hears. Strangely, nothingness is a thing-in-itself: the absence of a loved one gouges a wound, and our wounds are emptiness that has left its mark. The man born blind has no concept of sight. The man who becomes blind knows exactly what he has lost.

There is an interconnectedness between all things, brushstrokes on a canvas that come together to form an image, and even the negative space contributes to the whole.

This is what Paimon showed me when I took his hand, in a moment that lasted forever and no time at all.

22

UNRAVEL

It took what felt like an entire day to recover from the after-effects of the mesfera. For a long time, I watched shadows dance along the ceiling. The tallow candles burned impossibly large, gleaming with all the colors of the rainbow. I tried to sleep it off, but in the darkness, I hallucinated monsters covered in accusatory eyes.

After several hours the sensation returned to my face. I cried with relief when Sensi wrung a wet cloth onto my lips. The dryness in my mouth was a greater torture than anything I had ever experienced. Eventually I could wiggle my fingers and toes; once that hint of movement returned, the rest followed shortly after. I sat on the floor, chin resting on my knees, focused on the candle-flames.

Sensi said nothing that whole time. Or at least I heard nothing. It had been a long, long time since anyone had treated me with such gentleness. I thought of my mother—maybe dead, maybe alive. I preferred not to know, letting her exist in that state somewhere between worlds.

Full consciousness returned by degrees. The first thing I said to her was, "Never again."

She nodded. "Did it work?"

"I know everything."

She nodded again, silent. She was part of Astaroth's plan and had been able to allow demons to infiltrate her establishment. Even with Paimon's power there was nothing I could do about it. He said I could nullify the powers of others, but even if I took away her control of shadows, she could probably still kick me around.

I was the first to speak again. "I may be able to unravel the tesseract. Paimon seems to think so. Not while I'm like this, though."

"Take your time," she said. "Mesfera is particularly unforgiving to beginners. There are more mild hallucinogens, but I have developed too much of a tolerance to keep them stashed away here."

"I think I may be able to do without them in the future." I stood, bracing myself against the wall. The world spun.

"When you are recovered, we shall try to make our escape. Increate bless us."

"Where is Felix?" I asked.

She offered her best smile. "He insisted on staying to watch over you, but given his condition, he could not stand vigil the entire time. I let him sleep in one of the bedrooms. They've been occupied by some of my girls, but one was generous enough to let him stay in her bed for the time being. She, of course, doubled up with one of the others."

We spent the next hour in silence, lost in our respective thoughts. She meditated on the floor, shadows swirling about her like fish in a pond. Finally, my body returned to normal, and the fog in my head disappeared. I emptied my mind, reflecting on what little I had retained of the void. It had all made sense when Paimon had grabbed my hand. Now it felt like a half-remembered dream.

That was enough.

The tesseract blocked my control over time, but it held no power over the void. I extended my hand and squeezed it into a fist. The void begged to rush out, a wave of nothingness. Releasing this power felt like it would be effortless. Rather than channeling my own innate power, I was only the conduit for a being who made me look like an insect.

I reined the void back in, unwilling to reveal the power yet. While experimenting with its capabilities would grant us a greater chance of survival, if the Captain sensed something amiss, we were not prepared for its attention.

Now that I could think properly, we planned.

"The most obvious course of action is to go to the first floor and break through the barrier," said Sensi. "Once we do that, hopefully we'll have an exit into the real world. Fortunately for us, Vasely is the Archon of Sound. If we scream the instant we emerge, he should come to our rescue quickly. There is still a limit to how fast he can travel, and the Captain will not be pleased. We'll have a few seconds at most."

"Do we tell the others?" I asked. "They should help if they know there's a chance to escape."

"No," said Sensi. "The Amelies will come with us. The others are not our allies. The Captain is not the only minion of Astaroth's here. Some are already loyal to him, here to ensure nothing interferes with their master's design."

"Are you sure the Captain can't hear us planning all of this?" I asked.

"If so, we never had a chance in the first place. If we act like we have lost before even trying, the outcome will be inevitable. We wait until you and Felix are able to travel quickly. Then we make it out of here. Another day or two should not make a difference."

"No," I said. "Paimon told me the purpose of the tesseract. A challenge to see who remains at the end. The survivor becomes an Echo of Astaroth. Was that your plan this whole time?"

Sensi stood from her meditative position and stalked my way. "If I wanted to kill you, I would have done it while you were under the mesfera trance. Likewise, I could have finished Felix at any point. I was mistaken to allow this to happen. When we make it out of here, ask anyone who knows me if they have ever heard me admit to weakness. Well, I will admit it now. I am weak. The fate for everyone here is unspeakably cruel. So, yes, I want you to save us, even if this is karma being repaid."

I snorted but said nothing. She ruffled my hair.

Condescending, but I did kind of enjoy it.

Time to let the others know. Sensi knocked on each of the closed doors in a specific pattern. Three Amelies emerged, two from their shared room. Even without their masks I recognized them. Dragon-Amelie, with her tanned skin and long, dark braid. Fox-Amelie with her auburn hair and smattering of freckles. The third was the girl I had seen when I first entered the tesseract. Short brown hair and a sad face. Somewhere in her early twenties, a couple of years younger than the others. Without their masks they looked like any pretty girl one might see at the markets.

When Sensi knocked on Felix's door, I was relieved to see my friend look well. The color had returned to his face, even if he held his bandaged arm stiffly.

We explained the plan to the others. They listened without comment. None of them knew about my power over time, but I had declared myself as an Echo of Paimon. An enemy to mankind. It was a bold declaration even if they had no room to judge.

"Should we wait until Felix has recovered?" asked the Dragon-Amelie, taking all of this remarkably in her stride. If I had to guess, she was the real one.

I reached my magical awareness out toward the women. Nothing, from what I could tell.

"No," said Felix. "I can fight well enough with my left hand. Even if I was at my best, nothing I do will matter against the Captain. The goal is to make it out of here and pray for the Archon to save us."

"We do it now, then," said Sensi.

I nodded in agreement.

There was nothing more to be done. As vague as our plan was, obsessing over details beyond our control would waste time.

We took a few minutes to steady our resolve. Felix and I checked our blades for the hundredth time. Fox-Amelie balanced a long knife on one hand before returning it to the scabbard strapped to her thigh. Her yellow dress shifted back into place, concealing the weapon. Dragon-Amelie clenched and unclenched her fists. Sad-Amelie kept her eyes on the floor, nodding to herself to muster some semblance of courage. Sensi remained poised like a queen, shadows lapping at her feet.

If I failed, all of us were dead. At least it would not be a prolonged suffering.

"Ready?" asked Sensi.

Everyone made some sound of acknowledgement.

The black door materialized.

I stepped out first, the others trailing behind.

The Captain remained at the table in the center of the room, head bent over as it worked on another of its endless letters. Nearby prisoners took notice of our appearance, sullen eyes lingering on our weapons and the young women.

I walked so quickly I may as well have just sprinted. Eyes focused ahead, I spread my awareness through the room. Nothing from the Captain, but two different figures started to head in our direction as we approached the stairs. Not time to draw my sword. Not yet.

I thought we had escaped the area unhampered until we reached the stairway. Someone cleared their throat behind us. A hard-looking man with a scar bisecting his left eye, hand on the hilt of the sword at his side.

"Heading somewhere?"

None of us responded. Pretending to not have heard, Sensi descended the stairs. The man followed, ignoring the rest of us, baring a few inches of steel. Halfway down Sensi turned and lashed out, grabbing him by the head and smashing it into the wall once, twice, until the swordsman crumpled to the stairs, unconscious. A trickle of blood leaked out of his ear.

Shouts from the other prisoners.

"Quickly," said Sensi.

We rushed after her.

Some of the mad and sick lounged on the beds on the first floor, watching the violence unfold. We ignored them and continued on until reaching the barrier in front of the door. The Amelies spread out like some sort of shield.

"Let's see it, Leones," said Felix. He faced the stairs, sword drawn in his left hand.

Time to go. My heart raced in my chest. Slow breaths, clear mind.

"Remember your father," Sensi whispered.

Yes, I remembered him. How could I not? How many times had I dreamed about the day he died? Everything that had happened to me sprouted from that moment. I stopped trying to clear my mind and instead focused on that knot of rage throbbing in my heart. Fuck clarity. I will be great.

I stretched my hand out until it collided with the barrier. In my mind's eye, interconnected threads of silver energy trembled against my touch. The power of nullification pulsed out. It was easy, remarkably easy, to access this reflection of Paimon's power. The void and my anger mixed into something new and assaulted the barrier. The invisible force of the prison trembled beneath my hand. Trembled but did not give.

"Oh," I said.

The Captain appeared at the top of the stairs, head cocked to the side. Black lips stretched into a wicked grin. It descended the stairs with a practiced grace, like a lady making her entrance at a ball.

The swordsman stirred as the demon walked past. Without a glance it stamped on his head. Flecks of red and gray sprayed across the walls and the demon's robes.

"Try again." The calm in Sensi's voice stilled some of my rising panic. With confidence she strolled forward, a pair of throwing knives slipping from her sleeves. One thudded into the demon's neck, the other into its left eye. Ichor leaked from the demon's wounds as it continued its descent. Its long tongue lapped up the blue trailing along its cheek.

Focus. The threads of time energy around my hand had dimmed but remained intact. Summoning most of my remaining void magic, I tried once more. Another burst of nullification slammed into the barrier with even less effect than the first.

We had made a terrible mistake.

Shadow flared around Sensi like dark flames. "Huntress, grant me your—"

As she spoke, the Captain reached the last step then sped forward, crossing over twenty feet in an instant. I felt the impact of their collision more than I saw it, a blur of speed followed by a thunderclap.

Dark energy met pure force. Pure force won. Sensi shot through the air, arms flailing with a sickening wrongness, as if the impact had shattered every bone. Her trajectory carried her into the barrier, close enough for her blood to speckle my face and clothing.

I reached for her. With a snarl she snapped her teeth at me. Only the barrier and willpower kept her on her feet, slumped, arms dangling. Blood stained her mouth, ran thick down misshapen limbs; spurs of bone peeked through her forearms. Her face revealed no pain, only rage.

"Live," she said in a voice so weak I may have imagined it.

Shadows swirled at the Captain's feet. The demon glanced at them, back to Sensi, and clapped in admiration. Expression blank, it stood in place while great fingers of shadow emerged from the floorboards. Like a fist clenching they wrapped up and over the Captain, expanding until a perfect sphere encircled the demon.

Nothing happened for several seconds. Strength fled Sensi's body, and she collapsed onto her knees. Her chin wavered, eyes drooping. Blood trickled from the corner of her mouth. She shook her head in defiance, clarity returning to her eyes.

Five seconds. Six.

The sphere of shadow rotated, slowly at first, gaining momentum until it picked up a physical wind. Gray energy leaked through fractures in the prison; they widened as the sphere gathered speed, until sections of the Captain became visible. The demon grinned, head tilted to the side, as the sphere dissolved into black ribbons around it.

Sensi muttered under her breath. The swaths of shadow energy began to reform, clutching.

Laughing, the Captain dashed forward. Its hand lashed out and skewered her though the chest. The demon looked into her eyes as the life gasped out of her. Her hands looked ridiculously tiny as she wrapped them around the demon's arm. A wave of shadow crashed into the Captain; its purple robes billowed, but it looked otherwise untouched.

"Clever," it said. "Astaroth could have made use of you after all. A pocket realm containing a psychic assault. Very talented for a mortal, but such illusions would not pass muster in Desolada. Be proud of what you accomplished in such a short life."

With a flourish of its arm the Captain tossed Sensi's body across the room. The Amelies cried out as their mistress crumpled against the far wall. A random madman's scream was abruptly cut off as someone covered his mouth.

I watched, frozen, as the demon advanced on Felix and swiped at him with one hand. Lucky as always, he managed to parry the blow with his blade. The impact threw him off his feet and slammed him into the barrier.

"I smell Paimon's taint upon you." The Captain's sinuous tongue licked the blood from its hand. "He has no power here."

Here came death. I had become too reliant on my control over time to overcome any adversity. Without it I was nothing more than an overconfident boy. Paimon had not claimed the power he granted me would overcome the tesseract with certainty. We made our attempt too soon. The Amelies held their ground in front of me, though they would be dead in moments.

The ivory sword impaled through the Captain's heart. The keystone that held the tesseract together.

Hope blossomed in my chest.

I saw the strands of time that converged on that sword, the impossible knot they formed.

"Run," I told the Amelies.

They obeyed without a second thought, rushing as far from the demon as they could.

Once more I reached for the void and found it eager, willing. Nullification magic spread across my hands.

The demon flickered forward and, before I knew what was happening, wrapped its hand around my head. It squeezed, increasing the pressure until I was sure my skull would implode. The scent of rot choked me. Crushing, impossible strength.

I fumbled blindly for the ivory sword. Thick fabric, flesh like stone. Something solid. A handle. I wrapped my other hand around it. Nullification magic rushed into the sword.

It emitted a sound like a bell chiming.

In my mind's eye those threads of time unraveled, infuriatingly slow, as the demon's hand sank into my skull. Its claws drew forth trickles of blood.

Do not unravel the knot. Cut through it.

Yelling, I released all of the remaining nullification power I could muster. Through my hand, into the sword.

White light flared from the ivory blade, a short-lived supernova that dimmed to nothingness.

The Captain released my head.

"What have you done?" it squealed.

I stumbled back, expecting to hit the barrier, instead passing through empty space. Blood coursed from my head where the demon's fingernails had penetrated deep. The Captain roared, a sound of terror and remorse that reverberated through the room.

"I have failed, I have failed, I have failed." The Captain shook its head like a dog. "Oh, the Lord will punish me. He will punish me. There is one hope to escape him. Only Morningstar may reach through the Gate of Death and bring me back." It stopped shaking. "Oh, you have triumphed today, child of Paimon. But the game is endless and so are the players. Remember that."

I won't forget, I thought.

The Captain examined its claws, giggled, and skewered itself through the head in an explosion of gore. The demon sank to its knees. Its chest heaved in what must have been a silent laugh until it stopped completely.

People emerged from their hiding spots. Even the mad ones ventured forward. A half-dozen men and women gathered around the demon, maintaining a healthy distance. The Amelies held each other tightly.

Everyone was looking at where I sat, beyond the perimeter of the timeless loop.

23

FREEDOM

Shouts rang out through the first floor when the prisoners discovered their freedom. First came the Amelies, hurrying past without a word of thanks. One remained: Dragon-Mask. She cradled Sensi's body against her lap. Tears dripped down her face. Something about that scene broke through the numbness, but as callous as it was, I had no time for sympathy.

Some of the madmen and the few people who volunteered as their caregivers followed. One lunatic screamed in exultation, arms raised to the sky as he burst out into the morning sunlight. Captives from the second floor crowded the stairs, pointing as they discovered the cause of the commotion.

The sensation of time magic in the back of my mind felt like an old friend, back after a long journey. My reserves had fully recovered after a week inside of the tesseract. Beside it, the power of the void yearned to be used again.

The tesseract had limited my power to almost nothing. I had been able to sense the knot of time and unravel it, but I suspected that had more to do with the sword than me. I reversed time for a few seconds as a small experiment. A success, though it felt strange, like walking again after several days of bedrest.

Prisoners flooded into the first floor. I avoided them as I made my way toward Felix. He sat on the ground, good leg pulled up to his chest.

A sliver of steel as long as a finger protruded from his left thigh. In all of the chaos I had not realized his sword had shattered when he used it to deflect the Captain's blow. The bleeding did not look serious, but my friend was beginning to run out of functional limbs. From the dazed look in his eyes, he was blinking off another concussion, but at least he was conscious.

"I'm going to get us out of here," I said.

Felix grunted and touched the piece of broken sword in his leg. "Yeah?"

Without another word I used my power to return backward in five second increments. No matter how many times I practiced, these rapid reversals left me disoriented; my mind struggled to adjust to my new temporal reality for a split second before moving on to the next.

Usually, I would have enough confidence in my internal clock to reverse back to the moment I wanted; this time I wanted no room for error. While there was not much information readily available on the subject, I suspected the paradox of my power returning me back to my powerless self inside a time-distorting dimensional construct would end poorly.

I returned to the moment when I first stepped outside the fallen barrier. A small chuckle escaped my lips, a touch madder than I'd expected. This time I fled Amelie in Yellow as soon as possible. That first breath of fresh air when I emerged into the sunlight was like nothing I had ever experienced. Cool and refreshing. It felt warmer than it had in months, though the occasional snowflake still drifted past.

It felt like a bittersweet freedom while Sensi's body cooled behind me.

I slipped to the side, making room for the escaping prisoners to flee. They ran in all directions, like ants after someone had stepped on their colony. I took almost no notice of them, though in retrospect I should have minded who looked relieved and who glared about as if something precious had been stolen from their grasp.

Instead of following, I hid behind an adjacent building, peeking over the side of the wall to observe from a distance. Archon Vasely did not come as I expected. Over time I had grown so used to the soft melody of the Archon meditating that my mind no longer registered it. Now that I focused, I could find no trace. If he was not lost in meditation or coming personally to investigate, what was he doing?

After a minute and thirty-eight seconds, a spot cut through the sky, growing as it approached until I could make out the figure of a flying man. His speed must have been incredible; he crossed the city from the Archon's palace in less than a minute. When he came to a stop, hovering over Amelie in Yellow, his tanned skin and shaved head identified him as Barrow. A long golden spear dangled from his hand.

My magical awareness revealed an aura of wind lashing about him. Spreading his power throughout his body must have enabled him to fly. Diffuse as it was, I could not gauge his exact strength. Less than the Captain, more than a match for Sensi.

He descended until he floated over the heads of the gathered survivors, raising eddies of snow from the cobblestones. "The Archon bid me to come here immediately. He heard a rogue demon speaking forbidden words. Tell me, quickly, what has occurred."

No one spoke. Blood trickled down my face. I moved to wipe it away, stopped. What if he could sense movement?

The winds grew stronger, throwing my hair in a frenzy. Invisible currents lifted a nearby man into the air until he floated next to Barrow's slippers.

"You," said the North Wind. "Where is this demon? Are you aiding it?"

The man stared at the ground ten feet below, mouth gaping. He gathered his courage and said, "All of us were trapped within that place, Amelie in Yellow. It was like one endless day. It's over now. The demon is dead, I think. In there."

Barrow descended to the ground, landing lightly. The man drifted behind him, eyes squeezed shut, and collapsed when he touched the ground.

"Nobody leave." The North Wind strolled through the open door, spear balanced against his shoulder.

Such confidence. He walked right in there with his head held high, as if he already had some idea of what awaited him. A magical sense, or was he corrupted as well? His minion Jokul had stabbed me when I hinted at the possibility.

The Champion had failed to end my life, but he was just a man. Barrow could wipe out a legion of soldiers with a thought. Though my borrowed power to nullify magic might have theoretically countered him, escaping the tesseract had not been as simple as erasing any magic

I desired. Part of me expected the power of a demon lord to overwhelm anything it encountered, but it was still filtered through a mortal who had not quite reached seventeen.

The idea of Barrow strolling in there while Felix bled in some corner made me dig my fingernails into my palms. The urge to check on my friend was hard to resist, but I needed to gather as much information as possible. If Jokul had acted independently then perhaps Barrow was an ally. As unlikely as it was, he might at least be willing to fly Felix to the closest healer.

Arms crossed, I waited another thirty seconds until Barrow's reinforcements arrived. A platoon of soldiers marched in from all directions, apprehending the stragglers trying to make their escape. Felix and I should have plenty of time to escape before their arrival.

I prepared to reverse time. Then she arrived.

A flurry of snow billowed outwards as a figure appeared in the center of the guards. A Narahven woman in loose black clothing, her hair pulled back in close braids. With confidence she strolled toward the lieutenant of the platoon. The cobblestones appeared to ripple with each step of her boots.

Too far for me to overhear their conversation. The Narahven, who must have been the female Wind, gestured in several directions. Guards hurried to obey, weapons at the ready.

When they returned, they carried limp bodies over their shoulders like sacks of grain. As far as I could tell, the prisoners were alive and intact. When the guards deposited them on the ground in an untidy row, their bodies did not so much as twitch at the rough handling.

Could the Narahven have killed all of them in a way that did not show? Unconscious people usually did not stay unconscious long unless they had sustained significant head trauma. Minutes passed and still none of them moved. The guards continued to bring more and more bodies—less than the total number of escaped prisoners but not by much. No sign of the Amelies.

I could not afford to spend too much time here. Get to the other side of the Civilized Lands, then start thinking. Maybe go beyond. Paimon may even control some small territory within a reasonable distance. Becoming the Echo of one of the Goetia had to have some benefits.

Deciding to make the most of the situation, I snuck toward the Narahven and the lieutenant. A guard noticed and shouted a warning long before I came within earshot. Not worth the risk of trying again; the next person who spotted me might put a bolt through my head.

I reversed time, again careful to bring myself close to the initial moment of freedom without returning to the tesseract.

This time I returned immediately to Felix and, ignoring his complaints, helped him to his feet. Between the injured right arm and left leg there was no good side to support.

"You're an absolute bastard," said Felix.

"Would you rather lie there and die?"

He kept silent. Most of his weight rested on me as we hobbled toward the door together. As we passed by the Captain's body I noticed the sword protruding from its chest.

"Support yourself against that table for a minute," I said.

Felix grumbled but listened. He was in no shape to argue.

The Captain had fallen onto its side, hand impaled through its head. The demon seemed even more bizarre in death. A halo of blue ichor painted the floorboards around it. The ivory sword jutted from its chest. I shoved a boot against the demon's shoulder, intending to push it onto its back, but it must have weighed more than a horse.

I gave up and knelt beside the demon. No movement. A voice in the back of my head yelled to run. Ignoring it, I planted a boot on the corpse and wrapped my hands around the sword handle. Heaving with all my strength accomplished nothing. Its edge was dull and caught in the demon's ribcage. I worked it up and down, freeing it by degrees until it finally tore loose. Precious time wasted, but no doubt it would be worth it.

The weapon possessed no innate power. Perhaps the nullification had destroyed its magical properties. A shame, but it would still have its uses. I wrapped Felix's left arm around my shoulder, and we set off, the weapon dangling awkwardly in my hand. If we encountered Barrow or the female Wind, I would have to reverse time and leave the sword. Every second mattered.

Random passersby avoided us as we hobbled past. They seemed keen to leave in general, which was understandable, given the crowd of people fleeing in all directions. I was all too happy not to talk to any strangers with more curiosity than sense.

After five minutes we managed to put a surprising amount of distance between us and Amelie in Yellow. I expected the woman to find us at any second. Her powers seemed terrifying, even compared to Barrow's mastery over flying. She could appear out of nowhere, as if she transformed herself into the wind. Not to mention how she had managed to immobilize most of the prisoners. If she found us, we had no chance against her in our current state. Maybe in any state.

No point worrying. If she was going to capture us, she would have done it by now; if everything was going as it had before, she would be speaking with the lieutenant right now. In the end, the woman didn't find me.

Barrow did.

The North Wind streaked out of the sky before coming to a sudden halt twenty feet in front of us. "Leones. I did not realize you were part of this. I sensed your presence in the area, though you feel different than before."

A warm and stupid glow built up in my chest. Maybe there was a way out of here if Barrow wasn't involved. Not many people had witnessed the actual confrontation between me and the Captain.

"Well," he said. "I should have listened to Jokul. He told me to kill you before you ever left my home. At the time it felt like a senseless murder. I regret not heeding his warning. There is a wrongness to you, but you are not one of Astaroth's. I have no obligation to keep you alive. Not to mention you are holding the keystone of the tesseract. How curious."

The hope died as quickly as it came. I looked down at the weapon in my hand, still stained with the demon's ichor. "You know about the tesseract?"

"It is only one of several within the city. Escape should have been impossible. You will come with me and explain."

Felix slumped into me as he gave up hope. His voice was strained. "Bastard."

Barrow leveled his spear in my direction. The beginnings of a tempest stirred to life at the point of its blade. Presumptuous of him to think I would actually fight.

I reversed time to around ten seconds before his sudden arrival. Head tilted upward, I could just make out a figure high in the air. From his vantage the North Wind would be able to see half the city, but I knew, despite the hundreds of feet separating us, he was looking right back at me.

"Barrow is coming to kill us," I said to Felix. "I'll take care of him. Lean against that wall."

Taking a few steps back, I summoned the power of the void and pointed at the sky. The figure of the North Wind plummeted downward like a meteor, confident in his dramatic entrance.

A wave of nullification rippled outwards. And missed. My body felt heavy, lethargic, as if all my will had been drained. Terrified energy had powered all of my actions since the tesseract fell. Using the power of the void once more caused a different type of fatigue than the piercing migraines from overusing my time magic. Both were equally annoying.

I had at most two more tries before my body was in worse shape than Felix's.

I reversed time and tried again.

"Help me, Paimon," I muttered.

Maybe it worked, maybe it didn't. The nullification magic struck Barrow as he plummeted downward like a falcon on the hunt. His limbs flailed as control abandoned him. Desperate, he pointed his spear at the fast-approaching earth.

The impact disintegrated him into a fine pink mist.

The air whistled, and something stung my right cheek. When I reached up to touch it, blood came away. What must have been a piece of bone had left a thin laceration behind as it flitted past. My hand trembled.

Felix shouted.

Nothing recognizably human remained once the mist settled. Only a disgusting mess and a wide expanse of fractured cobblestones.

Bile rose in the back of my throat.

Most of the city saw Barrow as a hero. Caedius spoke of him in awe. A noble, divine warrior. A protector of mankind. Killing him felt different from the Magister. Though the Magistrate was respected back home, in Odena the North Wind was revered.

His death was only temporary if I wished to reverse time. Murdering the child of an Archon would have disastrous consequences. There was no place I would be free to walk the streets without fear. But he had tried to kill me and had ended up dead.

That is karma.

24

ZEPHYR

"We need to get out of here," I said to Felix. Never before had I seen a look of such disbelief on his face. He looked back and forth between me and the site of Barrow's impact. "You killed the Archon's son."

If only we had the time to think, I would have considered the situation more. Perhaps reversing the North Wind's death was the best action. What I had done to another human was horrible. Killing the Magister and his guards felt like justice. Something about the way I had ended Barrow felt different.

How much pity could I have for someone who intended to kill me? I was a loose end that Jokul had wanted dead from the beginning. Leaving Barrow alive kept an enemy at my back who knew far more about me than I wanted. There was no evidence I was the one to kill Barrow. Jokul might suspect my involvement, but who would believe some teenage acolyte had killed a half-divine being?

No, it was best if Barrow stayed dead. If I reversed time and regretted it, there was no guarantee I would get another lucky shot on him. He was just one more addition to all the corpses dropping around me.

"Yes," I said. "I killed him."

My friend remained silent. Keeping the ivory sword in my offhand, I passed my Bakkel to Felix. He used it as a crutch, and we set off as fast as we could together. No use in trying to mask the site of

Barrow's death. Traces of gore had spread far. Our priority was to leave the area.

After a minute of limping, Felix spoke up. "I'm glad you killed Barrow. We were nothing but an inconvenience to him. No one would have noticed if we disappeared."

I grunted in agreement.

"Where are we going?" he asked.

"My safehouse," I said. "We'll get some funds and travel supplies. I know some people who can get me out of the city in a pinch. We'll visit them and go as far as possible."

"You're well prepared for this sort of situation. I bet my people are better. I'll give you their names."

I quit walking, forcing him to stop with me if he wanted my support. "Why would you not just take me to them?"

Felix took a deep breath. "I'm not going with you. I can't leave Odena. Not now. It's not because of you killing Barrow. Astaroth still has plans for this city, and my life is in his hands. You can maybe escape Archon Vasely and his people. But if I come with you, Astaroth will be your enemy as well. At the very least, you should make it out of this alive. After all, you're strong enough to kill Barrow."

"I was lucky," I said. "I doubt he was using much of his power to control his flying. That would just be fine control of the wind around him instead of brute force. If it came down to his full might against me, I wouldn't have had a chance. I only disrupted his landing attempt and caught him by surprise."

"Something being lucky doesn't invalidate it." Felix touched the sliver of sword embedded in his leg. Too risky to pull it out and open an artery. "I'm just slowing you down. I chose my fate here. Don't feel obligated to protect me. Lyra knew the risks as well. You don't have to be some heroic crusader on our behalf."

"You know why she died?" I asked.

"Not the specifics." With a great sigh, Felix started limping away, forcing me to follow so he wouldn't collapse. "The demons used her paintings to do something. I'm not sure what the specifics are, but she painted that mural in Amelie in Yellow. I don't think that's a coincidence. Many rich and influential people purchased her art. It's displayed all over the city. Whatever is happening here, the tesseracts are only the beginning. Get out, Leones. Go."

I shook my head. One more thing to meditate on when I had the chance. "At least let me make sure you get to a healer."

Felix agreed begrudgingly. He knew of someone within a mile, though that distance seemed like forever at our current pace. The voice in the back of my head agreed with his warning to leave. No time to waste. But he sustained his injuries helping us gain our freedom. I could manage another full hour of time reversal; if too much time passed, I would go back and abandon him. The least I could do was try.

Signs of the guards mobilizing became obvious. Pressed against an alley wall, we waited for several armored soldiers to rush past before we slipped back onto the road.

We kept to the shadows and backways as much as we could. Anyone whose gaze lingered too long would realize something was off about us immediately. I had to use my time magic three different times after guards or perceptive civilians noticed us. My magical awareness proved unhelpful, but I maintained it as widely as I could just in case.

We moved in silence so Felix could save his breath. What was there left to say? Just before we arrived at the healer's, we reached the point of no return. An hour had passed since I killed Barrow. I could never reverse my decision again. I tried not to think about it—the choice had been made. During the whole walk I tried to parse through everything I had learned, but far too many distractions required my attention.

The activity throughout the city had picked up to a near frenzy. Barrow's remains must have been discovered, and word had spread. No one knew exactly what was going on, though Felix and I probably had the best knowledge out of living humans. Jokul might be the only person with a greater grasp of what was happening, unless Vasely himself was the perpetrator.

The healer turned out to be a pleasant older woman who looked completely unsurprised at two blood-stained teenagers panting at her entranceway. She helped me carry Felix to a bed close to the door. By then my friend could barely keep his eyes open, and though most of his wounds had stopped bleeding, the overall loss concerned me. How much blood did a human body have overall? My mind taunted me with the memory of Barrow's body disintegrating on impact. A lot, it seemed.

A couple of silvers bought me some clothes and a strip of cloth to tie the ivory sword to my waist. The quality was rough and the fit terrible, perfect for disguising myself as a commoner. Feeling awkward,

I stripped to my underclothes and changed into the new shirt and trousers.

When the healer went to grab some supplies, Felix and I said our farewells.

His voice was weak. "You should go."

I grabbed his hand and squeezed. "Find your way out of here, brother. We will see each other again. If we don't meet back up within two years, find me in Khalan two years from now. We'll meet in the most expensive gambling den in the city."

"Bring a fortune. I'll take it from you at the tables." He offered me a smile. Blood stained his teeth. "I hope you ended up with the better master. None of what happened here is your fault, Leones."

The healer returned, arms loaded with equipment. Herbs, poultices, a mortar and pestle, bandages, and an assortment of other tools. She selected a pair of shears and without a word began to cut off Felix's clothes. Should I have said something else? The chances we would meet up again seemed miniscule.

I tied the sword to my waist with the cloth and slid the Bakkel back in its place at my side. The arrangement looked awkward, but it would have to do for now. I paused at the door before leaving.

We would both have to go forward. Were there no better final words to say? Despite only knowing each other for less than a year, we understood each other on a level deeper than words. Everything that had happened spoke for itself.

I left the healer's home.

Despite my fatigue I ran the mile and a half to my safehouse. Since I did not have my keys on me, I broke a window and forced my way in. I raided the packs for coin, swung one over my shoulder, and hurried to the closest smuggler I knew.

Getting out of the city would be a service in high demand after the events at the Amphitheater. Given the escaped prisoners and word of Barrow's death, the exodus from the city would clog the roads for miles. Leaving would be expensive, but my coin purse was near bursting. As long as I had a few coppers and my time magic, I would be able to financially recover anywhere. Worst case scenario: my training had strengthened me enough that there would always be some physical labor work available.

I almost made it to the smuggler's place by the time the Narahven woman found me.

She appeared on the street directly in front of me, some twenty paces away, loose clothes flapping about wildly. The currents of wind heralding her arrival almost threw me off my feet.

The ground rippled as she strolled forward. "I should have never let Barrow chase after you alone. You will pay for what you've done, boy."

"What's your name?" I asked.

"Zephyr, the West Wind." The question made her pause but only for a moment. She unsheathed her sword as she closed in. The look on her face promised death. "The sister of the man you murdered. Your justice. Submit to me peacefully, and you will face a trial for your crimes."

Zephyr. Good to know. I wanted to figure out her abilities, but that curiosity could mean my death. Spreading my magical awareness revealed a compact orb of wind rotating within her core. Strong, though not on the level of her brother in terms of sheer power.

"No, thanks." I reversed time a few minutes.

I took a different route toward the smuggler's house that wasted an additional fifteen minutes.

Were they detecting me through sensing my magical ability? I was keeping both powers at the forefront of my mind, ready to use them at a moment's notice. Perhaps it would be better to relax and give others less of a beacon to follow. I forced myself into as normal of a state of mind as I could manage.

The reality of the situation was beginning to weigh on me. The time had long passed for me to reverse Barrow's death. This woman knew who I was and would tell her father, the Archon.

I had made an enemy of at least two gods in quick succession. Perhaps using my power frivolously in the past had distorted my sense of danger. Being able to reverse time for an hour had not stopped me from making the wrong decision.

Part of me wanted to visit the philosophers one last time. Maybe Brother Augur would even be in the city. But it would be a pointless goodbye, and the Gardens were too far away. If it ended up being a waste of my power, that reckless indulgence could be what killed me.

I made it to my destination without encountering Zephyr again. The smuggler answered my knocking promptly. He was a short man named Callos, a suspicious fellow with his greasy hair and small eyes.

Despite his appearance, he had a jolly voice. "Nice to make your acquaintance, young man! Come in, come in."

He ushered me into his home. A quaint and cheap place, poorly maintained, permeated with a strange musk. Callos's reputation held him up as one of the best smugglers in the city, honest and humble. Also, one of the richest, though he put on appearances to fend off the constant robberies most smugglers dealt with. I half-expected to see a private guard in his place, but if there was one, he stayed out of sight during business.

"I need to get out of the city immediately," I said.

"Understandable, understandable," said Callos. "Very bizarre times we are living in. I am thinking of leaving myself, but the business right now is just excellent."

After his spiel he watched me with expectant eyes. I handed him ten sols from my coin purse. Enough to make it across the Civilized Lands and back.

Callos's beady eyes noted the remaining bulge of my coin purse but, like any good smuggler, he knew not to be too greedy. "I have some horses hitched outside of the city as a getaway. I have an arrangement with one of the guards stationed at a side gate a few miles away. Another gold for his bribe, if you don't mind—yes, thank you, good man. I have a carriage ready to go. You'll climb under the blanket in the back. Not a peep until I get you out. Have you ever ridden a horse?"

I followed him out of a side door to where the carriage awaited. "Once, when I was a child."

"Well, I assume that was a pony. This will be different. You'll chafe something else. But it's faster than anything short of flying." Callos winked.

I forced a tight-lipped smile.

The smuggler went about preparing his carriage for departure. To my annoyance he kept up the conversation as he worked.

"Don't see a lot of young men with a sword," he said. "Let alone two."

"Good time to keep a sword on you."

He laughed. "True words, friend! I won't ask you too many questions, don't worry. I just like to tease. Now come on, get back there."

I bundled myself and my pack under the scratchy woolen blanket in the back of his carriage. Awkwardly splayed out, I attempted my best impression of a random bit of cargo.

When we set off, I realized I had been holding my breath for far too long. I inhaled the musty air under the blanket and had to hold back a coughing fit. Not exactly leaving in style, but it looked like I was on the right track.

Escape. A bloody, messy escape, but I would survive for another day. Relief washed over me like a wave. Even smothered under the blanket I was able to slip into a meditative trance and try to order my thoughts.

The carriage moved no more than a few paces at a time. An hour passed. Two. Finally, merry voices started up as the smuggler talked with one of the guards. The flap to the back of the carriage rustled open. A snort, then the flap rustled again.

"Try to be less obvious next time, Callos," said the guard.

My heart pounded in my chest, but the carriage started along.

We made it out.

I pushed the blanket off of my face and sucked in a huge lungful of relatively fresh air. After thirty more minutes the carriage rattled to a stop.

"Come on out, boy," said Callos.

I was all too happy to burst out into the sunlight. Outside, three mercenaries stood around a cluster of horses tied to a post. We were off some random branch of the main road heading east of the city. Quite the operation being funded here, though the smuggler would still rake in a massive profit even after paying a few random cutthroats to protect the horses.

Callos chatted with the mercenaries. They prepared a horse, a fine enough looking breed, mostly black except for its white feet. I clambered up onto the saddle awkwardly while they briefed me on the basics of riding.

After the impromptu lesson, Callos loaded my pack onto the horse. True to his excellent reputation, he even provided a map. "Closest village is Journey, about ten miles eastward. Remember to recommend me—"

The smugglers' voice was cut off as a titanic boom rang through the air. A figure shot overhead like a meteor, a warped explosion of air distorting his trail. Faster even than Barrow. Much faster.

Only one person was capable of such speed. The figure disappeared out of sight after it entered the city. But I could still hear the Archon when he spoke, a calm, mature voice that sounded like he was speaking right next to my ear.

"The city of Odena is under lockdown," said Vasely. "No one is to enter or leave. Report all suspicious activity directly to the nearest authority. I repeat . . ."

Before the smuggler or the mercenaries could react, I pulled the reins. The horse started forward at a trot. I leaned back into the saddle and stirrups and encouraged it with my legs. The horse picked up speed, and though it did not seem like nearly enough, I started to put distance between me and the city.

At any moment I expected the Archon to appear out of nowhere and apprehend me. But now that he had returned to the city, it would take some time to learn what happened in his absence. He may not even know Barrow was dead.

I left Odena behind. Hopefully never to see the god-cursed place again.

25

MISTAKES

I encountered a few other people as I rode in a panic, my mind racing, but they had their own worries to tend to. After seeing the Archon, I had briefly considered going back in time and squeezing out every additional minute of escape that I could. A little extra gold could have encouraged Callos to move faster. But buying myself another ten minutes did not seem worth depleting my time magic.

My whole body was sore, my mind in tatters. The land was flat enough to stay off the main roads, but I soon chafed on top of everything else.

By the time I reached Journey the sun began to set. The town looked idyllic in the twilight; small but not too small, smelling of bread and industry, silhouettes of people working or simply enjoying the vibrant skies.

My flight had left me sweaty and stinking. The horse plodded behind me, too exhausted to fight my loose hold on the reins. It looked like a wonderful place to rest, though soon enough this place would be swarming with soldiers from Odena.

Consulting the map revealed what seemed to be an accurate enough depiction of the surrounding land. Several villages like Journey lay within a twenty-minute radius of Odena. Any pursuers would not know which direction I headed in, if they even were aware I had left the city.

Callos could have reported me after seeing me rush off, but I was not too worried. He had a trustworthy reputation, and my reaction was not completely unwarranted after hearing the Archon's declaration. The smuggler would have to make a serious mental leap to conclude I was involved with Barrow's death, with enough conviction he would report me. But doing so would risk exposing his entire operation.

I should not have gone into the village at all, but I was willing to trade off some of my time magic in return for information.

Despite my appearance the people of Journey were a welcoming sort. A few of them waved or nodded. Word of chaos in the city must not have reached them yet.

I stopped next to the closest person, a rugged-looking man in his thirties. A long day of work had soiled his clothes and dirtied up his face, but his smile was wide and friendly.

"Hey there, son," he said. "Heading out of the city? What's the word?"

I raised a hand in greeting. "Came out a couple hours ago. Family left after all the craziness last night. I stayed behind to settle a few things before meeting up with them farther along."

"Having the son handle business? Why not your big man?"

"Just me, my mom, and my sister." I offered him a weak smile, head bowed.

He pointed a blunt finger at me. "Well, make sure you treat them right. My mom passed while I was still a little hellion. Lot of nights I wish I did right by her."

This playacting was beginning to make me feel uneasy, though these sorts of situations are why I wanted to learn how to manipulate others with the staccato. The man had an implicit trust for everything I said. How could you let yourself be deceived so easily? Maybe that was the sign of a life well lived.

"To be honest," I said, "we are a bit low on funds. I'm supposed to meet up with them farther along in Forest's Way. Think it's around twenty miles due east. I was wondering if there was any shelter nearby where I could sleep for the night?"

I feigned an embarrassed look. Avoiding eye contact with him was all too easy. How ridiculous, that I had killed several people recently but still felt ashamed of lying.

Even if I couldn't see his face, the pity in his voice was clear. "You can stay with me and mine. We'd be happy to have you. I added a guest room recently, would love for you to try it out."

"Oh, no," I said. "I wouldn't want to be a burden."

"That's nothing to worry about. Listen—"

"No, really. It's too much." I started to move along.

Confused, the man shook his head. He gestured northeast. "Well, there's an abandoned farm about three miles that-a-way. Nothing too wrong with it; the land there is just harsh, and all the recent cold drove the owners out. I can't encourage you to break into their home, but sometimes we catch people squatting in their barn. Most of the time we leave them be until they move along. Might be some others there, but you could take a gander."

"Thanks," I said.

The man looked like he wanted to say something else. A gale of wind crashed into me from behind, sending me stumbling forward. Some of the nearby villagers shouted. My horse made a run for it, jerking the reins from my hand. I nearly fell, caught myself in a crouch with a hand supporting me against the ground. Reflexively I reached out with my magical awareness and sensed a familiar figure behind me.

The Narahven woman had made her grand appearance.

Zephyr sauntered forward with her annoying confidence. "You've done an impressive job of evading me. That weak scent makes tracking difficult. I don't know how you managed to kill my brother, but I should have never let Barrow chase after you alone."

She had refined her speech since the last time we met.

"What's all this now?" asked the kind man, wide-eyed.

"What kind of power do you have?" I asked Zephyr, ignoring him. "You can track me, and travel so quickly without a horse?"

The West Wind spit a glob of phlegm to the side. "Why would I tell you a damn thing? If every criminal was stupid enough not to know me, my job would be far easier."

Worth a try. She would not be so easy to kill as her brother, though maybe there was something I could do about her sudden appearance. If she also moved quickly but along the ground, could I take advantage of nullifying whatever air magic she utilized? In much the same way as I had disrupted Barrow's landing, I could stop her motion enhancement.

Maybe she would trip over her own feet and turn into a long streak of red along the road as well.

The thought of it sickened me. How had I become so morbid? This woman did not deserve to die. If necessary, I could experiment and reverse time if it killed her, but what would it do to me as a person, if I treated killing people as something I could casually undo with no consequences? The coldly rational part of my mind agreed, though for a different reason: wasting more of Paimon's power would only slow me down.

I returned fifteen minutes back in time. Back to being on horseback, with the sight of the village on the horizon. This time I turned off of the road, completely avoiding Journey, taking a long route in the general direction of the abandoned farm. Even though that would leave me dangerously low on time magic, I would go back an entire hour if Zephyr caught me again.

I retracted my magical awareness again on the hunch that the weak scent she mentioned was me using my powers. The abandoned farm took longer to find than I would have preferred, but I made it without any issues.

There is something forlorn about the sight of an unoccupied home. It looked like it had been a well-maintained area, with carefully laid plots and a sturdy barn. Random pieces of equipment such as a rusted shovel littered the area. No other footprints disturbed the snow.

The sky was beginning to darken noticeably. Yawning, I led the horse into the barn. The stalls inside looked like they were meant for cows, but the animal fit just as well.

The interior of the building was mostly empty except for some shredded bales of hay and more rusted equipment. A corner housed some signs of human life—a threadbare blanket that looked like it had been ripped into strips of cloth, a fork coated in dirt, what looked like a handkerchief covered in crusted stains. Disgusting. All of it looked like it was months old, at least.

I set my pack down near a bale of hay near the barn doors. As good a place as any to sit down. I spread my bedroll out but did not climb in. As long as Zephyr was in the area, sleep was not an option.

I gathered some twigs from around the farm. After sprinkling them around the entrance, I settled into the lotus position on top of my bedroll.

Though meditation was not a replacement for true sleep, I would at least be able to relax and think. Staying too long was begging to be captured. Once I recovered and the horse had a chance to rest, we would continue on. Traveling through the chilly night held no appeal for me, but my options were limited.

Eyes closed, I focused on my breathing and spreading my awareness. Thoughts competed for attention in my exhausted mind—the bond with Paimon, leaving Felix behind, the West Wind's pursuit. The more I thought, the flimsier my plans seemed. Just run away as far as possible. Grow stronger. Get your revenge.

After three hours and forty-seven minutes, a twig snapped. I opened my eyes in time to see the Zephyr slipping into the barn, a specter in the moonlight.

I noticed her first; she wasted a second looking down at the little sticks I had scattered around the entrance for this exact purpose. A curse formed on her lips.

I sprang off the floor and caught her in a wild tackle, hoping to overwhelm her with my greater size. She locked her arms around me and twisted. Instead of me pinning her against the wall we collided into it at the same time. The impact reverberated through my body.

Before I could recover, her elbow caught me in the temple. I stumbled, managed to stay conscious.

Enough. I reversed time fifteen minutes.

Stupid of me to spend so long in a trance. I was honestly impressed that she had managed to find me. Had she been able to find me just from me spreading out my awareness? That required so little power that it seemed unlikely. Only way to find out: wait and see if she came if I wasn't using it.

I peered through the window, rubbing my side. Phantom pain lingered from the impact. Our brief exchange of blows made it obvious she had the upper hand. She had that easy command of leverage and gravity that marks a master. If she managed to knock me unconscious before I could turn back time I would be completely at her mercy.

Live like a hunted animal or risk everything? I had come too far to keep running. No matter where I hid, she found me. Endurance is one of the greatest strengths of human hunters. Chase, chase, chase, relentless, wearing down their prey. I could bleed all my magic away trying to avoid her, or I could stand my ground.

In the end, there was only one choice.

A ladder toward the back of the barn granted me access to the loft. It would have been the perfect location to sleep if the platform hadn't been half-rotten. I pressed one foot onto a nearby rafter, shifting my weight onto it until I became certain it would hold.

Heart pounding, I shuffled sideways along the thickest beam, prepared to reverse time the moment it snapped. Less than a dozen feet separated me from the ground; Avarus had taught us how to fall safely from greater heights, but I did not wish to test my luck. I paused several times, wincing at the groaning wood, but eventually reached my destination.

I perched like a monkey above the entrance. The Bakkel remained sheathed at my side. If possible, I preferred a captive over a corpse.

Ten minutes and twelve seconds later, the woman snapped a twig underfoot. Her head turned toward my pack in the corner.

I dropped.

The creaking rafter gave her a moment's notice. She glanced up and crossed her arms overhead in time to block my boots from crushing her skull. We collapsed in a tangle of limbs. A lucky elbow to the stomach knocked the wind out of her. I slipped on top, confident I could subdue her from that position.

Even surprised and breathless she was the superior grappler.

First mistake: I planted my hands to either side of her to support myself. Like an eel she wrapped herself around me, her hands twisting my elbow and wrist to pin my arm behind my back, one leg slipping around my lower back to brace herself. My shoulder screamed as she exerted more force, slow and inexorable.

I reversed time before it snapped.

Second mistake: I rained hammerfists down onto her head, hoping to overpower her. She deflected each blow with forearms and elbows like iron. Bruised and aching, I stopped my assault, weighed my options. Her hands flickered out, slipping past my defense, tap-tap connecting with my chin. I saw stars.

I used my magic to return a few seconds back. My vision swam, corrected as my brain realized there was nothing physically wrong. I would not beat her with my fists. Sword it was, then. I rolled off of her and, landing in a crouch, unsheathed the Bakkel.

"Move and you die," I said.

Her eyes flicked between my sword and my face. Unimpressed, she somersaulted backward, regaining her feet in one smooth motion. She drew her sword, a so-called suicide blade due to the missing crossguard. Still panting, she tilted her chin in defiance. The meaning was clear: *come then, asshole.*

Killing her would have saved me a lot of trouble.

She waited, happy to remain on the defensive as she sucked down measured breaths of air. Her stance was unfamiliar, body pivoted away from me, suicide blade held behind her with the cutting edge up. I nodded, unsure if I meant to acknowledge her or encourage myself.

I pushed off the balls of my toes, closing the distance in an instant. Her blade whipped forward to meet me, an upward arc meant to cleave my chin in two. I flinched away, a white-hot line of pain searing my cheek.

Time reversed. The wound disappeared.

I charged again, danced back from the blow, charged again. The swing threw her off balance, and she took a step forward in time for my shoulder to smash her to the floor. She somersaulted backward again, came to her feet with her free hand supporting her against the ground.

Annoyance flashed across her face. I smiled.

That set her off. She came at me, viper-quick, each blow meant to kill or cripple. Nothing like the legato's fluid forms and tricky footwork. A street style not meant for the dueling circle. Either she neglected her swordwork or I was better than I thought. Whatever ability allowed her to move so quickly did not enhance her speed with the sword. I held off her barrage, and when she overextended, I drove my blade into the opening, meaning to skewer her through the shoulder.

My sword met air.

Dust swirled upward from the floor, caught in an eddy of wind. I turned and saw the woman on the other side of the building, some thirty feet away. She leaned against the wall, gasping for air through a crazed smile.

From what I could tell, her ability was some sort of incredible speed isolated only to running.

I had tricks of my own.

I reversed time to the moment before she disappeared away from my sword thrust. A second power surged through me: the numbness of the void. Paimon's power nullified her ability to run, and this time

I skewered her through the right shoulder. I moved forward, concise, rapid steps that forced her to backpedal with me until her back slammed into the wall. The Bakkel's blade sank into the wood with a satisfying thud.

"Got you," she said.

Third mistake: I did not reverse time instantly after she gloated.

I looked down at my leg, surprised to see a gash along my thigh. Pain flared, brilliant and overwhelming. I blinked and discovered I was kneeling on the ground like a vassal before his queen. Another heartbeat sent the poison coursing through my body.

The pain was too much; I could not focus enough to use my power. The muscles in my thigh cramped, a hard knot of agony, then the poison spread, locking my body in place. I collapsed face-first into the ground as I lost control of my torso. In seconds I was paralyzed, unable to blink, head turned enough that I could see the woman.

With a scream she ripped the blade out of her shoulder and flung it aside. She snapped words at me in Narahven, guttural and damning. I'd spent enough time in taverns to understand the gist behind the words. I tried to focus on her tirade, something to anchor me away from the unbearable agony. Unable to scream, unable to concentrate enough to summon my power.

She tore a strip of cloth from her shirt and wrapped it around her bloody shoulder. Her right arm dangled at her side, useless.

"Bastard," she finally managed in Avanchean. "Got you, you bastard."

I stared.

She kicked me in the side. Hard enough to crack ribs but nothing more than a dull thump in comparison to the fire streaming through my veins.

"I'm tempted to kill you now. One more cut, and you stop breathing. Your respiratory muscles seize, and you asphyxiate, helpless. Helpless as my brother falling from the sky."

Her boots appeared in front of me. They appeared to be made of some bizarre liquid metal, something like quicksilver that glowed in the moonlight. Helpless, mesmerized, I waited for her to end my suffering.

Instead, she crouched and gripped my face, turning it this way and that.

"Look how young you are." Tears moistened her eyes. She laughed at herself, shook her head, but she couldn't stop the tears from falling. "Do you understand the pain you have caused me? My family? The people of Odena? I pity you, I do. But I am glad I was the one to find you. There is hope as long as people like me exist to stop people like you."

She set my head back on the ground and pulled a rolled cloth from one of her pockets. I could not see what she did, but I felt a needle enter the crook of my arm. With it came relief, euphoric and consuming. I sank into blessed darkness.

26

MORTALITY

I woke up on a battlefield littered with corpses. Humans, broken and twisted and bloody. A cluster of them to my right surrounded a demon in the form of an enormous bull. It bristled with arrows and spearheads and even a few swords, blue ichor obscuring most of its golden fur.

The sky was pure white, the sun a black hole. Every detail, down to the lines and creases, expressed in perfect clarity. Desolada.

Memories came flooding back. My fists clenched. That damn woman. I should have found a way to finish her.

Paimon appeared at my side. Again, he wore the appearance of an older brother, or perhaps it was supposed to be me a decade in the future. He wore a soldier's uniform, pristine white, with four golden epaulets on the shoulder.

What battlefield was this? Did it matter? Mankind had warred with the Goetia for over a thousand years. Paimon must have witnessed so many of these that they merged into a single battlefield stretched across time.

I was forced to speak first. "Greetings, master."

"Come."

I followed, avoiding stepping on the dead.

We stopped before the corpse of a praying-mantis demon. No human bodies rested in its vicinity. I recognized her, though she looked slightly different here. The demon Jokul had killed in the Amphitheater. Lyra's murderer.

Black chitin covered most of her body, shining and unmarked. Her arms ended in wicked organic scythes. Her head, decapitated in one smooth slash, lay in a pool of blue beside her body.

Paimon knelt next to the corpse. "This was Tasura. A great artist who identified much with the feminine aspect of mankind. She was not one of the Goetia, but she was much beloved by us. She possessed an understanding of aesthetics no human has ever imagined. Her art in the Mental Realm rivaled anything I have witnessed in the physical universe. Creation, destruction. Like the stars that burn themselves to birth light. And some mortal brutes executed her in public."

"She . . ." I trailed off.

"I already know your thoughts," said the demon lord. "Speak them aloud."

"Was she not the demon who killed Lyra?"

Paimon stepped away from the corpse. Her wounds healed in seconds, and an invisible hand lifted her to her feet. She had a striking face—not quite beautiful but memorable.

"You are young, so I will forgive such foolishness," said the demon lord. "Tasura would never harm an innocent, particularly one she favored. She was unique among our kind. She viewed mortality as precious, deserving of our protection. If violence had never struck her down Tasura would have lived forever, safe within Desolada. Instead, she chose to mingle among your kind in a suicidal attempt to assist you against the coming storm. Demons view humans as a weak species, but she alone considered mortals sacred. How can one truly value life if it cannot be taken from them?"

I swallowed. "I am sorry to have accused her."

Paimon waved, and Tasura collapsed, lifeless. "Do not mistake me. This is no chastisement. Your victory over Barrow paid great honor to her memory. Not that a memory is much. She is less than a ghost now. None of the others favored her enough to remember her spirit. As eternity progresses, I too will forget her, and no trace of her will remain."

I remained silent as we continued along the battlefield.

"This war has ended many," he said. "You bested two great enemies yet succumbed to Zephyr, the weakest of the Four Winds."

I looked at the ground. "A valuable lesson. It makes me hopeful that justice does exist. If that's true then perhaps no one is free from judgment."

Corpses returned to life as we walked past, groups of soldiers locked in eternal combat against their resurrected foes. Closest was a demon in the shape of a whitesteel fox. A cluster of metal ribbons formed its tail, waving languidly in the air. Three men faced it with spears ready. The demon pounced, a blur of movement. Tails flashed, and the soldiers fell apart in chunks of gore.

"Nothing can survive eternity," he said. "Over a long enough period of time everything must happen. Reality shall end, irreality shall become. We all have infinite destinies. You cannot avoid failure any more than you could avoid triumph."

The past few days had turned me into little more than an animal, reacting on instinct and fear. I closed my eyes, reflecting on everything that had happened. The tesseract, killing Barrow, the fight with Zephyr, and now being forced to discuss philosophy with an ancient demon lord in the Mental Realm. I was in no state to figure out what he meant.

"You have given me much to think about," I said.

"You will learn," said Paimon, drawing my attention back to him. "Mortal philosophers have corrupted your mind with their paradoxes and parables. Time is the universe acting upon itself. It is change. It cannot exist as a single frozen moment. A great power compels the universe to breathe. Some call it the Increate, others call it the anima. Because of it, nothing lasts forever."

His words resonated with me. Exploring my mental library had been a humbling experience. Much of what I believed contradicted itself or made no sense. What I did know about most subjects could barely fill a couple of pages. All my philosophical texts and personal musings about time amounted to no more than a couple of sentences.

"I've been limiting myself," I mused aloud. "Time is not just the past. It's the moment I live in. The future in front of me. I can't continue to see my power as nothing more than a way to correct mistakes."

Paimon nodded. "You understand more than I hoped. The Mental Realm is beyond the comprehension of any being, even myself. Attempting to define and limit your mind will only restrict your potential. Though time is only a fragment of the anima, understanding it is a path toward power. To my knowledge you are the first among your kind to display this ability. Some of the Goetia know cantrips, but if you can overcome Astaroth's tesseract, the others will pose little threat."

Even though I had lost an unnecessary fight against another mortal, he spoke as if I had personally bested Astaroth and by extension could hold my own against other demon lords.

"You honor me," I said.

Paimon looked at me for the first time. The weight of his regard froze me in place. His presence surrounded me, suffusing the landscape and the sky, The demon lord was far more than just the uniformed figure standing before me. I was like an intruder in another person's dream, encompassed within this vast and unknowable mind and subject to its uncertain rules.

"Honor yourself," he said. "I have chosen you as one of my Echoes because I know what you are capable of. You are not perfect. Nothing is. Do not fail me excessively, and do not betray me. In light of your recent triumphs, allow me to grant some knowledge you will find most interesting. First, the sword that once powered the tesseract is known as Dasein. It is, and has always been, your blade. Across all times and all realities, it is destined to always find you. Meditate upon it and discover the truth.

"Second, I must warn you about your situation in the mortal world. Zephyr wears a crude replica of the seven-league boots, allowing her to travel large distances with a single step. She makes haste toward Odena, and you will be arriving soon. I cannot reveal to you what the Goetia plan for that city, but it will challenge you like nothing before. Astaroth has made a great declaration against mankind, and though most of us remain neutral, the coming chaos will change everything."

The scene around us distorted into one much different than the others. Our steps carried us through a black void. No signs remained of our former path.

A string of bright lights glittered in the distance. At first I thought they were stars. Then the scene shifted abruptly, and I stood upon the source of the luminescence. We rode upon the back of a winged serpent as it undulated through the void; the lights I had seen were its golden scales, shining in defiance of the surrounding emptiness.

Paimon stood next to me on the back of this great beast. I recalled Sensi's tarot card, the Lord of the Void. The one who slew the last angel.

"How can I escape what's coming?" I asked.

"There is no escape. Astaroth has bound you to his destiny." The demon lord settled into a lotus position on the angel's back. Even a single scale dwarfed us. Its size was incomprehensible. "You have already been asleep for an hour and thirty-seven minutes before coming to the Mental Realm. Zephyr spent much of this time recovering. Hunting you depleted most of her power. It is only a matter of time until she reaches Odena, and there you will meet your fate. Your body has metabolized Zephyr's sedative, though the paralytic will last a while yet. Soon you will wake of your own accord."

His words should have made me feel panicked, trapped. Instead, I felt nothing. Here I was only a mind. Divorced from my body, the usual signals of distress no longer distracted me.

"You may think these are unworthy gifts, given your recent accomplishments," said Paimon. "Once you understand everything, the true worth of my words shall be revealed. Conquer those who would stand before us, Leones."

Pain brought me back to reality. Not as bad as before but still enough to make me yearn for more time with Paimon and his cryptic warnings. The world blurred past, vague glimpses of snow and the stars above. Each of Zephyr's steps propelled us forward a thousand feet; the effect was disorienting enough I closed my eyes and tried to fall unconscious once again.

Wind burned my face raw, a small distraction from the spasms wracking my body. Zephyr carried me like a sack of grain, each step driving her bony shoulder into my gut, the side of my head bouncing against her lower back. Ropes bound my wrists. When my hands stopped spasming I unclenched my fingers and experimented. No fine motor control, but I could rotate my wrists against the ropes and bend my elbows a touch.

The West Wind must have felt my movements and came to a halt, depositing me on the ground with casual disregard. The snow felt like a thousand needles prickling my wind-chafed face.

The spasms were infrequent enough that I could grasp my time magic between bursts of pain. As of now it was useless. Reversing time would only prolong this ordeal.

Zephyr crouched beside me. Sweat glistened at her brow, and her chest rose and fell in a deep, steady rhythm. As vicious as she was, the combination of our fight and my bulk must have taken its toll. "We've made great time. Almost back to Odena."

She watched with gleeful malice as my lips twitched nonsense threats. When her breathing returned to normal, she scooped me back up and resumed her march.

As we continued along, I experimented more with the limits of my movement. I counted time in my head as a mantra against the pain. The more time I spent conscious and unable to move, the more I panicked. Complete helplessness frays away at one's sanity.

Minutes passed. Breathing no longer felt like sucking air through a reed. I focused all my willpower on bending my pinky finger and, miraculously, it curled on demand. Progress. I adjusted to the pain as well as possible, accepting the rhythm of agony, each pulse coming slightly later until over a minute separated them.

Ten minutes and forty-three seconds of torture later, we came to a halt.

Voices murmured at the edge of my hearing. Again, I collided with the ground, grateful for the blanket of snow. We were on the outskirts of Odena, within shouting distance of the outlying farms and supply stations.

Thousands of people occupied a haphazard crescent of makeshift tents and shelters skirting an invisible barrier around the city. Smoke curled from hundreds of fires. At first, I thought it was a horde of refugees, but many wore the rich clothing of the upper class. It was as if a large, random section of Odena's population had decided to spend the night camping.

"What the fuck is this?" asked Zephyr.

She grabbed my legs and dragged me to the nearest people clustered around a fire. Fresh blood blossomed from beneath her bandaged shoulder.

My cheeks flushed with windburn and indignation.

One of the group noticed us, a large, bald man in a furs worth more than a commoner's yearly wage. He pointed us out to his companions.

"I'm Zephyr," she said. "I've been gone less than a day. What happened?"

The bald man offered her a sickly smile. "Oh, we all came out here."

She waited for him to continue, but he remained silent. "Why did you come out here?"

He frowned and turned to his companions. They all had the refined air of the relatively well-off—diplomats or owners of small industry, perhaps. A crone with a puckered face and an abundance of pearl jewelry coughed up something foul and spit to the side. The others had the decency to look abashed, as if they were witness to Zephyr committing some tactless gaffe.

A cold pit formed in my stomach.

Annoyance and impatience tinged Zephyr's voice. "It is a simple question, citizen. I am an authorized authority of Odena. Simple questions, simple answers. Why are so many people out here?"

"We came out here," said the bald man. The others muttered amongst themselves. Some glanced at me with fleeting interest.

Zephyr forced her response out as if it caused her physical pain. "Too simple. What is stopping you from going back?"

Silence.

None too gently, Zephyr snatched my legs and dragged me to the next group of people. Common workers from the look of them, most of them passed out around the fire beneath threadbare blankets. Only two of them were still awake, sipping from flagons and staring into the fire as if it contained the mysteries of the universe.

Zephyr's interrogation fared no better than her last attempt. She screamed in frustration. The men drank, ignoring her.

"Fine," she said. She slipped them a couple of silver coins and muttered some instructions.

Silent and dull-eyed, they hoisted me up by the arms, trying to balance me on my feet like parents guiding a toddler through its first steps. My boots sagged against the ground; I could still barely bend my knees, let alone support myself.

"For the love of mercy," said the Narahven. "Pick him up and let's go."

I struggled against them, which amounted to little more than me twisting my elbows and rolling my head. One of the workers heaved me onto his shoulder. Back to the grain-sack treatment. A spasm of pain left me docile.

We cut through the camp in the direction of the city. Large, finely-wrought tents belonging to the gentry stood out amongst the shelters of the commonfolk. Though the social classes did mingle in Odena, it was an unexpected sight, as if everyone had set up camp at random.

When we came to the invisible division between the ring of emigrants and the city outskirts, the men dropped me to the ground, turned, and began to walk back toward their camp. Zephyr shouted and chased after them.

Shivering in the cold, I looked toward the city and the horror that awaited us. The distant figures of guardsmen stood at attention outside the city. They remained motionless, as if they were toy figurines arranged against some artificial tableau.

Zephyr returned, alone, and muttered to the sky, "What the fuck is going on?"

She rolled her injured shoulder and grimaced. With a nod she made her decision, grabbing one of my ankles with her left hand. She heaved, digging her boots into the snow for purchase, our progress blissfully slow.

My screams escaped as a low whistle. A pathetic voice in the back of my mind begged me to get up, to run away as fast as possible. I had regained enough control to flail out with my free leg, thumping it against the side of her knee. Her stare promised murder.

Part of me hoped I was wrong. But everything I had discovered pointed toward one truth: we were heading in the direction of another tesseract, this one large enough to encompass all of Odena.

27

ARCHON

Now that the pain was bearable, I could focus on my time magic. Wanton use of my powers had left me exhausted, but anything was better than the horror awaiting me. As soon as I realized what was coming, I returned a few minutes in time to consider my options, to when Zephyr's hired men still carried me through the camps. Though the paralytic still affected me enough to make deep breaths impossible, I focused on calming myself against the rising panic.

Paimon had mentioned that my fate was sealed as part of Astaroth's destiny. Struggling should be hopeless, but the Goetia were not omniscient. If their karmic magic truly fastened reality itself on an immutable path, they would be the undisputed rulers of the world. There must be a way.

How could I convince Zephyr not to enter the tesseract without being able to speak to her? Though lacking fine motor control, I could attempt to write something in the snow. Whatever pathetic struggle I could manage would not be enough to overcome her. If she was not willing to listen, it would be impossible to convince her of anything.

How could I get her attention?

After the man carrying me dumped me on the ground, I enacted my first plan: writing in the snow. I could flail my arms about enough to displace snow in an uneven line. Any true message was impossible. Perhaps if I delayed her long enough, I could regain enough function to communicate.

When Zephyr returned from chasing my oblivious carriers, she once more looked at the sky and cursed.

For the first time I noticed she wore my ivory sword at her hip, fastened in its makeshift loop of cloth. She must have left my Bakkel behind, but there were hundreds of the things out there. The sword was a priceless treasure even without considering Paimon's words. Dasein, he had called it, mentioning something about how it was bound to find me across all of time.

The implications were staggering. If I had just claimed the sword within the past day, that meant we had a future together. Which meant I would not—could not—die soon, because at some point I would have to have bonded with it. Maybe? What if I killed myself and chose to eliminate any possible future where that happened? Would it disappear as if it never existed? Dasein defied the principle of sufficient construction, Heizel's indeterminacy of time, the entropic loop . . .

I could not afford to waste my energy on such thoughts. Even forgetting the poison, I had exerted both of my powers frequently and had not slept since before the tesseract unraveled. Traces of mesfera still lingered in my system. Defeating Zephyr would require everything I had left.

The second plan worked no better. Loath to waste my time magic, I reached for the void and released a small burst at her boots. The ripples spreading outward from her feet flickered before returning to normal. Just enough to get her attention. She unsheathed her poisoned blade. Too much attention. I reversed time to right before the nullification, uninterested in another taste of the paralytic.

Was it truly hopeless? The migraine thumping between my ears was beginning to overwhelm the agony coursing through my veins. Even that small burst of nullification took its toll.

Was this the true nature of the Echo of Paimon, the one who unraveled the tesseract, who killed one of the Four Winds? The powerful being who would reverse time far enough to save his father from the Archon of Flames? In the end, nothing more than a weak, sniveling boy, begging his enemy for mercy.

If I gave up hope, everything I had done since the beginning was pointless. All the suffering, the indecision, all the times I questioned my own sanity. All of it could have been avoided if I had just let the Magister's flames consume me.

I screamed with all of my might. Though it was nothing more than a low whistle, I put everything I had into it. Zephyr sneered at me as I flailed in the direction of the city. I whistled until my eyes burned from hemorrhaging blood vessels. Her expression turned to disbelief, then even a touch of concern, as my whistling screams dragged on. Over and over, I smashed my face into the thin layer of snow, abandoning all reason. With everything I had I tried to communicate my intention.

Not a warning to turn back from the city. No begging. The fire in my chest grew, washing away the pain and the fatigue. These people put me through so much. More than any man should suffer through.

Not even I knew what words I attempted to scream. Intention overwhelmed everything else:

Take me, then. I will be the end of everything. Demon lords, divine children. Every sneering face and mocking tone. Tie your destiny to me, if that is your wish. After me, there will be nothing.

Zephyr unrolled her cloth of vials and selected a needle.

Do it. Bring me in. This time, I will be the only one leaving.

When she pricked my arm with the sedative, I grinned wide and wild. As the darkness closed in, Zephyr could not bring herself to even look at me.

Desolada, the realm of air and fire.

Some few great minds anchored it to reality. The One Who Rages. The One Who Waits. The One Who Yearns. The One Who Feasts. The One Who Rules. It was only their existence that revealed the truth of the cosmos. Before these beholders, there was only nothingness, since nothing could comprehend existence.

In a way, they were the entire universe.

A new mind blossomed. Within the tempest of flames that raged throughout the cosmos, a crown of horns materialized. First came the tips, so infinitesimal they seemed to emerge from irreality. They grew downward in an expanding fractal, forming great prongs, secured to a forehead of pure white. And below that a face, fine and noble. A neck. A body. Molded from the void. Something from nothing.

Within the Universal Conflagration, Paimon opened his eyes.

* * *

I woke up in a comfortable bed. In that first moment nothing made sense. It was the opposite of dreaming, a certainty that what I was experiencing was not real—that it could not possibly be real. I sorted through the events I could remember over the past several days, arranging them in a sequence that seemed correct enough. This moment happened in the Mental Realm, that event was just a nightmare. I wondered how accurate I was at telling the difference.

Most of all I remembered my last thoughts. That all-consuming rage. Though sleep had calmed the rising fury, ripples of it still sent twitches through my body. My hands clenched as I remembered what Zephyr had put me through.

And that vision . . . the birth of a god, a being so far beyond me that it defied comprehension. Sensi said that Echoes experienced some of their patron's thoughts, incongruent moments the mind attempted to piece together in dreams. The depth and complexity of Paimon's memories made him seem so much more real than me, so much greater a presence, that it felt as if I were nothing more than an insect attempting to comprehend a human's thoughts.

A migraine pounded behind my temples. I felt like I had been dragged behind a horse all the way back from Journey, which was not so far off. Trussed up and brought back. Inside Odena. Inside the tesseract. I rubbed my wrists, raw and bloody from straining against the ropes.

"You're awake," said a voice.

A middle-aged Narahven man sat in a plush armchair beside my bed. His bald head and the laughter lines around his eyes gave him the appearance of an old monk. A stylized tattoo of the cardinal directions divided his forehead into quadrants. Gray suit. Legs crossed at the knee, teacup in one hand, saucer balanced on his other palm, he looked like an illustration from an etiquette manual.

I extended my magical awareness toward him. Nothing. More concerning than even a blaze of power.

My mouth felt like a desert. "Which Wind are you?"

He took a sip of tea. Porcelain clinked as he placed the cup back on the saucer. "All of them, I suppose."

"The patriarch himself." I felt nothing after the realization. Not hatred, not fear. He may be divine, but he was still just a man.

"None other," he said. "By all rights you should be in a cell a mile below the earth. You are curious, though. I've always been fond of curious things. Water for the gentleman, please."

We were the only two people in the room, but he spoke with complete confidence. A servant slipped in and set a decanter of water on my bedside table. Most of it over spilled over my face and chest as I drank. What little made it into my mouth was pure heaven.

Someone had changed me into loose-fitting cotton. Ointment glistened on the dozens of little wounds on my arms. Sunlight streamed through an open window. After being paralyzed and dragged around, I had to admit finding myself in a nice infirmary was a surprise.

"At the risk of sounding arrogant," said the man, "did you really not know who I am? Perhaps I should commission more statues."

His casual tone and the fact I wasn't shackled in some torture chamber reassured me that the situation was not completely hopeless.

"Archon Vasely," I said.

He winked. "I must admit I am not so noble as they say. You are a guest in my palace, but this entire time I have been watching you, arguing with myself about whether I should strangle you in your sleep. My city has been your shelter, and how have you repaid me? Consorting with demons. Killing Barrow, sent to lawfully detain you. I hope your explanation is excellent."

"Your son drew his spear against me," I said. "It is the fate of all warriors to succumb to a greater foe, whether man or death itself."

His smile was broad, tombstone teeth gleaming white. "The philosophers have educated you well. Iniver's *War as Life*, chapter three, paragraph ten, sentence two. You are, of course, correct, but what use is there in being a god if your will does not supersede such absurd tenets? Fortunately for you, Barrow is—was—not my son. None of the Winds are my spawn. They are merely the most promising members of my tribe, brought to these so-called Civilized Lands to become my Echoes. If Archons could have divine children, we would all create our own clan of godlings. But the common man does not think about such things. I say something, they listen."

A disgusting, pathetic hope flared to life within me. "Then what are your intentions?"

"I merely wanted to question you about what is occurring," said the Archon. "You see, Barrow has been a very bad Echo. The man has always despised this world of stone buildings and paved roads. Most of my people yearn to escape the desert. To no longer wage great battles, just to claim water from an oasis inhabited by monsters. But Barrow was that special breed of man who hungers only for power. To be worshipped and acclaimed. His sister is also desperate to prove herself, but at least she is civil."

Zephyr was supposed to be civil? I wanted to laugh.

The laughter lines around Vasely's eyes crinkled as he judged my reaction. "You must realize, many of you Civilized Folk consider us savages. If I was not an Archon, they would have waged war against my people and annexed us forcefully. We speak a different language and look a little different, which somehow makes us barbaric. Though every child learns at least three dialects from infancy. Every one of us is literate, even if each tribe only has a small library of sacred books, faded by age and sand and a thousand hands flipping through it. So imagine how much a man like Barrow despised your kind."

Given his cheerful demeanor and the lack of fiery brands sizzling against my flesh, it was best not to antagonize the Archon. I had many words for him, but none of them seemed smart to voice. My time magic could reverse any serious gaffes, but if I could detect traces of magic in others, I had no doubt the Archon would immediately notice. Chances were, he already knew everything just by looking at me.

I had not forgotten my rage. Only the insanity that came with it. Screaming and attacking the Archon would accomplish nothing. If revenge was possible, I would have to be cold.

"Respectfully," I said, "what is your point?"

"The point is that Barrow was compromised. He came to kill you, to tie up all of the loose ends that would reveal his deception. While I was conferring with other Archons outside of the city, he laid plans without my knowledge. The spectacle in the Amphitheater was specifically designed to bind us closely to Desolada. The oracles are their priesthood. To slay them is one of the greatest sins among the demons. The karmic bond this forged is unfathomable."

"The demons have priests?"

"Us Archons have priests," said Vasely. "I heard what the demon called you when Amelie in Yellow broke open, for lack of a better term. 'Child of Paimon.' His taint is thick upon you. You are a clever boy, Leones Ansteri. Between me and your master, which of us do you think deserves to be worshipped as a god?"

Denying the truth would get me nowhere. Vasely could do as he wished, and no one would think twice. Odena was legendary in part because of his tolerance and willingness to permit individualistic freedoms. People who would be ostracized anywhere else called Odena their home. He had done nothing to earn my ire. If I could make an ally of the Archon, being trapped within such a massive tesseract was . . . survivable.

"You already seem to know almost everything," I said. "I may have some interesting knowledge to fill in the gaps."

Vasely leaned forward, sipping his tea. "Excellent. Go on."

"First, can you tell me what is happening within the city?"

The laughter lines around his eyes disappeared. After explaining so much to me, those were the words that enraged him?

"For the past seven days, it has been impossible to leave Odena," he said. "There appears to be a boundary approximately a hundred feet outside of the city walls. Once someone passes that boundary, they say that the world around them completely changes. From the outside they cannot see what is occurring within the city. From the inside, not even I can escape this barrier. I imagine at some point nearly every citizen has tried their luck at escaping. There are so many that the guards can only bind them with ropes and cart them back once they've captured enough."

So the people within Odena had experienced seven days compared to less than a day spent outside. Good to know.

"Do things return to their prior state after an entire day passes?" I asked.

"No," said the Archon. "We have interrogated the survivors of Amelie in Yellow extensively. That demonic construct served a different purpose to the barrier around the city, though I suspect they share many similarities. The time distortion remains, but the regenerative properties do not seem to extend to the city. The amount of power required to do something like that to such a large area would extinguish the sun itself within a few months. So, what is it that you can tell me, that others cannot?"

Paimon had never told me to lie or keep what he told me a secret. Could he possibly be offended by this conversation with the Archon? If he wished to place such restrictions on me, he could have forced some sort of oath. Instead, our relationship seemed built on a mutual understanding: I would serve him and carry out his will in exchange for power and knowledge. If I failed to do this, consequences would surely follow, but outside of such restrictions I had free rein.

"The demonic construct is known as a tesseract." My voice cracked. I took another sip of water, careful not to spill it everywhere despite my shaking hands. "Its purpose was simple. Whoever survived would become one of Astaroth's Echoes. If you haven't discovered this already, Amelie in Yellow was not the only tesseract within the city."

The Archon's locked eyes with me for what felt like an eternity before he responded. "No new tesseracts have been uncovered since the one you came from. Their goal must not yet be accomplished. Do you know why Astaroth is selecting a new batch of recruits within the city? I have suspicions, none of which I like."

"I'm afraid not," I said.

Vasely rubbed his jaw. "Then I have one last question for you. When Zephyr returned you to the city, you possessed a certain sword. It bears an uncanny resemblance to the weapon within the demon's chest, and we found no trace of it at Amelie in Yellow. What compelled you to take that sword?"

Revealing the whole truth behind Dasein would spring an entire new conversation I did not want to go down. I forced myself to admit some of it. If the weapon was destined for my hand, not even an Archon could keep it for himself.

"The sword was the keystone to the tesseract," I said. "I could feel something strange emanating from it. The power Paimon bestowed upon me allows me to nullify magic, at least to an extent. I unraveled the tesseract by directing his power into the sword. When the tesseract fell, the demon killed itself. It said that it wanted to escape retribution from Astaroth for failing."

The Archon nodded. "I must say, I do appreciate your candor. Unfortunately, given everything that has happened, I cannot allow you to roam the city as a free man. You will remain within the palace for now. You will be provided a suite and servants, but you are not to attempt to leave. In the meantime, I will investigate your claim that other tesseracts exist within the city. We shall speak again soon."

As soon as he finished speaking, soldiers filed into the room. The Archon slipped past them without another word.

"One more question," I said.

Vasely paused, turned on his slippered heel. "Yes?"

I kept my voice neutral, light. "With all due respect, how could this have happened right under your nose? Barrow? Champion Jokul? Who knows how many others are involved on something of this scale?"

The Archon's face went blank. After a second the mask of joviality returned. "It appears there are places, like the tesseract, where I cannot hear crucial details. There are always fake plots, contrivances, distractions to annoy me. There were rumors, but it seems the people I sent to investigate were compromised. And thank you for making me aware of Champion Jokul. I will have him questioned."

The Archon left.

A pair of soldiers hoisted me to my feet roughly, ignoring my complaints. This wasn't an alliance. How arrogant of me to think that Vasely would treat me as some sort of partner or friend. I was a prisoner once again. A fancier cage but a cage nonetheless.

I was growing tired of prisons.

Still weak as a babe, I dangled between the guards' arms, seeing no reason to help them in moving me. Their curses fell on deaf ears. Most of all I cursed myself: still sniveling, still begging my enemies for help.

Down a hallway festooned with art. We came to a spiral staircase leading up several floors. They had to drag me up it.

As we climbed one of the flights of stairs on the way to my new cage, a pair of soldiers led a familiar figure down past us. Incandescent rage filled me at the sight of him. Champion Jokul. The men escorting him were too scared to lay their hands on him; their fingers hovered a few inches from his arms. His sword still dangled at his side.

As he passed by, Jokul smirked and nodded. "Be seeing you."

28

HERE

As far as prisons went, my room within the palace wasn't bad. I would have preferred Sensi's suite, but they provided more than necessary. An ice box stocked with vegetables and fruit, a soft bed that served as the only bit of furniture, a few books on basic philosophy stacked in a corner, a weathered chamberpot. Judging from its size, it must have been a guest room for undistinguished servants. The metal bars along the windows served as a reminder of my situation.

After spending a week locked in with other killers at Amelie in Yellow, the solitude was appreciated.

The only other people I saw were the two guards stationed outside of my door. Once, a young servant bringing my meals tried to sneak a peek into my room as he delivered my tray, only to be shoved back by the guards.

They remained silent despite my probing them with questions about what was happening. I made no wasteful attempts to escape. Without a weapon, there was no defeating two grown men with halberds and full plate. Their only weakness was the open window in the front of their helms. Even with a sword and full use of my powers, they were a better match for me than someone like Barrow. At least I could trick that bastard.

Escaping would not benefit me for the moment, anyway. Something would soon descend upon the city of Odena, and there was no place safer than the inside of the Archon's palace.

Six hours into my first day, Jokul visited. The Champion pushed open the door with a casual grace and slipped into the room. His fingers toyed with the green ribbon sprouting from his sword handle as he watched me in silence. Dense wind energy cocooned his sword, though he seemed to have no innate magic I could detect.

I refused to speak first.

He set one boot in front of the other with exaggerated care as he circled around the room. His gaze drifted along the confines of my prison, a little smirk tugging at the corners of his lips. I remained in the center, sitting in the lotus position, as he walked behind me. There he remained, looming. I did not look back.

Hot breath washed over my cheek. He whispered into my ear, "You told the Archon I'm involved in this. With no proof."

"You are."

The Champion circled back around to my front. He crouched until we were eye-level. "I deny your accusations fully. Did Barrow say something? I know you killed him. Why would he falsely implicate me?"

"You deny it?" I asked. "You lied to the Archon's face?"

Jokul wiped his thumb along his lower lip, shaking his head. "You are the servant of demons. Yet at your word he has confined me to the palace. Warden and prisoner at the same time. If I could, I would execute you here on the spot, but the Archon forbade me from a little well-justified vengeance."

The Champion stood and attempted to draw his sword. The weapon remained in its scabbard. With lightning speed, he pivoted on one heel, the other leg snapping out in a vicious kick. I forced myself not to flinch. The blow met invisible resistance a foot from my face.

"Remember, boy," he said, settling back onto both feet, "you are trapped in here with me. At some point, the Archon will realize you are far too dangerous to let live. I'll be waiting for that moment."

I laughed. The threat would have seemed a lot more serious if he hadn't revealed how crippled he was. "We're both trapped, aren't we? Not just here but in the tesseract. Right in the middle of whatever act of war the Goetia intend." My voice was steady, casual. "I bet you thought you would be long gone from the city by the time everything was set into motion. You're a loose end, Jokul. You'll die here along with everyone else."

The Champion sniffed, bloodshot eyes glaring. Without another word he turned and left.

I breathed a long sigh of relief once the door slammed behind him.

One of my questions answered itself as time wore on. The city of Odena did not experience a normal day-night cycle. Sunlight streamed through the windows constantly. By my guess, the time dilation extended a day to approximately a week, so the sun would set after around three-and-a-half days. Disturbing. Despite my ability to tell time perfectly, my body refused to rest normally, even when I covered the windows with my bed linens to mute the sunlight.

On the bright side, it seemed possible for me to use time magic within the tesseract around Odena, unlike the one in Amelie in Yellow. I could only speculate on what the difference was. Archon Vasely's palace was fairly deep into the city. It was possible that if I went closer to the barrier around the city, I would begin to feel the time magic interfering with my own. I would never know until I attempted to escape the tesseract itself, but it seemed wise to take precautions, just in case.

I learned early on that the water they brought me dulled my magical power. Its slightly bitter taste and the white residue coating the bottom of my cups made it obvious, but they didn't care if I knew. My only other option was dying of thirst. The inconvenience proved to be minimal: while my powers felt weaker, they regenerated at the same, steady pace.

At this proximity the melody emanating from Vasely as he meditated shook my teeth for hours on end. Otherwise, I felt nothing from him. There must be some method of shielding oneself from being detected by others' awareness. Perhaps the void could be used to form a shroud, but such control was beyond me.

In my mind's eye, the void and time magic appeared like two small orbs hovering in the aether, white and silver respectively. Though the void came from Paimon, it seemed its qualities were derived from some characteristic native to myself. Their agonizingly slow regeneration only served to worsen my already foul mood. Discovering what enhanced their power would have to be one of my primary avenues of research.

I spent most of my waking hours in the Mental Realm. Whenever the Archon meditated, I was trapped in his song, my mind tossed around like a locust caught in a hurricane. I was able to focus best when Vasely concealed himself, but attempting to stabilize against the tempest of his mind helped steady my own willpower. My resistance built up; though I still shook under his might, after the third day I was able to imagine my family manor even while he meditated.

The walls of my memory palace shook as I sat in my room, reading through some of the books there. While altering my own memories required an unacceptable amount of mental power, reading through what I already knew required little effort. Three new additions to the library caught my attention: *Tesseract, Echoes, and Enemies.* They each contained no more than a few pages.

The first book discussed what little I knew about the demonic construct: it was a four-dimensional seal of sorts, powered by an external source that would supply a colossal amount of power. Some formulae were scribbled on the bottom of the second page, crossed out, attempted again. Feeble attempts at dimensionalism that my subconscious mind must have tinkered with.

Vasely claimed the tesseract around Odena also possessed a recursive element that would drain the power of the sun within a few months. From there, it could be possible to determine the amount of energy required to power the tesseract. I devoted a few minutes to the problem before giving up. There were far too many unknowns and, even if I knew all the variables, I had no idea where to begin.

I closed the book and opened *Echoes.* This one basically repeated Sensi's lecture and included a short mention of the dream I had about Paimon's birth. At the end was a list of known Echoes.

Barrow (deceased)
Jokul?
Sensi (deceased)
The East Wind
The Magisters of Velassa (# ?)
The South Wind
Zephyr

I swallowed a knot that formed in my throat at the second name. Returning that book to the shelf, I took up *Enemies* instead. A sobering thought, that I had reached a point where I had a list of people who wanted me dead. I skimmed through it, tracing the words with a finger; it paused on Jokul's entry. Most of it derived from speculation, Caedius's effusive praise, and talking about the bastard with Felix during our time in the tesseract. But one particular speculation made me clench my fists.

Jokul, the Champion of Odena

Rumored to be at least a sixth-legato blademaster, the Champion has never lost an official duel. Rumors about the man hold him to be an equal to the former North Wind, Barrow, though they refused to ever face each other in a sanctioned bout. Whether or not this includes Barrow using his divine wind magic is a matter of much debate. He wields a sword of unknown make, thought to be a gift from Archon Vasely himself. It seems likely Jokul may be an Echo.

Unlike the Magisters of Velassa, Odena has no magical enforcers in appreciable quantity. The Four Winds presented a formidable front, but the Magisters would annihilate them through sheer numbers. Though Vasely is not as authoritarian as his Velassan counterpart, it would be reasonable to assume he has some unknown force of equal strength. Of all the public warriors, Jokul seems the most likely to have received the Archon's blessing.

At Amelie in Yellow, Jokul would have murdered me, if not for the forced activation of my ability to slow time.

Avoid the Champion at all costs.

My hands shook. I had never really thought this consciously, but of course Jokul would be an Echo. That was obvious. It was the other part that made my heart pound in my chest. The forced activation of my power to slow time. I thought back to when I encountered the Champion inside Amelie in Yellow.

We had been sitting on cushions next to each other. When I voiced my insane speculation about him working with demons, he found the words sufficient cause to try to put a knife in my heart. Given the tesseract erecting itself in Amelie in Yellow that night, I had not thought much about the near-death experience as much as the rest.

Now I remembered clearly how time had seemed to slow to a crawl in that moment. I had assumed it was a trick of the mind. It was, in a sense, but if this book was correct, I had actually used my power to dilate time.

As when I manifested my reversal ability, I first used this technique subconsciously to save my life. Hopefully understanding my magic more in the future would not require a close brush with death.

I wanted to strangle myself. How had I not realized sooner? Around that time, I had received so many revelations back to back that something like this had just slipped from my notice. With that ability, how much easier would my fight have been against Zephyr? How much could I have changed?

The anger I felt toward myself built up until the memory palace fractured around me. I opened my eyes, no longer able to maintain my concentration. I wanted to leap to my feet and throw the furniture around like a child. That would just enrage the guards. Even if my time magic was available, it would be foolish to use it right below the Archon's feet unless necessary.

I settled for pummeling the bed for a while, feeling vaguely ridiculous and immensely satisfied at the same time. The guards did not hear it or did not care enough to investigate. When this lost its luster, I started moving through the forms of the legato. Though the latter parts of the first form required a sword for proper practice, I visualized the dance well enough to make it a useful exercise. My body would remember when the time came, as long as I practiced the same motions until perfection.

Moving through the bladeform always helped bring me back into a trance state. My breathing settled into the proper rhythm. Calm settled.

Slowing time . . . what was required to accomplish such a feat? If such a thing was possible, time must not move at a specific speed, steadily along an arrow to the future. It could be twisted. Distorted.

Once, in a moment of pique, I had asked Lyra if she experienced time the same way I did. Back then I was thinking of how my ability to reverse time made me experience a completely different reality from other people.

The implications had gnawed at me for a while. An entire universe ceased to exist whenever I reversed time. Or did it simply continue on, and some part of my mind transferred into a new reality, leaving my former self still trapped in whatever situation I found myself in? The thought made me paranoid about putting myself into truly awful situations, but there had still been times when I may have killed some ghost of myself through carelessness.

Time, then, and existence itself, must be relative. To me, with my pathetic mortal lifespan, the saga of my life spanned everything. To Paimon, I was an amusing distraction. Over the passage of aeons, the demon lord would cease to consider even years worthy of recognition. His purpose stretched across eternity.

And at some point in their lives, each person experiences that moment where everything around him seems to pause. A moment of revelation. In all these ways, the passage of time is malleable.

As I approached the end of the first legato, I began to visualize dripping water. Each droplet collided with the calm surface of a pond, birthing a chorus of ripples. A steady, constant rhythm, one second per droplet. Tap. Tap. Tap. I knew I could slow the droplet any moment I wanted, but that would activate my time magic and alert Archon Vasely.

I stopped after ninety seconds. The entire first form of the legato, completed. Flawless. I shouted, fists raised to the heavens in defiance. By the Increate, I wished Felix had seen that. Even if there was a massive difference between a dance and a real fight, it felt damn good. Thinking about my friend dampened my mood. What was he up to?

Despite using none of my power, a deep exhaustion had settled into my bones. What I intended to be a brief nap ended up lasting six hours. A distant, shrill sound woke me up from a deep slumber. At first, I had no idea what had happened and merely laid there, blinking against the wash of color through the window.

The sun had finally begun to set, a brilliant wash of orange and pink and lavender. Beautiful. One of the only good parts about this tesseract: such a lovely palette would last that much longer.

Then the sound came again. Distinct and disturbing. Almost like a distant cry, but it was not the kind of sound a human would make. Too shrill, too furious. The kind of sound a lunatic would make. It sounded both close and far, bypassing the ear, directly into some shadowy crevice of the mind.

No, certainly not a sound a human would make.

For the first time, I experienced a proper glimpse of the Archon's power. Sound surged, so dense it almost seemed visible. The windows and wall-mirror shattered into fragments of glass. Fortunately, I had not been using my magical awareness, or the sensations may have overwhelmed my mind.

An explosive thunderclap of air boomed as Vasely launched himself from the palace. His streaking figure flew into the city, the sky around his feet distorted from the speed of his passage. He was heading toward the source of that scream.

No, it was not a scream. It was a declaration:

We are here.

29

LEGATO (I)

I meditated as a demon shrieked in the distance.
 I had been preparing for this moment ever since I had first been trapped within Amelie in Yellow. Before that, even, from the beginning, when the Magisters burned down my family manor and started this chain of events. Everything I had been through led to this moment. I knew something was coming, and when that happened, I could not falter.

The white and silver orbs floating in the back of my mind appeared to be close to full strength; that helped ease some of my worries, but with no idea what the future held, it seemed best to err on the side of caution. Focusing on the silver orb revealed three hours, fifty-six minutes, and seven seconds worth of time magic if used purely for reversal. Without experimenting, I had no inkling of how much of a drain it would be to slow time. It would have to be enough.

Fifteen minutes after I woke up, the guards stomped into my room. Their halberds gleamed wickedly.

"You're coming with us," said one of them.

I kept my face blank. "Where are we going?"

"Underground," said the guard. "It's not safe here. In the dungeons, we can keep you all together under the Archon's protection."

"I don't like the sound of that screaming," I said, remaining in the lotus position. "Seems like you're rounding us up for a slaughter if the palace ends up falling."

The second guard felt left out of our conversation. "You don't have a choice here. Get up and come on."

"There's always a choice."

Still, I complied, curious as to what would come next. For a maximum of fifteen minutes, I would indulge them. No matter how I made my escape, the guards were the first obstacle. Best to see what openings they left me.

"Creepy kid," the second guard whispered to his companion.

They went so far as to bind my hands with rope. One guard in front, the other behind, they led me toward the staircase. Brave of them to only send two people to escort Barrow's murderer to the dungeons.

My magical awareness billowed throughout the area, searching every nook and cranny within a ten-foot radius. Now that the Archon had left, I could at least experiment with my powers.

Both of the guards both gave off a weak gray aura—at least, weak compared to the likes of the Captain. Normal men would not possess such auras. Either they were some of Vasely's Echoes in disguise, or they were outfitted with divine protection. If it was the former, I was going to have some problems. Two of them, and clever enough to disguise their power until now.

Stairs took us down into the dungeons below the palace. At the entrance, another pair of men in full plate stood at attention in front of a double-locked door. Iron chains around the guards' neck bore keys as pendants. After noticing my escort, the men guarding the dungeons grabbed the keys from around their necks and plunged them into their respective holes. The metal-banded door slid open without a sound. We descended, torches throwing wild shadows along the walls.

Behind us, the door slammed.

The stairs descended several floors deeper, but they intended to keep the prisoners on the first floor. Figures wandered through the communal cage, large enough to house a hundred prisoners. Separate cells in the back housed several men presumably barred from socializing. The guards shoved me into the communal cage and took up posts outside.

Around twenty others occupied the space as well. The closest, a man and a woman, were fellow prisoners from the tesseract. We had never spoken, but I felt a sense of kinship. They, too, had suffered through this farce—in fact, their incarceration within Amelie in Yellow had been far longer than mine.

The man nodded; the woman stared with suspicious eyes.

I did not intend to stay here long, but I was curious. If they were here, then . . .

My magical awareness revealed a familiar presence in one of the isolated cages.

Felix.

Part of me hoped that my friend would have escaped, but his presence here was inevitable. He was no more likely to escape this hell than I was. Felix looked resigned after he noticed me; he must have shared my thoughts.

The Champion stood outside Felix's cell, frowning. It must have chafed him, watching over a prisoner while his master fought in whatever battle was occurring in the city. When he saw me, his expression shifted to one of predatory amusement.

A knot formed in my throat.

Was this me, then? A boy without pride, without confidence, a passive observer watching others strive toward greatness. Bestowed with the power of a god and using it to run every chance he had. A god, refusing to believe he was anything but mortal. Part of me shied away from this thought. Arrogant, dangerous. I was no one special, only lucky, an aberration.

What is it that separates a man from a beast? A man from a god? How had the Archons convinced the world they were not simply powerful mortals blessed with longevity? They had the spark of the divine, ineffable, displayed with such pride that just doubting them invited retribution. They were not good in the way society tells us that we should be good: kind, lawful, humble. Yet our society deified them in a way no good man would ever experience. No one questioned them because they allowed no questions. Most of all, they never questioned themselves.

Deep down I believed I was nothing. A void. Witnessed by others and promptly forgotten. But that was not quite the truth. The void is much more, just like time is more than the passage of seconds.

"Felix!" I called out. "If I came to your room earlier, how would I get you to fight the Champion with me?"

Jokul's head swiveled toward my friend in disbelief.

A few seconds passed before Felix's voice drifted back. "I'm always ready. Just say the word."

"Where are you?" I asked.

"Third floor off the staircase. Fifth room on the right."

My time here was up.

I reversed time forty minutes, back to my suite. Three hours, sixteen minutes, and seven seconds of power left.

That would have to be long enough to meet up with Felix before they attempted to move us to the dungeons. Otherwise, I would have to find a way to retrieve him from his cell in the dungeon, through Jokul and an unknown number of soldiers in the palace. This time, instead of waiting for the guards, I would bring them to me.

I took position next to the door, spread flat against the wall. Once I was ready, I began to scream as loud as I could. At the same time, I closed my eyes and focused.

Water droplets, falling steadily against a placid lake. One per second. And now, half speed.

The guards burst into the room. Their moment of confusion as they looked around offered the perfect opening.

At first there was no immediate difference. Only when I focused on my breathing did the truth become evident. Everything around me was slowed to around half. My body itself did not move faster, but my attention sharpened, and I could move with more grace despite stretching my body to the limit. Not to mention how obvious my opponent's movements would become.

I emerged from my hiding spot, pressed against the wall to the left of the door, and leaped into the air. With all my might I kicked outward with both legs, intending to knock the closest guard into his companion. My first try was slightly off, my feet slipping off his pauldron and barely forcing him to stumble. Even with the time dilation, the perfect connection was difficult.

On the third try I landed a respectable blow against his shoulder and upper arm. Pain tore through my legs from the impact. I managed to twist and land in an awkward crouch.

With time slowed, it was almost comical to watch them stumble into each other. In his surprise, the closest guard fumbled his halberd. It clattered to the floor between us. I was faster, scooping the weapon up. I visualized the perfect movement, using the haft to sweep his feet completely out from underneath him. My body followed an instant later. The jolt of connection was almost as satisfying as the sight of the bastard toppling to the ground.

Terrible fighters. Avarus would have drilled such awful habits out of them in the first month. That made it more likely they were Echoes in disguise instead of trained guards. Before the guard even hit the ground, I lashed out with a wave of the void, wiping out all traces of their weak auras. When the guard finally landed in a cacophony of metal, the haft of his halberd followed right behind, crunching directly into the center of his forehead.

Not a fatal blow. Probably. The other man recovered from the shock of his power being nullified. For a moment he looked like he wanted to run. I might have let him if he had tried. Already a small jolt of pain shot through my mind as the time dilation drained my power away.

Our engagement was brief but fierce. The halberd was an unfamiliar weapon, but I was able to press him against the wall. He managed to land a counterattack along my left arm, steel grating against bone.

Gritting my teeth, I reversed time. That pain was nothing compared to Zephyr's poison.

On the second attempt I deflected the blow properly. His desperate counter left him wide open. Instead of attacking with the halberd, I leaned back and kicked out in front of me, driving my heel through the open front of his helmet. Blood sprayed. The back of his head smashed into the wall, and he crumpled in a heap.

I released the time dilation. The disorientation of returning to normal made me nauseated. Shaking my head, I looked at the two unconscious men. Leaving the two of them behind seemed like a mistake, but killing them was a bold declaration. I had not yet made a complete enemy of the Archon.

The entire fight had taken less than thirty seconds. Two hours, fifteen minutes, and nineteen seconds of time magic remaining. A hefty price to pay but well worth it.

Halberd at the ready, I crept down the hall. No other guards manned this floor. The entire area looked deserted. It made sense to separate me from the others, particularly Felix. But that would not stop me in the end from reuniting with my friend.

Judging from Felix's description, my friend's room was a couple of floors below mine. My first instinct was to make haste his way. But we could not confront the Champion without proper weapons. I wandered through the corridors for a while, searching for anyone who looked like they belonged.

The palace looked near abandoned. Most of the stationed forces must have been deployed elsewhere. It took a couple minutes of searching to find an old man in expensive robes hurrying down one of the corridors. He fled at the sight of me, but I caught up easily.

I seized him by one frail arm. "Who are you?"

"Just an old servant," he said. "Ecurus is my name. Please, I am just trying to leave."

"How familiar are you with this place?"

The old man remained silent.

"I'm not going to hurt you," I said. "Show me where the armory is, and you're free to go."

Between the halberd in my hand and my unblinking stare, Ecurus gave up in the end. His shuffling gait eventually led me to the top floor, wasting a precious five minutes of my time. At least he did not attempt to mislead me.

The armory was a cramped room with a basic assortment of weapons along the walls. An unimpressive selection, but the real prize rested on a table in the center of the room. Dasein, its ivory blade laid bare. A pair of magnifying glasses and other tools were arranged around the weapon. Whoever had messed with my sword at least had the decency to include a serviceable scabbard to accompany it.

The idea of someone fiddling with my sword made me grit my teeth. But the scabbard was a perfect fit and felt far more natural at my hip than some loop of cloth around the waist.

I reversed time to completely eliminate the encounter with Ecurus. No use wasting all of my time when I could head there immediately after defeating the guards. This time I ascended the stairs as fast as I could, keeping my breathing steady. No need to weigh myself down with the halberd, either.

Having wasted no more than two minutes to reach the armory, I buckled Dasein and an additional sword at my side. Just for good measure, I held a third one in my hand. Felix would need a blade as well.

I took a much needed ten seconds to steady my breathing and my mind. Then, I was ready.

Down the stairs. The world around me shone with perfect clarity, every detail gorgeous in its intensity. Down. Down. To the third floor. The whole time my mind remained utterly blank. Numb. Fearless.

Both my time and void magic remained healthy enough. I knew my limits, and I was not even close. And I knew I was not alone.

"Felix!" I shouted as I sprinted down the corridor.

And there the Champion waited, guarding my friend's room. This time, his expression remained blank as he drew his sword. No more restrictions now that Vasely had greater concerns.

I assumed a fighting stance. Jokul was content to wait at his post. Light from the setting sun streamed through a window opposite him, soft oranges and pinks gleaming along his blade and accenting the hollows of his face.

What other signal did my friend need? Was his name not enough?

"Let's kill this bastard!" I shouted.

Jokul's eyes hardened. He took a step toward me.

After a long, breathless moment, the door tore open. Felix charged out, wielding a chair leg like a club. The Champion's sword lashed out in a casual backhand. For a moment it seemed the blow would sever Felix's head from his shoulders. Then Felix moved just enough, ducking underneath the blow so close it almost shaved his scalp. He feinted with the chair leg, just enough that the Champion assumed a defensive posture.

Felix seized the moment and slipped around him, coming to a stop beside me. My friend tossed his club aside and accepted the spare sword I offered him.

Jokul pointed his blade in our direction.

I was going to enjoy this.

30

LEGATO (II)

Felix and I stood side by side, breathing in unison. We had fought together many times but never against another opponent. Still, Avarus had taught us both the same techniques and habits. Perhaps, combined and working together, we had a chance if we could find our rhythm.

"Trust me," I said. "If I say something, listen."

He nodded.

I was unsure which of us charged first. The moment I saw my friend in motion, I was moving too, focusing on the air filling my lungs, the blood circulating through my body. When Felix veered to the left, I went right, blades flickering. The Champion backpedaled, twisting his body to avoid my blow while catching Felix's sword on his own. Sparks flew. Clever of the Champion—he parried blade-to-blade, whittling down the integrity of our steel with his superior blade.

The hallway was too narrow to fully take advantage of flanking tactics. We pressed forward with quick, darting attacks, seeking any weakness in his defense. There was none. The Champion's blade was longer, giving him the reach advantage, and he lashed out along diagonal angles to keep us at a distance. But we had advantages of our own. While Jokul might be aware of Felix's luck, my time and void magics should give us an edge. I had kept the former power a secret for so long I was loath to reveal it, but if there was any time to do so, it was now.

I kept the power of the void at the forefront of my consciousness. My magical awareness suffused the area but mostly focused on the Champion, watching for any surprises. As long as he did not instantly kill me, we would find a way eventually.

The sound of clashing steel rang through the halls as we engaged, disengaged, engaged again.

Once, the Champion stumbled, and I leaped forward to take advantage, utilizing my quick-step technique from the second legato: a twitch of the calves, a sideways chop directed at his neck. I fell right into his trap. The Champion's sword was in place to deflect before my blade even started moving. He guided my sword aside at an angle, throwing me off balance, and a casual kick slammed into my ribcage like a battering ram.

I reversed time immediately, back to the moment before I attacked. This time, I feinted the quick-step and leaped aside instead, leaving Jokul standing there awkwardly. Felix swooped in from the side, slashing at the Champion's wide-open gut. For a second, I thought it would be that easy, then the Champion's hand snaked down and grabbed my friend's sword-wrist. The lazy arc of his blade took out Felix's throat in a spray of bright red blood.

Another time reversal.

"Stop!" I said to Felix before he moved in for the kill.

He shot me an aggrieved look but backed away, falling back into place at my side.

The Champion stalked forward, slow and menacing. A smug little grin twisted his lips. I half-expected him to gloat, but he remained silent. So far, he had only experienced a couple of teenagers flailing through second-legato movements at best. Nothing to be concerned with.

In my mind's eye, I slowed the water droplets. Half-speed.

When the Champion moved to the offensive, he came at me like a whirlwind, having identified the weaker opponent. Each parried blow sent jolts of pain down my arm. The reduced speed allowed me to hold my own against the onslaught for a few seconds before he picked apart my defenses; the Champion seized his moment and thrust at my heart.

Felix intercepted the blade, taking the lead while I recovered.

Their steel flickered in a beautiful sequence that almost seemed planned; in that moment I realized my friend was much better than I ever realized. Both seemed to predict the others' strikes perfectly, as if they possessed some sort of clairvoyance, lost in the rhythm as their bodies danced. Each movement was flawless, joints bent just so, the path of their blades unerringly straight.

I slipped around the Champion, coming at him from the side, certain we could pincer him between our two attacks. He leaped up and sideways, body corkscrewing through the air. He landed a safe distance away, unruffled. It felt like he was toying with us, as if this entire battle were a farce in some play.

Then, he tilted his head and smiled.

"Leones!" Felix shouted. Time dilation elongated my name into one long, distressed sound.

The Champion flicked his wrist. A throwing knife flipped end-over-end.

I slowed the droplet even more in my mind's eye. Quarter-speed. Roaring, half in rage and half from the pain lancing through my head, I flung myself to the side. The knife buried itself in a painting hanging from the wall behind me.

Jokul rested a finger on his chin in contemplation before shrugging.

Another flick of his wrist, but this time there was no flash of steel.

A feint?

Something blossomed in my mental awareness: invisible, shaped like a knife, and fast. I jerked aside, taking the air-blade to the shoulder instead of the heart. It punched through flesh and bone easily.

Time reversal.

Void magic intercepted the blade of air. Instead of annihilating it from existence with an uncontrolled burst, I conserved my power, sending just enough to disrupt the magic into a gentle breeze.

The baffled look on the Champion's face made me laugh wildly. His eyes narrowed as Felix and I charged. He pivoted, presenting only one side to us, backpedaling to maintain some distance. Smart, but the sheer cowardice of it only invigorated us. We pressed the advantage, our movements becoming more synchronized.

In the end, Jokul was still a sixth-legato blademaster. One of his counters skewered Felix though the gut. Another opened my throat, air wheezing out and blood filling my lungs, until I reversed time. I needed a moment to reorient myself while Felix weathered the storm.

We accumulated wounds as fast as I could reverse them. After each reversal I would bark directions to Felix. It felt like my friend responded right before the words left my mouth.

If I was only reversing time, I could have kept it up indefinitely. The quarter-speed slowing drained my reserves of time magic at an alarming rate. Less than half of the silver orb remained, and we had not landed so much as a scratch on the Champion. I dropped back to half-speed, just enough to distinguish Jokul's lightning-fast movements.

Another flare of magic as the Champion launched a barrage of wind-knives. I imagined the void rising in front of us in a shield thin as a hair. The disrupted wind felt refreshing against my sweat-soaked face.

Jokul followed right behind, leveling a slash at my neck that would have taken my head. My blade intercepted his in time, but after so much abuse the steel finally snapped. Jokul's sword took a notch from my cheek; fragments of my broken sword rained sharp around me.

At my side, Dasein pulsed.

I reversed time and threw my near-broken sword at Jokul; he knocked it aside contemptuously. When I unsheathed Dasein the weapon felt perfect in my hand. The blade held no edge, but it was better than a sword one blow away from exploding.

In the distance, a demon shrieked.

For the first time, Jokul spoke. "What is that?"

At first, I thought he meant the screaming, but his gaze was focused on Dasein.

No point in trading words with the bastard. I slowed my panting, ignoring the burning in my muscles and my growing migraine. Felix and I nodded at each other before charging back in. Though my sword could not cut, it would function well enough as a club.

This time Jokul was even faster. With his off hand, he drew a dagger from his belt. Wind magic augmented his limbs with such speed and strength that each blow threatened to disarm me.

More tricks. I had not yet revealed all of mine, though I did not want to waste all of my strength on a single threat.

I held out as best as I could. Jokul buried his dagger in my gut. He slid his blade down mine and chopped through the fingers of my sword-hand. Once, when Felix circled around him, he tossed the dagger over his shoulder without looking and split my friend's skull in half.

Time and time again I reversed our wounds. Their memory remained, phantom pains and aches accumulating. The Champion was butchering us.

Deep breath. I focused inward, fighting for stillness against my rage and the ever-growing voice begging me to just escape.

The placid lake appeared in my mind, water droplets falling at half speed. Dasein trembled in my hand. Usually, I directed my willpower against the image to slow time. Instead, I flooded the sword with my magical awareness, filling it with myself. And the sword responded, awakening—not a sentient being, more like an extension of my body. A third arm.

Time magic poured into the ivory blade. Dasein absorbed the energy, amplified it, a prism of silver lattices that reflected my power back tenfold. Magic flooded my mind, euphoric, the world becoming more real than real.

I slowed the falling droplets. Slower. Until the movement was barely perceptible, even the ripples subdued.

At such a dilated speed, I watched with detached interest as Jokul unleashed a somewhat familiar sequence against me. Moves from the fifth legato, far beyond my current mastery. I had only seen it illustrated in a book once. Though I could not do it, I could remember its refutation.

Void magic flooded through my hand, into Dasein. A risk, but if Paimon was right, this sword was special. The weapon accepted the void and likewise amplified it. A wave of pure negation washed over Jokul, stripping him of his magic. Even his face went blank for a moment, as if his mind itself had been washed away.

Still, he came forward. My body carried out my will exactly, if not gracefully. Dasein met a blow and held; then another; then another. Even without his magic, Jokul's strikes made my arm go numb. To him it looked effortless on my end, my sword in the perfect position each time. For me it took ten tries. The entire time it felt as if my mind was being split apart.

And at the end, the most difficult part of the refutation: the counter. Visualizing what I needed to do, I thrust my sword forward. Parried. Deflected. On the third reversal I found the precise rotation and path of the blade. This time, Jokul blocked it, but I did not care. The strike, made as perfect as I could, knocked him off balance for a moment. And in that breath my friend slipped behind the Champion and slashed through his hamstrings.

Jokul fell to his knees, face twisted, his breath coming in heavy gasps. Seeing how defeated he looked broke through the numbness that had settled over me.

I released my magic. Time returned to normal.

The brilliancy from the sunset seared my eyes. I stumbled, supported myself with a hand against the wall.

"Do you want the honors?" Felix asked me, offering his sword.

Jokul smiled, teeth bloody. "Fine deals you have made in exchange for those powers. I wish I could have granted you the mercy of ending you here."

"Your friend Barrow helped the demons this entire time," I said. It was hard to get the words out, but I could not stand the bastard's arrogance. "All of this is because of him. Who are you to speak of deals?"

"I am not Barrow. And I do not lose to children. You saw the gorgeous work I made of your friend Lyra, did you not?" The Champion paused to catch his breath. "In the end she was stronger than I thought. What a stubborn girl."

Felix lunged forward to kill him.

The Champion screamed. Blades of wind whipped outward, tearing long gouges from the walls. I nullified the magic heading our way. Everywhere else was shredded in the razor tempest, paintings and rugs disintegrating, doors exploding into storms of splinters.

Felix stumbled backward, and I stopped him with a steadying hand between his shoulders.

"I do want the honor," I said, sheathing Dasein. Every movement felt like torture, but some things need to be done personally.

Clenching his jaw, Felix shoved his sword into my hands.

The Champion had collapsed, barely managing to prop himself off the floor with his elbows. Strands of disheveled hair fell over his face as he glared up at me, panting. One last feeble blade of wind shot my way. Though my magic was near exhausted, I still had enough to disrupt it.

Reversing the sword and holding it in both hands, I rested the tip of the blade on his back. Up and slightly to the left; directly above the heart.

Smiling, I drove the blade downward.

31

GRAVITY

I sat hard, my breath coming in gulps. Felix kneeled a touch more gracefully, supporting himself with his sword. The Champion's corpse leaked blood along the ornate carpets. The after effects of abusing my powers so much were beginning to settle in, transforming the world into a blurry haze. The migraine I had grown used to by now, but the physical strain of using the void added its own punishment.

After Felix had mustered enough energy, he pinned the Champion's sword wrist to the ground with his boot and pried his sword from his fingers. After a moment of contemplation, he stabbed the Champion several times in the torso. Just to be sure. Jokul made no sound except the sickening squelch of steel plunging into his flesh.

Felix patted Jokul down, searching his pockets and coming up with a coin purse and several wicked throwing knives. My friend pocketed a set of keys from the Champion's belt.

"Bastard doesn't keep much on him. We can't stay long. Increate knows where the Archon is. Tending to a much bigger problem than us, I imagine. We don't want to be here when he comes back."

I calmed my breathing enough to speak. "Where do we go?"

"Home, of course. There are powerful people there who should have some allegiance to us. Our only other option is to find somewhere random to hide where no one would expect us."

"I have a safehouse I've been paying for in case something happens." I spoke mostly to distract myself. "It's not far from here."

"This qualifies as 'something.' I have one too. But we want to avoid residential areas for now. Too high density. Clusters of people will draw the demons. It'll be utter chaos."

"Should we try to release the other prisoners?" I asked.

Felix buckled Jokul's sword onto his hip. "I never really trusted any of the others from Amelie in Yellow. We were competing for Astaroth's attention, after all. Leave them."

He grabbed my arm and hauled me after him. I gritted my teeth and stumbled in his wake.

We wandered through the palace for five minutes until finding a side exit. The emptiness of the palace was eerie, silent save for the occasional shriek in the distance.

We stumbled out into the light of the setting sun, clasping each other for support. The fight with Jokul had exhausted most of my power, but I still had around twenty minutes of time magic and a couple uses of the void left.

The side exit must have been for delivery of goods into the palace. They were likely usually manned by some guards, but now the unattended gates had been flung wide open. We followed the path until we came across the main roads.

People rode horses at full gallop down the streets, mindless of the others in their path. At least there seemed to be very little in the way of children. As innocents they would have been spared being trapped within the tesseract. Felix and I looked to be the youngest people around.

We avoided others as much as possible. Some people ran down the street clutching random belongings. A guard rode past on an unsaddled horse, not bothering to spare us a glance. Our bared weapons did not make us look suspicious under the circumstances. Most people clutched something, even if it was no more than a steel rod.

Every once in a while, an inhuman shriek stirred people into a greater frenzy.

A resounding boom cracked in the distance. The ground shook below our feet.

"What was that?" I asked.

Felix shrugged and hobbled along.

The Gardens seemed impossibly far away. One moment at a time we advanced forward. Easier to keep going when your battle is only with the present. The voice in the back of my head that loves to sabotage me whispered the time in fifteen second intervals. A unique sort of torture.

"There was something about the way you fought," I said, finally having caught my breath enough to converse while talking. "You've improved. Significantly."

Felix remained silent for a full minute. I gave him his space to talk whenever he was ready. I had my suspicions about what Felix had been hiding. He had killed the oracle and been trapped within the tesseract, but his involvement with Astaroth went deeper than that. Not that I had much room to criticize.

"Astaroth first began speaking to me a year ago," he said, his voice going stronger as he went on. "At first, I thought I had gone insane. This voice just appeared in my head. I was at Amelie in Yellow that night, smoking that damn opium. You know how you used that mesfera hallucinogen to communicate with Paimon? Whenever I smoked opium I would hear Astaroth, whispering to me. He told me things I couldn't possibly know—mostly mathematical formulae and the like. When I looked them up, everything he told me was true. After that, I had to believe him."

"So you were talking with Astaroth the whole time," I said. "Whenever we were gambling together and you were smoking opium. You were hearing his voice."

"Not really," said Felix. "Most of the time when I was around you, the voice kept silent. As if you were some sort of blind spot. I don't think he can see what I see. It's not a possession, just communication. But eventually Astaroth noticed your presence and took interest."

"And the reason you've become so much stronger . . ." I said.

"Astaroth accepted me as one of his Echoes already." Felix looked away. "If he hadn't ended up having a use for me, I would have been dead. It's my fault, Leones. Lyra's involvement, yours. If we never met, you would have never been dragged into this."

"No," I said. "I think we were always destined to be trapped here. What power did Astaroth grant you?"

He sounded relieved to be discussing something besides his guilt. "It's almost like I can see the future, but not quite. It's a mental enhancement more than anything. I can calculate the trajectories of everything. The most likely paths to occur. It's like a hyper-awareness of my spatial boundaries and how they function. It's almost impossible to describe."

That sounded almost like a far more advanced version of my magical awareness. The benefits for someone like Felix would be enormous. I was almost jealous. Would my void magic nullify his ability? As much as I hated thinking about fighting my friend, he might not be the only Echo of Astaroth we encountered.

If we were going to make it through this, I needed to start trusting Felix. Defeating Jokul was only the first step of surviving this ordeal.

The second appeared within a half mile from the entrance to the Gardens.

A man in an expensive suit sprinted out of an alleyway, face contorted in pure terror. When he noticed us in his way, he attempted to shove Felix to the side. My friend tripped him, sending the idiot tumbling into the cobblestones.

Seconds later a woman in a luxurious fur coat followed him out of the alleyway, screaming. Disgust tinged her face as she passed her companion, who was stumbling to his feet and cursing.

The abomination in pursuit of them emerged, humanoid enough to make its wrongness all the more evident. Like a grotesque spider it balanced between a dozen chitinous legs sprouting from its scalp; their tips punctured through the cobblestones as it swayed forward. Organs the color of bruises pulsated beneath translucent skin. Its head swiveled my way. A dozen black, bulging growths that must have been eyes dominated its face.

A mad part of me considered seeing what it was capable of.

I reversed time by a couple of minutes.

"Let's take a quick rest," I said.

Felix was all too happy to agree. We stopped for a minute and thirty seconds before continuing along. Though I wanted to avoid the area altogether, it offered the quickest path to the Gardens. Going another route might lead us to a pack of the spider-demons. At least the one I saw may have already moved along. If not, more of my precious reserves of time magic would have to be wasted.

A little past the alleyway we found the woman's corpse facedown in a puddle of blood. Her bisected lower half had been tossed a dozen feet away into a nearby wall.

"Increate bless." Felix put a hand over his mouth. "What did this?"

I gestured at thick strands of glistening material stretching between buildings in front of us. "Spider-demon."

At least the man appeared to have escaped. Suppressing my guilt over not attempting to save them proved disturbingly easy.

We made it to the Gardens without further incident. We did not even speak after noticing the iridescent trees marking the beginning of philosopher territory.

One of the trees had been sliced cleanly in half so it fell directly along the path. The cut was so smooth it appeared to have been made with a single stroke from a giant ax. I stopped to run my hand along its smooth trunk. It was a peaceful being that had basked in the light of the sun since ancient times, after all.

Strange, to pay homage to a tree when demons would soon take countless human lives in the city.

Farther along we found a woman's corpse. Philosopher Vera, a kind and uncommonly humble person I had spoken with a handful of times. She strolled down the path every morning to—she would say with a smile—stretch out her old knees. Her head was a dozen feet from the remains of her body. Felix insisted we had no time to waste staring.

I muttered a prayer for her under my breath.

A couple minutes later we discovered a spider-demon corpse. Ichor seeped from dozens of puncture wounds along its humanoid torso. All of its limbs, including the spider-like legs once attached to its scalp, had been dismembered and laid in a careful pile behind it. The head rested on top, like a marker on a cairn.

Felix pointed above us to Philosopher Aeron's body; a thick branch skewered him straight through the heart. I swallowed bile.

"At least they don't kill like spiders," I whispered, a strange attempt at a joke I immediately regretted.

"Demons have no need to eat. They kill only for pleasure." Felix's gaze lingered on the man.

How did it feel to be him, looking at all these corpses of people you knew, knowing that you were in some way responsible for it? Each disturbing sight brought a new numbness. But from the tension in Felix's face, I knew he felt each and every one of them.

The nervous knot in my stomach grew the deeper we went. Dasein's weight offered some small reassurance. I would have loved nothing more than to lie down for a twelve-hour nap.

Once I thought I saw a figure scuttling between the iridescent trees.

"We aren't far from Augur's place," said Felix.

Would we find my teacher's corpse there, impaled on one of his precious trees? I picked up my pace—more of a frantic shuffling than a dignified march, but it would get us there.

We turned the corner to the arboretum. The sight made us pause.

At least five spider-demons scuttled around the immediate area, suspended on their webs. Their movements were purposeful, encircling the lone man in the center. Surrounding him were several massacred demons as well as the body of an unfamiliar woman. Judging from her expensive clothes, she may have been a random noble who had fled toward the safety of the philosophers.

The top half of her skull had been completely sheared off.

Judging from the look on Augur's face, he was taking that personally. The difference from his usual tranquil expression made my heart speed up even more. His snarl transfigured his face into something feral.

The defeated foes around him had either been crushed or dissected into neat chunks. Soon, I understood why.

Augur disappeared and reappeared in a tree some thirty feet away, poised on a heavy branch next to one of the spider-demons. No flurry of snow or wind marked his location. One second, he stood in one place, the next he was in another.

The spider-demon sensed his presence and lashed out with one chitinous leg. Augur's hand sliced the air in front of him. The leg scything toward him simply disappeared, ichor leaking from the perfect wound left behind. Another gesture, and its entire upper half vanished. The remains of the demon collapsed from the branch, throwing up a plume of snow on impact.

Simultaneously two other bodies plummeted to the earth. The missing leg had skewered one of the spider-demons through the head, teleported directly through its skull. The other sight was more gruesome: the upper half fused directly into another demon, forming a gruesome collection of frantic limbs until it slammed into the ground.

Everything stopped moving. The remaining spider-demons must have had enough intelligence to recognize they were in trouble.

Augur noticed us.

He appeared at our side. No displacement of wind. The snow around us didn't so much as shift.

"You boys have some explaining to do."

Neither of us spoke.

My teacher pointed at the tree containing the last two demons. Wood groaned. Leaves trembled. Hairline fractures appeared in a spiral pattern over every inch of the tree before it collapsed in on itself, fragments of glimmering wood and occasional demon exploding into a controlled storm. It coalesced into an orb no wider than a man's head, rotating at a gentle speed.

"Talk."

32

ECHOES

"Do we have much time?" I asked. "It's a long story."

Brother Augur closed his eyes. Something quivered through my magical awareness, a disturbance as another mind spread itself through the area. His senses encompassed every blade of grass in a wider radius than I could imagine. Just how powerful was my teacher? Looking at him revealed no visible aura.

My investigation was interrupted as the orb spinning next to the philosopher collapsed into a pile of organic matter. Could he not maintain that power while also expanding his senses throughout the Gardens? That gave some idea of his limitations.

"There are other spider-demons within the Gardens," said Augur. "They are avoiding this area for now, but two of them are heading toward the center. Mara and a couple of the Karystans still remain. Avarus and some of the surviving philosophers are there to protect them."

The memory of Mara's betrayal sent a pang through my chest. "Why are they inside the tesseract? Haven't most innocent people left by now?"

The philosopher paced along the once-tranquil arboretum. "Well, if that is the criteria, I suppose they must not be very innocent. You do not have to be a terribly evil person to be stuck here, however. The Goetia consider breaking a serious oath, for instance, to be a crime as grave as murder. Likely worse."

"I still don't really understand what karmic magic is," said Felix.

"Powerful demons may alter their own destinies," said Augur, not bothering to glance back at us. "So can we, of course, but they are creatures of bonds and curses. Their words have a power that ours don't. The human act of promising is a twisted reflection of what they can do, corrupted by our free will. We can always break a promise by lying. They cannot. Still, it is no small thing for a mortal to break his oath to a demon."

Felix stared down at his feet. "Is it impossible?"

"Of course it is not impossible." Augur held up a fist and began to raise fingers as he listed out the ways to do so. "The Increate can always descend from Paradise and grant your wish. The universe may end, and the contract is made null. You can die, or your master is banished from reality. Otherwise, it's unlikely either of you will escape your obligations."

"So you know we've made oaths with the Goetia," I said.

"That much is obvious," said the philosopher. "Both of you have expended much of your magic recently. The traces of it still linger around you. You could have become Echoes of Sound, but I know the two of you well enough to guess the truth. Despite your cursory studies of the staccato, both of you remain completely transparent."

"I still do not really understand what karmic magic does," said Felix.

"The use of karma is not exclusive to the Goetia, though they have a greater individual connection than we do. Think of mankind as a collective consciousness. United as a common people against the outside world, our will influences reality. This is why we have created a religion centered around the Archons. Our belief in them and their divinity strengthens us as a people. We generate our own karma through our collective actions, though no single person can do much to influence things on a greater scale."

"So when the Goetia wage war, it is against our psyche," I said.

Augur nodded. "Invading the Civilized Lands acts in contradiction to the will of its people, and so it acts as a sort of karmic defense. When the Goetia undermine our beliefs and our traditions, they weaken us at certain points. When their oracles were sacrificed within the Amphitheater, it was not for the benefit of mankind. It was to make us afraid of the Goetia's retribution and to give justification to the demons for their invasion."

Felix cursed after a thorn scratched his cheek. "Can we win? Those spiders were annihilated easily enough."

"Lesser demons such as them contain no trace of the divine. They are nothing more than scouts."

"Your own power earlier," said Felix. "That was remarkable."

"Masking your curiosity as a compliment." Augur observed his fingernails. "Not the worst idea. To answer your unspoken question, my powers are a consequence of a rather tumultuous youth. I am afraid I cannot reveal too much about my benefactor."

An immensely unsatisfying answer, but as long as he was on our side, we could not complain much.

"Seems like you can't toss a coin without hitting an Echo nowadays," said Felix.

"Oh," said my teacher, "we are a rather small community, but in times of crisis we are forced to reveal ourselves."

"For what purpose?" I asked.

"The title of Echo means very little by itself. Many of the powers bestowed upon us vary wildly in usefulness. Sensi, for instance, was by no means a traditional combatant. Still, her talents would have been useful during these times. Her passing is a great tragedy. Tell me what happened."

We followed Augur off of the main trail, pushing our way through overgrown foliage. Despite the long winter, the undergrowth this deep in the Gardens remained dense.

As we continued along, Felix explained most of what had happened, starting with him being trapped within the tesseract. He glossed over my contract with Paimon, instead mentioning the Captain killing itself one day and the tesseract collapsing. Not the full truth but not exactly a lie, either. Augur merely listened without comment.

I paid more attention as Felix described what had happened to him after I left. The healer reported him to the authorities in exchange for a reward. No great surprise, though she had seemed trustworthy enough at a glance. How naive we both were, despite everything.

When he began to talk about our escape from the palace, I held up my hand. "You never know if he's listening."

"'He' is not so powerful that he can listen in on every conversation in the city," said Brother Augur. "Especially now, with so many other distractions. I can feel the tremors through the ground from him expending his power elsewhere. Whatever is happening over there is destroying a significant portion of Odena."

"The thing I don't understand," I said, "is why you are helping us."

"Good question," said Augur. "Would you prefer I abandon you? Or strike you down where you stand? I also made some mistakes in my youth, but in the end, I think I have been able to find the right path. Out of all the culprits here, you are some of the least. Besides, if I did not want to be here, I would have never entered this place."

Felix unsheathed his sword and chopped at a particularly thorny cluster of vines blocking his way. "You chose to enter?"

"Yes," said the philosopher. "Interesting things have been brewing in Odena for a long while. It is my responsibility to ensure this land does not fall. What the Goetia have set in motion here is only part of a greater plot. The fighting along the Frontier has been especially deadly as of late. Winter himself has become involved. The consequences have led to this endless snow. I do not want to know how many innocents have died from that alone."

"What is the point of this tesseract?" I asked. "What designs does Astaroth have on this city?"

Augur stopped and shot me an annoyed glance. "Careful what names you use here. Now the Archon may be listening. If so, let me remind him that we have an agreement that I will not be eavesdropped upon."

For a moment, silence, then there was a sound like a bell chiming.

The philosopher nodded in satisfaction and continued along. "Good to see that Vasely is not pressed that hard. But he may not have been the only one who heard. The Duke you speak of is one of the Goetia who despises humanity the most. He was the right hand of Morningstar until the Great One's fall. While most of the demon lords maintain their independence, there is a great faction amongst them that opposes the existence of mankind. That is what you have agreed to serve. Whatever their intention is, it must be stopped."

Felix looked away. "But I can't defy him, can I?"

"Has he asked anything of you so far?" Augur inquired.

"Not yet."

"Then you may live for now, Felix," said the philosopher. "But if he asks you to oppose me, there will be no mercy. Understand?"

My friend grunted something that may have been agreement.

Something nagged at the back of mind. Would he really allow Felix to live after the boy had revealed himself as one of his enemies? He claimed he sought to protect this land in defiance of Astaroth. Brother Augur did not strike me as a sentimental person. I would never allow him to execute Felix, of course; I still had around an hour of time magic, enough to head elsewhere in the city far from the philosopher. But shouldn't he at least make a move?

There were still so many questions I wanted to ask.

Before I could, the philosopher raised a hand to stop us. "There is a spider coming in our direction quickly. Two hundred paces to the north. Let me see what you boys are capable of."

Then he disappeared without a trace.

"Is he serious?" asked Felix.

"Give me your extra sword," I said.

He tossed the scabbarded blade that had finished off Jokul my way. I snagged it from the air, and both of us assumed defensive postures.

Dasein would be useless in this situation. The spider-demon had no magic for me to nullify, and using my time power in front of Brother Augur seemed a poor idea. After the fight with Jokul, my body was wracked with various aches and pains. Ordinarily I would do my best to avoid such an unnecessary encounter. But Augur would not let the spider-demon tear us apart, would he?

The abomination appeared as a blur in the distance, leaping from tree to tree. Now that one was coming straight at us, its speed seemed incredible. The dozen chitinous legs sprouting from its head flexed and propelled it forward, humanoid body bobbing about like some useless sack of meat. What would be the best way to kill such a creature?

The spider-demon was upon us before I could figure on a plan. Its legs speared into the tree right beside us, and it perched there for a moment like a tumor upon the trunk. Then the spider-demon launched itself at us with such force the upper half of the tree bent backward, wood groaning.

Felix and I rolled in opposite directions. The ground shook from the spider-demon's impact as it landed between us. Luckily it fell onto a patch of ice and lost its balance for a moment, teetering on its rightmost legs.

My friend came to his feet and slashed sideways. His new sword sliced through two of the supporting limbs in a spurt of blue ichor.

The remaining legs crumpled, unable to support the demon's precarious weight. I leaped into the opening as the humanoid body collapsed to the ground. My blade chopped into the demon's neck, halting after a couple inches. The gristle felt as hard as bone—it must have been unnaturally strong to support the body as it bounced around.

Its legs speared into my body from multiple directions. With no other choice but to reveal my power, I reversed time.

That plan had been a failure. Hell, it may still be able to move as a head suspended between legs even if I decapitated it. Best to go for its remaining limbs first.

This time, I wrapped both hands around the handle and brought my sword down in an overhanded chop. Another leg down—nine to go. The demon recovered, its remaining limbs moving in unison to spear at Felix. He backpedaled out of its range, deflecting a chitinous limb to the side. The demon attempted to chase him, but it moved awkwardly due to its missing limbs. We had to end this fight before it adjusted its balance.

Compared to the Champion, the spider-demon was not such an intimidating opponent. Up close, its stench was horrendous enough to be nauseating—like mold and rotting meat. The mere sight of it invoked disgust. But it struggled to keep up with us as we circled around it, lashing out to chop gouges from its desperately flailing legs. Ichor leaked from dozens of small wounds, and it looked like it was on the verge of collapsing.

The demon bunched all of its legs together into a point beneath it. They flexed, and the demon launched itself high enough to latch onto a nearby tree.

Unacceptable.

I reversed time. Deep breath.

When the spider gathered itself for a leap, it left itself wide open. I leaped forward and thrust my blade into one of the largest central eyes. No more than a thin membrane, it burst beneath the steel, spurting a foul black humour.

The demon's deafening shriek made my ears ring. Its legs flailed madly, desperate to put some distance between us. I followed, unrelenting. My next thrust caught it in the same spot, splitting its skull and burying the sword deep within its brain.

Its flailing continued for a few more moments, non-purposeful, before finally subsiding into little twitches.

I panted, trying not to vomit from the smell of the thing.

Augur appeared, sitting on a thick branch above us. He clapped a few times. "Perhaps there is a chance, after all."

33

INTEREST

"What was the point of that?" asked Felix. "You could have taken care of that thing yourself in a few seconds."

Augur slid off the tree branch and plummeted fifteen feet to the ground. He landed in front of us, knees slightly bent, cloak whipping around him. "Curiosity. While you both are impressive for your age, I do not see what the Goetia hope to accomplish with you as their Echoes. I suppose if they had several hundred like you, that would supplement their forces, but was it worth all of this effort?"

His glib tone made me clench my hands into fists. If I had not used my time magic, that demon would have torn me into pieces after I failed my first attack. Was the philosopher so in control that he could save my life at the last minute? Or would he have watched it slaughter both of us if we failed?

My biggest concern was about whether or not he had sensed any traces of my time magic. If so, he had not given off any reaction, but that meant nothing when dealing with Brother Augur. The temptation to flee an hour back in the past remained. Even if he could sense some disturbance in the surrounding area from my time magic, would he be able to trace it back to me?

But after witnessing Augur display his power, staying by his side seemed to be our safest bet. He was the one who had taught me about the memory palace, allowing me to expand my powers and bond with

Paimon. The latter may have made me a puppet of the Goetia, but at least I was alive. Could I have managed without the void? It was possible I would still be trapped within the tesseract. Though such a delay may have even been beneficial in the end, granting more time to train my powers. Maybe Sensi would still be alive . . .

There were plenty of regrets from the past to linger on.

The philosopher rested a hand on the trunk of a nearby tree. "The last two demons are heading toward the center. Stay here while I handle them."

He disappeared in front of us. Into the tree? The ground? Something else?

Felix stared at the empty space for a few moments. "Do you think he's really gone?"

My magical awareness picked up nothing around us. Not that it meant much. "I think so. Why?"

"I don't trust him," said my friend. "All his muttering about a mysterious past and being an Echo. But he just accepts us having bonded with the Goetia? Shouldn't we be his enemies? He taught you some things, sure, but I've never exchanged a word with him until now. He knows I'm associated with the Goetia and just . . . doesn't care?"

"Would you prefer he fused our bodies together?" I asked.

"Look." Felix rubbed the patchy stubble invading his jawline. "He pretty much said that he's here to stop whatever the Goetia are planning. I can't imagine working with him is in my best interest. We are sort of trapped here though, aren't we? He can find us easily."

Not necessarily. I still had enough time magic for us to avoid the Gardens. That would also drain most of my reserves. Perhaps I could experiment with Dasein amplifying my time magic. It was possible using the sword would allow me to use less power for the same effect. That carried its own inherent risks. Best to stick with Brother Augur but keep our guards up.

Something was certainly off about the man. He seemed so casual about this entire situation, even choosing to enter the tesseract of his own free will. After such a striking demonstration of his magic, he had done nothing else but walk around with us and have us challenge a spider-demon, seemingly for his amusement. Shouldn't he be protecting the people of Odena? Aiding the Archon in his battle on the other side of the city?

"Well?" said Felix, snapping me out of my reverie. "What do you think?"

"Look, I thought the same thing, but what choices do we have?" I asked. "Why don't we just ask him what he is going to do?"

Felix crouched down, back against a tree. His eyes drooped as if he was struggling to stay awake. "And you think he will just tell the truth?"

"Well, what was your perfect plan again? Maybe we should find one of your spider-demon friends and ask it to protect us? Funny, that thing took a swipe at you as well."

Felix started raising a finger in my direction. Halfway through he thought better of it, leaning back against the tree trunk and closing his eyes. Silence hung heavy between us.

I crossed my arms and waited. The argument seemed petulant the more I thought about it. I considered taking my words back, but damn, Felix's surliness and contrarian nature could be grating at times.

After a while, my friend sighed. "Sorry. I just don't know what to do. It doesn't seem like there are any good options left."

I nodded, my anger dissipating just as quickly as it had appeared. "I'm sorry too. The stress of everything is just squeezing me. I feel like I'm holding up fine mentally, but when I focus on it, I realize how clenched up my entire body is."

We nodded at each other. That settled that.

One Step carried Zephyr into the Gardens.

The boy's scent wafted through the air. It had not been long since he walked this path.

The wind had spoken to her since she was very young. Now it said that Leones Ansteri had spent much of his time within this place. Unsurprising for an acolyte, but to her knowledge the boy had spent less than a year in Odena. His scent was everywhere, and the wind disagreed with itself on how long he had spent where.

She had not been to the Gardens in over a decade. Her work did not permit much time for leisure nowadays. Back then Vasely had brought her and the other Winds he had selected from the tribes. Including, much to her pride, her blood sibling Barrow. The place had been overwhelming then too, permeated deep with a bouquet of magics. Its very existence had blossomed from the Archon of Earth's divine blessing. Mystical land warped reality.

It still made her uneasy.

From what she could gather, Leones was an Echo twice over. He smelled white and silver to her—an impossible scent to define to others, but Zephyr had smelled colors and seen scents as far back as she could remember. No accounts existed of any dual Echo who had not succumbed to madness within five years. Those were all honorable men, the strongest and wisest, bestowed with gifts that were truly curses. All of them went insane.

Leones Ansteri never had a chance. Heretic blood ran through his veins. So much trouble could have been avoided if she had executed him at that abandoned farm. The way evil prospered was by taking advantage of the good. Now . . . she squeezed her eyes shut . . . now the city she had sworn to protect had become a domain of the Goetia. A stronghold in the heart of the Civilized Land.

The familiar scent of Odena had turned to blood and fire.

She directed a small stream of Will into her seven-league boots, activating them. Her next Step took her to the strongest source of blood in the area. A decapitated female philosopher. With a sigh, Zephyr retrieved her head from some distance away and placed it above the stump of the woman's neck. She muttered a prayer before rubbing snow between her hands to clean off the congealed blood.

Another small Step. A male dangling from a tree branch and a butchered demon, its limbs and head arranged in a pile. She forced herself not to look away. The dead should be remembered.

She was preparing to activate her boots again when a figure appeared on the path in front of her. A male philosopher, arms crossed, with sad eyes and thin scars all over his exposed skin.

The air around him screamed of wrongness in a way she had never experienced, even with the spawn of Desolada. It was as if reality itself wished to expel him from existence. So many contradictory scents. An inscrutable miasma.

Half of her wanted to execute him at once, the other half wanted to flee.

"You have made yourself into a problem, Zephyr." His voice was dead. Low and flat and hollow. "You were doing so well before."

She went for her sword.

He pointed.

A deep, irresistible pressure settled into Zephyr's chest. She directed a sliver of willpower to activate her seven-league boots.

Too late.

Bones crunched as her arms and legs retracted into her body, drawn into the hungry gravity at the core of her being. Red crept into the corners of her vision as the compression intensified. Excruciating pain; then, mercifully, blackness.

A few seconds later, Brother Augur stepped forward. Sighing, he plucked an organic marble from the air. He observed it for a moment before flicking it off to the side.

Brother Augur reappeared thirty seconds later, calm as if he just returned from a leisurely stroll through the Gardens. He stood with his hands clasped behind his back. No weapon. Radiating the simple confidence of a man fully within his element, certain he would conquer whatever came next.

"Quite the dour expressions, you two," he said, a hint of laughter in his voice.

Felix glared at the philosopher with intense eyes. "What is your purpose here?"

Augur tilted his head and looked off into the distance. His lips twisted into a little smile. "To bear witness. There are certain events that are inevitable, so tightly woven into the fabric of the cosmos perhaps not even the Increate could reverse them. In a place like this, one finds the most interesting things." He glanced my way. "I must admit some fondness for my student as well. You have progressed as well as one may hope. And you've even found a fascinating companion along the way."

"Did that seem like an answer to you, Leones?" asked Felix. "The only thing I got out of that is that he has a strange liking for us."

The philosopher's face remained blank. For a moment I had the ridiculous thought that he wanted to end Felix's life then and there. Just . . . compress him into an orb the size of a marble. Instead, Augur touched his forehead with two fingers before resting them against his heart.

"I make an oath on my mind, my soul, my being," he said, "I intend you no harm. Both of you. Consider me a sword and a shield. I am here to protect you and all of the other worthy souls within this dark world."

"Why me?" Felix slammed a fist against his chest. "I understand why you would protect Leones, but why me?"

"When you put it like that, there is only one reason to do anything," said Augur. "Because I want to."

The ground quaked beneath our feet for several seconds.

My friend shook his head in frustration. "What is going on out there? How much do you know about Astaroth's plans, Brother Augur?"

The philosopher smiled. "You should have some idea. Your master accounts for every eventuality. He is fluent in the language of fate. So many variables to take into account here. To exert this much influence on the Mortal Realm, he must have one grand intention."

"Which is?" I asked.

"To descend."

34

EXHALE

Archon Vasely had always wanted to be revered as a wise and benevolent ruler. Like one of the ancient philosopher kings, dedicated to justice and equality and prosperity. In that, he shared a dream with Nony of Velassa. Long ago they had spent many a day drinking and debating the optimal way to achieve their utopia. Not so much, as of late.

Hovering over the panorama of his dying city, he conceded Nony might have been right.

What that boy Leones said had struck close to Vasely's heart. All of this had occurred right beneath his nose. The wise, all-hearing god would not leave his imprint on mankind's collective consciousness as a beloved leader ushering in a golden age. He had suffered the worst defeat since Tenlas and the Fall of Arostara. Worse, even.

The Goetia had learned their lesson.

Encompassing the entire thirty square miles of Odena and extending above and below the earth, the tesseract was as flawless as one expected from Astaroth's work. It vibrated on a frequency Vasely had never seen before. Since its formation the Archon had dedicated most of his time studying its intricacies, but he doubted more than a handful of people within the Civilized Lands could analyze even its conceptual foundation.

The only hope now lay in all of the Archons gathering for the first time in centuries. Such a feat was next to impossible in modern times, and they would never agree to set foot in an unknown domain like the tesseract. Too many cowards in this generation of the mortal pantheon. They would only care when their own lands were threatened.

Thousands of disparate screams reached him from his perch miles above the city. Glass shattering, demons chittering, babies crying. Filtering through the noise revealed nothing new.

Vasely flew down to the establishment known as Amelie in Yellow. Citizens on the street pointed and shouted when they noticed his descent among them. He muted their pleas as he stepped into the building. He could not afford to focus on any individual plights. Twenty people would perish in the time it took to save one.

Discordant vibrations lingered in the area, traces of the proto-tesseract. The Ansteri boy had unraveled this construct, but the barrier around Odena existed on a completely different level. Perhaps he may be the key, but Vasely was unwilling to trust any of Goetia's minions. The Archon had thought he had more time to come to a decision before relying on the boy.

Astaroth had calculated everything to perfection.

Vasely floated up to the second floor. Something there called to him.

A mural of a golden skull surrounded by runes.

He traced each of the symbols with the tip of his finger, straining to decipher their meaning. Over a century ago he had studied some of the incomplete lexicons purported to translate the demonic language. Since then, he had grown lax with his studies, favoring new avenues of knowledge instead of reinforcing old ones.

All of them had grown so complacent over the years.

What little he did understand concerned him. The mural was some sort of anchor, meant to work in conjunction with the tesseract to overwrite physical law. The Increate's workings could not be destroyed, but they could be mixed, like an artist blending paints. The domain within a tesseract existed not in the Physical Realm or Desolada, but in a purgatory between the two. As the bastard child of different realities, it combined the laws and possibilities of both.

Vasely thought he knew what Astaroth intended.

An unfathomable blasphemy. Melding the two worlds into a pocket dimension was one thing. But Increate only knew how many of these had been distributed throughout the city. Each of them the site of their own separate tesseract, depositories of karma and bloodshed.

Together they could integrate his city into Desolada, his citizens made slaves in a foreign universe. Their minds and souls trapped, perhaps forever, divorced from their incongruent physical bodies. And in reverse Odena would be a portal back to the Physical Realm, an impenetrable stronghold from which to conquer the Civilized Lands.

An unprecedented disaster. Potentially the end of mankind's empire. If only it ended there.

None of the Goetia had ever descended to Savra in recorded history. Perhaps in one of the ancient cataclysms thousands or millions of years ago. Their existence defied the fundamental nature of the Physical Realm. It would be like plunging fire into water. Or darkness being pushed into the sunlight. But perhaps, in the steam or in the shadows, Astaroth could find a way to step into the land of mortals.

No time to waste. Go to the Ansteri boy and force him to help. Brother Augur would be a problem, but if they worked together, a solution would still be possible. Vasely might not be remembered as a philosopher king, but perhaps he could stop his home from being the epicenter of the universe collapsing.

Vasely whispered, and the roof of Amelie in Yellow disintegrated into a million splinters. His speed tore the air around him as he shot off in the direction of the Gardens.

A tempest of energy exploded out from the direction of the Amphitheater. The Archon stopped, torn between the nearby Gardens and investigating the source of that disruption.

The Ansteri boy remained a priority. Before Vasely could take off, he sensed smaller storms of power erupt all over the city. Amelie in Yellow was one of dozens, all vibrating to the same cosmic rhythm, spaced out in perfect intervals to form a giant sigil throughout the city. The Heretic Star, three orbs clustered around each of its five points, bisected on both sides by sphere-tipped lines.

In the very center of the pentagram lay the Gardens. Geometrically it would be the perfect place for Astaroth to manifest. Vasely resumed his journey toward Leones; the energy near the Amphitheater started to move in that direction as well.

Whatever was capable of emitting that tremendous aura was a city-level threat. Something precious to the Goetia, fielded on rare occasions. Such a being attracted the Archons like moths to a bonfire, and if they eliminated it, the blow to its master would turn the tides of battle for years. Decades, even.

It could not be allowed to reach the Gardens.

Vasely closed his eyes and whispered, dispersing sound in the direction of the Amphitheater. The returning vibrations registered to his ears, and his mind translated it into an image. A humanoid figure. As it floated over the city streets, it held its six arms aloft, many-jointed fingers twisting into complex shapes reminiscent of runes.

All mortals that witnessed its passage committed suicide. Those with weapons jammed them into their own vital organs. Those without bashed their heads into walls or the ground until they stopped moving. Lovers strangled each other. A woman watching from a third-story balcony climbed onto the railing and leaned forward.

A General.

It watched as the Archon plummeted toward it. The demon gleamed as if made of pure gold. Its eyes were a pair of white runes painted onto its face, together translating roughly to "Lost Moment." It lifted its arms in greeting, fingers tying themselves into combinations of blasphemous runes.

His mother's face loomed enormous over him as she cooed a gentle lullaby. He rocked side to side. Hunger, confusion, annoyance evaporated as the tune washed over him. Such a beautiful sound. His eyes closed.

Vasely shook his head. A torrent of wind blasted into the demon, carried it high into the sky. The Archon manipulated the current, carrying the General high enough that it nearly vanished, a speck in the distance. Adjacent clouds rippled when Lost Moment collided with the barrier of the tesseract at the speed of sound. It disintegrated. Wind scattered its shreds far and wide.

Energy surged to Vasely's left. The woman who had leaped from the balcony was no longer a woman. The General came to its feet in the exact spot where her corpse had landed. Its body shook in silent laughter, all six hands pointing at the Archon.

Panic. Screaming. His family tent lay in ruins around him, furniture scattered, loose pages torn from books floating through the air. The desert sun flared high above him, its searing light revealing what he had done. No, this was not his fault. He looked toward the distant dune where his mother lay, unmoving, neck twisted at an unnatural angle. The wind had spoken to him. All he had done was say something back.

Vasely bit his tongue. Pain brought him back to reality. Hot blood like copper in his mouth. He exhaled, and his breath tossed the General backward, through a brick building and the one behind it.

Behind him, Lost Moment stood in place of a man who had sawed halfway through his own neck with a dagger. The hands of its upper arms covered its mouth, shoulders bouncing up and down. The middle arms clapped. The bottom ones pointed before resuming their frenzied movements.

When the last breath left Hariza's body, Vasely captured it in the palm of his hand. She would never move again. She would never smile or slap his arm or nudge him whenever she noticed a baby. Hariza had always wanted children, but Archons were incapable. Someone like her should have had a legendary brood, unruly boys and surly girls tamed under her iron will. She spent her life with him instead, suppressing her maternal spark, until she went gray and barren, and he remained the same as ever. He stole her life for a few selfish decades of personal joy.

He released her last breath, letting it flow back into nature.

Vasely screamed. Windows within a mile shattered. Buildings collapsed. Bodies flew like trash in every direction. Lost Moment perished in the furious outburst.

A surge of energy, not far off from the Gardens. The Archon set off in pursuit, arriving in time to watch Lost Moment climb to its feet once more. A horizontal crease split the bottom half of the demon's head. A mouth opened, rows of teeth like ivory, and it emitted the most horrible laugh he had ever heard.

Vasely silenced everything around him. Reached deep into his soul, to the heart of his connection with the wind around him. An updraft of warm currents rose to shear against cold, dense air above, forming a spinning column as they competed against each other. He had spent long hours observing thunderstorms, learning the ways of the wind at their most chaotic. Calling upon those memories, he manipulated the vortex, linking it with a cloud above, forcing the wild mass of wind into a funnel.

A cyclone descended from the heavens, touched base right behind the General. The Archon's laughter joined in with the demon's amused croaking. Its fingers weaved complex patterns.

Screams. Dead faces. Accusatory glances. Broken promises. Failure after failure after failure over the centuries.

Debris swirled through the air. The tornado tore the world apart as it approached. It gathered the demon in its grip, sucked it into a rotating mass of wind and dust, tore it apart at hundreds of miles per hour of rotating force.

Vasely was still laughing when the currents swallowed him as well, flung him at a nearby building. How easily he could have manipulated the air around him, to dwell untouched within this all-consuming storm.

Pointless.

He hit a brick wall.

The cyclone continued along the street, an avatar of destruction devouring the city. It headed east, away from the Gardens.

The shattered mess of the Archon's corpse reformed into a golden humanoid, three arms sprouting from either side.

35

FAREWELL

We contemplated Brother Augur's words in silence as we strolled down the path of the Gardens.

In the distance a continuous roar shook the world. Through the leafless canopy I witnessed a cyclone descend from the heavens, far too close for comfort. The sudden squall lifted sheets of snow from the ground. Branches shook and bent. Brother Augur clapped a steadying hand on my shoulder.

The force died down as the cyclone wandered in the opposite direction.

"That must have been the Archon, right?" I said.

Augur took a few seconds to respond. "Yes."

"Is he coming for us?" asked Felix. "Is he going to help?"

The philosopher closed his eyes and whispered something under his breath. A prayer? "No, I believe we will have to rely on ourselves. Everything has been set in motion now. It is only a matter of time until the inevitable."

I shook my head. "There must be something we can do."

He gestured at Dasein. "Learn as much as you can from that sword. You have acquired a treasure beyond compare. Go join the others farther along. I will be staying behind to deal with a new complication."

Felix and I shared a look before obeying. The philosopher remained on the trail, facing the way we had come from, hands clasped behind him. Before we turned out of sight, I cast one last glance back; the philosopher had not moved.

The wind died down. The vibrancy of the setting sun waned as the canopy overhead grew thicker, and the world made its slow transition into night. Treading the familiar path with my friend by my side was almost enough to forget the recent horrors we had gone through. The iridescent trees seemed to have lost some of their luster, even the snow more gray than white, but that may well have been a manifestation of my fatigue and low mood.

Avarus was the first person we saw. Noticing our approach, he drew his sword and proceeded forward until his old eyes recognized us. Sheathing his blade, he took a few more hesitant steps forward before rushing over. He gathered us both in a tight embrace, shoving our faces into his chest.

"Boys," he whispered. The emotion in the grizzled old man's voice was thick and welcome.

Tears stung my eyes. I blinked them away.

The blademaster squeezed us tight for another moment before holding us out at arm's length, searching our faces for something. "You made it back."

"Yes, master," we said in unison. Using that title to refer to Avarus felt far more natural than Paimon.

"Come, come," he said. "The others will be thrilled to see you."

He led us to the clearing where we had spent so many days studying the blade.

The others did not look thrilled to see us.

Mara sat off to the side by herself, knees pulled up to her chest, arms wrapped around her shins. She hid her face between her legs. Her mane of red hair was a wild mess. No sign of Caedius. Lisara and Johan stood in the center of the clearing, wooden spears dangling from their hands; our arrival must have interrupted a sparring session.

Two familiar figures in brown robes came to their feet. Yuri and Elena, a pair of middle-aged philosophers relatively unknown to me. The most interaction I had with them was attending one of Yuri's lectures on ethics, a dull affair best forgotten.

"Thank the Increate," said Elena. A blonde woman with flushed cheeks, she exuded a motherly warmth. "Some more surviving acolytes. Where did they come from, Avarus?"

The old blademaster rested one huge, gnarled hand on the back of my neck. "I did not feel a pressing need to interrogate them on sight. They are here now, and that is what matters."

"Are these all of the survivors?" I asked.

Yuri spoke up in his gruff voice. "No. At least half of the philosophers left during the initial mass exodus from the city. Several acolytes are unaccounted for. Lakken and Elys are here as well, though he refuses to abandon his home."

Johan approached, spear resting against his shoulder. "Good to see you two again. Did you see what we did to that disgusting scout?"

At first, I was unsure what he meant. He must be talking about the dismembered spider-demon displayed near Philosopher Aeron's corpse.

"We did," I said.

"Proof we can fight back. At least, with Brother Augur's help. Lisara and I got that bastard good."

Felix snorted. Johan's eyes lingered on him for a second before returning my way, awaiting my response.

I offered a sickly smile. "Excellent work. I know we just arrived, but would all of you excuse me for a while? I need to have a talk with Lakken."

"You know," Felix said to Johan. "We never did have that sparring match. How about a little fun? You and Lisara against me."

Uninterested in watching that particular massacre, I made my way to the elderly philosopher's residence.

Smoke drifted from the chimney.

No response to my knocking. I tried again, with the same result. A cold pit formed in my stomach.

I pushed open the door, steeling my nerves.

Lakken rested on his usual cushion, eyes open, hands wrapped around a cup. His granddaughter sat on the floor beside him, surrounded by a pile of ruined books, little more than spines with ragged scraps of paper clinging to them. One half-intact tome rested on her lap. With deliberate care she tore out a page, crumpled it, and tossed it into the hungry fire.

"Thank the Increate," I said. "My apologies for barging in, but . . ."

Lakken fell into a rattling coughing fit. When it finally subsided, he groaned and laid his head back on the cushion. "Just like old times, Leones. While I am glad to see you again, I hate that I lived long enough to see this moment come to pass. Just as he said it would."

Elys cast another crumpled page into the flames.

"What do you mean?" I asked.

Lakken lifted his feeble head enough to sip from his cup. He grimaced. "Tell him, Elys."

The woman stopped halfway through tearing the next page from her book. "The man who calls himself Brother Augur first came to the Gardens a little over a decade ago. I was younger than you, back then. He had recommendation letters from all sorts of renowned folk. Even Aramadat, the Archon of Earth. He settled in fast. Didn't take long to befriend most of the people here. A few people, like Sensi, saw right through his charisma, but in time he won them all over to his side."

"What exactly is Brother Augur's side?" I asked.

Lakken's voice was soft, weak. "Have you noticed yet, Leones? Colors becoming duller. The barrier between dreams and reality crumbling. You fall asleep and wake up . . . somewhere else. If there is judgment in the afterlife . . . I hope the Increate forgives an old fool . . . his curiosity."

So it was not just fatigue. Colors had become duller, lines and edges more blurred. The light and heat from the fireplace did not quite match the intensity of the flames.

Elys hauled herself to her feet and rested a hand on the philosopher's quivering cheek. His eyelids drooped, closed. Slow and careful, she leaned forward and planted a kiss on his forehead. Lakken did not move again. His granddaughter pried the cup from his fingers, peered down at the contents.

I rushed over. "He's dead?"

"On his own terms, yes." Elys sniffed and stepped away from me. "And I will be following him soon, to whatever awaits us beyond. Brother Augur sowed the seeds of corruption throughout this city. Those who opposed him vanished or repented. Now he pretends to protect us from whatever he has wrought. Whenever he achieves his goal, I do not want to be here to see it. Like Grandfather said, the barriers between our world and Desolada are growing thinner. When the two merge, your consciousness will be trapped here until the end of time."

Lakken's pale face looked serene in death. I rested my hand on top of his. "And you think you can escape through death?"

"What benevolent goal do you think Brother Augur could possibly seek that would be worth sacrificing a hundred thousand souls? The options are eternal enslavement or worse. We decided to take our chances with the Increate," said Elys, extending the empty cup. "Will you join us?"

I knelt and pressed my lips to the old philosopher's cold hand. Though I had not heard it in years, the Guiding Prayer came to mind. Under my breath, I plead with the Increate to show mercy and bring that wayward soul back to His bosom. When I came back to my feet, his granddaughter had already walked over to the teapot on the table and refilled the cup.

"We make our own chances in this life," I said.

Elys smiled bitterly, raised the cup in a salute before drinking deep.

I left them to their peace.

The sun had finally almost set, the vestiges of its soft light soothing the sky above Odena one last time. Artists call twilight the blue hour, that mesmerizing lull before the dark of night. Shadows disappear, and the world smooths out, taking on an almost mystical quality.

My feet carried me to the barracks. Memories of a simpler time, when my biggest worries were becoming stronger and figuring out how to get along with the other acolytes. Easy to imagine everyone settling in for the night. Mara and Caedius retiring to their adjacent cots. Irele snored in her little corner, fast asleep before any of us even yawned.

So easy to imagine that I hallucinated their figures throughout the building. Felix tied his boots, ready to head out into the city for a night by himself. I even saw myself lying in bed, hands crossed behind my head, staring at the ceiling as I reflected on something or another.

Hallucinations are a symptom of insanity. How simple it would have been, if going mad was my only problem. No, this was the blurring between my world and the realm of Desolada. Where reality becomes a dream. Maybe I was nothing more than a product of Leones's wild imagination as he lay there in his cot, and all that had happened was nothing more than me deceiving myself into believing I was the real one.

The barracks door opened.

I blinked, and the imaginary figures disappeared. Mara stood in the doorway, arms crossed, not quite able to look me in the eye. Her once-vibrant mane of hair looked copper in the light of that fading world.

"I wasn't wrong to report you, you know," she said.

The old rage I had felt at her betrayal was nowhere to be found. "Probably not."

"I think Caedius is dead. I forgot about him until just recently. I had these dreams of someone holding me. A shadow by my side in so many of my memories. I couldn't remember his face until maybe an hour ago. But he didn't come back. You and Felix did."

I walked over to my cot, smoothed the wrinkles out of the thin blanket. "He might not be dead. He may be on his way here now."

"No," she said, wiping her eyes. "I don't think he is. I wish he was, though. I wish he was here now to comfort me like he always did. I never even got to say goodbye. This seems like a good time for farewells, doesn't it?"

I sat down on my cot. "Probably."

"Farewell then, Leones."

"Farewell, Mara."

When I looked back, she was already gone. Had she even been there in the first place? I settled into the cot, pulled the blanket over me, and closed my eyes.

The realm of the One Who Rules exists within a point where eleven dimensions meet. As such, to experience it is to have one's mind fractured into unimaginable shapes. No physical thing can exist within it: all interactions occur within the Mental Realm, anchored to this multidimensional nexus. The One Who Rules is banished from existing anywhere within the Increate's wonders; He must find his place within the gaps.

Though Paimon holds no bonds with the One Who Rules, he responds to the summons in respect of the eternal traditions.

The Fifth, the Betrayer, Morningstar. His power is incomprehensible, to be able to create a bridge from his prison to the Mental Realm. He even creates a representation of a physical space, allowing one to anchor their mind to a familiar scene. Such an effort is useless amongst the Goetia, who require no such tricks. Which means The One Who Rules is entertaining a mortal guest.

The physical manifestation Morningstar has chosen is of an aesthetic plot of land from Savra. A little hut in a stand of iridescent trees, with a calm river winding through. A black-haired man, middle-aged, sitting in the lotus position next to a bonfire. Pale lines of scarring cover his flesh. A humble way to present oneself, in a place where any form is possible. Neither of the Goetia have yet created a homunculus to interact with him. They wait.

Who is this mortal? says Paimon.

Morningstar's words are neither grand nor overwhelming. He does not force his willpower into them for the purpose of intimidation. Such things are beyond Him. *He calls himself Augur.*

36

TIME AND SPACE

I woke up in Desolada.

This time, it had taken the shape of a vast, featureless plain of white marble. My feet floated a few inches above the stone, my weightless body rotating slowly. The view was like nothing I had ever seen before: an infinity of black around me punctuated with countless stars. Without the plain to orient me to what was "below," my sense of direction would have been lost in that endless expanse. To the right, a planet blessed with verdant lands and crystalline oceans, capped with brilliant ice.

"A lovely view, is it not?" Paimon's voice resonated within my being.

He appeared upon the plain, wearing the form he had taken the first time we met: a tall humanoid carved from solid moonlight, a great rack of antlers sprouting from his brow. Malevolent sparks of bloodviolet glowed within his eye sockets.

"It is," I said, breathless.

Experiencing Paimon's memory confirmed that the Goetia had no need for such visual images within the Mental Realm. Even the existence of a physical space known as Desolada was questionable. The clergy taught that the Goetia live within the moon, but the demon lords seemed to have no true corporeal forms. In the end, perhaps it was nothing more than a celestial object, part of the Increate's beautiful painting for some privileged few to witness.

"One of the memories I implanted within you has come to life," said Paimon. "The moment I first encountered the one who calls himself Brother Augur. I made an oath that I cannot speak much of that situation, but its memory is an innate part of me. When our minds merged, that memory became part of you as well. Over the millennia one learns these loose interpretations of the laws that bind us."

"What does that memory mean?" I asked.

"I cannot discuss anything with you beyond what you have already seen, but the connections are there for you to find, if you figure out how everything is connected." The sparks within his eyes brightened. "I can tell you a few things, or at least, I will allow you to consider a new teleological paradigm about purpose. We Goetia understand fate, and that gives us responsibility as its caretakers. The Increate keeps His distance for unfathomable reasons, leaving us children to supervise His great project. Some of my kin do not care to preserve order, but all of us must find a purpose that suits our nature. An immortal without purpose will discover that its existence is useless; it becomes no more than a stagnant mind rotting through eternity, each moment indistinguishable from the last."

No doubt Paimon could sense my frustration, but the demon lord offered no sign that it bothered him.

"I follow you so far," I said. "You are the caretakers of fate."

"Understand that means that I care little about your individual life, or even the collective lives of the human race. If fate wills your souls to be extinguished, so be it. Some, such as Astaroth, believe their purpose is to exterminate mankind. This is contrary to the Increate's self-evident purpose, the reason He created your cosmos in the first place. To create something that encompasses everything he is capable of and hoping that something beyond Him sprouts from it. Only in this way can the ultimate consciousness learn something new."

"An experiment?" I asked.

The demon lord chuckled, a sensation that overwhelmed my mind until it abruptly cut off. "Yes. Over an eternity, what happens? Particularly if enough stimuli are applied to the correct places. What is learned? How are the laws of nature manipulated? Now, to understand the brilliance of our supreme creator, you must attempt to appreciate the scale of what He has wrought. An obscure philosopher from your world was executed for positing a line of questioning: what if there is not simply our reality but an infinite number of realities? What if, each time a choice is made, a divergent universe is created in which each possibility is explored? Infinite events occurring over infinite timelines."

The thought made me pause. It was a hard thing to begin to comprehend. No doubt Paimon was correct about the very idea being suppressed within the Civilized Lands. The implications could inspire an entirely new field of ethics and ideas. The verdant planet captured my attention again: an illusion of the world I lived in, revealing just how small everything I held dear was in the grand scale of things.

"Even the minds of the Goetia are not capable of comprehending the exact nature of your universe, though the conclusion is undeniable," said Paimon. "The anima is a great project, not only to know everything, but to learn what exists beyond the scope of understanding. Much is possible within the Mental Realm, but each of us immortals exist within it as a singular entity. Over an eternity, all of the Goetia will discover something that pleases the Increate. But that would require an infinite amount of time. Instead, He created the framework for an infinite number of your parallel universes to overlap, and in this way, He will constantly be fed novel stimuli. As such, many anomalies will manifest throughout your reality."

"Like Brother Augur," I said.

The bloodviolet sparks of Paimon's eyes intensified. The pressure of his mind weighed heavy, but he was careful not to crush me. "Precisely. A mortal man who made himself so useful, few beings would dare oppose him. He even sought a bond with Morningstar, an immortal banished from all creation by the Increate Himself."

"Why? What happened?"

"I cannot reveal such a thing to a mortal Echo. It is far beyond you. But due to his banishment, outside of the minds of the Goetia, he only exists within the memories of a few beings who have questioned us about his existence. As of now, you will become one of them. Morningstar, the One Who Rules, is one of the five original immortals. The power he grants is that over space itself."

I nodded slowly, absorbing the demon lord's words. "What is it you wish me to do?"

"We observe," said Paimon. "Outside of that, do as you wish. Every possibility has already been accounted for. You would be wise to listen to the mortal's advice, however. Take this opportunity to meditate upon your sword, Dasein."

Before I could protest that I did not have it on me, the weapon materialized within my hands. Of course. I settled into the lotus position, floating in that vast space, sword held horizontal before me with the flat of the blade resting on the palm of my free hand.

Slipping into a trance was as simple as breathing. Perspective shifted, and I was looking down upon myself, a disembodied soul. Without a second thought I propelled my consciousness into the ivory blade.

Whiteness everywhere. The void? Stretching out my awareness revealed a seemingly endless expanse of nothing. Then a black point appeared, infinitely large and small at the same time, the only thing in existence. A second appeared some distance away. A line emerged from the first point, connected it to the second. The first dimension, length.

The process repeated, forming another line that intersected the original. The second dimension, width.

My perspective shifted again, and now I meditated in the center of these lines. They grew around me, folded, forming a three-dimensional cube like a prison. Depth.

Another shift. Again, I looked down on myself, now seated in the dimensional cube opposed to floating through space. The strain on my mind felt like a tearing—something deeper and more fundamental than a migraine, but similar, in a way. Instead of trying to understand, I observed, and the sense of being split vanished.

A second cube with a second Leones appeared in the space next to the first. Then another formed on either side of those two, then another on either side of those four, and so on until an infinite number of Leones meditated within an infinite number of three-dimensional cubes arranged in a row. My mind flitted through the void, past dozens, hundreds, thousands of Leones. Each one subtly different, an instant younger than the one before, until I saw my fifteen-year-old self, myself as a small boy, myself as an infant.

The fourth dimension. Duration. Time.

I returned to the original Leones cube and looked down the opposite direction: to the future. What could I find out if I traveled along that path? My mind headed that way, then the row of cubes branched off into another direction, then another branched off into another. More and more branches, twisting upon one another, impossible twisting, stretching, straining . . . the fifth dimension . . .

A jolt shocked my mind. I blinked and was once more meditating in Desolada, Paimon by my side. The verdant planet shone in the distance.

"Your mind cannot go down that path," said the demon lord. "Not yet. If I allowed you to pursue any deeper, you would have been lost forever. Now that you have glimpsed the foundations He laid down, you can begin to comprehend how the Physical Realm is truly the masterpiece of creation. In our arrogance, we Goetia believe we can influence it. Bend it to our purpose."

Paimon's laughter shook the universe around me. Threatened to tear my soul asunder. After an eternity it ended.

"Yes," said the demon lord, voice full of mirth. "The time comes. This will be a memory I shall never forget. Return, Leones Ansteri, and bear witness to something great."

I took a deep breath, looking about Desolada. "How do I get back to Odena? Should I somehow force myself to wake up?"

"Boy," said Paimon. "Do not be ridiculous. You are already awake."

I blinked and found myself standing in the center of the barracks. The last vestiges of light streamed through the windows, shaded the world in white and black and gray. I held my hands out; they looked translucent, as if they were themselves made of moonlight. Another blink, and they appeared solid again.

Not much time left until the realms merged. Unless they already had while I was jaunting about within Dasein. I removed the sword from its scabbard at my side, ran my fingertips down the length of its white blade. What had I witnessed, precisely? A deeper visual representation of dimensionalism, which had made no sense to me as diagrams and formulae on a page? What was I supposed to make of that?

Well, I thought to myself. At least I will have plenty of time to think it over.

May as well go outside and enjoy nature before reality dissolved into some abstract dream. I took a step toward the door.

Perspective shift.

I stood in the middle of Brother Augur's arboretum. Heavy snowflakes drifted past. His firepit burned white, illuminating enough of the area to confirm most of the color had drained from the world. Hints of brown still stained the wood of his hut. The philosopher himself, seated next to the fire, appeared untouched by the loss of color affecting everything else.

"You have returned to us," said the philosopher, rubbing his hands together for warmth. He smiled. "Just in time, as expected. While I do not mind missing the beginning, I am afraid my presence is required for the grand finale. Did you learn much from the sword?"

I took a seat next to the philosopher. The white fire produced no flames, more the . . . idea of heat. I copied Brother Augur, rubbing my hands together, enjoying the tactile sensation of calluses rubbing over calluses while I still possessed a sense of touch.

"Maybe?" I said.

"It's good to never be too sure about this sort of thing." The philosopher's voice was smoother and more casual than ever. For the first time, it felt as if he were no longer acting. Or perhaps his mastery of the staccato was just that good. In the end, I did not care either way. "What have you pieced together so far?"

"Not much," I admitted. "The sword contains some sort of dimensional capability related to time. Maybe to higher dimensions. Not really my field of expertise."

Brother Augur clapped a hand on my shoulder. "No, I would imagine not. Before the apocalypse occurs, will you indulge me in one last elenctic discussion? Good. What is a tesseract?"

I narrowed my eyes, frowning as I recalled Paimon's description. "A four-dimensional construct, encompassing time as well as physical reality."

"If it is something that one can construct, what would one use to construct it?"

I leaned forward, closer to the false-fire, peering into its white depths. "Time. And space."

The philosopher nodded. "In all of Savra, what two beings are able to harness these forces?"

"Me. And you." I buried my face in my hands as if I sought something in the darkness there. "But I would never agree to something like this. Merging Odena and Desolada. The end of mankind's freedom. Even if society has betrayed me, even if I'd be executed simply for existing, I would never sacrifice so many innocents."

Brother Augur stood. "No. But perhaps one day you would. Open your mind's eye and look upon me."

I had tried in the past, but the philosopher had always masked any trace of magic. Now I spread my awareness through the area.

From all directions, from the heavens and the earth, millions of silver threads like moonlight congregated upon the philosopher. I felt more than saw the black threads interwoven with them, forming braids of space and time magic. Immediately I recalled how Dasein had served as the keystone for the tesseract in Amelie in Yellow.

Except this time, Brother Augur was the keystone.

"You have to understand," said the philosopher, "I would never tell you this if it affected anything in the end. I will not drop the tesseract. Not now and not ever. They say over the course of eternity, everything that can happen, will. In that case, I will not allow an eternity to pass. Once this tesseract finishes merging with the Mental Realm, I will be in complete control of all laws, including time and space. Astaroth has agreed to make me the master of this place, as long as I assist him in his endeavors."

"Why?" I asked. "What could possibly make you do something so insane?"

He leaned close and whispered one word:

KARMA

Perspective shift.

Brother Augur and I sat within the Odenan Amphitheater. Looking over to my left revealed Mara, still as a statue, hands folded in her lap, wide eyes focused on the arena below. On the other side of Brother Augur sat Lisara and Johan, holding hands, fear leaking through their determined expressions. None of them so much as glanced our way.

Much of the seating in the Amphitheater was occupied. Here and there, terrified humans sat in clusters. The demons far outnumbered them.

They made a bizarre spectacle, bright as peacocks compared to the mortals; only Brother Augur retained his original coloring. Most of the demons favored a humanoid shape, though each had their own unique appearance. Hundreds, perhaps thousands of them. Some had heads like lions and eagles and bulls. Upside-down faces. Horns of chitin. Women of unearthly beauty with lotuses tattooed all over their porcelain skin. Giants so large their frames took up several seats, next to dwarves with variegated beards or multiple heads or . . .

I could have spent hours observing all the different forms the demons had assumed. But the one in the center of the arena drew all of my attention. A six-armed being that gleamed as if it were made of gold, hands contorting in a constant stream of gestures. Instead of eyes, a pair of white runes had been painted onto the upper half of its face, and though I had never seen them before, deep within I understood the idea they represented. Missed opportunity. Desperate failure.

Brother Augur glanced over at me. "Lost Moment."

When the demon spoke, its voice transmitted directly into my mind. It sounded soft, mournful.

"We begin," it said, "with the main event. Afterward, four bouts of single combat, followed by an interlude at the end."

It bowed to the crowd four times, once in each cardinal direction.

"Violence, my friends, violence," it said. "No demon has invaded a mortal city for centuries. We have brought them to you for this special purpose. Every warrior has been personally evaluated to make sure they are not in danger. The humans are priests of the imposter-god Vasely, unused to combat. Those who refuse to sully their hands with filthy blood will fight one another for our entertainment. Let it be said that no one is forced to participate."

A familiar speech. We had been sitting in much the same arrangement when Barrow made his own declaration. It felt right that the end should loop back to the beginning, or at least this grim parody of it. Only Caedius and the other Karystans were missing. Most likely dead, though part of me that somehow remained optimistic thought perhaps they had been judged innocent and made it out before the tesseract swallowed the city.

My biggest concern was where Felix had gone.

"Tonight, we host a special Game in Odena," said Lost Moment. "You have the option to leave at any time, but there is no cause for alarm. I am here to protect you, and there are others hidden among you. Tonight, the warriors of Desolada will face humans."

The crowd of demons went frantic in precisely the way the mortals had not. They cheered, clapped whatever number of hands they had, threw silk scarves high into the air, as if they were attending some bacchanalia and the wine had been distributed generously.

Chanting nonsense, Lost Moment proceeded to dance in mockery of the sacred movements meant to consecrate a battlefield. As it moved, sand swirled, buoyed on currents of wind. I recognized the pattern of movement as the inverse of what the Four Winds had demonstrated to open the ceremony.

"As planned, Lost Moment consumed the Archon. You can see it using his power." Brother Augur leaned back, grim amusement writ clear across his face. "Almost makes you yearn for a cup of sweetbark, doesn't it?"

Mara shook her head at the comment, life returning to her glazed eyes. She drew both hands up to her chin, like a child clutching a blanket, her voice horrified. "Oh, Increate. Increate. The visions stopped. How long . . . how long has it been?"

"If I were forced to guess," said Brother Augur, "I would approximate around a minute and fifty-seven seconds. Quite a while to remain sane under Lost Moment's spell, but you never really did much to deserve all of this. The visions cannot be too bad, though I admit I never have asked."

Lost Moment ceased dancing. Its fingers returned to their frenzied contortions. The vitality drained from Mara's face, pupils drifting to the back of her head to reveal only whites. Johan's hand drifted to his side, removed a dagger, and placed it against his neck. Without looking, Brother Augur reached out with preternatural quickness, seizing the boy's wrist a moment before the steel tip pricked his throat.

"Too much of a mess," the philosopher explained, taking the knife from Johan. The big boy lapsed back into his trance. "The demon known as Lost Moment forces all who witness it to relive the worst moments of their lives. Eventually even the strongest wills and most innocent souls will commit suicide. Any who do so are under its thrall until the day Lost Moment is finally destroyed."

Searching the crowd revealed several human bodies slumped over. Pink blood leaked from their wounds; after leaving their body it swiftly faded to gray. Horrified, I moved to stand and try and help the others however I could. Brother Augur forced me back into my seat.

The philosopher shook his head. "There is no point."

"Why is it not affecting us, then?" I shoved his hands off me. "Are you trying to pretend you have no regrets? I certainly have plenty. If it can steal the Archon's power, what would it do with yours? With mine?"

"Simple," he said. "It is not affecting us because I politely asked Lost Moment not to. More of a courtesy than anything. And even if it acquired our powers, it would have to learn to use them. Imperfectly at that. Why waste prime magics on a General?"

Politely asked it not to. So absurd I wanted to laugh. Perhaps my mind had already been dominated, forced to live within this terrible vision for all eternity while Lost Moment learned to master my time magic.

A man in the robes of an Odenan clergyman stumbled out of the south gate. When he saw the howling crowd, his knees buckled, and he fell to the sand on all fours. Lost Moment floated toward him, all three sets of hands pressed together in front of it as if it were about to pray. The mortal priest pressed his face into the sand, either in supplication to the demon or to blind himself to its approach.

Lost Moment knelt in front of the priest, a horizontal crease forming along the lower half of its face. A primitive mouth full of teeth opened wide, lowered until it touched the back of the man's head. Even from the middle seats of the Amphitheater I could see the man shaking uncontrollably. Nothing happened. What was that? A kiss?

The demon stood and gestured back toward the north gate. The clergyman must have felt the motion deep in his soul, because he complied despite having his face in the sand. Keeping his gaze focused on the ground, he stood in his assigned spot.

"What is this?" I asked. "Is this supposed to be the main event?"

"I believe it was referring to the dance it did earlier," said Brother Augur. "The demon fancies itself to be clever. Watch."

The scene repeated three more times with nearly identical results. The four priests stood in the four corners of the Amphitheater, heads bowed.

"And now," said Lost Moment, "for the interlude."

From the Gate of Death emerged Felix.

I wished I was surprised, but the dread had been building ever since I realized our location. This whole farce had to include him. One final parallel to complete the karmic tale.

My friend held his head high, not reacting to the crowd of demons, or even the General standing in the center of the arena. He moved with the same restrained grace he adopted whenever his pride took a blow, as if he was on the edge of beautiful violence. As he neared Lost Moment, he held his scabbard aloft and unsheathed his blade in one fluid motion.

The last of the sun's light disappeared behind the horizon as the blue hour ended. Complete silence fell over the crowd. Nothing moved. Except for Brother Augur.

The philosopher stood. "That boy has more courage than we ever will, Leones. He is a greater hero than any you have ever heard of. Without him, mankind will fall, city by city, person by person. If not in our lifetime, then the next, or the one after. No matter what I attempt, no matter how many times I try, nothing works without his sacrifice."

The edges of reality began to blur, refocused into perfect clarity, blurred once more. I rubbed my hands together and barely felt anything—a memory of touch, not the real thing.

High above, the full moon shone bright. A black point appeared within its center, expanded, an eclipse that swallowed every speck of white until only darkness remained. The expansion spread, eating into the night sky, turning it into the flat white void. A sky I had seen before.

Desolada.

From the black moon came an overwhelming presence, a sinuous thread of gold that drifted through the white heavens. A being of incomprehensible size, capable of swimming between the stars. As it descended it grew larger, more defined, taking on a serpentine outline.

"Astaroth is an angel?" I asked.

"The Goetia were something like that, in the beginning." Brother Augur's fists clenched at his sides. For once his voice sounded strained, angry. "What you see is not his true form. He is nothing more than an ancient consciousness. Incapable of learning anything new. Destined to repeat the same mistakes for eternity."

On the sands below, Felix offered his sword to Lost Moment. The General accepted the blade and pointed it at the figure approaching from the heavens. Astaroth's approval echoed throughout the world, overpowering my own mind long enough to feel some echo of the demon lord's mind. Dark and unfathomably deep, like the ocean depths.

With a flourish, the Lost Moment reversed the blade of the sword and plunged the weapon into its own chest. Blue ichor splashed across the dull sands. The demon collapsed to its knees; at the same time each of the priests echoed the exact same motion, clutching their hearts.

Felix watched as the life bled from the General. Lost Moment's chin slumped to its chest. It fell to the side, did not move again.

"Astaroth," announced my friend, his voice ringing throughout the world. I could hear him as if he stood right beside me. "Accept me as your vessel. All of me is yours. My heart, my mind, my soul, unwavering in devotion. Tread upon the mortal world with my feet. Speak truth with my tongue. Conquer with my hands. May this body never fail you until the end of time."

His speech ended, Felix pushed the corpse of the golden demon onto its back. With both hands he drew his ichor-stained blade from

Lost Moment's chest. Reality trembled. The golden serpent in the sky drew closer, hundreds of wings flexing as it sped toward Savra.

Brother Augur turned toward me and smiled. "There is so much I wish I could teach you, Leones, but you would be destined to repeat my mistakes. You must find your own path forward, but know that you are not alone. Throughout the Physical Realm, there are infinite versions of us, but there is only one Astaroth. I am proud of what you have accomplished, even if you have so much farther to go. Though I must admit, you and Felix have made an art out of finding creative ways to die. Finding the right path took longer than I'd hoped."

I was at a loss for words. "I . . . I don't understand what you mean."

"One day you will," said the philosopher. He gestured at Dasein. "I appreciate you taking care of my sword, but I am afraid I will be needing it."

Down below, Felix plunged his own sword through his heart.

Reality flickered.

Astaroth opened His eyes.

What a fine vessel. A most pleasing golden form, though retaining much of that boy's appearance. The final result of Lost Moment merging with the sacrifices matched every calculation precisely. As pathetic and fragile as the human body was, it could be sculpted into perfection once one discovered the right instruments.

No physical form on Savra could match him. Every whisper, every brush of wind against a surface—even the snowflakes. Astaroth heard everything. Though merging with Desolada had muted most of the colors within the tesseract, what a wonder it was to view the workings of the Physical Realm from within. Infinite shades of gray and white and black. Infinite shapes. And the sense of touch. Phenomenal. Cool air along exposed flesh. Millions of grains of sand, shifting in response to the lightest adjustment, settling into new configurations.

There was, however, a problem.

It was too much. Without the burden of a physical form, Astaroth could analyze, calculate, and sort through such information in moments. Adjusting to corporeal reality would take some time. Sixty-four years, eight months, three days, ten hours, five minutes, twelve seconds, according to his mental calculations.

Until then, Astaroth could not so much as twitch a finger, but nothing on Savra could harm him. Even if this body were destroyed, his mind would return to Desolada. After countless aeons of waiting, sixty-four years meant nothing. The tesseract would last until the end of time, a bridge between realities that the demon lord could cross at will.

That was not the problem.

The problem was Morningstar's Echo, that paragon of human arrogance. The so-called Brother Augur. He sat beside Astaroth on the sand in the lotus position, ivory sword resting across his lap.

"Look at you," he said. "Astaroth, Great Duke of Desolada, lying in the sand and drooling on himself. Calculated every possible circumstance, did you? I must admit, it took quite a few attempts to make it here. You are right to never trust us mortals. All those contingencies you made. Forcing me to bind the tesseract to my soul, so I can never destroy it without ending my own life. Even if I wanted to, that would not be the end of you. You would manifest back in Desolada, moving on to your next plan."

Let the foolish mortal prattle. Astaroth continued working on his calculations.

"I accept every oath I have broken," said the man. "All the trust I have lost. Again and again, the same faces with the same betrayed looks. All the corpses in my path. I embrace all those foul deeds. The loss of my humanity. Every mistake. Every stupid decision. Every action I took led me here, and I regret none of it. I am only relieved that it is finally over.

"You see, Astaroth, I know that I cannot destroy you. But the tesseract and everything within it are under my control. I was never much for mathematics, let alone dimensionalism. You provided that. But the magic comes from me. I can rewrite the physical laws here. Dilate time. Speed it up. We can experience eternity in a second, or a second as eternity. I can shrink it, even, down to the size of this arena. Even now the forces of the mortal world are sweeping through the newly-freed city of Odena, rescuing the survivors, sending your forces back to that afterthought you call a realm.

"It's just you and I, on the sand, forever. Allow me to introduce myself in truth this time. My name is Leones Ansteri, and here, you will worship me as your god."

EPILOGUE

ZERO

If you are the dreamer, I am what you dream.
But when you want to wake, I am your wish,
and I grow strong with all magnificence
and turn myself into a star's vast silence
above the strange and distant city, Time
— "I Am, O Anxious One," Rainer Maria Rilke

Once upon a time, before he revealed his true nature to the world, Leones's companions had named him Brother Augur for his ability to apparently predict the future. Often he presented himself as an oracle or fortune teller, influencing the paths of Archons and other renowned heroes. Over the years he learned to disguise himself, lest anyone too clever noticed the similarities between Aramadat's vizier and the foreign Desert Prophet.

A grim irony, considering his world no longer had a future. Though he navigated through time, cultivating his power to the limit, fate is the domain of demons. In thirty-five years, he lived thirty-five lifetimes. It was still not enough to prevent the Frontier from collapsing. Not enough to save the other Archons from their destinies. Even as the unquestioned leader of the pantheon, directing mankind to the best possible path in as short a time as possible, the ending remained inevitable.

In this moment, he wandered through the streets of Velassa, reminiscing about his childhood. Or at least, he remembered his memories of his youth, distorted over the years to the point he was not sure if it was his story or someone else's.

His boots made no sound against the cobblestones. The streets were empty, though on occasion he glimpsed people through windows. Drained of most color, like statues whose paint had faded over time. Cowering in their homes. A mother holding her bundled child close to her chest. A determined youth clenching a nicked and rusty sword, mouth open as he argued with his parents; that one stirred something deep within him, a small ripple in the placid lake of his soul.

All these figures frozen in place, never to move or think or love again. No signs of life remained in their faces. Though he knew it was foolish, he hoped their souls had escaped to a better place.

Not even the wind stirred.

Once upon a time, Astaroth had mocked him from atop his golden throne. That bastard of bastards. The architect of Savra's collapse. The demon lord claimed everything Leones had done had only helped the Goetia. Twisting time, tampering with fate, disrupting the foundations of reality enough for them to widen the cracks. A magic that could disrupt and confound even the Goetia could likewise affect the Physical Realm.

As his reward, he alone was left to wander the corpse of his world.

Light exists in a special realm outside of time; it resides, strangely, in an infinite moment, defined only by itself. Slightly slower than the speed of light, time dilates. Slightly faster, it goes backward. But at the speed of light itself, time does not exist. It is zero. Much like himself—the only light in a world drained of color, experiencing eternity through movement. And so he wandered, forever.

The demons left him alone for the most part. Sometimes they would manifest nearby, mocking the mortal they had once feared above all, like fools taunting a caged lion. Before the Stasis, they would never have dared step within a hundred miles of him, lest they be trapped within a temporal prison. Cut off from Desolada, left to reflect on their foolishness.

Once Savra collapsed, all of them had been freed. Some sought revenge, though he retained enough prowess to break down their corporeal forms and return them to the mindless collective consciousness from which they had sprung.

The dead world held many secrets. With nothing to oppose him, he plundered every forbidden library. He journeyed far beyond the Civilized Lands. He harvested the cores of feral gods and learned the languages of other sapiens. His feet carried him over beaches of bone dust, through palaces carved from jade. Far and wide he searched, seeking something. Anything. Someone to converse with besides the mocking demons. A way to uncouple his universe from its unholy union with Desolada.

And, eventually, he found something. Not a solution, but perhaps an escape. A recording within the Great Web of the mind-arachnids. A tale told in spun silk. Of one of the Goetia, banished from reality, existing within his own pocket dimension beyond Creation.

Brother Augur's feet now carried him to the site of his family manor, rebuilt from memory into a holy temple dedicated to Archon Leones. For a while, he reminisced about the past. Then he settled into the lotus position and began to meditate.

A massive door appeared within his mind, stretching to the heavens above and the hells below. Ornate, golden, with countless runes etched along its unfathomable length. In his mind he recited the chant recorded within the Great Web. He begged, cried, threatened. His tenuous sanity slipped. For an eternity, he sat before the door.

Finally, he made an oath. Help me, and I help you.

And slowly, inexorably, the door cracked open.

ABOUT THE AUTHOR

Louis Kalman is an ICU travel nurse who dreamed of becoming an author ever since he was young, when his parents would give him whole boxes of science fiction and fantasy books for the holidays. Kalman spends most of his free time reading a wide variety of genres; working out; skiing; playing tennis, poker, and chess; and mapping the recession of his hairline. Sometimes he even writes.

Printed in Great Britain
by Amazon